WHAT THE CRITICS SAY ABOUT ANNE RICE AND HER MAGNIFICENT FICTION

"BOLD AND EROTIC, LACED WITH LUXURY, SEXUAL TENSION, MUSIC . . . DAZZLING IN ITS DARKNESS. . . . There are times when Mrs. Rice seems like nothing less than a magician. It is a pure and uncanny talent that can give voice to monsters and angels both."
—*The New York Times Book Review*

"ANNE RICE HAS A TALENT FOR THE PAN-ORAMIC, FOR THE LARGE STRUCTURES OF PLOT. . . . [She] deserves a place among those responsible writers who strive to combine the accuracy of history with the vitality of fiction."
—*Chicago Tribune*

"SPELLBINDING, EERIE, ORIGINAL IN CONCEPTION. . . . Anne Rice has created a preternatural world that parallels the natural one."
—*The Village Voice*

"HER POWER OF INVENTION SEEMS BOUNDLESS. . . . She has made a masterpiece of the morbid, worthy of Poe's daughter. . . . It is hard to praise sufficiently the originality of Miss Rice."
—*The Wall Street Journal*

"AN INTRICATE, STUNNING IMAGINATION."
—*Los Angeles Times Book Review*

EXIT to EDEN

ANNE RAMPLING

A DELL BOOK

Published by
Dell Publishing
a division of
Bantam Doubleday Dell Publishing Group, Inc.
1540 Broadway
New York, New York 10036

This is a work of fiction. Any similarity to persons living or dead is purely coincidental and exists solely in the reader's mind.

The trademark Dell® is registered in the U.S. Patent and Trademark Office

ISBN: 0-440-12392-5

Reprinted by arrangement with Arbor House Publishing Co.

Printed in the United States of America

One previous Dell edition

New Dell edition

October 1989

10   9

RAD

For Stan

Lisa

1

MY NAME IS Lisa.

I'm five foot nine. My hair is long and it's dark brown. I wear leather a great deal, high boots always, and sometimes glove-soft vests and even leather skirts now and then, and I wear lace, especially when I can find the kind I like: intricate, very old-fashioned lace, snow white. I have light skin that tans easily, large breasts, and long legs. And though I don't feel beautiful and never have, I know that I am. If I wasn't, I wouldn't be a trainer at The Club.

Good bones and big eyes, that's the real foundation of the beauty, I suppose—the hair being thick, having a lot of body—and something to do with the expression on my face, that I look sweet and even kind of lost most of the time, but I can inspire fear in a male or female slave as soon as I start to talk.

At The Club they call me the Perfectionist, and it is no small compliment to be called that in a place like The Club, where everyone is after a perfection of sorts, where everyone is striving, and the striving is part of the pleasure involved.

I've been at The Club since it opened. I helped create it, establish its principles, approve its earliest members and its earliest slaves. I laid down the rules and the limits. And I imagined and created most of the equipment that is used there today. I even designed some of the bungalows and the gardens, the morning swimming pool and fountains. I decorated over a score of the suites myself. Its many imitators make me smile. There is no real competition for The Club.

The Club is what it is because it believes in itself. And its glamor and its terror evolve from that.

This is a story of something that happened at The Club.

A great deal of the story doesn't even take place there. It takes place in New Orleans and in the low countryside around New Orleans. And in Dallas. But it doesn't matter really.

The story began at The Club. And no matter where it goes from there, it's about The Club.

Welcome to The Club.

Lisa
2

The New Season

WE WERE WAITING for landing clearance, the enormous jet slowly circling the island in the tourist route, I call it, because you can see everything so well: the sugar-white beaches, the coves, and the great sprawling grounds of The Club itself—high stone walls and tree-shaded gardens, the vast complex of tile-roofed buildings half hidden by the mimosa and the pepper trees. You can see the drifts of white and pink rhododendrons, the orange groves, and the fields full of poppies and deep green grass.

At the gates of The Club lies the harbor. And beyond the grounds, the ever busy airfield and heliport.

Everyone was coming in for the new season.

There were a score of private planes, winking silver in the sun, and a half-dozen snow-white yachts anchored in the blaze of blue-green water offshore.

The *Elysium* was already in the harbor, a toy ship it seemed, frozen in a sea of light. Who would guess that there were some thirty or more slaves inside it, waiting breathlessly to be driven naked across the deck and onto the shore?

The slaves all make the journey to The Club fully clothed for obvious reasons. But before they're allowed to see the island, let alone set foot on it, they are stripped.

Only naked and subservient are they admitted, and all their belongings are stored under a serial number in a vast cellar until time comes for them to leave.

A very thin gold bracelet on the right wrist with a name and number artfully engraved on it identifies the slave, though in the first few days much would be written with a grease pen on that stunning naked flesh.

The plane dipped slightly, passed closer to the dock. I was glad the little spectacle had not begun yet.

I'd have a little time before inspection to be in the quiet of my room, just an hour or so with a glass of Bombay gin and ice.

I sat back, feeling a slow warmth all over, a diffused excitement that came up from inside and seemed to cover all the surface of my skin. The slaves were always so deliciously anxious in those first few moments. Priceless feeling. And it was just the beginning of what The Club had in store for them.

I was unusually eager to be back.

I was finding the vacations harder and harder for some reason, the days in the outside world curiously unreal.

And the visit with my family in Berkeley had been unbearable, as I avoided the same old questions about what I did and where I lived most of the year.

"Why is it such a secret, for the love of heaven? Where do you go?"

There were moments at the table when I absolutely could not hear anything my father was saying, just see his lips moving, and when he asked me a question I had to make up something about having a headache, feeling sick because I'd lost the thread.

The best times oddly enough were those I hated when I was a little girl: the two of us walking around the block together, uphill and downhill in the early evening, and him saying his rosary, and the night sounds of the Berkeley hills all around us, and not a word said. I didn't feel miserable during those walks as I had when I was little, only quiet as he was quiet, and inexplicably sad.

One night I drove into San Francisco with my sister and we had dinner alone together at a glossy little North Beach place called Saint Pierre. There was a man standing at the bar who kept looking at me, the classically handsome young lawyer type wearing a white cable-knit sweater under his gray houndstooth jacket, hair cut full to look windblown, mouth ready to smile. Just the sort I always avoided in the past, no matter how beautiful the mouth, how brilliant the expression.

My sister said, "Don't look now but he's eating you alive."

And I had the strongest desire to get up, go to the bar and start talking to him, give my sister the car keys, and tell her I'd see her the next day. Why can't I do that, I kept thinking? Just talk to him? After all, he was with a couple and he obviously didn't have a date.

What would that have been like, vanilla sex as they call it, in some little hotel room hanging over the Pacific with this wonderfully wholesome Mr. Straight who never dreamed he was sleeping with Miss Lace'n'Leather from the grandest exotic sex club in the world? Maybe we'd even go to his apartment, some little place full of hardwood and mirrors with a bay view. He'd put on Miles Davis, and together we'd cook dinner in a wok.

Something wrong with your head, Lisa. Your stock and trade is fantasies, but not fantasies like that.

Get out of California right away.

But the usual distractions hadn't done much for me afterwards, though I'd raided Rodeo Drive for a new wardrobe, spent a whirlwind afternoon at Sakowitz in Dallas, gone on to New York to see *Cats* and *My One and Only,* and a couple of Off-Broadway shows that were great. I'd haunted the museums, been to the Met twice, seen the ballet everywhere I could catch it, and bought books, lots of books, and films on disc to last me the next twelve months.

All of that should have been fun. I'd made more money at twenty-seven than I'd ever dreamed I'd make in a lifetime. Now and then I'd try to remember what it was like when I wanted all those gold-covered lipsticks in Bill's Drugstore on Shattuck Avenue, and only had a quarter for a pack of gum. But the spending didn't mean very much. It had left me exhausted, on edge.

Except for a very few moments, sort of bittersweet moments, when the dancing and music in New York had been utterly exalting, I'd been listening to this inner voice that kept saying:

Go home, go back to The Club. Because if you don't turn

*around right now and go back, it might not be there anymore. And
everything you see in front of you is unreal.*

Odd feeling. A sense of *the absurd* as the French philosophers
call it, making me so pervasively uncomfortable that I felt like I
couldn't find a place just to take a deep breath.

In the beginning I had always needed the vacations, needed to
walk through normal streets. So why the anxiety this time, the
impatience, the feeling of being dangerous to the peace of those I
loved?

I had ended up the vacation finally watching the same video
disc over and over again in my room at the Adolphus in Dallas,
of a little film by actor Robert Duvall called *Angelo, My Love.* It
was about the gypsies in New York.

Angelo was a shrewd, black-eyed little kid about eight years
old, really street wise and brilliant and beautiful, and it was his
film, his and his family's, and Duvall let them make up a lot of
their own dialogue. It was realer than real, their life in their own
gypsy community. Outsiders in the middle of things, right in
New York.

But it was crazy for me to be sitting in a darkened hotel room
in Dallas watching a film seven times, like the reality of it was
exotic, watching this sharp little black-haired boy call up his
preteen girl friend and bullshit her, or go into the dressing room
of a child country-western singing star and flirt with her, this
fearless and good-hearted little boy immersed in life up to his
eyeballs.

What does all this mean finally, I kept asking like a college kid.
Why does it make me want to cry?

Maybe it's that we are all outsiders, we are all making our own
unusual way through a wilderness of normality that is just a
myth.

Maybe even Mr. Straight at the Saint Pierre bar in San Francisco is some kind of an outsider—the young lawyer who writes
poetry—and wouldn't have shocked out over coffee and croissants the next morning if I'd said: "Guess what I do for a living?
No, actually it's a vocation, it's very serious, it's . . . my life."

Crazy. Drinking white wine and watching a movie about gypsies, and turning out the lights to look at nighttime Dallas, all
those glittering towers rising like ladders to the clouds.

I live in Outsider Heaven, don't I? Where all your secret

desires can be satisfied, and you are never alone and you are always safe. It's The Club where I've lived all my adult life.

I just need to get back there, that's all.

And here we are circling over Eden again, and it's almost time to have a very close look at those fresh slaves coming in.

I wanted to see those slaves, see if this time there wasn't something new, something altogether extraordinary . . . Ah, the old romance!

But every year the slaves are different, a little more clever, interesting, sophisticated. Every year as the The Club gets more famous, as more and more new clubs like us open, the backgrounds of the incoming slaves get more diverse. And you never know what will be there, what new form that flesh and mystery can take.

There had been a very important auction only days ago, one of the only three international auctions worth attending, and I knew we'd bought heavily, full two-year contracts on some thirty men and women, all of them ravishing, with excellent papers from some of the best houses in America and abroad.

A slave doesn't get shown at one of those auctions unless he or she has had the best prior training, unless every test has been passed. Now and then from other sources we get an unwilling or unstable slave, some young man or woman who, flirting with the leather paddles and straps, got swept up in things more or less accidentally. And we liberate and pay off those slaves very fast. We don't like the losses. But it's not the slave's fault.

Yet it's amazing how many of them show up a year later on the most expensive auction blocks. And if we snap them up again—and we do if they're beautiful enough and strong enough—they tell us later that ever since they were liberated they've been dreaming of The Club.

But to continue, these mistakes don't happen at the big auctions.

For two days prior to the sale, the slaves are worked before a board of examiners. They have to show perfect obedience, agility, and flexibility. And the papers are checked and rechecked. The slaves are rated for endurance, temperament; they're classified according to a series of physical standards, and you could, if you wanted, make a very satisfactory purchase from the extensive catalogue copy and photographs alone.

Of course we do all this evaluating again for our own purposes and according to our own standards once the slaves come to us. But it means the merchandise at these auctions is first rate.

And no slave reaches the auction preview room who isn't a gorgeous specimen, expertly mounted on the lighted platform to be examined by thousands of hands and eyes.

In the beginning I used to go to the important auctions myself.

It wasn't only the pleasure of picking what I wanted from these fledglings—and no matter how much private training they've had they *are* fledglings until we train them—it was the excitement of the auction itself.

After all, no matter how well a slave is prepared, the auction is a cataclysm for him or her. There is a lot of trembling, the free flow of tears, and the frightening aloneness of the naked slave on the carefully lighted pedestal, all that delicious tension and suffering displayed as exquisitely as a work of art. It's every bit as good as any Club entertainment that I ever worked out.

For hours you drift about the huge, carpeted preview room, just looking about. The walls are always painted in soothing colors: vermillion or robin's-egg blue. The lighting is perfect. And the champagne is delicious. And there's no distracting music. The rhythm is the beat of your heart.

You can touch and feel the candidates as you inspect them, asking a question now and then of those who are mercilessly ungagged. (Voice trained, we call it. It means trained never to speak except when spoken to, never to express the slightest preference or wish). And occasionally the other trainers draw your attention to a fine specimen, maybe one they don't think they can afford themselves. Now and then there is a gathering of buyers around some extraordinary beauty who is being made to assume a dozen or so revealing positions, respond to a dozen commands.

I have never bothered to paddle or strap a slave at an auction preview. There are others only too willing if you just wait and watch. And the few blows dealt on the block itself at the moment of bidding can tell you all you need to know.

And you hear so much gratuitous wisdom: this slave marks much too easily, you'll never get your money's worth, and this skin feels kitten soft but it's very resilient, or small breasts like that are really the best.

It's an education all right if you can keep away from the champagne. But the really fine trainers reveal little of themselves or the poor shuddering victims they examine. A really fine trainer can learn all he wants by slipping up to a slave and closing his or her hand very suddenly on the back of the slave's neck.

And no small part of the fun is seeing the other trainers who come from all over the world. Gods and goddesses they seem sometimes, slipping out of those black limousines lined up before the doors—everywhere that brand of high fashion that seems luxuriously friable: threadbare denim and open-down-the-front shirts in the thinnest Indian cotton, the off-the-shoulder silk blouse that is about to fall apart. Savaged hair and dagger nails. Or the colder, three-piece-black-suit aristocrats with the square, silver-rimmed glasses, and the perfectly combed short hair. A babble of languages, (though the international language for slaves has pretty much been established as English) and the special imprint of a dozen different nationalities on what is almost invariably an air of command. Even in the sweet-faced ones, the seemingly innocent ones, there is underneath the air of command.

I know trainers when I see them in other places. I have spotted them everywhere from the dirty little pavilion in the Valley of the Kings at Luxor to the veranda of the Grand Hotel Olaffson in Port au Prince.

There are dead giveaways like the broad black leather watchbands and the high heels you could never find in an ordinary shop. And the way that they undress with their eyes every good-looking man or woman in the room.

Everyone is a potential naked slave to you once you become a trainer. And you carry with you an aura of supercharged sensuality that is almost impossible to shake off. The naked backs of women's knees, the little crease where a bare arm presses against the body, the way a man's shirt stretches across his chest when he puts his hands in his pockets, the movement of a waiter's hips as he bends to retrieve a napkin from the floor: you see all that everywhere you go, feeling that perpetual low hum of excitement. All the world is a pleasure club.

But there is a special pleasure too at the auctions in seeing those few very rich individuals who maintain trainers in their homes or country houses and are permitted to buy slaves through the auction for their own use. They are often stunning, the private owners, a curious lot.

I remember one year there was a handsome eighteen-year-old in the company of two bodyguards going through the catalog with great seriousness and peering from a distance through his violet sunglasses at each victim whom he would then approach and quite deliberately pinch. He was dressed all in black except for a pair of dove-gray gloves that he never removed. I could almost feel those gloves myself when he would pinch one of the slaves. Everywhere he went the bodyguards went, and the trainer, one of the best I should add, was also right at his arm. His father had been keeping a trainer and two slaves for years, and now it was time for the son to learn to enjoy "the sport."

He settled on a very robust boy and girl.

Understand when I say a boy and a girl, I don't mean children. The Club and the reputable auction houses don't deal in children for obvious reasons. The private trainers know better than to send them to us. When teenagers do get in sometimes, through trickery or with false papers, we fly them right back out.

By boy or girl, I mean a kind of slave who regardless of his or her real age looks and acts young. There are slaves thirty years old who qualify as boys or girls. And there are slaves of nineteen or twenty who even in bondage and humiliation retain an air of seriousness and injured dignity that makes you think of them as women or men.

Anyway, the eighteen-year-old master bought two very youthful and well-muscled slaves and I remember it because he outbid The Club in the auction for the girl. She was one of those darkly tanned blond-haired creatures who never sheds a tear no matter how hard she is punished, and the master becomes more and more enflamed. I wanted her badly, and I remember being a little out of sorts when I saw her bound up and packed off. The young master observed this and I saw him smile for the first and only time that day.

But I always worry about them, those slaves who go to individual owners. It's not that these owners aren't trustworthy. To buy from a reputable slave auction house or a reputable private trainer, you have to be trustworthy, and your staff must be tested and approved and your house must be safe. It's just that it's lonely and eerie being only one of two or three slaves on a great estate.

I know because that is what I was when I was eighteen. And

no matter how handsome or beautiful the master or mistress is, no matter how often there are parties or other entertainments, no matter how vigorous and good the trainers are, there are too many moments when you are left alone with your thoughts.

The Club frightens the slaves at first. It terrifies them. But in a real way, The Club is a great womb. It's an immense community where no one is ever abandoned, and the lights never go out. No real pain or damage is ever inflicted. There are never any accidents at The Club.

But as I was saying, I don't go to the auctions now, and haven't for some time.

I'm simply too busy with my other duties—supervising our little newspaper, *The Club Gazette,* and meeting the insatiable demand for new souvenirs and novelty items sold in The Club Shop.

White leather paddles, straps, boots, blindfolds, even coffee mugs with The Club monogram—we can never design or supply enough. And these items don't end up in bedrooms back in the States. In San Francisco and New York, they are selling, along with back issues of the *Gazette,* for four times the original price. That means this merchandise has come to represent us. All the more reason to make it first rate.

Then there are the new members who have to be guided on their first visits, have the naked slaves personally introduced to them.

And then there is the all-important indoctrination and training and perfecting of the slaves themselves, which is my real work.

A good slave is not merely a thoroughly sexualized being, ready to serve your every whim in bed. A good slave can bathe you, massage you, talk to you if that is what you want, swim with you, dance with you, mix your drinks, feed you your breakfast with a spoon. Just make the right phone call from your room and you can have a specially trained slave ready to play master or mistress expertly, making you the slave as you desire.

No, there is no time anymore to go to the auctions.

And besides, I've found it's just as interesting to wait for the new batch of slaves to be delivered and then choose the one I want to train.

We buy enormous numbers, at least thirty at a time if the auctions are big enough, and I'm never disappointed. And for two years now, I've had first pick. That means I choose before any other trainer the slave whom I want to develop myself.

It seemed the plane had been circling for an hour.

I was getting more and more anxious. I was thinking, this is like an existentialist play. There is my world down there but I cannot get into it. Maybe it is all something I've imagined. Why the hell can't we land?

I didn't want to think anymore about dreamy Mr. Straight in San Francisco or a dozen other clean-cut faces I'd glimpsed in Dallas or New York. (Was he just about to come over to our table at the Saint Pierre when we left so abruptly, or did my sister make that up?) I didn't want to think about "normal life" or all the little irritations of the vacation weeks.

But as long as we were up here I was still caught in the net. I couldn't shake the atmosphere of big city traffic, the endless small talk, or those hours with my sisters in California, listening to the complaints about careers, lovers, high-priced psychiatrists, "consciousness-raising groups." All the easy jargon about "levels of awareness," and the liberated spirit.

And my mother so disapproving as she made out the list for the communion breakfast, saying what people needed was to go to confession, and there didn't have to be psychiatrists, old-guard Catholicism mixed up with the tired expression on her face, the irrepressible innocence in her small black eyes.

I had never come so dangerously close to telling them all about "that certain spa" that was always being mentioned in the gossip columns, that scandalous "Club" they'd read about in *Esquire* and *Playboy.* "Guess who created it? Guess what we do with 'levels of awareness' at The Club?"

Ah, sadness. Barriers that can never be broken.

You only hurt people when you tell them the truth about things that they cannot respect or understand. Imagine my father's face. (There wouldn't be any words.) And imagine a flustered Mr. Straight hurriedly paying for the coffee and the croissants in that Pacific Coast hotel dining room. ("Well, I guess I better drive you back to San Francisco now.") No, don't imagine that.

Better to lie and lie well, as Hemingway put it. Telling the truth would be as stupid as turning around in a crowded elevator and saying to everybody: "Look, we're all mortal; we're going to die, get buried in the ground, rot. So when we get out of this elevator . . ." Who gives a damn?

I am almost home, almost okay.

We were crossing the island now, and the sun exploded on the surface of the half-dozen swimming pools. It flashed from a hundred dormer windows in the main building. And everywhere in the verdant paradise below I could see movement, crowds on the croquet lawn and on the luncheon terrace, tiny figures running beside their mounted masters or mistresses along the bridle paths.

Finally the pilot announced the landing, the gentle reminder to fasten my seat belt.

"We're going in, Lisa."

I felt the air in the small cabin subtly change. I shut my eyes, imagining for a moment some thirty "perfect" slaves, that it would be difficult for once to make my choice.

Give me one really unusual slave, I was thinking, one true challenge, something really interesting . . .

I felt suddenly, unaccountably, like I was going to cry. And something happened in my head. There was some little explosion in slow motion. And then fragments of thought or fantasy like the bits and pieces of dreams left over the next day. But what was the content? It was disintegrating almost too quickly for me to know.

Some image of a human being broken open, penetrated, but not in any literal sense. Rather a being laid bare by the delicacy of sado-masochistic ritual—until you reached out and you touched the beating heart of the person and it was this miracle, because the truth is, you've never seen anybody else's beating heart and up until this moment of touching you thought it was just a myth.

Not in good mental shape. Almost unpleasant thought.

I hear my own heart. I have heard and felt the pulse of hundreds and hundreds of other hearts. And no matter how good the slaves are, no matter how exquisite, it will all be the same in a couple of hours.

That's why I want to be back here, isn't it?

That is what I'm supposed to want.

Elliott

3

The Voyage In

THEY TOLD ME to bring any clothing I would want when it came time to leave. How did I know what I'd want when it came time to leave? I'd signed a two-year contract for The Club, and I wasn't even thinking about when I would leave. I was thinking about when I would arrive.

So I filled up a couple of suitcases pretty quickly, and put on the "dispensable clothes" they'd told me to wear for the trip. And then there was an overnight case with what I might require on board.

But at the last moment I threw in my tuxedo, thinking, what the hell, maybe I'd go to Monte Carlo as soon as it was over and gamble every cent they'd paid me for the two years. It seemed a perfect thing to do with the hundred grand. I mean it was such an irony that they were paying me anything. I would have paid them.

And I packed my new book too, though why I wasn't sure. It might still be in a few bookstores when I got out, if the wars in the Middle East were still going on. Photography books tend to stick around that way, but then again maybe not.

I just had this idea that I should look at it as soon as I left The Club, maybe even page through it on the plane out. It might be really important to remind myself of what I'd been before I went in. But what were the odds that I'd still think I was a pretty good photographer by then? Maybe in two years it would all look like trash.

As for El Salvador—the book that didn't get done, the book I was leaving undone—well, it was too late now.

All I cared about on that score was shaking this eerie sense that I *ought* to be dead, just because some asshole had almost seen to it, this feeling it was some kind of special miracle that I was living and breathing and walking around.

It was strange the last evening. I was sick and tired of waiting. Ever since I'd signed the contract, it had been nothing but waiting, turning down the assignments from *Time* I'd ordinarily jump at, drawing away from everybody I knew. And then the final call.

The same genial, well-bred voice. An American "gentleman," or an American behaving like a British gentleman without the British inflection, something of that sort.

I closed up the house in Berkeley and went to Max's at the Opera Plaza and had a drink. Nice to look around at the crowd against all that brass and plate glass and neon light. Some of the most beautifully finished women in San Francisco pass through Opera Plaza. You see them in the Italian restaurant, Modesto Lanzone, or in Max's. Gorgeously painted ladies with professionally done hair and couturier clothes. Always wonderful to look at.

And then there's the big bookstore, true to its name, "A Clean Well Lighted Place," where I could pick up half a dozen Simenon mysteries for the voyage, and some Ross MacDonald and Le-Carré, same high-grade escapist stuff I'd read in the hotel room at three o'clock in the morning when the bombs were dropping on Damascus.

Almost called home to say good-bye again, but then didn't, and then I took a cab to the waterfront address.

Nothing but a deserted warehouse, until the cab had pulled away, and then a well-dressed man appeared, one of those nondescript guys you see everywhere in the financial district of a city at noontime, gray suit, warm handshake.

"You must be Elliott Slater." He led me out onto the pier.

A handsome yacht was anchored there, dead quiet like a white ghost ship, with its string of lights reflected in the black water, and I went up the gangplank alone.

Another man appeared, this one a lot more interesting, young or at least my age, with nicely unkempt blond hair, and very tanned skin. His white shirt sleeves were rolled up to the elbows, and he gave an extraordinary display of beautiful teeth when he smiled.

He showed me to my cabin, and took the suitcases off my hands.

"You won't see these again for two years," he said in a very friendly manner. "Is there anything perhaps you want, Elliott, just for the trip? Everything in your cabin will be put in these afterwards, your wallet, passport, that watch of yours, anything you leave."

I was a little startled. We were standing very close together in the passage and I realized this meant he knew what I was, where they were taking me. He wasn't somebody who merely worked on the yacht.

"Don't worry about anything," he said. He was standing right under the light, and it showed a few freckles on his nose, the sun streaks in his hair. He slipped something small out of his pocket and I saw it was a gold chain with a name plate. "Give me your right wrist," he said.

It raised the hairs on the back of my neck, the touch of his fingers as he put the bracelet on me and snapped the clasp.

"Your meals will be pushed through that slot. You won't see anyone, or talk to anyone during the voyage. But the doctor will come for a final check. The door won't be locked until then."

He opened the cabin door. Soft amber light inside. Dark-grained wood under a sheen of plastic lacquer. His words had set up a din in my head. *The door won't be locked until then.* And the little bracelet felt annoying, like a cobweb clinging to me. I read my first name on the plate and something like a code of numbers and letters beneath it. I felt hairs rise again on my neck.

The cabin was okay. Rich, brown leather armchairs, mirrors all over the place, large bunk with too many cushions, built-in video monitor with a library of films on laser disc under it, lots of books. Sherlock Holmes of all things, and the erotic classics, *Story of O, Justine, The Claiming of Sleeping Beauty, Beauty's Punishment, Romance of the Rod.*

There was a coffee grinder-maker, beans in a glass canister, a refrigerator full of French mineral water and American soda, a tape player, and unopened decks of exquisitely decorated cards. I picked up one of the paperback Sherlock Holmes.

Then the door opened without a knock. And I jumped.

It was the doctor, obviously, in a starched white coat. With an easy, amiable expression, he set down the inevitable black bag. I wouldn't have guessed he was a doctor without the coat and the bag. He looked like a weedy adolescent, even a little pimply still and washed out, and his short brown hair was as messy as short hair can get. Maybe he was a resident just off twenty-four-hour duty. And with a polite but preoccupied look, he had out the stethoscope immediately, asking me to take off my shirt. Then he removed a manila file from the bag and opened it on the bed.

"Mr. Elliott Slater," he said, scratching the back of his head, and looking at me for definite verification. He was already thumping on my chest. "Twenty-nine. In good health? No major problems of any kind? Regular doctor?" He turned to consult the file again, and glance over the signed report of physical examination. "All this has been checked out," he hummed half under his breath. "But we like to ask you face to face just the same."

I nodded.

"You work out, don't you? You don't smoke. That's good."

Of course my private physician hadn't known what the examination was for when he filled out the report. "Fit to participate in a long-term strenuous athletic program," was jotted on the blank portion at the bottom in his near indecipherable hand.

"Everything seems in order, Mr. Slater," said the doctor, putting the file back in his bag. "Eat well, sleep well, enjoy the voyage. You won't be able to see much out of the windows; they're covered with a film which will make the scenery something of a blur. And we have one recommendation, that you refrain from any private sexual stimulation during the trip." He was looking me directly in the eye. "You know what I mean . . ."

I was startled, but I tried not to show it. So he understood everything, too. I didn't answer.

"When you arrive at The Club, you should be in a state of sexual tension," he said as he moved to the door. He might as well have been telling me to take an aspirin and call next week. "You'll perform much better if you are. I'm going to lock the door now, Mr. Slater. It will open automatically if there is any emergency on the vessel and there is more than adequate lifesaving equipment, but for no other reason will it be opened. Is there perhaps any last question you want to ask?"

"Hmmmm. Last question!" I couldn't resist laughing under my breath. But I couldn't think of anything. My heart was clipping along a little too fast. I looked at him for a moment. Then I said: "No, thank you, Doctor. I think everything's been covered. That's tough about not jerking off, but I never did want hair to grow in the palms of my hands."

He laughed so suddenly that he looked like somebody else. *"Enjoy* yourself, Mr. Slater," he said trying to get his smile under control. The door shut behind him, and I heard the lock turn.

For a long moment I sat on the bunk staring at the door. I could already feel a stirring between my legs. But I decided I would try to play the game. It would be like being twelve years old again and feeling guilty just on general principles. And besides, I knew he was right. Better to land at The Club with all systems revved and ready for action rather than on an empty tank.

And for all I knew they were watching me through the mirrors. I was theirs now. It's a wonder it didn't say "Slave" on the bracelet. I'd signed all the papers myself.

I took one of the books off the shelf . . . one that wasn't erotic, and making myself comfortable on all the pillows, started to read. James M. Cain. Terrific stuff, but I'd already read it. I reached for the Sherlock Holmes. It was a wonderful facsimile of the original *Strand Magazine* printing of the stories, complete with little ink drawings. I hadn't seen anything like it in years. Very nice, being with Holmes again, remembering just enough to make it interesting, not enough to ruin it. What they call good clean fun. After a while, I put the book down and consulted the shelves again hoping they'd have Sir Richard Burton, or Stanley's book about finding Livingstone. But they didn't. And I had Burton in my suitcase where I'd packed it and forgotten about it days ago. First feeling of being a prisoner. Trying the door to see it was locked. What the hell? Get some sleep.

At times, playing the game was hard.

I showered a lot, soaked in the bathtub, did push-ups, read all the James M. Cain again, *The Postman Always Rings Twice* and *Double Indemnity* and *Serenade,* and watched all the films on disc.

There was one film that really got to me. It was brand new, still in the brown paper mailing envelope, and I opened it last. It was a little thing about the gypsies in New York called *Angelo, My Love.* I wished there'd been a couple of sequels, all about the same gypsies, the same little kid Angelo.

But it seemed strange, a film like that in this collection of Bogart *film noir* classics and hard glossy *Flashdance* trash. I took the packaging out of the waste basket. The disc had been sent out express mail from a Dallas video store of all places only a couple of days before we left. Odd. Like maybe somebody saw it and loved it and ordered it impulsively for the cabins on the yacht. I wondered if anybody else on board was watching it. Not a sound ever penetrated the room.

I slept a great deal. In fact, I would say I slept most of the time. I wondered if there weren't drugs in the food, which was slipped through the door. But I don't think so, because I felt so good when I woke up.

Now and then I woke up in the middle of the night and realized what I'd done.

I was headed to The Club, this strange place, for two years, and no matter how I begged or pleaded, for two years I wouldn't be allowed to split. However, that was the least of it. It was what was going to happen there. And I remembered my master, my trainer, my secret sexual mentor, Martin Halifax, saying over and over, right up to the end, that two years was too long.

"Go for six months, Elliott, a year even. You can't really imagine what The Club is. You've never been incarcerated anywhere longer than a few weeks. And these are small places, Elliott. The Club is enormous. We're talking about two years."

I didn't want to argue with him anymore. I had said a thousand times I wanted to be lost in it, no more fortnight trips and exotic weekends. I wanted to drown in it, get so deep into it that I couldn't keep track of time, believe in a day when the time would be up.

"Come on, Martin, you've sent in all the papers," I'd said.

"And they've examined me, accepted me. If I wasn't ready, they wouldn't take me, right?"

"You're ready for it," he had said wistfully. "You can handle what happens there. *But is it what you really want?*"

"I want to go off the proverbial deep end, Martin. That's what I've been saying all along."

I had practically memorized the rules and regulations. I'd be paid one hundred grand for my services. And for two years I'd be their property to do with as they pleased. I wondered what they charged their "guests," the ones who would use us, if they paid us that much.

And now I was on board the yacht, and already there was no turning back. I could hear the sea, though I couldn't see it or really smell it, and rolling over I went back to sleep.

The truth was, I couldn't wait to get there. I wanted to be there now. I got up in the night and felt the door again to make certain it was locked, and that made the desire in me uncontrollable so that it erupted in a half tangle of painful and delicious dreams.

I was kind of regretful afterwards, but there was only one mistake—coming like that, like a Catholic boy in a wet dream.

A lot of the time I thought about Martin, about the way it had started, "the secret life" as he called it and I called it to myself.

There had been so many mentions of "The House," before I had finally made somebody spell it all out. And it had been so hard to call that number, yet so easy to wind up outside the immense Victorian at nine on a summer night. The traffic was almost gusting past me uphill as I turned to make the short walk under the tall, straight Eucalyptus trees to the wrought iron gate. ("Come to the basement door.")

Forget the hackneyed whores in black corsets and spike heels ("Have you been a bad boy? Do you need a whipping?") or the dangerous little baby-faced hustlers with the tough-guy voices. This was going to be the Deluxe Escorted Tour of Sado-Masochism to the max.

And the civilized conversation first.

Small lamps in the big, sprawling, darkly paneled room, no brighter than candles as they illuminated the paintings, the tapestry on one wall. Oriental screens, deep red and gold paisley window shades. Dark, lacquered french doors with mirrors for glass along the far wall, and a big comfortable leather wing chair, my foot on the ottoman, and the shadowy figure of the man behind the desk.

Martin, soon to be my lover, my mentor, my therapist, my unstinting partner in the inner sanctum. Tall, black haired, youthful voice, gray at the temples, the fiftyish college professor at home in the brown V-neck sweater with the open shirt collar, small, but brilliantly inquisitive eyes. Eyes that seem forever to be examining something wondrous. Gleam of an old-fashioned gold watch against the dark hair on his arm.

"Do you mind the smell of a pipe?"

"Love it."

Balkan Sobranie tobacco, very nice.

I was nervous, sitting quietly in the chair, my eyes scanning the walls, the old landscapes under the crazed lacquer, the small enameled figurines on the mahogany chest. Otherworldly here. Mass of purple flowers in a pewter vase against the marble clock. The carpet that smooth plum-colored velvet kind you only see these days on the marble staircases in the very old hotels. Sounds from the house above. The creak of boards, the dull resonance of a music.

"Now, I want you to talk to me, Elliott," he had said with an easy authority, as if none of this was rehearsed, had ever happened before. "I want you to relax and recount for me the sort of fantasies you've enjoyed over the years. You don't have to be graphic. We know how to be graphic. We're geniuses at it."

He sat back, his eyes moving over the ceiling, touch of gray in the eyebrows, the pipe smoke rising thickly for an instant, then vanishing.

"And if it's difficult for you, describing the fantasies to me, you can always write them down if you like. I could leave you alone for a while with paper and pencil, the typewriter if you prefer . . ."

"But I thought you made things happen, that it was an environment, so to speak, a world . . ."

"It is, Elliott, don't worry about that. We'll take control. Complete control. Once you go through that door. We have a thousand ideas, a thousand proven ways of doing things. But it's important that we talk first, about you, about your imagination. It's a good way to begin. Do you want a cigarette, Elliott?"

How unnerving it had been to realize I had to begin it, start the wheels turning. I had seen myself surrendering when I came to the door. "Yes, I'm guilty. Punish me." How unnerving to discover myself saying, "I want to go through that door now."

"Soon enough," he had answered, with a little smile. Eyes softening, getting larger, more mellow as they studied me. It was the easiness of a man who had known you all your life. A man like that could never hurt anyone. Face of the family doctor, the college professor who understood and respected your mania for the subject matter, the perfect father . . .

"You know, I'm not the type you would expect for this," I had said uneasily. God, he was a good-looking man. Had some constitutional elegance a young man never has, no matter how beautiful he is.

"As a student I was something of a nuisance," I said. "In my family, I'm considered testy. I don't take orders well. I'm almost a cliché when it comes to macho tastes. I'm not bragging about it, you understand." I had shifted in the chair a little uneasy. "I think it's ludicrous, risking your life at 150 miles an hour around the Laguna Seca track, skiing down the most treacherous slopes you can find anywhere, pushing a goddamned ten-pound Ultralite plane as high and as fast as it will go on a teacup of gas."

He had nodded for me to go on.

"There is something compulsive, stupid about it all. For two years I've been working as a photographer. But in a way it's the same routine. More and more danger. The scrapes I've gotten into are obscene. Last time, I nearly bought it in El Salvador, ignoring the curfew, like some rich kid on vacation . . ."

Don't really want to talk about that. Those awful endless seconds in which for the first time in my life I could hear my own watch tick. Couldn't stop running it by over and over afterwards, what *almost* happened: TIME-LIFE PHOTOGRAPHER GUNNED DOWN BY DEATH SQUAD IN EL SALVADOR. The end of Elliott Slater, who could have been writing the great American novel in Berkeley, or skiing in Gstaad instead of doing this.

Wouldn't have made the network news for two nights.

"But that's often the *type* of man who comes here, Elliott," he said calmly. "The kind of man who submits to no one and nothing in the real world. The man who's used to wielding power and fed up with intimidating others. He comes to us to be turned inside out."

I smiled at that, I think. Turned inside out.

"Don't edit the fantasies, Elliott. Just talk to me. You're obviously articulate. Most of the men who come to us are articulate. They have keen and elaborate imaginations, well-developed fantasies. I don't listen to these fantasies like a doctor. I listen to them as stories. Like a literary man, if you will. Do you want a drink to help you talk? Maybe some Scotch, a glass of wine?"

"Scotch," I had said absently. I didn't want to be drunk. "There was one fantasy in particular," I said, as he stood up and went to the bar. "A fantasy that used to obsess me when I was a boy."

"Tell me."

"God, you don't know how felonious it all was, having those fantasies, thinking I was some sort of lunatic when everyone else was gaping at the *Playboy* centerfold and the cheerleaders on the football field."

Johnny Walker Black Label. Good luck. Just a little ice. Even the aroma and the thick crystal glass in my hand had its effect.

"When people discuss their fantasies they often talk only about the acceptable," he said as he settled behind the desk again, leaning back. He was not drinking, merely drawing on the pipe. "They talk about the clichés, not about what they really imagine at all. How many of your classmates had the same fantasies, do you think?"

"Well, I used to imagine something of a Greek myth," I said. "We were all youths in a very great Greek city, and every few years seven of us—you know, like in the Theseus myth—were sent to another city to serve as sexual slaves."

I took a little sip of the Scotch.

"It was an old, sacrosanct arrangement," I said, "and an honor to be chosen, yet we dreaded it. We were taken into the temple, told by the priests to submit to everything that would happen to us in the other city, and our sex organs were consecrated to the god. It had happened for countless generations, but the older boys who had been through it never told us what would take place."

"Nice," he said softly. "And then . . ."

"As soon as we arrived in the other city, our clothes were taken away. And we were auctioned off to the highest bidder to serve for several years. It seemed we brought luck to the rich men who bought us, we were symbols of fertility and masculine power, like the Priapus in the Roman garden, the Herm at the Greek door."

How strange it felt to be telling it, even to a man who seemed the perfect listener. Not the faintest indication that he was shocked.

"We were cherished by our masters. But we weren't human. We were utterly subservient, meant to be played with." I took another slow drink. Might as well get it all out. "Meant to be beaten," I said, "and sexually tormented and starved—driven through the city for the amusement of the master, made to stand at the gate for hours in a state of sexual tension while the passersby stared, that kind of thing. It was a religious thing to torment us, while we kept our fear and humiliation inside."

Had I really said all that?

"Terrific fantasy," he had said very sincerely, with a slight lift of his brows. He appeared to reflect. "All the best ingredients. You not only have 'permission' to enjoy the degradation, but it's religious, good."

"Listen, my mind is a three-ring circus," I had laughed, shaking my head.

"That's the way it is with all sado-masochists," he said. "The 'circus animals' almost never desert *us.*"

"There has to be the framework," I said. "All very neat. It would be unthinkable if you were really forced. Yet there has to be coercion."

I had put the glass down on the desk and immediately he rose to fill it.

"I mean there has to be consent and coercion for it to be a really good fantasy," I said, watching him. "Yet it has to be a humiliation, with a struggle inside between the part of you that wants it and the part that doesn't; and the ultimate degradation is that you consent and grow to like it."

"Yes."

"We were objects of scorn as well as veneration. We were mysteries. We were never allowed to speak."

"Just priceless," he whispered.

What had he really heard in those hours as we talked? Anything really different, new or unique? Maybe all he had learned was that I was like a thousand other men who had passed through his doors.

"And your master, the man who buys you in the other Greek city . . ." he had asked. "What does he look like? How do you feel about him?"

"You'd laugh if I told you. He falls in love with me. And I fall in love with him. Romance in chains. Love triumphs in the end."

He hadn't laughed, merely smiled agreeably, drawing on his pipe again.

"But he doesn't stop punishing you or using you when he starts loving you . . ."

"No, never, he's too good a citizen for that. But there's something else." I could feel my pulse accelerating. Why the hell mention it at all?

"Yes?"

I felt a slowly heating anxiety for the first time, a confusion as to why I had come here.

"Well, just that there is this woman in the fantasy . . ."

"Hmmmm."

"She's the wife of the master, I guess. Well, I know she is. And it sometimes works towards her."

"How does it work towards her?"

"No. I don't want to be involved with women," I said.

"I understand."

"There are a thousand reasons why you choose a man or a woman as a love partner, a sex partner, aren't there? It's not like it used to be, when the lines were hard to cross."

"No, not like that anymore," he said. But he had paused for a second before answering. "And you've been with women as well as men?"

I had nodded. "Too many of both."

"And she's in the fantasy."

"Yeah. Damn her. I don't know why I brought her up. I sort of look to her for some sort of mercy, tenderness, and she becomes more and more interested in me—her husband's slave—but then she's worse."

"How is she worse?"

"She's tender, and she's loving, but she's harsher, stricter, crueler at the same time. The humiliation is like keening. You know what I mean? Strange."

"Yes . . ."

"She isn't always there. But sooner or later . . ."

"Yes."

"But this is really off the point."

"Is it?"

"Well, I mean I want male lovers, male dominators, if you will. That's what I really have to say. That's why I came here, for men. I've heard you've got beautiful men here, the best . . ."

"Yes," he said. "I think you'll like the album when it's time for you to make your choice."

"I get to choose the guys who dominate me?"

"Of course. That is, if you want to. You can always leave the choice to us."

"Well, it's got to be men," I said. "Men are the exotic sex to me, the hot sex. The sex for romps and for rough adventures . . ."

He nodded, smiled.

"There's nothing like it, that sense of being with somebody as tough as yourself. When women come into it there is something sentimental, high pitched and romantic . . ."

"Whom have you *loved* in the past—really loved—men or women?" he asked.

Silence.

"Why is that important?"

"Oh, you know why it's important," he said very gently.

"A man. And a woman. At different times." Close those doors, please.

"You loved them equally."

"At different times . . ."

It wasn't three months before we were talking again in that same room—though I would never have thought after all that happened upstairs I could sit in a room, fully clothed, and talk to him again—and he was saying: "But there is no need for you to pay me anything anymore, Elliott, that's what I'm telling you. I can arrange it with three or four interested 'masters' who will cover all expenses. You'll come here as before, but on their nickel. While you are here you will belong to them."

"No. Money doesn't mean a damn thing to me where all this is concerned, and I'm not ready for that . . ." The complete domination of another, his fantasy supplanting my fantasy. No, not yet. Keep it careful. It's hard enough.

But it was like a staircase spiraling upwards from the basement room, and I was going to climb it right to the very top.

"I'd like a woman," I said suddenly. Did *I* say that? "I mean I . . . Well, a woman," I said. "I . . . think it's time for that, a really good-looking woman who knows what she's doing, and I don't want to know anything about her, and I don't want to pick her picture out of any album. You pick her. Make sure she's good at it, great at it, that she can take over. It's time . . . I mean, to be dominated by a woman, don't you think?"

Martin was smiling agreeably.

"As the genie says when he rises from the lamp, 'Yes, master.' A woman it shall be."

"She'll be good looking—she doesn't have to be beautiful you understand—and she'll know how to do what she does . . ."

"Of course." He nodded patiently. "But tell me . . ." He drew on his pipe, letting the smoke out slowly. "Do you think you'd like to meet the lady in a Victorian bedroom, you know, an old-fashioned setting? I mean in a very ladylike room—lace curtains, a four-poster, that sort of thing?"

"Oooooh, God. Is this really happening to me?"

Up and up the staircase, through one lovely layer of dream after another.

And now, half a year later, where was I headed? The Club.

"It's just what I want," I had said. I had driven over as soon as I finished reading the rules and regulations, waiting an hour to see him in the little waiting room, glancing again and again at my watch. "Why didn't you tell me about this place before?"

"You have to be ready for The Club, Elliott."

"Well, I'm ready for it now. The full two-year contract, that is exactly what I want." I was steaming as I paced the floor. "How long will it take to get me in there, Martin? I could be ready day after tomorrow. I could be ready this afternoon."

"The two-year contract?" he had asked, weighing each word equally as he spoke. "I want you to sit down, have a drink. I think we should talk a little more about what happened in El Salvador, Elliott. What happened there with the death squad and all of that."

"You don't understand, Martin. I'm not running from anything that happened there. I learned something there about violence, that it didn't have to be literal for it to work."

He was listening very intently.

"When a man seeks out violence," I said, "be it war, sports, adventure, he wants it to be symbolic and most of the time he believes it really is. And then comes that moment when somebody *literally* puts a gun to your head. And you *literally* almost die. Then you realize that you've been confusing the literal and the symbolic all along. Well, El Salvador is the place where I learned that, Martin. I'm not running from it. It's merely the reason I'm here. I want violence just as I always have. A sense of danger, Martin. I love it. I think I even want to be annihilated by it all. But I don't really want to be hurt and I certainly don't want to die."

"I understand," he had said. "And I think you put it very well. But for some of us, Elliott, sado-masochism may only be a phase. It may be part of a search for something else . . ."

"So it's a two-year phase for me, Martin. So The Club is the perfect landscape for my search."

"I'm not so sure, Elliott."

"It's too much like the boyhood fantasy I had, don't you see? Being sold to the Greek master for a period of years. It's too perfect . . ."

"Time doesn't mean much in a fantasy . . ." he objected.

"Martin, the die was cast when you told me about the place. Now if you won't sign the papers, I'll find some other way . . ."

"Don't get angry." He had cooled me off at once with that easy smile. "I'll sign the papers. And for the full two years if that's what you want. But let me remind you that there were a lot of elements in that boyhood fantasy you told me."

"This is too beautiful!" I said.

"You may be searching for a person rather than a system," he went on. "And when you go to The Club, Elliott, the system—in all its remarkable splendor—is exactly what you get!"

"I want the system," I'd said. "I can't turn away from this! If it's half as good as what you've described, I wouldn't miss it for anything in the world."

So the contract for two years at The Club with its male and female slaves, male and female guests, its male and female handlers, trainers, staff. All right.

Okay. That's *exactly* what I want. I don't think I can stand it. How could anyone stand it? It is just exactly what I want.

No good to think of all that while trying to refrain.

After six days at sea I was like a male dog tormented by a bitch in heat when I finally heard a key in the door.

It was afternoon and I was just coming out of the bathroom, showered and shaved after a really late sleep. Maybe they knew that. Saved them work.

It was the young blond-haired kid with the deep-bitten suntan and the white sleeves rolled halfway up his arms.

He came in smiling again.

"All right, Elliott," he said. "We're eighteen hours away from port. You're not to speak at all unless you're spoken to. And just do as you're told."

There were two other men with him, but I didn't really see them. Instantly, they had swung me around, pinning my hands behind my back. I got a glimpse of a white leather blindfold before it was slipped into place. Secret panic. If only they wouldn't use the damned blindfold. I felt my pants being unsnapped, and the shoes being pulled off my feet.

It was all beginning, really happening. My cock was immediately hard. But it was hell, absolute hell, not being able to see.

I waited for the gag to come but it didn't, and as soon as I was stripped, my wrists were being shackled with leather cuffs and lifted over my head. Not too awful. Nothing as awful as being tied up tight.

I was led into the corridor, and in spite of all the training I'd had, I was sort of stunned.

But it was like an aphrodisiac had been pumped into me. When they hung my wrists up on a hook above me I was sorry I'd played by the rules all those nights in the cabin when I was alone.

I didn't know where I'd been taken, except that for some reason it sounded like a large room. I could feel the presence of others there. I could hear them making small sounds. I could hear a sort of whimpering as though one of the slaves nearby was about to cry. I realized it was a woman slave.

So we really were mixed together, males and females, just like they'd said we'd be. I couldn't picture it. And the sound of the woman confused me. Maybe I felt more powerless because I couldn't protect her. Or it tantalized me to know I was suffering silently in the same manner that she was suffering. I just couldn't tell.

I hated the blindfold. Couldn't stop hating it. I rubbed my face against my arm trying to get it off but that was useless. And I had to make myself quit.

And it crossed my mind as it would a hundred times that maybe Martin was right and I'd made an awful mistake. Training in Martin's house in San Francisco, what was that? And the brief stays at the country place, scary as they were, what had they been compared to this? But with the strongest, sweetest sensation of relief, I thought: "It's too late now, Elliott. Can't say, 'Let's call it quits now, gang, and all go out for a steak dinner and a couple of beers.'" I mean it's over because it's begun. That's the beauty of it. It's for real, as Martin had said.

There was this glorious sense suddenly of really being *in* it for the first time over my head. I'd done this inalterable violence to my own life, and this was exhilaration, this feeling. I wouldn't have gone back then for anything in the world.

The sounds I heard undoubtedly meant that more and more slaves were being brought in. I heard the pat of their bare feet and the click of the heels of the handlers. I heard a groan here and there, the creak of a chain or the chink of the metal of the buckle sliding over the hook. The leather cuffs were tight around my wrists.

There were mostly small sighs, moans. Both male and female noises. And it seemed some of these cries came from behind gags.

I was sure that some distance away someone, a man, was struggling, and a scolding voice confirmed this immediately, calling him by name and telling him to "behave." It was almost cajoling. The "you know better than that" tone of voice. The sharp crack of a strap sounded and I heard a loud moan. Then came a real thrashing, sounds so keen they were like fingers stroking my skin.

I was trembling. It would be awful to be punished like that for bad behavior. It wasn't like being humiliated for someone's pleasure, being an exotic champion of pain. No, it was being a failure down here in the hold of the ship, a bad slave.

The thrashing seemed to go on forever. Then I heard random cracks of the belt drawing nearer, grunts, groans. I could feel movement around me. And the belt caught me on the thighs and then on the butt, but I stood very still and didn't make a sound.

Hours passed.

My arms and legs ached. I'd doze for a while and then awaken, feeling naked all over, the passion in me like a knot.

Once I woke up and found myself writhing as if trying to touch another body, the desire was so keen, and I felt a whack from a thick belt.

"Stand straight, Elliott," said a voice, and with a flush of embarrassment I realized it was the young blond one with the pretty teeth.

Then I felt his large, cool hand open against the flesh he had just struck. He squeezed it hard. "Only six hours to go, and they want you in prime form." And I felt his thumb on my lips telling me to be quiet, as if I had dared to speak.

The sweat broke out all over me. I couldn't tell whether he'd moved away or he was right beside me. It was awful to me that I hadn't been perfect, and yet I was so aroused it was exquisite, that perfect stab in the loins of pleasure and pain.

When I awoke again, I knew it was deep night.

Some inner clock told me and also the dead quiet of the ship, though what the noises on board had been before I couldn't have told.

It was just quieter now, that's all.

Unwelcome flash of home, the last weekend with my father in Sonoma, the blaze of the log fire in the game room, him standing opposite me across the green felt of the pool table, getting ready to call his shot. Last rain of the season washing down the windows over the olive-green hills, and a wholly unexpected rebelliousness rising in me, something that too sadly resembled malice. *You think you are so very sophisticated, you think you have always anticipated everything, understood every little twist and turn, analyzing and evaluating and predicting the eventual pattern of every "phase" before it even began, handing me the treatises on masturbation, and the* Penthouse *and the* Playboy *magazines when I was fourteen, and the pair of two-hundred-dollar call girls in Las Vegas on my sixteenth birthday—not one but two, goddamn it, two call girls—and then that brothel, that gorgeous brothel full of black-eyed smiling little boys in Tangier. All the sophisticated blather about the health of it, the unwholesomeness of Mother's ideas, the necessity of the word being made flesh again, the poetry of the expanded vision, well, I have something to tell you now that will scorch your balls off, Dad, do you know what your son really wants!*

"You cannot be serious. You are not going to such a place for two years!"

The last time I spoke to him on the phone, he said: "You're not going to do this. I want you to tell me who these people are. I'm driving down to Berkeley tonight."

"Dad, give up, will you? Write to me at the New York address I sent you. The letters will be opened but I will get them. And don't try anything dramatic, Dad. Don't hire any Philip Marlowes or Lew Archers to track me down, okay?"

"Elliott, do you realize I could have you committed for this? I could have you put in the state asylum in Napa. Why are you doing this, Elliott?"

"Come on, Dad. I'm doing it for pleasure, the word made flesh, *(just like the call girls and the Arab boys),* for pleasure, pure and simple, this is going all the way to the moon." *And it is something else too that even I can't grasp, some harrowing of the soul, some exploration, some refusal to live on the outside of a dark and heated inner world that exists behind the civilized face I see in the mirror. It goes way, way back.*

"I'm scared shitless over this. Do you hear what I'm saying? The Middle East thing I could put up with. I had you out of El Salvador in less than two hours after you called. But this thing, Elliott, this sex club, this place . . ."

"Dad, it's a hell of a lot safer than El Salvador. There are no guns or bombs where I'm going. The violence is make-believe. I thought that a man of your sophistication would be the last one to . . ."

"You're out too far."

Too far?

Dad, we have already left the earth's atmosphere. We are landing on the moon.

I knew it was morning because I heard people stirring all around me. And about an hour later, the ship really came to life. Doors were opened. There was the sound of feet, and my bound wrists were unhooked and the leather cuffs taken off them, and I was told to clasp my hands to the back of my neck.

"Take off the damn blindfold!" I thought. I was pushed and felt another naked body right in front of me. Hands steadied me when I lost my balance, and moved me a step back.

I was crazy. I could hardly resist the urge to tear off the blindfold myself. But the moment had come and I wasn't going to freak out. My heart was going in rapid staccato. I realized my mind was going absolutely blank.

Suddenly hands were touching me again and I stiffened. A leather strap was being fitted round the base of my cock. My balls were lifted and pulled forward, the loose skin bound against my cock as the little strap was snapped tight.

And just when I thought I'd go bananas from this, the blindfold was finally pulled off.

For one second my eyes were squeezed shut against the light. Then I glimpsed a narrow corridor over the heads and shoulders in front of me, and a metal ladder that led up to the almost blinding sunlight on the deck.

There was a lot of noise on the deck. Shouts, talking, even laughter, and I saw a slave being forced up the ladder and a handler beside the ladder driving the slave with his belt. It was a woman slave with very fine, full red hair, the kind that looks like a cloud, hovering around her shoulders, and the sight of her nakedness absolutely paralyzed me, and she ran very fast up the ladder and disappeared into the sun. I've never been able to make up my mind who is more naked when stripped, a man or a woman. But seeing those full feminine hips and that tiny waist made me even more frantic than before.

But we were all rushing forward.

I felt myself pushed, then lashed. I saw the dreamy blond man for a moment before he ordered me to the ladder.

"Up on deck, Elliott," he said with that same genial expression, and I felt the smack of his belt. "And keep your hands on the back of your neck."

As I reached the top of the ladder, I heard the command "Eyes down" and "Forward" and yet I saw the blue water and the white beach.

I saw the island itself.

Lush low trees, roses trellised to the whitewashed stucco walls, and terraces stacked one on top of another, like the hanging gardens of Babylon, broken everywhere with bursts of fluorescent bougainvillea, deep tropical green. There were people at tables on the terraces, hundreds and hundreds of people, maybe thousands. This is it. Really it. The lump in my throat hardened to a rock.

Martin's many warnings came back, that nothing could really prepare you for a system that worked as well as this one. They could tell you all about it but the sight of it, the size of it, was always an incalculable shock.

The commands were coming sharp and fast. Slaves right in front of me were running across the deck and down a broad gangplank. Perfect bodies, muscles rippling with the exertion, hair flying, the jiggling, prancing movements of the women in sharp contrast to the swift, powerful strides of the men.

I couldn't accept or rebel against what was happening. And for an odd moment I doubted not the reality of what was going on around me, but the reality of all that had ever happened to me before.

I had the positive sensation as I came down the gangplank with the others that all my comfortable life before had been an illusion, and that I had always been this. I can't explain how unaccountably real this was. I had always been this.

And I had to keep up with the others, do exactly as I was told. The blond kid appeared again like some kind of demon (I almost said "You again, you little bastard."), his suntanned arm flexing as he hit me almost caressingly with his belt.

"Good-bye, Elliott," he said in the most friendly voice. "Have a good time at The Club."

I flashed him my most venomous smile, but I was disoriented. Clearing the gangplank, I stared up at the vine-covered walls and that endless stack of terraces, and the soft blue dome of the flawless sky.

Another strong young menace was whipping the slaves up a zigzag path. There was nothing to do but pass him, to take the licks as I ran with the rest.

The handler shouted impatiently for us to pick up speed. And I wondered why we obeyed, why it was so important to do what he said. I mean we'd all been brought here for the pleasure of the thousands up there on the terraces. And why wouldn't it give them just as much pleasure to see somebody stumble, and be singled out for the strap?

But if anybody stumbled, it wasn't going to be me. That's the genius of it, I thought. I want to please them. We're not only acting like slaves, we're thinking like slaves too.

4

Love at First Sight

IT WAS DIZZYINGLY warm, and the grounds were so crowded I could hear the loud steady hum of conversation even in the empty corridor as I hurried to my room.

There wasn't time now for that quiet drink, or a walk in the garden, or even to see the slaves driven off the yacht.

They would be in the receiving hall in an hour and I hadn't even been through the files.

A complete description along with history and commentary is collected on every slave, along with detailed photographs, and I've learned to pay as much attention to the file as to the slave.

As soon as I opened the door, I saw Diana waiting for me, unadorned, hair brushed free, the way I like her best. Some trainers think that subtle little adornments make the slave more naked. I don't agree.

In rooms like our rooms, with the thick wool carpets and antique velvet draperies, and all the little accoutrements of civilization, a naked slave burns like a flame.

Amid the dark flowing colors, and the video screens and the

low sculpted furnishings, she is purely animalian and infinitely mysterious the way only the human animal can be.

Put her in rooms as outrageously decorated as my own—among the Haitian paintings and the potted ferns, the barbaric stone sculpture—and you have something so lush and ripe that you can smell the incense where there is no incense, taste the smoke and salt of flesh on sight.

There is nothing quite like the moment of first discovering her there, no matter how many I have seen in the halls and the gardens, and seeing those heavy swaying breasts, and the moist triangle of pubic hair, as she waits for my command.

Diana was always like a dancer, sleek and languid, her snow-white hair falling straight over her graceful shoulders and back. Her face is the contradiction because it's all pluck. Large, almost pouting lips and the roundest, most alert eyes I've ever seen. But it's the French accent that really gets to me. I've tried to analyze it, the effect, tried to get used to it. But it's one of her indefinable assets that simply will not quit.

I couldn't pull her into my arms and kiss her. There wasn't time to start all that. I could see the enormous stack of manila files before the white computer screen on my desk. All the data was in the computer but I still liked to hold the photographs and the hard copy in my hands. I always sent for the folders, no matter how primitive they looked.

"Open the windows, my dear," I said.

"Yes, Lisa."

The Bombay gin was waiting, glass already packed with ice, the limes just cut. Bombay gin is the only gin I can drink straight, and I never drink it with anything else.

Out of the corner of my eye I watched her move with that same feline speed and agility, her long hands reaching slowly as if they were in love even with the cord that pulled the heavy purple drapes.

For three years, she has lived within these walls, as the expression goes. Once a year for a six-week vacation, she vanishes. And I have to confess I have wondered where she goes, what she does, what she is like during that time. I'm told that Club members have offered her film contracts, marriage, luxurious private arrangements in exotic places. But that's nothing too extraordinary for the slaves here. That's one reason we make them sign up to stay for a while and pay them so much.

I saw her once, dressed and on her way out for her holiday, walking arm in arm with another slave to the waiting plane. Someone said that five of them had clubbed together to rent a castle in the Swiss Alps. And Diana was already dressed for snow in a white fur-trimmed coat and a white fur hat. She looked Russian, like a giant of a ballet dancer, dwarfing the other girl as she moved in big easy strides over the landing field, her chin up, her little French mouth puckered naturally as if always ready to be kissed.

But I don't know that Diana. I know only the naked subservient slave who is here for me night and day. She is perfection if there is such a thing, and in the unbroken quiet of the night I've often told her so.

The sunlight poured in through the french windows, the great leafy limbs of the California pepper tree like a veil over the blue of the summer sky.

It was too clear, that sky. The faint sound of wind chimes came from the garden; a wisp of cloud gusting south suddenly disappeared.

And as she crouched near me, I reached down, slipping my fingers over her breasts—perfect breasts, not too large—and felt her silent yielding as she knelt, her bottom back on her heels as I liked her, her eyes moistening as she looked down.

"Pour," I said, and started with the files. "You behave yourself while I was gone?"

"Yes, Lisa, I tried to please everyone, Lisa," she said. I took the glass from her hand, waiting a few painful seconds for the gin to chill, and I drank a deep cold swallow, letting the immediate warmth spread through my chest.

She was poised like a cat, ready to spring and slip her arms around my neck. I should have been unable to resist it really, but I still hadn't shaken the anxiety of the vacation. It was as if we were still circling up there.

I went ahead and made the little indescribable gesture that said all right to her. And she knelt up and pressed against me, the incarnation of softness, and I turned and kissed her large and puckering mouth. I could see the feeling penetrating her, coursing through her limbs, her nakedness offering up everything. Could she feel the stiffness in me? She tightened her eyebrows, her lips open, when I let her go.

"There's no time now," I whispered. It wasn't necessary, really, to tell her that. She was as well trained as any slave I'd ever had. But there was that softness between us, and it excited her just as much as the remoteness that always brought the tears to her eyes.

I turned on the computer video display, quickly tapping out Preliminary Report on the bed of white plastic keys. At once the silent string of glittering green letters began its march across the screen. Fifty new slaves. I was astonished at the number.

Thirty I knew about from the auction, but there were twenty independent sales. *All* two-year contracts! So our new rules and regulations were working. I hadn't expected it so early, I'd thought surely we'd be stuck with some six-monthers or at least yearlies who would be released just when they had reached their prime. We need two years really to train a slave, and get our money's worth out of him or her, but many just aren't ready for that.

Now time for the hard copy.

Each file has a large picture of the slave on the inside cover. I went through them fast. I threw aside six, seven, ten immediately. Beauties all, and someone would love them and torment them. But not me.

But here was a gorgeous woman, with heaps of brown hair in big natural ringlets, American oval face.

I released myself slowly from Diana, guiding her down to put her arms around my waist. I could feel her delicious weight against me, her forehead nudging my belly, and with my right hand I stroked her hair. She was trembling. She was always jealous of the new slaves. And her breasts felt very hot. I could almost feel her heart beating.

"Did you miss me?" I asked.

"Desperately, Lisa," she said.

Kitty Kantwell, I memorized the name of the slave in the file. She was tall by the chart, five foot six inches, that would make her fun to handle, and the IQ was listed as remarkably high. Master's Degree in journalism, well traveled, television weather girl in Los Angeles, own talk show in San Francisco for a while, trained in a private club in Bel Air by a Parisian named Elena Gifner. I didn't know the trainer. But we had bought good merchandise from Gifner before. I flipped back to the picture.

"And were you worked much?" I asked. I had deliberately left permission Diana could be worked. She needed it. Maintenance wasn't enough.

"Yes, Lisa," she said. I could hear the break in her voice. I lifted her hair back from her neck. She was hot all over. I knew the hair between her legs would be drenched.

The brown-haired girl in the picture was definitely an American Beauty—*Playboy* centerfold type, perfect weather girl all right. I could see her on the nightly news. Round-eyed, big-eyed, like Diana, but something mundane about her, even with the lovely bone structure. But then, there was the strong intelligence in the face, the touch of inquisitiveness. Wholesome American girl, with cheerleader breasts.

Definitely have a look at this one.

I sipped the gin and hurried, cracking back the stiff covers one after another. Diana was kissing me.

"Be still."

I was staring at a photograph of a man.

Blond-haired, six foot two by the chart. But I looked back to the photograph, unable for a moment to understand my reaction, its intensity, unless it was the expression on the man's face.

They don't often smile in the pictures. They stare straight forward as though they were being photographed by the law. Sometimes all the vulnerability is revealed there, the fear. They're going into captivity, they don't know what's going to happen, maybe it's all a mistake. But he was smiling, or at least there was some amusement, some cleverness there.

Thick blond hair, almost curly, falling a little down on the forehead, well shaped around the ears and the neck. And his eyes gray or blue maybe, behind the pale smoke tint of a large pair of glasses, the kind shaded only lightly at the top so that the glass is clear over the cheeks. And that smile. He wore a black turtleneck for the picture, arms folded instead of at his sides. An amazingly relaxed picture.

I flipped to the back of the file to see him naked. I sat back staring at the photograph, sipping the gin.

"Look at these," I said. Diana raised her head and I showed her the two pictures. "A beauty," I whispered, tapping the picture of Slater. I motioned for more of the ice and the gin.

"Yes, Lisa," she said, putting as much injured feeling into the words as permissible, and filling my glass as if the gesture had tremendous significance. I kissed her again.

In the naked picture, he stood with arms at his sides but there was the same faint amusement, though he'd tried to conceal it a little. Maybe somebody told him not to smile. And a startling sense of presence emanated from the picture. He wasn't shielded behind an attitude, a fantasy image of himself. Flawless body, a real California body, with fine gymnasium muscles and powerful calves. Not overdeveloped, and a real beach tan.

Elliott Slater. Berkeley, California. Age twenty-nine. Trained in San Francisco by Martin Halifax.

Well, that was interesting. My hometown. And Martin Halifax was only the best in the world, and a friend to me like no one else had ever been. A little crazy maybe, but then aren't we all?

I had worked in Martin Halifax's Victorian house in San Francisco when I was twenty. Only fifteen dimly lighted and elegantly furnished rooms and yet it seemed a universe, as vast and mysterious as The Club. It was Martin Halifax who had perfected the solarium for slaves, with the little treadmill and the exercycle that slaves were made to pedal as they were punished. Leave it to a Californian, even one as pale as Martin, to think of something healthy like that.

But Martin Halifax and The House had existed when there was no Club, and in a way he was as responsible for The Club as I was, or the man who had financed it. It was Martin's choice not to come in with us. He could never leave San Francisco or The House.

I flipped to the handwritten report by Martin. Martin loved to write.

"This slave is a man of unusual sophistication, financially independent, possibly wealthy, and in spite of a variety of interests, obsessed with becoming a slave."

A variety of interests. Ph.D. in English literature from the University of California at Berkeley. My old alma mater. For a Ph.D. he should get the Purple Heart. IQ not as high as Kitty Kantwell, but nevertheless extremely high. Occupation, freelance photographer covering rock, celebrities, frequent war assignments for Time-Life. Author of two books of photographs, *Beirut: Twenty-Four Hours* and *San Francisco Tenderloin Down and Out.* Owns a Castro District art gallery, a Berkeley bookstore. (Which bookstore? I knew all of them. Didn't say which one.) A fanatic for dangerous situations and dangerous one-man sports.

Now that was unusual, like the face.

I glanced at my watch. The slaves wouldn't be coming to the hall for another forty-five minutes and I already had my two, I was sure. Either Kitty Kantwell or Elliott Slater, and all I had to do was look at Elliott Slater to know that I'd go mad if I didn't have first pick.

But I did have first pick.

So why the anxiety on the upsurge? The sudden feeling that something terribly important might somehow be out of reach? Damn it, I was off the plane. Vacation was over. I was home.

I shoved the other files aside and began to read on Slater.

"Slave presented himself for training on August seventh of last year." (Nine months ago. Absolutely phenomenal that he was here. But then Martin knew what he was doing.) "Determined to submit to the most intensified programs we offer, while resisting any alliance with a master outside the house, though several were enthusiastically offered after almost every group activity in which the slave was used.

"Extremely resilient and strong. Requires hard punishment to make an impression, but surprisingly easily humiliated, almost to the point of panic, in a variety of circumstances. . . . A subtle stubbornness surfaces in this slave that won't be discerned except—"

I stopped. This sort of thing I would find out my way and with exquisite pleasure. I flipped forward a few pages, knowing Martin's penchant for description.

"Slave incarcerated briefly at Marin County country estate, and obviously found the full week's program very strenuous yet requested almost immediate return. Sleeps extremely well after all sessions. Reads constantly during rest period at the end, a wide variety of classics, trash, and sometimes poetry. Addicted to mystery stories and James Bond thrillers, but then reads great Russian novels apparently word for word." (That was too juicy. Who would notice it, but Martin, the spy?) "Slave is a romantic. Yet shows no attachment *so far* to any master after any session, asks only for whatever I recommend in the future, saying that *he wants what he fears most.*"

I glanced at the picture again. Squarish face, even features except for the mouth, which was a little full. And the smile could be construed as having just a touch of mockery in it, a little bit of a sneer. There ought to be some word for a sneer that isn't quite as crude as a sneer. He had a "nice" face, rather antithetical to the word sneer.

God, two weeks ago I might have passed him in Berkeley on the street, seen him at the bar at . . .

Take it easy, Lisa.

You've read a thousand files on slaves from San Francisco. And we don't have any life beyond this island, right? The information in this file, as you've told the new trainers over and over, is supposed to help you *here*.

I flipped to the digest of the training history.

"Surprised to find slave returned immediately after two-week session in the country during which he was worked almost relentlessly by series of out-of-town guests. Old Russo-Prussian countess in love with the slave (see later notes). Slave says if longer incarceration can't be arranged he will go elsewhere. Money no object. Slave mentioned several times that the younger masters terrified him, yet he makes no request to avoid them. Says it is particularly terrifying to be humiliated by someone weaker than himself."

I flipped to the end. "Sent with the highest recommendations *(ideal* for The Club!), *but must emphasize this slave is a novice. Watch.* Though I can vouch for his readiness and mental stability, I must add that his training has not gone on very long! And though he passed tests with women handlers here, these were very stressful situations for the slave, who obviously fears the women more than the men. Slave refuses to talk about the women, however, saying he will do whatever he can to be accepted by The Club. Repeat. Watch. Slave responded well to the women, *obviously profoundly excited by the women,* but this produced intense conflict in the slave."

I had a suspicion about the face. Paged through the file until I found several small pictures. I was right. In the profile shots, when he wasn't addressing the camera, Elliott Slater looked hard, almost cold. Something really formidable in the preoccupied face. I flipped back to the smile again. Very lovable.

I closed the file without reading "Notes on Masters and Mistresses Who Favor the Slave." And God knows how much else Martin had written out. Martin should have been a novelist. Or maybe Martin should have been exactly what Martin was.

I sat there just looking at the manila cover. Then I opened it and looked at the photograph of Slater again.

I could feel Diana beside me. Feel her warmth and her need. I could feel something else in her, too, a little concern about the tension in me.

"I won't be back for supper," I said. "Now get the hairbrush and quickly, and I want some cool Chanel to splash on my face."

I jabbed the button on my desk as soon as she was on her way to the dresser.

She kept the Chanel cold for me in a little refrigerator in the dressing room and she brought it with a clean flannel cloth.

I patted my cheeks with it as she brushed my hair. No one brushes it quite as well as she does it. She knows how to do it.

The door opened before she was finished. Daniel, my favorite attendant, was there.

"Good to see you back, Lisa, we've missed you," he said. He glanced at Diana. "Richard says the slaves will be in the hall in forty-five minutes. And he needs you. Special matter now."

Worst luck.

"All right, Daniel." I gestured for Diana to stop with the brushing. I turned her, looked at her. She bowed her head, her white hair falling down around her. "I'm going to be very busy," I said. "I want Diana worked."

I could feel her mild shock. The hottest moments for us were always right after we'd been separated, and in the late afternoon there would be time, wouldn't there? And she knew that, of course.

"Count Solosky's here, Lisa. He's already asked for her, been told no."

"Yes, good old Count Solosky who wants to make an international star out of her, right?"

"That's the one," Daniel said.

"Make him a present of her. Bind her nicely with ribbon, something like that."

Diana threw me a stunned look, but she was pouting beautifully.

"If he doesn't have any immediate use for her, see that she's worked in the bar until very late."

"She hasn't displeased you, Lisa."

"Not at all. I'm just suffering from jet lag. We circled for two hours up there."

The phone was ringing.

"Lisa, we need you in the office." It was Richard.

"Just got in, Richard. Give me twenty minutes, and I'll be there." I put down the phone.

Diana and Daniel were gone. Blessed quiet.

I took another long cool drink of the gin as I opened the folder again.

"Elliott Slater. Berkeley, California . . . Trained in San Francisco by Martin Halifax."

Not just home, those places—Berkeley, San Francisco—where you go to suffer the particular penance called vacation. No. They were the landmarks of the long journey that had brought me to this very island, this very room.

In a half daze, it seemed I remembered things, or rather reinvoked them—the way it had all started. And in the beginning there had been no Martin Halifax for me.

I saw the first hotel room where I had ever made love, if that is what it is called, remembering that steamy and forbidden encounter, the smell of the leather, the lovely feeling of abandoning all control.

Was there any heat like that first heat? How strange it had been, those long hours beforehand of dreaming about it—a ruthless master, a cruel master, a drama of punishment and submission without real hurt—not daring to describe it to another living soul, and then meeting Barry, handsome as the boys in the romance comics, in of all places the University Library in Berkeley, just a few blocks from home for me, and having him ask so casually about the book I was reading, the dreary imaginings of masochists chronicled by their psychiatrists that proved . . . what? That others like me existed, people that wanted to be bound, disciplined, tormented in the name of love.

And then his whisper in my ear on that typical first date that it was what he wanted, that he knew how to do it and well. He worked weekends as a bellhop in a small but elegant San Francisco hotel, we could go there now.

"Only as far as you want to go," he had said, the blood thudding in my ears when the kisses had done so little.

I'd been so terrified as I climbed the marble steps—we couldn't use the elevators from the front lobby—criminals together as he unlocked the dark little suite. Yet it was precisely what I wanted, yes. Strange surroundings. And his firmness, his direction, his unerring sense of timing, and limits, and how to push them ever so gently.

It was the blaze at last consuming all the more swiftly because I hardly knew who he was.

I couldn't remember his face even now. Only that he was good-looking, that he was young, that he looked wholesome, like every other young man in Berkeley, that I knew the house, the street where he lived.

But then the thrill had been the near anonymity, that we were two animals, that we were mad, that we knew absolutely nothing really about each other. A quiet young high school girl too serious for sixteen, and a college boy scarcely two years older who read Baudelaire, made enigmatic statements about sensuality, smoked fancy pastel-colored Sherman cigarettes that you ordered direct from the company, wanted what I wanted, and had a place to do it, a plausible technique.

We would make dissonant but beautiful music. And the danger? Had that been thrilling? No, that had been an ugly undercurrent, dissipated only when the night was finished, when drained and silent I had followed him out of the hotel, slipping through the side door, relieved that nothing "horrible" had happened, that he wasn't insane. Danger was not a spice, only what I had to pay in those days.

In the womb of The Club there was never that price . . . that was its genius, its contribution, its raison d'etre. No one was ever hurt.

Had I seen him two times more before he suggested a meeting with his friend, David, and the afternoon session with the three of us together, when it lost its intimacy, when it seemed suddenly we were not all equal participants, when I became afraid? Sudden attack of inhibition. When he called with yet another friend, another proposal, I felt betrayed.

Long agonizing evenings after that wandering in downtown San Francisco searching faces that passed me, peering into the lobbies of the grand hotels, thinking, yes, somewhere, somewhere a man, an elegant and experienced man, a new beginning, someone infinitely more clever, commanding, more discreet.

Sitting by the phone at home with the personal column from the newspaper before me. Is it a cryptic code for what I think it is? Do I dare to call the number? Drifting through the regular experiences—senior prom, movie dates—murmuring lies now and then to excuse apathy, restlessness, that appalling feeling of being a freak, a secret criminal. Wandering past the counters where the leather gloves lay in the glass case looking faintly sinister for all the white tissue paper in the shallow box.

Yes, I would like these, these long, long tight black gloves . . . And the broad leather belt around my waist cinching me like an exotic girdle, yes, and black silk and the high tight fitted boots as soon as I could afford them. And finally discovering in a bookstore near the Berkeley campus, in silent disbelief and blushing excitement, that shocking French classic which others must have known for years, looking so innocent in its smooth white book jacket, *The Story of O.*

No, you are not alone.

I felt everyone in that store was looking at me when I paid for it. Yet flushed and glaze-eyed I sat in the Cafe Mediterranee turning page after page, defying someone to see it, comment on it, come up to me, closing it only when I had finished all of it, and staring through the open doors at the students hurrying through the rain on Telegraph Avenue, thinking I will not live all my life with it being fantasy, not even if . . .

But I had never called Barry again. And it hadn't been one of the mysterious personal advertisements, nor the blatant communications between sadists and masochists that shocked everyone so in the pages of the underground newspapers. Rather it had been a most innocent-looking little advertisement in a San Francisco neighborhood paper:

> *Special Announcement. Applications still being taken for the Roissy Academy. At this late date, only those entirely familiar with the training program should apply.*

Roissy, the name of the mythical estate to which O had been taken in the French novel. Impossible to misinterpret it.

"But you won't use a whip, I mean something that can really damage, inflict bad pain . . ." I had whispered into the phone after all the arrangements had been discussed, the interview at a San Francisco restaurant, how we should recognize each other.

"No, my dear," Jean Paul said. "No one does that, except in books."

Oh, the pure agony of those long ago moments, the secret hopes and dreams . . .

Jean Paul had looked so European when he stood up from the table at Enrico's. Velvet jacket, narrow lapels. Like a beautiful dark-eyed French actor I remembered from a Visconti film.

"A truly sensuous American woman, what a treasure," he had whispered as I finished the coffee. "But why do we waste time in this place? Come with me."

Yes, agony, that was the word for it, being that young, that compelled, that frightened . . . Some pagan angel had been watching over me in those days, surely.

But my mental clock had sounded its silent alarm. Richard was waiting, and now we were the pagan angels. And we had less than half an hour before the new slaves came into the receiving hall.

Elliott

A Walk on the Wild Side

I GUESS I figured those terraces facing the sea were the whole club, and once we were inside the garden, we'd be sheltered from adoring eyes by the sprawling branches of the trees. No such luck.

I bowed my head, trying to catch my breath, only half believing what I saw. The garden stretched out endlessly, linen-draped luncheon tables everywhere crowded with elegantly dressed men and women, and waiting on the crowd quite nonchalantly were hundreds of naked slaves with trays of food and wine.

Scores of guests moved back and forth from the buffet tables, under the lacy foliage of California peppers, laughing, talking in small clusters, and of course there was still the throng on the terraces of the main building gazing down as before.

But it wasn't just the size of the gardens, or their crowds that shocked me again.

It was the odd way that the crowd resembled any other, except for the dazzling spectacle of the naked slaves.

There was the flash of gold jewelry on tanned arms and throats, the sun exploding in mirrored glasses, the clink of silver on china—men and women in dark tans and Beverly Hills chic lunching as if it were perfectly normal for a horde of scrumptious nude men and women to be waiting on them—and of course there was the usual gathering of some fifty abject and trembling newcomers with their hearts in their mouths at the gates.

It was as devastating to see backs turned, faces in earnest conversation, as it was to see bold stares and smiles.

But again, everything happened very fast.

The mass of new slaves was huddling together, and a new flock of handlers was closing in. They waited just long enough for us to catch our breath, then we were ordered to run along a garden path.

A strong, red-haired male slave broke into the lead when ordered, and another followed, whipped on by the handlers, who seemed a little more sophisticated than the bunch on the yacht.

They were powerfully built like the blond sailor, but they were decked out all in white leather, including tight pants, vests, and the straps with which they drove us along.

They seemed made to go with the pastel tablecloths, the huge flowered hats worn by the women, the white or khaki shorts and seersucker jackets of the men.

I braced myself for the sight of a woman handler but there was none, though there were plenty of knockout women scattered all through the garden, and everywhere I looked I saw short skirts, exquisitely shaped legs, bright sandal high heels.

The grass, soft as it was, scratched at my feet. And I was dazed by the lush growth on all sides, the fragrant jasmine and roses everywhere, and the birds I glimpsed in gold cages, giant blue and green macaw parrots, pink and white cockatoos. In one enormous gingerbread cage there were dozens of chattering capuchin monkeys. And the final spice were the free-wheeling peacocks picking their way here and there through the flowers and the grass.

It's paradise all right, I thought, and we're pleasure slaves in it, just like something out of an ancient Egyptian tomb painting, where all the slaves had been naked and the lords and ladies exquisitely dressed. We were here to be used and enjoyed like the food being eaten, the wine being poured. We'd slipped into an unexpurgated history of decadence, and found ourselves being driven right through the garden of the quintessential lord.

I felt my breath give out, but it wasn't the running. It was the flood of sensation, the desire reaching a new pitch.

The slaves waiting the tables were incredibly poised. I got glimpses over and over of well-oiled bodies adorned only with a bit of silver or collar of white leather, pubic hair and nipples startling me wherever I glanced. And I'm one of these characters, I thought. This is my role and there's no getting away from the script.

We were driven faster, the handlers smacking us pretty hard with the straps. And the blows were beginning to sting.

There was that creeping, swelling warmth that excites and weakens at the same time. And while the other slaves pressed to the middle of the path to escape the straps, I didn't bother. I got stubborn and just let the blows fall.

The path twisted and turned a thousand times. I realized we were going around the garden. We were being shown off. A tiny psychic explosion went off in my brain. There wasn't any escape from this. I couldn't give some code word and check out for a bath and massage.

In fact, everything was out of my hands. Maybe for the first time in my life.

We passed very close to a flagstone terrace of tables. Heads turned, members, guests—whatever they were—pointing, commenting. And a young dark-haired handler started really putting on a show with his strap.

On some level, my reason said: "It's his job to whip the hell out of us, so why resist it? We're here to be reduced to nothing, to surrender our will." But I couldn't keep this in my head. I was already losing some vital perspective, "getting lost"—which was just what I'd told Martin I wanted to do.

But the scene around us was looking familiar. We were passing the swimming pools again and the high mesh fence of the tennis courts.

In fact, we'd come around almost to where we started, and now we were driven towards the center of the garden, where the tables fanned out from a large white stage. It was a kind of pavilion you see in small town parks where the band plays on Sundays, but there was a catwalk jutting out from it like the kind they use in fashion shows.

My blood went cold, or hot, depending on how you see it, when I saw the stage.

Within seconds we'd been crowded under the mimosa trees behind the pavilion, in the shade. The handlers pushed us roughly together, then told us not to touch one another, and over the loud speaker system there came one of those smooth, liquid radio announcer voices saying, "Ladies and gentlemen, the postulants are now at the pavilion to be viewed."

For a second the sound of my heart pounded over everything else. Then I heard a roar of clapping rising from the tables. It seemed to echo off the banks of terraces, and then to lose itself in the empty blue sky.

I could feel the trembling and the anxiety around me as if we were all connected to the same live wire.

A tall female slave with a lot of sleek golden hair pushed her lovely breasts against me.

"They aren't going to make us walk down that ramp one by one?" she asked under her breath.

"Yes, ma'am, I think they are," I found myself whispering back, red-faced at the realization we were two naked slaves trying to talk to each other, scared as hell the handlers would hear.

"And this is just the start," the red-haired male slave said to my right.

"Why the hell can't we just serve drinks or something?" the blond said without moving her lips.

One of the handlers turned around, smacked her with the belt.

"Beast!" she hissed. I pushed between her and the handler, as soon as he looked the other way. When he turned back he didn't seem to notice, just smacked somebody else.

The blond sort of snuggled against me. And it occurred to me for the first time that the women had it a little easier because you couldn't tell what they were feeling. There wasn't a single male who wasn't fully and humiliatingly erect.

Whatever the case, this was going to be hell. Being tied up, that was one thing, being made to run with the gang, that was bad enough. But forcing myself down that ramp on my own steam? *If I wasn't ready for it, Martin, they wouldn't take me, right?*

The crowd seemed to be growing by cell division, as there was a movement everywhere towards the pavilion with a lot of empty tables being instantly filled.

I wanted to run. I don't mean I really thought to do it. I couldn't have gotten two feet away, but I was really panicky that if they put me up alone on that stage, I'd back off or bolt. My chest was heaving and it was like somebody had given me another shot of aphrodisiac at the same time. And the blond was pressing against me with her sweet soft silky little arms and thighs. I can't go bonkers like that, I was thinking, I can't fail the very first test.

A white-haired young man with ice-blue eyes was carrying his hand mike back and forth across the pavilion as he told the audience the new postulants were a stunning crop. He had on the same white leather pants and vest as the handlers, shirt open at the throat, but he was wearing a well-tailored white cotton jacket that gave him an even more tropical look.

Members were crowding up to sit on the grass right by the catwalk. There were clusters of people standing back under the trees.

Immediately an absolutely delectable tidbit of dark female flesh was forced up into the middle of the pavilion, a handler holding her wrists together over her head. It was better than an out-and-out slave auction, the nude merchandise wriggling in the handler's grip.

"Alicia from West Germany," the man with the mike announced to a round of applause. And the handler turned Alicia in a circle before pushing her forward to make the long walk down the ramp.

No, I was thinking, maybe even whistling through my teeth. Just not ready for this. And I ought to feel sorry for her, damn it, instead of staring at her plump little bottom and the blush on her face. I'm in the same fix.

In a kind of delicious agony, she turned at the end of the walk, and rushed back to the master of ceremonies, obviously straining not to break into a run.

The crowd was getting louder. Even some of the women had folded themselves up nicely to sit close on the grass.

Nope, impossible. They can do anything to me where I'm passive, but I can't make myself do that. Yet how many times had I said that at Martin's, and always I managed to do what I was told, right?

These are small places, Elliott. The Club is enormous . . . Yes, but I am ready for it, Martin. Even you said that.

The next one up was a young man named Marco with a hard tight little backside and an extremely beautiful face. He was blushing as badly as Alicia, and he was stiff as a battering ram.

He made the walk awkwardly, but I don't think anybody cared much about that, and it seemed the crowd got rougher, as if a male slave released something in it that the girl had not.

When I felt the handler gripping my shoulder I couldn't move. I mean, my God, there are fifty other slaves here, give me a break.

"You gotta do it!" the little blond whispered.

"You gotta be kidding!" I whispered back.

"Silence. And move it, Elliott!" The handler went to shove me forward, and was obviously startled that I didn't budge. I couldn't make myself budge. The master of ceremonies turned around to check out the delay. And another handler grabbed hold of my wrists immediately while a third pushed me forward towards the steps.

I'd always heard the expression "dig in your heels" but I'd never done it till this moment, and I knew then I was totally out of control.

And now they were hauling me by force onto the pavilion, just like this was a Roman marketplace, two other handsome strong-arm types helping the first three so that I didn't have a chance.

"I can't do it!" I said, struggling.

"Oh, yes, you can," said one of them ironically, "and you will and right now." And abruptly they let me go, pushing me forward in front of the master of ceremonies as if they knew I'd be too ashamed to turn and bolt.

Thunderous applause came from all around. It was just the kind of racket they make at a horse show when a thrown rider gets back on a balky horse. For a second, I couldn't see anything in front of me but light. But I wasn't moving. Just standing helpless on the Roman auction block like all the other imports. I'd scored at least that much.

"Come on, Elliott, down the ramp," said the master of ceremonies, in a nice pampering lunatic tone, his hand over the mike. And from the front-row spectators on the grass there came a chorus of whistles and cajoling shouts. It seemed to me that I was going to back up, to get off the stage as fast as possible, but what I did was put one foot in front of the other and start walking down the ramp.

My brain had gone to the moon—this was beyond humiliation; it was execution, it was walking the damned plank. The sweat had broken out all over me again, yet I was as hard as I'd ever been.

But I started seeing everything again, the eyes working me over, and I started to hear the clapping and the little comments that were all tone and no words. *The system—in all its remarkable splendor.* I deliberately slowed my pace. I belonged to these people, and it was a feeling halfway to orgasm. I took a deep breath.

Turning around and coming back was just a shade easier, so why the hell did I force myself to look right at those watching me, look into their eyes? Smiles, nods, little whistles of approval. You bastards, you.

Don't do anything smart, Elliott. Don't do it. But I could feel the smile spreading on my face. I stopped, folded my arms, and deliberately winked at the lovely dark-skinned lady who was grinning under her white hat. A roar went up from the front rows. Loud clapping. Hell, don't just smile and look out of the corner of your eye at all the others. Blow a little kiss to the little brunette in the white culottes. In fact, why don't you smile at all the pretty girls, give them all a wink and a little kiss?

Laughter and cheering from all sides. I had a real rooting section spreading all the way back to the trees. I was getting kisses from everywhere, "right on" fists from the men. Why not make a little fashion model pivot, nothing camp, you understand, just taking my time, looking them over, what the hell?

Then I was staring straight down the ramp at a gang of the angriest-looking guys I'd ever laid eyes on, the crowd you don't want to meet in a dark alley, all of them glowering at me while the master of ceremonies just sort of gaped.

"The show's over, Elliott!" one of them said in a stage whisper between clenched teeth. "Come on, Elliott, now!"

I froze. But there was nothing to do but wave good-bye to my fans and walk right into it. I wasn't going to let them drag me off.

I bowed my head and moved towards them like I hadn't seen them, was just being a good boy again, and in two seconds they took hold of both my arms and threw me right down the steps and onto my hands and knees in the grass.

"Okay, Mr. Personality," I heard one of them say in a voice vibrating with anger. Another pushed me forward with his knee.

All I could see in front of me was a pair of white boots as my head was pushed down so that my lips touched the leather whether I liked it or not.

Then I felt a hand on my hair, and my head was pulled up until I was looking into a pair of very dark brown eyes. Pretty terrific looking, like all the rest of them, and I sensed that it was going to be part of the sweetness and torture, that even the pastry cooks in this place could bring your blood to a simmer against your will.

But this one had a voice that could throttle your soul.

"Oh, you're really clever, aren't you, Elliott?" he asked with a kind of chilling outrage. "You've got a lot of tricks up your sleeve."

"And no sleeve," I thought but I didn't say it. Things were bad enough. In fact, they were awful and I didn't really understand how they could have gotten that way so fast. In fact, I couldn't believe what I'd just pulled.

The other handlers closed in as if I were a dangerous animal, and the slave show was continuing against the tidal wave of noise from the crowd as before.

Impossible to analyze this sense of shame, this sense of disaster. I'd blundered already, goddamn it, I'd panicked up there, and I'd failed.

I tried to look submissive, knowing the worst thing was to try to speak in my defense.

"That was a first for us, Elliott," the brown-eyed guy said, "that little number you just did. You really made your mark."

Fine face, and disturbingly resonant voice. His chest was almost bursting out of his shirt.

"What do you think the Master of Postulants is going to do with you, Elliott," he asked, "after he hears about that little stunt?"

He held something before my eyes and I saw it was a broad grease pen.

I think I said shit or hell under my breath.

"Don't make a sound," he threatened. "Unless you want to be gagged, too."

I felt the pressure of the grease pen against my back and heard him spell out what he was obviously writing, the words "Proud Slave."

I was pulled up onto my feet. And somehow standing up was

worse. I felt the wallop of one of the handler's straps. And then a nice little hail of blows that made me wince.

"Keep your eyes down, Elliott," said the handler. "And your hands behind your neck." He touched the grease pen to my chest, and I tried not to grit my teeth as he wrote the same words, spelling them very deliberately again. I couldn't figure why a little thing like that was so mortifying, and the sense of regret in me was turning into panic again.

"Why not the whipping post?" one of the others asked. "That would soften him up for the receiving hall awfully well."

Really, guys, I'm just the new kid on the block.

"No, we'll keep him fresh for the Master of Postulants," said the first one, "and for whatever the Master of Postulants decides."

He lifted my chin with the tip of the pen.

"Don't try anything else, blue eyes," he said. "You don't know what trouble you're in."

I glanced back at the "good little boys and girls" as I was shoved to the side and told to stand still.

The red-haired male slave was just making the promenade, with all the appropriate humility, bringing a chorus of whistles from the crowd. And the little blond was staring at me like I was some kind of hero or something. The hell.

What was wrong with me that I started that clowning? I'd been doing okay until I had to look at them, had to smile.

And now I was at odds with the very system that I wanted to be embraced by; fighting it instead of yielding to it, just the way I fought everything outside.

You're ready for it, Elliott. You can handle what happens there. But is it what you really want?

Yes, goddamn it, Martin. And somehow this little fuck-up had made the discipline and the humiliation seem even more real than before.

Lisa

6

Business as Usual

RICHARD WAS AT the window of his office when I came in, sunglasses shoved up into his thick reddish-blond hair, obviously watching the new slaves through the garden below.

He roused himself, and smiled immediately, sauntering towards me in his usual slow graceful manner, his thumbs hooking in his back pockets. He had deep-set eyes, eyebrows a little bushy, and those deep lines in his tanned face that Texans get very early from the hot dry heat there and never seem to lose. I never laid eyes on him that I didn't think of his nickname at The Club, which was the Wolf.

"Lisa, my darling," he said. "We missed you. Don't ask how much, it'll only make you worry. Give me a kiss."

At twenty-four, he was the youngest chief administrator and Master of Postulants we'd ever had, and he was one of the tallest trainers in The Club.

I like to believe that the height doesn't matter, that it's all in the manner, but when you have the manner of Richard, the height adds a hell of a lot.

He handled the slaves effortlessly, whipped them around,

shook them up, and all his gestures were so slow and languid that the power continuously astonished them. And he had a particularly disarming expression in spite of the deep-set, often squinting eyes, an expression of openness, curiosity, an immediate affection for every slave he saw.

He was perfect as Master of Postulants because he could explain things so well. As an administrator, he was the best. He was forever exhilarated by what he had to do, endlessly absorbed in the essence of The Club. He riveted himself almost painfully to the slaves under his immediate command. He "believed" in The Club, an obvious fact that struck me now with a startling freshness, disconcerting me slightly as I slipped my arm around him, pressed my lips to his cheek.

"I missed you too, all of you," I said. My voice sounded funny to me. I wasn't all right yet.

"Little problems, beautiful," he said.

"Now, when they're just about ready?" I meant the postulants. "Can't it wait?"

"I think you can manage it quickly, but it requires your touch." He slipped behind his desk and pushed a file forward. "New member. Jerry McAllister. Full service for the year. Sponsored by half a dozen other members and they're all here, talking to him, telling him what to do, but he doesn't know how to begin."

Full services meant the man had paid the top membership fee of $250,000 yearly to come and go any time that he wished. He could have lived here year round if he wanted to. But they never do.

The Club works sort of like a bank in that way, depending on the fact that everybody won't cash in on the same night.

I sat down behind the desk and flipped open the file. Forty-year-old home computer millionaire from California's Silicon Valley, huge estate in San Mateo County, private Lear jet.

"He's had several drinks with his friends on the terrace," Richard explained, "and now he's in his room waiting for a little help. Wants a young female slave, dark hair, dark skin. I sent Cynthia in, but he sent her back. Says he needs a little guidance, a 'hands on demonstration' as they call it in computer world. Thought maybe you could stop in, talk to him, promise to come back this afternoon."

"Not if I can help it," I said. I picked up the phone. "Get me

Monika right away." Monika was the only trainer whom I trusted with this sort of thing, and if she wasn't in, I'd have to go. She was in.

"Hi, Lisa, just on my way down."

"Detour, will you, Monika?" I gave her the details on Mr. Jerry McAllister—heterosexual, light smoker, light drinker, probably cocaine user, workaholic, et al. "Ask for Deborah to work with. Tell him you'll be back right after the indoctrination. Deborah can probably take it from there. She could turn Peter Pan into the Marquis De Sade with not a word said."

"Sure, Lisa, leave him to me."

"Thanks, Monika. Fifteen minutes. Don't miss the indoctrination. Promise him we'll both come in the afternoon."

I hung up the phone and looked at Richard.

"Okay?"

"Sure. I just thought you'd want to handle it yourself. We could have held things up for a few minutes . . ."

Same look on his face I'd gotten from Diana and Daniel.

"I'm a little tired from vacation," I said before he asked the inevitable question. "The plane was late."

I glanced at the other papers in front of me. The human pony trainer was here from Switzerland, the man who wanted to sell us the slaves all done up in harnesses and bits and reins to pull rickshaws, carts. Hmmmm. Lovely. So why did it give me a headache at once?

"Never mind all that," Richard said. "We'll see the lovely little stable tomorrow." He had settled in the chair on the other side of the desk.

"And what's this—" I picked up the scribbled phone message —"about some kid claiming he was coerced?"

"A lot of nonsense. Handsome young faun, strictly the Persian Boy type, told the boys on the yacht last night he's a captive, that he was kidnapped in Istanbul no less. He's lying. He came from New Orleans and he's got cold feet."

"You're positive."

"We brought him right on in early this morning. Lawrence is working with him now. Ten to one he has already confessed he's just frightened. If he was captured it was in Darius's palace right before the invasion of Alexander."

I reached for the phone.

None of us like to disturb a master with a slave in his private studio, but this had to be settled right away.

The bell that rings is very soft, and it is always interesting how different slaves react to it. For some slaves and masters, the phone breaks the spell completely. With others, it heightens the sense of subservience. The master stops to answer the phone while the suffering slave waits for further examination, ordeal.

Lawrence's voice was the usual discreet whisper.

"Yes?"

"How's it going?" I said.

Slow, rich laugh.

"He's confessed to everything. It was all a lie. He was just panicked. But you should hear the story he made up. I'll give you the tapes." He turned his mouth away to give a command to the slave in the room with him. "The best part was about his being drugged," he said, "stripped naked, and shipped north on the Orient Express. The Orient Express! Now the big question is, do I send him below stairs for three days to thoroughly chastise him, or take him in hand?"

"Take him in hand. If he's that scared I think it's important you do that. Punish him for the lying, but you know, not hard labor. He'd be lost."

"My thinking exactly, but punished he will be."

"And do give me the tape. I want to hear that story." I put the receiver down.

A gorgeous scenario flared in my head, something as elaborate as an amusement park ride. That we should have a train on the grounds with a big old-fashioned steam engine and ornate old passenger cars—ship slaves to various parts of the grounds on it, have them auctioned to the members from the platform, have slaves available for little sessions in the sleepers on the train itself.

Not the Orient Express but the Eden Express. I liked that. Could see the gold scrollwork: the Eden Express. Yes, everything very Edwardian on the Eden Express. And maybe when we got bigger, covered the whole island, we'd really need the conveyance. We could lay miles of track . . .

And suddenly I saw the track going on forever, as if land and sea were no longer substantial, and the Eden Express just went steaming ahead, its cyclops eye boring steadily through the nighttime darkness, as it left this little Eden for parts unknown . . .

"My, but you're getting soft," Richard said suddenly.

It seemed sudden anyway to me. I had just seen myself in a white dress getting aboard the Eden Express.

"Last year you would have had that boy on hard labor for two weeks."

"Is that so?" I wore a white hat and I had a white handbag, dressed sort of like that girl the old man remembers in *Citizen Kane,* the girl he glimpsed years before on the ferry and never forgot. "A white dress she had on . . ." Is that what he says? Sweet madness to think someone could remember me like that. Somewhere in my luggage there was a new white dress, and a white straw hat with long white ribbons . . .

Now how will that go with your black leather watchband, your boots?

"I think you made the right decision, of course," Richard was saying.

I looked at him, tried to listen.

"Either way it will work," he went on. "That's the sublime thing. As long as there is firmness and direction, everything will work."

"The kid is scared," I said. He was talking about the kid, wasn't he?

"What time is it?" I asked.

"Fifteen minutes until they're in the hall. And don't tell me whom you have your eye on. Let me tell you."

"I don't want to hear it," I said, forcing a little smile.

Richard was always right. He could go through the files and match the slaves to the prospective trainers, knowing without fail who would pick whom. Of course the others had to compete for the slaves, haggle with one another. I was first.

"A certain blond-haired gentleman named Elliott Slater," he teased.

"How do you do it?" My face got warm. I must have been blushing. Ridiculous, when we'd been through these games a thousand times before.

"Elliott Slater's the tough one," he said. "The one that's really walking into it. And he's beautiful, besides."

"They're all beautiful," I said, not wanting to admit anything. "What about the L.A. girl, Kitty Kantwell?"

"Scott's in love with her already. I'm betting you choose Elliott Slater."

Scott was the Trainer of Trainers. He and Richard and I made up what the others called "the Holy Trinity" that really ran The Club.

"You mean you want me to for Scott's sake," I said. Scott was an artist of a trainer. And whomever he picked would be on show in the trainers' classroom as a working model half the time. Dazzling experience for a slave.

"Nonsense," Richard laughed. "Scott's just as much in love with Slater. But he's sort of given up, knowing you. And Slater comes from your mentor, Martin Halifax in San Francisco. Halifax sends us geniuses, philosophers, real madmen. How did Martin put it? 'Reads Russian novels word for word'?"

"Come on, Richard!" I said, trying to sound casual. "Martin's the romantic. What we get is the flesh and blood."

The conversation was making me uneasy. That desperate feeling again, like something terribly important was going to be missed. Headache for real. Never should have drunk that gin.

"Lisa loves Elliott!" he sang softly under his breath.

"Knock it off," I said crossly, surprising both of us. "I mean, you know, let's see how it goes. You guys are getting too clever for me."

"Come on, let's take our time getting down there," he said. "Get away from these phones before they ring."

"Good idea."

The slaves might be assembling already.

"I'm betting you choose Slater. If you don't I'm out a hundred bucks."

"No fair telling me, now is it?" I forced a smile.

Scott was waiting for us in the hall, his sleek black leather pants and vest fitting him exactly like skin.

He gave me the usual warm welcome home kiss, and slipped his arm around my waist. The trainers had given him the nickname of the Panther and he deserved it, just as Richard deserved the nickname of the Wolf. Physical affection was always easy with him, and we'd never been in bed together, which made for a nice tension, a nice bit of flirtation every time that we touched. You could learn things about sensuality from Scott just by watching him walk across a room.

I hugged him close for a second. He was all muscle, all heat.

"If it's about a certain slave named Elliott Slater," I said, "don't try to sweet-talk me. It's not fair."

"Whatever Lisa wants, Lisa gets," he answered with another lingering kiss. "But maybe not as soon as you think."

"What do you mean?"

"Your boy's a live one, honey. He just broke into a little vaudeville routine at the pavilion that brought down the house."

"He did what?"

"A perfect send-up of the whole exhibition." Scott laughed. "They pulled him right out of the ranks."

"Richard," I said turning to him immediately.

"Don't expect me to be as lenient as you were just now, my dear," Richard said. "I'm not the one who's getting soft."

Elliott
7

Judgment in
the Receiving Hall

MY HEART STARTED to trip when I realized the show on the pavilion was ending. And the others were being rounded up and marched off like naked school kids two by two.

One of the handlers finally came for me, ordering me to walk forward with my eyes down.

We got plenty of jeers and comments from the tables, the words Proud Slave flickering like neon in my brain.

A couple of times, in fact, the handler ordered me to stop and stand still for inspection. And somehow I managed to do it, keeping my eyes down, ignoring the talk that went on around me, the muted voices sometimes in English, sometimes in French.

The good guys were now out of sight.

But soon enough we came to a low-roofed building, half hidden by banana trees and foliage, and entered a carpeted corridor that led to a large well-lighted hall.

The slaves were already assembled when we entered, and some kind of indoctrination had begun.

I felt my face redden, as rather conspicuously we headed along the side of the group, all the way to the front.

A tall narrow-faced young man with reddish hair was talking and he broke off when he saw us to ask, "What's this?"

This was worse than the pavilion. I tensed all over, and tried to look really contrite.

"Proud Slave, sir," the handler answered with amazing rancor. "It took three handlers to force him onto the stage in the garden . . ."

"Oooh, yes," the tall red-haired man cut him off.

The words seemed to boom through the hall. All the meek were surely staring. Again, I tried to analyze the sense of shame I felt but it was no good.

"Pride so soon, Mr. Slater?" said the red-haired man. I was stung to hear him say my name. And he hadn't even looked at that tiny delicate gold bracelet with the nameplate. This was great. I didn't dare to look up but I could still see he was not only tall, but kind of sinewy in a graceful way, and real sea-tanned like he'd done his time on the yacht.

I could also see glass walls on either side of us, and men and women behind them. And a number of people assembled behind the red-haired man.

Everybody was watching this little debacle. And I knew this weird crowd had to be the trainers, the real heavies of The Club, because they were wearing a lot of black.

Black leather boots, skirts, pants, with their white blouses or shirts. They had black straps hanging from hooks on their belts. Martin had said only the top brass in paradise wore the black leather. And I was hardly immune to the effect.

The man started pacing, as if looking me over, and even his posture, the way he shifted his weight, exuded command.

With a dull, ugly shock, I glimpsed a row of four obviously anxious slaves to the far right of him, all turned to face the assembly, some wet faced, others just red. They had the grease pen writing on their chests or bellies. They'd all been very well worked over by the strap. My gang, the bad guys, I thought dismally. Not good at all.

This was the old-fashioned schoolroom I'd never been in, where the frock-coated schoolteacher dragged you to the fore to be whipped in front of the class.

"I've heard about your little performance in the garden, Mr. Slater," said the red-haired trainer, "your little beauty pageant walk down the plank."

They pick these guys for their voices, I was thinking. He *is* the frock-coated schoolteacher right out of the Dickens novel. Excuse me, please, I think I would like to read *Robinson Crusoe* now instead . . .

"You'd receive the Initiative Award of the new season if we had one to give."

I gave a little shake of my head to show I thought it was awful what I'd done. It was awful.

"But we don't want initiative here, Elliott," he said, drawing closer so that his height got almost as menacing as his voice. Men this tall should be immediately anesthetized and have four inches excised from both legs. "You are a slave. And it seems you have a little difficulty keeping that in mind." Nice pause for effect. "We are here to help you with your difficulty, to eradicate it, so to speak, along with your pride."

I didn't need to try to look miserable. He was flaying every inch of my naked skin. The stillness of the damned place was nerve shattering. I had the sense again, the way I'd had it on the yacht, that there was no reality anymore beyond this. I'd always been this bad little boy, in need of the worst correction, and now the real world had shaped itself around that simple fact.

To make matters worse, one of the female trainers was zeroing in. Okay, you knew it would happen sooner or later. So hold tight. But the word defenseless was taking on new dimensions in my head. I could see her shadow, smell her perfume.

Fragrances and sex, a kind of a tinderbox for reactions.

I saw her boots, small and beautifully molded to her ankles. I could hear my own breathing, my own heart. (Steady, Elliott. No more panic.) She was tall, though nothing as tall as the red-haired honcho towering over me, and she was delicate like the perfume, and she had a veil of long, dark brown hair.

The trainer took hold of my arm suddenly and turned me around. Now I didn't have to see them, but being exposed from the back made my heart freeze.

I looked at the floor, hearing a subtle clicking sound, which I knew was the unlinking of the strap that hung from the trainer's belt. Here it comes, class.

Nice, hard smacks on the thighs and the calves. The trick was not to flinch or make a sound. And then I was jerked around and pushed down on my knees in front of the man, and I had to put my hands out not to fall on my face.

This time it was the back of my neck that got whipped and I hadn't expected that. He smacked it so hard I had to bite down on a groan. I could smell the leather of his boots and his pants, and suddenly, I kissed his boots, kind of amazed I was doing it without being told. My mind went blank.

"Ah, that's much better," said the trainer. "Now, you're showing promise, even a little style."

I was in a sort of mild state of shock.

"Get up, and put your hands back on your neck where they belong, and move over there with the other punished slaves."

Couple of fast smacks, and the new humiliation of joining the wild bunch and standing motionless in the silence, facing the class.

Rows and rows out there of lovely bodies, naked thighs, pink organs in luxuriant tangles of hair. And for the first time I saw glass-walled observation rooms high above as well as on this level, full of attentive faces of both sexes.

It was a hell of an audience. And the whipping wasn't over. A new shower of smacks with the trainer's strap, and again that struggle not to flinch or make a noise.

I struggled for inner calm, for stillness, to fight through the sense of utter insignificance, to somehow give in. The pain was tingling and hot.

In a frantic moment I saw the tall female trainer on my right, caught the light and shadow of her angular face with its extremely large brown eyes. Gorgeous, absolutely gorgeous.

My heart was going to trip out. And so what. The other male slaves were broken down, weren't they?

"How is our pride now, Elliott?" the trainer asked, coming around in front of me. He lifted the strap, holding it taut between his two hands and he put it to my lips.

I kissed it, the way Catholics kiss the crucifix on display in the church on Good Friday, and the warmth spread all through me at the feel of the leather against my lips.

There was an odd moment of total release. I let my lips stay against the leather as he held it. My head was spinning. All the resistance was washing away in the heat.

I didn't even look at him, but I had the feeling he sensed it, that something a little profound had happened. I felt like I'd been unconscious for a couple of seconds when he took the strap away and stepped to my left.

Then another one of those reckless compulsive moments like the moment on the ramp when I had looked at the crowd. But this time it was at that female trainer that I looked, and only for a split second, and I don't think the red-haired guy even saw.

Face to die for, lady. I looked down without moving my head. Things had gone a little dim.

"Let's have a little lesson in lifting that chin and looking full at our obedient classmates," murmured the red-haired trainer. That bunch of goodie-goodies, you must be kidding. I looked at them exactly as he said.

"Class, you are to look at these punished postulants," he ordered. All eyes on the Gang of Five.

"Now we will resume our lessons, as if these little interruptions hadn't happened," said the trainer. "And if any of our bad boys and girls dares to move a muscle, to make a sound of complaint or suffering, then we will be forced to stop again."

He strode away from me and forward towards the first row of postulants and I saw him fully for the first time. Exceptionally tall, yes, with very broad shoulders for his slender chest, red hair a kind of thatch. The white silk shirt was pure pirate drag with full sleeves and lace at the cuffs. Handsome bastard, naturally, though his eyes were almost buried under his bushy brows, "like smoldering coals" as the bad books say.

"As I was saying before this lamentable interruption," he began very calmly, slowly, "you are now, all of you, the property of The Club. You exist for its members, for their pleasure in looking at you, touching you, whipping you, or humiliating you, working you as they see fit. You have no other identity here except that of slave, and by your individual trainers you will be fed, exercised, and groomed."

The voice was not only calm now, it was almost friendly.

But I could see the slaves squirming; he was looking at them again, and they were shooting their covert glances at him. Maybe it's harder for them, I thought, because they haven't screwed up. Maybe you could go the whole two years never screwing up and die at the end of a nervous breakdown. But what could be worse than this? The lower echelon. What fun.

"But you will also be studied," he said, "you will be learned. The trainers here, with or without your conscious cooperation, will discover exactly what shames you, excites you, weakens you, or strengthens you, exactly what causes you to perform best. But in all this it is the pleasure of your masters, the members of The Club, that they seek to increase.

"That you *need* this punishment, that you crave it and must have it, no matter how frightened and regretful you are at this moment, that you gave yourselves up to slavery to receive it, that you offered yourself on the fashionable auction block and through the best brokers for it—all this is one of the more interesting and delightful coincidences that nature provides. As you are mercilessly and tirelessly worked here, you will get what you crave in forms you have never imagined, and all your wildest dreams will be put to their most exorcising test.

"And again, this is all done for your masters, and for your trainers who represent your masters and know what your masters desire. You are perfected and brought to prime for your masters. It is for your masters and mistresses, the guests, that The Club exists."

He paused, pacing slowly before the postulants, his narrow back turned to me for a moment, his arms folded, the strap dangling from his belt. I could see several of the slaves shuddering. I could hear soft whimpers from one of the male slaves near my side.

"You will be both pleased and disconcerted to hear," the trainer went on, "that you will be the object of relentless attention in this place, that you will be constantly and tirelessly worked. Some three thousand members are here presently for the new season and suites and bedrooms are now three quarters full. Beauty, variety, intensity . . . these are what the guests expect, and their appetite is insatiable. You will never be neglected by the members of The Club."

I tried to imagine I was hearing these words with the others, that I'd made it through the gardens without freaking, and my training was moving right along.

"Of course, you will be kept in the best of health," he continued, "you will be fed three times a day, sometimes for the amusement of your masters and mistresses, other times in private, you will be massaged, bathed, exercised, suntanned, polished, oiled. And never will your punishment cause you real physical injury. Your skin will never be broken, burned, or in any way irrevocably marred. In almost any situation, you will be under surveillance, with your trainers near at hand. No accidents have ever occurred here, and we do our best to see that none ever will.

"But you exist to give pleasure, and you are tended to that purpose, whipped to that purpose, humiliated, and relentlessly sexually aroused to that purpose, to be made an object of amusement in any way the masters and mistresses desire."

He had stopped before me, his back turned still, and I saw him reach out and touch the breasts of one of the small female slaves who seemed most upset. She was crying, tears staining her small face. Her whole body seemed to bend to him as he ran his fingers across her small belly.

"Now, you have all been presented in a casual way to The Club," he resumed, stepping back. "But tonight, that presentation will be more dramatic, with special performances in which you will play important parts."

But did that include us? What the hell was going to happen to us?

"And to prepare you for that, to prepare you for all your training, you will now be given over to a trainer who will pick you on the basis of your individual characteristics to be part of his or her stable of regular slaves.

"Your individual trainer will come to know you better than you know yourself; he or she will supervise all your behavior, your physical condition, oversee your exercise and your special training, converse with the guests who request your presence and your services; he or she will discipline you, develop you, perfect you as you become one of the full-fledged slaves of The Club.

"And let me warn you now that if you think you are trained, if you think the paddle and the strap and the trainer and the master and the mistress have no surprises for you, you have much to learn at The Club.

"In fact, you would be wise to look upon your next few months of training as a series of shocks. That is: expect the unexpected, and resign yourself that the control of your mind and body in all their parts belongs to others.

"If you give your cooperation, if you surrender to your trainer in all ways, then it shall be all the easier, but with or without your surrender it will be done.

"What is mandatory from this moment forward," he went on, raising his voice as he glanced at us, the punished ones, "is your absolute silence and obedience, your absolute submission to all who train you and use you here and stand above you here. There is nothing on this island as lowly as you are, not the commonest servant in the kitchen or garden. You are true slaves, true property, and you must never make the slightest movement, gesture, or response—or lack of same—which can be construed as disobedience or pride.

"But your most severe offense," he said turning back to the other slaves, "is any mention of, let alone attempt to, run away. Any begging to be liberated shall be counted just as severely as an attempt at escape. And need I add there is no escape? And punishment for these offenses means time out from your contracts, no matter how long that punishment must last. For example, if you are here for two years, severe punishment for escape or rebellion will not count towards that time."

He paused and turned to face us. I could feel his eyes on me, though I still looked past him, forward, as that lovely black-haired female slave who was, in spite of her tears, looking back.

I couldn't see the tall brown-haired female trainer, where was she? Her power to move about in this room like a normal human being while I stood here captive seemed mildly terrifying. The male trainer approached.

I could see the soft glossy silk of his shirt, see the small band of lace stretched over his large-boned wrist. My legs ached. I struggled for steadiness as he moved up and down the row. I heard a loud whimpering from one of the others again.

"But those are rare offenses," the trainer said. "More common, as you see from this little display here, is pride. Obstinance, the impulsive rebellion, with which we must be concerned here today. Five disobedient slaves who must thoroughly disgraced themselves before their true service has even begun."

As he stopped once more, staring from one to the other of us, I saw a large metal rack being wheeled forward. A really ugly-looking thing. It was a white platform on heavy casters with thick steel rods rising at both ends to support a long high bar from end to end. It wasn't too different from a clothing rack used to move coats on hangers around a store. Only it wasn't meant for clothing. The rods were too high and too strong, and the hooks affixed to the overhead bar too large.

The trainer glanced at it, and moved to the first of the punished slaves on my right.

"Jessica," he said quickly. "Disobedient, fearful, cowering, trying to scramble away from those who examined her!" he said with a dry echo of scorn. I heard the whimpering again. "Five days in the kitchen, scouring pots and pans on her knees, the plaything of the kitchen staff, should give her some appreciation of her true purpose." He snapped his fingers, and there was a flurry of movement, the loud moaning of the slave.

In an instant I saw her, upside down, being held high, her hair streaming, as white leather cuffs were buckled around her ankles and by the lacing between them she was hung from the hook.

That cannot happen to me, being hung upside down like that! But guess what, it's about to happen. And you don't have to do anything this time. Just stand still and wait. Across her back very quickly was written the word kitchen in a rather ornate hand.

The next slave was already being condemned: "Eric, for obstinancy, reluctance to obey his handler's simplest commands. I should think five days in the stables grooming the horses, and being the horse of the grooms should do it," said the trainer, and then the spectacle in the corner of my eye of the powerful male slave being lifted just as easily as the woman, and hung by his shackled ankles from the rack.

My heartbeat was registering the predicament perfectly. Yes sir, they are going to hang you upside down like that within a couple of seconds, and then what? Five days beyond the pale! Oh, no, time to call home. Circuits overloading. Faulty equipment. Fuse about to blow.

"Eleanor, willful, independent, very proud, positively surly to the guests." And a blond already gagged with black leather was quickly carried by her ankles past me. "Five days in the laundry, a good education in washing and ironing," said the trainer as the appropriate word was quickly scribbled across her pretty back.

My head was teeming. There was one more slave next to me. Kitchen, stables, aaahh. No, this isn't going to happen. Rewrite the script.

I saw that woman trainer again to my left. Perfume. Click of those delicate little heels.

"Gregory," the red-haired trainer announced, "very young, very foolish, and very reckless, a crime more of clumsiness and nervousness I think than any other . . ."

The slave moaned supplicatingly, without the slightest restraint.

"Five days service with the maids should do it, cure some of that nervousness, a good workout with mops and brooms."

I stood alone now, watching the bronzed Gregory, his hair a close cap of black curls, quickly hung upside down from the bar.

Obediently he kept his hands in place as did some of the others, the disobedient Eleanor writhing frantically despite or because of the repeated blows of the belt.

"Elliott," said the trainer, as he stood beside me. I felt his hand quite suddenly under my chin. "Proud, willfull, a little too much of an individual for the tastes of his mistresses and masters, I should say."

It was unendurable. I thought I heard the son of a bitch laugh.

But from behind me I heard the woman's voice.

"Richard, I want this one," she said under her breath.

All systems on emergency power. The circuitry is burning through the insulation. There's about to be a major fire.

She came in closer, sweet floral perfume, dark shape in the corner of my eye, sharp angles of her little hips, pointed breasts.

"I know you do," the red-haired bastard answered, kind of low, "but the punishment . . ."

"Give him to me," she said. Voice like a velvet glove on my neck. "I just made an exception in the office because I knew it was best. And you know I can best handle this."

The hairs were rising all over me. The perfume was Chanel, and it came in little waves, like with her pulse.

"Lisa, that exception was your prerogative . . . But I am the Director of Postulants and this is a routine case . . ."

Lisa. I felt I was writhing, though I hadn't moved. The man's hand touched my chin again, lifting it.

"Elliott," he resumed.

"I have first pick, Richard," she said, voice a little crisper. "And I'd like to make it now." She pressed closer, her lace blouse almost touching my arm. I was about to combust. I could see her tight little black leather skirt, her long slender hands. Magnificent hands like the hands of saints in church.

"Of course, you do," said the trainer. "And you may pick him now, naturally, but he still must be punished before the training can begin."

He held my chin still, studying my face. I felt the thumb against my cheek. But my mind had gone white.

"Elliott, look at me," he said.

Steady, Elliott. Look at the nice man. Deep-set gray eyes, full of vigor, easy humor.

"Let's hear what kind of voice our proud young postulant has," he said, barely moving his lips as though thinking as he spoke. He was close enough to kiss. "Keep your eyes on me and tell me very sincerely that you are sorry for the disgrace you brought on yourself."

Elliott Slater is lost.

"Well?"

"I'm sorry, Master," I heard myself say softly. Not bad for somebody who had died five minutes ago. But it was like reinhabiting the situation, to speak, and he must have known that, the bastard, it was awful to look right at him and say it, to keep seeing her dark shadow, smelling that perfume.

Flicker in his eyes, quiver of the eyelids.

"I'll handle him, Richard—" she said just a little bit sharply.

I shut my eyes for a second. Do I want her to win this argument? What do I want to happen, and what does it matter what I want!

"We'll compromise," he said, his hand still firm as he held my face. He was studying me like I was a scientific specimen. "We'll say only three days hard work cleaning the lavatories and then to Lisa, the Perfectionist, as she desires."

"Richard!" she whispered. I could feel her anger like it was heat.

And this was my individual trainer, this shadowy lady, this was the future, and three days in the lavatories to think about it if I could still think.

"You're a very fortunate young man, Elliott," Richard, the trainer continued. I was visibly trembling. Why try to hide it anymore? "The Perfectionist has first pick of all the slaves; and those she chooses are the finest artists of The Club. But in the future, you might hope and pray for more punishment in the lavatories if she finds fault."

She had stepped in front of me, but still I didn't dare to take my eyes off his. Yet I could see she was delicate all over, and her dark wavy hair was more a mantle than a veil. Big dark eyes boring into me.

And there was something else about her, something palpable that I couldn't define. I don't believe people have auras, that they give off vibrations. Yet there seemed to emanate from her some primitive force. I could feel her. I'd been feeling her all along.

Like a sound was coming from her that was too low for the brain to consciously hear.

As the trainer gave the order in a louder voice, "Three days cleaning the lavatories," she reached out and took my head in both hands. I felt something so unfamiliar at her touch that I would have looked at her even if it hadn't been exactly what she was forcing me to do. It was like an electrical connection.

She was lovely all right, her face exquisitely boned and shadowed, her red mouth just a little petulant and her eyes staring straight at me with the faintest touch of innocence in them, seeming not to see me looking back at her at all.

My mind was blank again. I couldn't be tortured by her, belong to her! Have that fragile a creature hold me powerless. But my cock had gone from fourth gear into overdrive. And surely she saw that. She wouldn't miss anything, not her. She let me go.

I saw the goons in white leather coming for me and I couldn't think even enough to panic. They lifted me, swung me up heels over head.

Sheer astonishment, beyond panic—they'd done it, damn it— seeing nothing, and then the wide, smooth leather cuffs closing on my ankles and my weight being let down on the hook.

The grease pen cut into my back—I lost track of the letters which seemed a failure somehow—and I found myself desperately trying to stop the swaying of my body as the blood rushed to my head.

Then I did panic. I went completely screwy. But it didn't make any difference because I was completely helpless hanging there and nobody could tell. The rack creaked, started rolling and we went with it. It was as simple and excruciating as that.

The trainer's voice rang out, explaining that the punished postulants would work and sleep under the most uncomfortable of conditions, that their punishment would be relentless and wearying and not for the pleasure of anyone, and that in the next few days they would be visited by the class for a further understanding of disobedience and its results.

We were moved steadily towards the open door. My whole body felt swollen. The Club was swallowing us like a giant mouth. But inverted as we were, we might have been moving into another dimension. I tried not to look back at the upside-down vision of the room.

"Now," came the voice, "the trainers may choose their slaves."

Lisa

8

Anything You Desire, Master

Of course they had to send him below stairs, didn't they? Who had made all the rules about firm punishment in the beginning? And it was routine, even if nobody pulled that little scene before, Richard was right about that.

Nine o'clock when I finally shut the bedroom door.

Twilight through the curtains, and the inevitable night breeze that always cools our island. Why couldn't it cool the fire burning in me?

The bath slaves were two of my favorites, Lorna and Michael, both blond and small and perfectly adorable, and already lighting the lamps.

They drew the water without asking how I liked it, set out my nightclothes, turned down the bed. I got sleepy finally as they worked gently with the shampoo and the soap. With a light touch, Michael rubbed in the oil afterwards, dried my hair, and brushed it.

"We missed you, Lisa," he whispered, kissing me on the shoulder.

He lingered after Lorna had gone, doing a dozen little unnecessary things. Superb body, thick organ. Why not? But not tonight.

"That's all, Mike," I said.

He came silently across the room to kiss me again on the cheek. I slipped my arm around him just for a second and leaned on his shoulder.

"You work too hard, boss lady," he said. Mouth ready to kiss.

I closed my eyes and the plane went round and round in circles. My sister looking across the table at the Saint Pierre said, "Why don't you ever confide in us, tell us about your work?"

"Ah!" I opened my eyes, shuddered. I'd almost drifted away. "Gotta go to sleep now," I said.

"Two can sleep better than one."

"Michael, you're a treasure. But it's no good tonight."

I lay still and silent under the soft thick white bedspread. I stared at the thin tissue of cotton lace that made the canopy of the bed.

Okay. They had to send him down there. All right.

Couldn't stop picturing him as he'd been in the receiving hall. Ten times as good looking as his pictures, no, a hundred times. And blue eyes, yes, real first-class blue eyes, and the body U.S.D.A. Prime for certain. But it was the unshakable dignity, the way that he just stood there and took all of it, like Alcibiades in chains.

Cornball, Lisa, try to sleep.

Okay, he deserved it, three days in the lavatories. But did I deserve it, three days until he came up?

I hadn't had five minutes alone with Richard since then to tell him what I thought of him, or five minutes without thinking of Elliott Slater cleaning tile floors on his hands and knees.

Right after it was all over, I'd locked myself in my office and wrapped up correspondence that had been lying around since last year. Purchase orders, medical forms, bills, new equipment designs, approved, filed, sent out, whatever . . . Promised to talk to the pony trainer tomorrow. Then the usual dinner with the new members, answering questions, leading little tours around the grounds. Mr. Jerry McAllister was very happy. Everybody was very happy. Maybe even Elliott Slater was happy. Who knows?

In fact, First Night was going splendidly as it always did, and nobody would give a damn if I just disappeared.

And now what?

Staring at the canopy above me, as if that little moment of drifting off just now in Mike's arms had never occurred. Memories again. Bits and pieces of the past floating around me, faces about to take shape, voices about to speak.

Listening to the breeze through the open doors, the rustle of the leaves.

Don't think about him. It isn't like they sold him off to a foreign land.

And don't think about the memories either. But how can you stop them? When you go over the past like this, it's as if you think you can change it, put it in order, understand it maybe for the first time. The memories had been there all day, actually, prowling in the psychic shadows, like an enemy army ready to close in.

I saw the highway leading south from San Francisco, then the dense wood of Monterey Cypress, the high peaked-roofed houses behind their moss-stained brick walls, and the narrow gravel road, private road unwinding ahead as the gates shut behind us. I was sitting beside Jean Paul so primly on the dark blue seat of the limousine, my hands folded in my lap. I even tried once to pull down my skirt to cover my knees. How absurd.

Jean Paul was speaking in a calm voice.

"Now you will find the first few days the most difficult. There will come a point when you realize that you cannot escape, and you will panic. But your consolation will be this: there is nothing you can do about it." He paused, regarding me carefully. "How do you feel now?"

"Afraid," I whispered, "and excited." But the words dried up in my throat. I wanted to say, no matter what I feel I would not turn back for anything. I could see the wooden gates and the gatehouse above. The limousine was gliding towards a deep brick garage with a peaked roof, the same Tudor architecture as the mansion beyond the trees that had just been in front of us.

Darkness was closing around the car as we entered the garage, and in a sudden moment of terror I reached out and touched Jean Paul's hand. "You will always know how it goes, won't you?"

"Of course. Now, think. Is there anything else you would like to say or know? Because I'm to strip you now. You're only admitted to the estate naked. And I must take your clothes away with me. You must never try to speak to the master or to the grooms. They'll only punish you for it."

"You will come to get me . . ."

"Of course, in three months, exactly as agreed."

(Have to be in class at Berkeley in three months, have to.)

"Remember all I've taught you, the phases that you will pass through: when you are terribly afraid, remind yourself of how exciting it is. Be honest with yourself in that regard—and remember that you cannot do anything. You are relieved of responsibility to try and save yourself."

(Save yourself. Save your soul. My father looking at the books on the bed, the new novels, the paperback philosophy. "Lisa, you have never had any taste, any judgment, anything but a penchant for the worst trash you could find in a bookstore, but for the first time, I fear for your immortal soul.")

I could feel my nipples burning against my blouse, the thin panel of my panties soaking wet against my thighs. Jean Paul leaned over and kissed me on the cheek, brushing my hair back over my shoulders. My hair had been even longer then than it was now, and very thick it seemed, very heavy.

I felt Jean Paul's hands reaching for my wrists, taking them behind my back, and the cut of the scissors through the cloth of my blouse as the fabric fell away in a jagged patch on the dark blue carpet of the car.

When I was naked, he pulled me out of the limousine.

"Bow your head," he said, "and be still."

The cement floor was cool under my feet, and the light from the open door dazzled me. He kissed me again. And as I heard the motor starting up with a roar in the closed garage, I realized he was going away.

But a young uniformed attendant in gray had come forward, and taken my wrists, pushing me toward the door. I felt my hair around my naked arms like a merciful covering. My nipples throbbed, and I wondered if this stranger, this coconspirator in the secret sexual world, could see the dampness between my legs.

"We use the covered walkway in winter," he said. The voice of an older man. Educated. Neutral. "You will walk most of the way. When you near the house, you will fall on your knees, and remain on your knees. Always in the house you are on your knees."

We went down the walkway now. I felt his gloved hands tight

on my wrists, the light bright yet watery through the thick frosted glass of the barren windows. I could see nothing but bare wall up ahead. Greenery pressed against the glass. I thought with a sudden panic, the limousine has already reached the highway and I wasn't gagged. I might have screamed to be let go.

But then he would have gagged me. I was sure of it. I'd been told.

"Don't be deceived by the kindness of the servants towards you," the man said close to my ear. "If they catch you in anything other than the kneeling position, if they receive the slightest impertinence from you they will without fail report it to your master. And the reason is very simple for this: if they can find some fault with you, the master will give you over to them to be punished by them. They wait for that. They enjoy it. Especially a fresh young girl with such tender skin. A little novice. So again, don't be deceived by their attentions."

We had rounded the turn and the floor was now carpeted. For my knees of course. Down the long corridor ahead I saw a doorway. My heart was racing.

"You must show absolute subservience to everyone in the house. Never make the mistake of failing to do so. Now down on your hands and knees."

What did I recall after that?

The door swinging wide, the large luxuriously modern kitchen, the massive refrigerator doors, and the shining stainless steel sinks and the cook in her starched white linen, apron tied around her ample waist, turning to look at me from the wooden stool.

"Why, she's darling." A smile crinkling her round face.

And the shock of seeing the long polished hallway with its marble-topped tables and mirrors and the quiet parlors with the lace panels filtering the sun in a frame of heavy draperies. And I passing naked through this substantial realm, towards the master's study where he sat at his desk, telephone to his ear, pencil in hand.

First glimpse of the master. No more than a split second, as head down, I was made to crawl into the very center of the dark blue Persian rug.

Clocks chiming in the house. Canary twittering somewhere, soft sound of wings against the bars of the cage.

"Oh, yes, yes, well I have another call. Let me get back to you" —crisp British accent. Aristocratic and full of expression. Click of the telephone. "Yes, she's lovely, quite lovely. Kneel up, my darling. Yes, I *like* her. She'll do admirably. Come here, young beauty."

I moved around the desk as he directed me until I saw his shoes, the skirt of his dark satin red robe around a darker pant leg, a hand reaching out to touch my face, my breast. "Hmmm, quite nice." Each word so distinct, yet rapidly spoken. "Nicer than I had dared to hope."

"Yes, sir," said the attendant. "And no nonsense."

"Look at me, Lisa." Snap of the fingers.

Gaunt face, sharpened to the bone, the black eyes almost unnaturally vibrant. Gray hair thick and combed back from the forehead and the temples. Handsome, yes. Extraordinary, actually. Like the timbre of the voice, the eyes were ageless, or more truly mischievous and almost young.

"Leave her with me now. I'll send for you." Easy air of command. "I don't really have time for this," considering . . . "but I will make time. You follow me, young lady."

A door opening on an unusual room, narrow, harshly lighted by the sun through panels of leaded glass. A long polished table with leather handcuffs and anklets dangling on leather chains from the edges. The wall a rack of paddles, belts, cuffs, harnesses. Very like Jean Paul's studio where he teaches "discipline" to those who answer his discreet advertisements in the most unlikely papers. I have been well educated for this.

But this is graduation, this is the first job interview, this is the career world.

I moved silently on hands and knees across the dark, rose-colored parquet onto another soft rectangle of red Persian carpet. Heart thudding. The sound of his shoes.

"On your feet, my dear, that's it." I felt the thin leather straps enclosing my head. Panic.

"Shhh, now, now. Are we so frightened?" His right hand came around, cupped my left breast as I felt the smooth satin robe against my back. "There, steady, hands clasped at the base of your spine. You want to look pretty for your master, don't you?" Lips against my face. I melted at the tenderness. Anything for you, Master.

It seemed my sex was growing impossibly hot, full. I felt the thin straps encircling my forehead, my cheeks, narrow straps coming down the sides of my nose. My tongue darted to touch the opening for my mouth.

"Kitten tongue!" he whispered in my ear, pinching the underside of my bottom. Breath of cologne, and a low, toneless laughter. He had gathered all my hair up and was winding it into a coil with firmly placed hairpins. The helmet of straps was being clasped tight around my head, over the circle of hair with short tugging motions. I felt the corset go round my waist, slipped under my arms. I tried not to make a sound. I was trembling too violently.

"Shhh, now, my precious darling. You're just a baby, a lovely little baby, aren't you?" he said. He stood in front of me, hooking the corset tight at the bottom over the curve of my belly, then drawing it in impossibly with each new hook as he worked his way towards my breasts. The leather casing closed around me, pushing the breasts up and high with half cups that did not cover the nipples.

"Grand," he said, suddenly kissing my lips through the thin strap mask. Unbearable the tension. The corset was fastened now completely. It seemed to hold me up as if I had no weight or stamina of my own.

"Lovely," he said, lifting my nipples, nestling them carefully over the leather, pulling at the nipples to make them longer, harder. How accustomed to it all he was, how skilled and quick.

"And now those lovely arms, what shall we do with those lovely arms?" *Anything you desire, Master.* I stretched my neck, shuddered, tried to show by undulation my submission. Every breath seemed to strike against the burning sheath of the corset. Hungry spasms between my legs.

He moved out of my blurred vision, returning almost immediately with a curious pair of long leather gloves. I saw at once they could be laced together. Turning me around he quickly pushed my fingers into the black kid, working it carefully over my hand and wrist, then same thing for the right hand until the gloves were smoothed well above the elbows. I felt the jerk of the lacings, my arms being sealed against each other, pulled back hard so that my breasts were thrust out all the more. My face was burning under the straps. The tears were rising. Would that please him or anger him? I was bound now, unable to help myself in any way, my breaths coming faster, and more unevenly. Bound.

"There, there," he said again, that unfamiliar British intonation making the simplest syllable exotic.

I saw his long, gnarled hands—just a touch of black hair on the backs of the fingers—as he held out the high-heeled boots. It did not seem possible to walk in heels that high. He set them down, the long leather flank unzipped, and I stepped into them, feeling the leather drawn shut up to the knee immediately. Unbearably sweet the tight clasp of his hand as he smoothed the leather. It was almost like standing on my toes, except that my arch was bent so far back.

"Good, excellent. You know Jean Paul sent your size for these things and he is very exact. He never makes a mistake." He took my face in his hands, kissed me again through the straps. The desire burnt to an ache inside me. I felt I might fall.

"But we have more divine adornments for my little plaything," he said. He lifted my chin. I knew these adornments, the round black weights he clamped to my nipples, the pendulous earrings he hooked into my ears with their tiny prong that touched the inner core of the ear, sending the shivers through me. I could not remain absolutely quiet, or still.

"There, now you are properly outfitted," he said. "My delightful little girl, and we will see just what you're made of. Go before me and gracefully. Look sharp."

Finger snap.

The high heels of the boots clicked loudly on the parquet until I reached the carpet again, my body thumping with hunger, my body thrusting with heat.

He was leading me to the pair of soft velvet sofas that faced each other on either side of the fire. And I felt the warmth of the blaze on my skin keenly. Sweet warmth.

"Now kneel, darling," he said, "with legs apart." I tried to obey, the boots so high and stiff that I was awkward. He sat on the sofa before me. "Thrust your hips towards me, darling," he said. "That's it, divine. Your master finds you very beautiful indeed."

And as he went silent, I heard myself sobbing softly. The tears came in a flood. I was bound so tight by the gloves, the corset, the boots, I felt as if I were floating somewhere in a world where strength and gravity meant nothing. He bent over and kissed my breasts, pinching them and lapping with his tongue at the nipples, at the clamps of the weights. I felt my hips riding forward uncontrollably. I felt I would fall into his arms.

"Yes, precious darling," he whispered in my ear. He kissed my mouth. Hot, firm fingers supporting my breasts above the corset. "Now stand," he said lifting me. "Turn for me. That's it. Heels together. Yes, such lovely tears."

The room was a dim wonderland of shapes and light, the glare of the fire behind its brass screen, paintings on the walls, the thin figure of the black-haired man who had also risen and was some distance away from me, his arms folded as he watched, his commands almost a whisper.

"Yes, around again, very good, heels together, always together, chin high."

And finally I felt his arms around me. I couldn't keep from crying, sobbing at the strength of his arms, the sight of his shoulders, the feel of his chest. He enclosed me, pulling me against the satin smoothness of the robe, my breasts aching, his lips again touching my mouth through the straps. I felt I would brim over. I couldn't contain it.

What had I felt that first night when it was all over, and I lay beside him, my flesh still tingling from his flesh?

How to sum up those three months that followed? The countless supper parties, and the violent intimacy with those nameless foreign guests, the endless treks with that saucy, mean little maid and her flailing paddle, the morning runs through the garden when it was spring, the master riding his favorite gelding beside me, the world outside as distant and unconvincing as a fairy tale.

And the unavoidable humiliation of punishment by the servants when I had somehow failed to please, to submit, to answer, to respond with expressed willingness.

Had there ever been panic? Perhaps on the first morning that I saw the bridle path and knew I would have to run, arms bound to my back. Or the first time I was flung over the cook's knee, squirming and crying over the injustice of it. But I think not.

The panic came on a morning in late August when Jean Paul paced back and forth in the small whitewashed room off the kitchen where I slept and said over and over: "Think before you answer. Do you know what it means to have him wanting you again, for another half year? Don't you understand what you are throwing away if you refuse this offer? Look at me, Lisa. Do you understand?"

He had leaned down and peered into my eyes.

"You know what it means, incarceration like this. Do you think it's easy for me to find something for you like this! And you need it, you know you do. It's your dream. Are you going to wake from it? I don't know if I can find you another such position when you come to your senses. Such glorious imprisonment as this."

Cut the poetry.

"I will go mad if I don't leave. I do not want to stay. I told you from the very beginning I had to be at school when the fall semester started . . ."

"You can put off the enrollment. You can postpone a semester. Do you realize how many I have to take your place . . ."

"I have to get away for now, don't you understand? This is not my life, not my entire life!"

Within the hour we were driving to San Francisco. And how strange it felt to wear clothes again, to sit upright, to stare through the distant windshield of the limousine.

What did the city look like after those months? What was it like to lie in the hotel room staring at the phone? Two weeks until the beginning of the semester. My body was arching and stiffening with its fever. Orgasm. Pain.

I was on a plane to Paris that very first night with the money I'd earned without ever calling home.

For days I roamed the cafés of the left bank in a daze. I was shocked and bruised by the din of the traffic, the press of the passersby as if I'd been released from a padded cell. My body was aching for the paddle, the strap, the cock, the enormous, smothering, tormenting wealth of attention! Orgasm. Pain.

Two miserable dates with a student at the Sorbonne, supper and argument with an old American friend, a dull evening of tepid lovemaking with an American businessman picked up boldly in the hotel lobby for no reason at all.

And the long flight home, the crowds on the campus, the glaze-eyed young men, eviscerated by drugs and ideas, who seemed not even to see the bronzed girls in their braless T-shirts, talk of pot, sex, revolution, women's rights in the greatest social laboratory in the world.

Alone in the room at the Saint Francis Hotel, I'd made the inevitable call after hours of staring at the telephone.

"Yes," Jean Paul had answered with immediate enthusiasm. "I have just the thing for you. He's nothing as rich as our other friend, but has a beautifully furnished Victorian in Pacific Heights. He'll be impressed with your experience. And he's frightfully strict. How long is the Christmas vacation? When can you be ready to go?"

Was it an addiction? *This is not my life!* I am a student, a young woman. I have things I must do. . . .

There had been the man in Pacific Heights, yes, and then the couple, the young man and woman, both very skilled, who kept the room on Russian Hill only for their slaves. And another fortnight—"No more than that, Jean Paul!"—with the master again at that lovely Hillsborough estate, and his sitting beside me on the high four-poster, his hand hurting mine slightly as he talked:

"You know you are a fool to leave me. Jean Paul says I must not harass you, pressure you. But don't you see what you're throwing away? I'd let you go to school in the mornings if you wish. As long as you obeyed as always. I would give you whatever you needed, as long as you remained devoted as you've always been."

I was sobbing, his voice going on and on.

"I need you," he said. "I need to possess you, to possess you completely, to make you feel all that you can feel. Oh, if I had only less conscience and less delicacy I'd never let you leave here. It can be so exciting, don't you see, passing back and forth through the veil. I would dress you up to take to the opera, sit with you in the box, forbidding you to speak, to move your hands, then bring you back, strip you, possess you. Each morning after you returned from school, I would make you run naked through the garden—" *I would, I would, I would . . .* "Ah, you know you want it, you want to belong to me, you do belong to me . . ."

Out alone on the highway that night, I had hitched a ride into San Francisco, the driver saying over and over, "College girls like you just shouldn't get into cars with strange men."

After that, the months of refusing others, no I cannot, I will not, not again. I will study, I will go to Europe. I will be what the world calls normal. I will fall in love, get married, have children. I will, I will . . . I am burning. I am in hell.

Jean Paul was angry, disgusted. "You are my finest pupil, my work of art."

"You don't understand. It was swallowing me. If I do it again, I won't come back from it. Don't you see? It was eating everything up. I was losing my mind."

"It's what you want!" Angry whisper. "You can't deceive me. You were born for it, you are a slave, and all your life you will be incomplete without the master."

"Don't contact me again."

Knock at the door? Knock at the dream door?

I sat up in the bed. Dim sounds of conversation from the garden beyond, guests moving along the paths. The darkness thinning slightly as I stared into it, the shapes of the trees becoming distinct against the glass.

Yes, a knock, so soft that it seemed an auditory hallucination. And the odd feeling in me that Elliott Slater was going to be out there. Impossible. They had him below stairs, probably shackled. And why in the world would I think that even if he could he would come to this room?

I hit the little buzzer on the table and the door opened. Slice of yellow light from the hall, and a figure, naked, perfect as they are all perfect, but it was much too small a figure to be Elliott Slater. It was Michael come back again, unable to see as he looked into the darkened room.

"Lisa?"

"What is it, Mike?" I couldn't have been more dazed if I had been really sleeping, really dreaming. The past was its own drug, it seemed.

"They need you in the office, Lisa. They said that the phone must be off."

Impossible. I never turn off the phone, and this is First Night . . .

Yet in the corner of my eye I saw the tiny pulsing light of the phone. The bell, what had happened to the bell? And I remembered that when I had come in I had deliberately turned it off myself.

"Richard says they have a girl down there with some fake

papers," Mike explained. "She isn't old enough to go to her senior prom."

"How the hell do they get in here?" I asked.

"Lisa, if I'd known about this place when I was seventeen, I would have parachuted in." He was already standing by the open closet, ready to help me dress.

I sat there for a moment, hating it that they needed me. But it was better than this sleep that wasn't sleep, these dreams that weren't dreams.

"Michael, see if there's some good red wine in the bar," I said. "I can get dressed by myself."

Elliott

Visitor in the Shadows

IT WAS DARK.

I was standing on the balls of my feet again, head hanging forward, my wrists tethered to a hook, as I had been on the yacht. Second night in a row. Pleasant dreams. There were other slaves near me, and every so often the door would open and an attendant would come down the row, swabbing oil onto our sore butts and legs. Lovely sensation. Less often an attendant passed to offer water from which we were only allowed to lap.

All afternoon and evening we'd cleaned the lavatories—not the private baths of the bungalows and suites—but the public rest rooms on all floors of The Club buildings, adjacent to the many lounges and the swimming pools: full-fledged slavery with the mops and scrub brushes, a lot of it done on hands and knees. The brawny male attendants who worked us, a cheerful crew of real rough-cut gems, had a field day with the tips of their boots and their inevitable leather straps.

You couldn't cook up something this divinely degrading in a brothel—the sublime necessity of every humiliation and command. It was an eight-hour tease to the greatest climax you'd ever had, except they made sure the climax never came.

A thousand glimpses of salons, bars—the beautiful and the privileged passing us everywhere without a glance—added nicely to the gorgeous torture. And the attendants helped themselves to a little one-way fun and games when they had the chance, just to remind us what climaxes were all about.

But the genius of it, the real purpose, was that it wore you down. It wore down the nervousness, the inhibition, the raw feeling that around every corner was an impossible test.

I could feel the barriers going in my head.

And I was part of the system. It was working. I was grateful for the uncomfortable rest period, and oddly accepting that in less than six hours I'd be scrubbing again in a glare of lights as the fashionably dressed members came and went. Three days of this! And the real training hadn't even begun.

And the real training meant Miss Dark Hair Dark Eyes Beautiful Hands Called Lisa. Elliott, you drew a royal flush.

But back off from that. My mind went a little fuzzy every time I tried to picture her, remember the tone of her voice.

Better to think about anything else. Better to hope that after three days of mop-and-scrub-brush purgatory I'd be all toughened up for hell.

Or was it heaven?

That's the problem with all this, it's both.

I think I was half sleeping when I picked a strange sound out of the shadows. Boots on the marble floor, probably in front of me, in front of the narrow strip of thin carpet on which my aching feet were planted. But what was it? A lighter, crisper clicking sound.

I opened my eyes.

There was a figure in the darkness off to the right. Tall but not as tall as all the men were here. And there was that sweet, intoxicating scent of Chanel.

No doubt about it. She was there. The woman in my life.

I saw the light touch the long sleek fall of her hair. I saw it glint in her eyes.

All the rest of her except for the gleam of a ring on one of her fingers was dark. Then a flash of light on the instep of her boot and something sparkling in her hand as she stepped nearer, and the luminous white of her blouse with tiny glimmering pearl buttons on it, and her face coming visible as if the darkness were thinning with light.

If it hadn't been so dark still I would have dropped my eyes the way we're supposed to do. But I just stared.

She stepped closer, and I felt her hot little hand on my cheek, and the touch of something cold to my lip.

I smelled the rich, fruity fragrance of the wine, and opened my mouth. Delicious claret, and just cool enough. I drank deeply, and when the glass was drawn away, ran my tongue over my lips.

Her eyes were enormous and dark and clear.

"Are you enjoying your little penitential sojourn among the brushes and buckets?" she asked softly, without even a hint of irony.

I heard myself answer with a low laugh.

Not smart. I tensed, but I saw the light on her cheek as she smiled.

Her naked forearm brushed my hip and her hand stroked my backside.

"Hmmm!" I winced too quickly, stiffened too violently. And my leg muscles weren't the only thing getting stiff.

"Bad boy," she said. She pinched one of the welts and her fingers sent that shock through me just as they had in the receiving hall upstairs.

My pulse was racing. I could feel it in my temples. Her breasts were almost touching my chest before she stepped back.

"What have you learned down here?" she asked.

Again, I almost laughed. I was sure she had heard it.

"To be absolutely obedient, Madam," I said. It had a thin edge of humor to it, but it happened to be the truth.

What she was doing to me now, however, was worse than the brooms and mops. And every titillation of the day was making it worse. Sexual satisfaction was getting to seem mythical to me at this point. The dizzying arousal would go on forever with its peaks and its valleys, and this was one of the peaks. This was getting to be Mount Everest, as a matter of fact.

"Give me something in particular," she said earnestly. "Something you've learned that was new to you. If there *is* anything." Her voice had nothing of artificial drama in it. It was intimate and strangely raw. Soft pulse of Chanel. Light etching her little mouth.

I tried to think. But all I could think about was what was going on in the lower half of my anatomy, and how she looked and smelled, and what her fingers had felt like.

She lifted the glass of wine again and I drank slowly and took a deep breath. Not much help.

"What have you learned?" she asked again and there was a little steel in her voice. Like she was going to smack me with a ruler if I didn't say my multiplication tables at once.

"That I'm afraid," I said, surprising myself.

"Afraid," she repeated it. "Of the men who've been using you?" she asked. "Or of me?"

"Of both of you," I said. "And I don't know which I fear more."

Instantly I regretted it. I wanted to take it back. And I couldn't understand what had drawn it out.

I'd been voice trained, as Martin and all his clients called it, that is, versed in making sort of ritualistic answers. And ritualistic answers aren't just a turn on; they cover everything up.

"Did the broom and mop brigade . . . work you over?" she asked.

"Of course, when they had the chance," I said. My face went hot. "They're more into soap and water and name calling. There wasn't much time for anything else."

Was this me talking? To her?

"You're a tough guy, aren't you?" she asked. Again, no irony. In fact, she sounded vague.

"Only if it pleases you, Madam." Now that was a nice ritualistic answer. But it sounded as sarcastic as hell.

My heart was too loud, too fast.

But she appeared to smile again, yet not broadly, not easily. "Why are you afraid of me?" she asked. "Haven't you ever been punished by a woman?"

"Not all that much, Madam." I felt a distant catch in my throat. Just those exquisite creatures in Martin's house in those frilly Victorian bedrooms, giving me the barest taste of it, driving me wild. And that Russian countess at the country villa who merely watched. Now, that was a trip—but not enough of a trip to buffet me against what was happening right now.

"Are you too good to be punished by a woman, Elliott?" she whispered. Ritual question.

"Not if it's a good woman," I said. Goddamn it, Elliott. Knock it off.

But she laughed. She tried to hide it, turning to the side a little, but I'd heard it, one of those soft little laughs.

I saw myself kissing her suddenly, subduing her with kisses, and pulling down the lace and the pearl buttons of her blouse. I couldn't think of her in any other way, except in my arms with me kissing her and opening her mouth. Nice. This is real trouble, sport.

Why didn't she just draw a blank from me? I mean the white-light blot out of terror that came over me at the pavilion and in the receiving hall?

"Are you really *that* afraid of me, Elliott?" she asked. The blood was dancing in my cheeks. But she couldn't see it, it was too dark. "You don't sound like you're afraid enough."

I could see the white lace spilling down over her breasts. I could see the paler skin of her long throat. Her voice was touching some place deep inside of me that was as vulnerable as it was unexplored.

"I'm afraid," I said.

Pause.

"Maybe you should be," she said as if confiding an important secret. "I'm so disgusted you got yourself into this mess, I'll make you sorry you did."

I swallowed, trying not to make a little grimace, keep the ironic smile off my face.

She rose on tiptoe and her hair touched my naked shoulders, her perfume inundating me. I felt her lips against my mouth, high voltage, the lace of her blouse crushed against my bare chest. Double shock, taking the breath out of me, her wet little mouth opening. My cock touched the smooth leather of her skirt. I sucked at her hard, opening her lips wider, pushing my tongue into her, my cock pushing her. She let me go and danced back.

I strained forward on the leather tether as far as I could, and kissed her hard on the neck before she could get away.

"Stop it," she said, jumping back farther.

"I'm your slave," I whispered. I really meant it. But I couldn't resist adding, "Besides, I can't get loose from this damned hook."

For a second she seemed too steamed and too surprised to say anything. She was glaring at me. And she was rubbing the place where I kissed her as if I'd bitten off a little chunk, which I hadn't of course.

"You're fucking incorrigible!" she said furiously, but there was something tentative and uncomprehending in it, and in her face.

"I didn't mean to be," I said very contritely. This was a real mess. "Honest, I didn't. I really didn't. I came here wanting to obey all the rules. I don't want to keep getting into trouble like this."

"Shut up."

Tense moment. Blood pounding in my head, and a couple of other places. I wondered if they had a jail in this place for the really bad guys. Maybe the slave convicts dug ditches on a chain gang. Would I get a fair trial? Would she testify against me? Would Martin send a telegram begging for clemency? Probably not.

She moved in cautiously, like I was some sort of jungle beast. I didn't look at her.

"Now, I am going to kiss you again," she whispered. "And you keep still."

"Yes, Ma'am."

She drew in on my right, careful not to brush against me, and there came the 300-volt shock again, and this time I felt her burning up. I thought I'd come just kissing her, it was so hot. She was leaning against my side. She had her arm around me. And when she suddenly let go I turned my head. Mount Everest all right.

"I'll be waiting for you, Elliott," she said.

"Yes, Ma'am," I said, still unable to look at her, absolutely tortured by the sounds of her footsteps moving away.

Lisa
10

Miss Teenage America

I WALKED TOWARDS the administration building like I was being chased.

I was in a low-grade fever. I kept touching my mouth because my lips were tingling as if he'd done something to them, like the hero in a high school romance, kissing me that way. I could still smell him, the salty clean smell of his skin.

Yes, a hundred times more beautiful than his pictures.

But it was his manner that was the killer, his manner that put it all into some sort of perspective. Because when he smiled and when he spoke, the character came out.

Stop it, Lisa.

I mean this is a healthy, red-blooded American male, here to play slave for two years, who just happens to know how to put on the charm for anything female, how to use his eyes and his voice.

I was just too wired right now. Shouldn't have tried to check him out so early, should never have turned off the phone, and should never have kept everybody in the office waiting just to go down there and see him!

I mean sneaking down to kiss him on the mouth as if we were

in the back of a Chevrolet, this had to stop, that's certain, couldn't go on for three days. Three days. The voice was like the look in his eye. Really *present*. But that's what we want from all of them, right, that we take over their fantasies and become the fantasy. So what's so terrific that he is really there?

At eleven, The Club was still alive from one end of the island to the other, lights pulsing in a hundred curtained windows, the sky overhead a fathomless dark blue under the lamp of the full moon.

I walked fast past the doors of the darkly carpeted casino, not wanting to be seen or spoken to, only glancing out of the corner of my eye at the naked slaves navigating gracefully the endless sea of tables, trays held high as they hurried to take orders, to serve wine, liquor, exotically colored and decorated drinks.

Behind thick and dimly illuminated glass wall panels the slaves on display writhed and struggled in their bonds, limbs polished in gold or silver, pubic hair studded with tiny jewels. On the stage at the far end a little playlet was being enacted, two Greek slave girls in delicate chains and bracelets, being severely punished by their Roman lords.

In the quieter lounges the drama was more intimate, Club members having brought their slaves at heel to the tables. Above the dark, glittering bottles of the bar, a string of young men with heads bowed and arms bound high above them, a series of statues by Michelangelo, turned silently on a carousel.

I saw Scott, the Panther, my dark and handsome genius Trainer of Trainers, in fast conversation with an old English lord, a recent member who'd been hanging around for months, and a little jet of excitement warmed me at the sight of Kitty Kantwell crouched at his feet, her lips pressed to the carpet silently waiting his command.

So he had picked Kitty. Good for her. He'd probably taken Kitty right to the new trainers' class and used her for demonstration. I should have gone, might have learned something. Now that was thinking like the old Lisa, in the swing of things around here, as the old expression goes.

Wishful thinking, kid. Three days down there. No. The fact was, nothing had felt right since I landed. Nothing had felt right since before I even left.

Except kissing Elliott Slater just now, how about that?

Richard, the Wolf, got up from the desk chair as I came in.

"Sorry to wake you, Lisa," he said. "Tried to get you earlier but . . ."

"I'm here to be awakened. What's going on?" I asked.

Two handlers, looking a little smudged and dusty from the long day, were standing by with their arms folded doing their best to fade into the white walls.

And in front of the desk a girl, in a short, belted, white terry-cloth robe, sat sobbing theatrically, pounding her knee with her fist.

"Miss Teenage America," Richard said. "The doctors say she's not a day over seventeen."

If it hadn't been for the squabble over Elliott, I would surely have remembered her from the receiving hall. Luscious breasts bulging against the sagging lapel of the robe, and long, exquisitely sculpted legs. She tossed her black curls angrily, jutting her lower lip at me and then her eyes squinched, watering fearfully, as Richard gestured for me to take his chair.

"You can't do it! You have to take me!" she said shrilly, her lips looking almost bruised from her crying. And her whole face knotted as she shook her head and pounded her fist again. It was difficult to believe it just looking at her, but when she spoke, it was clear.

Richard pushed the medical report at me. He looked sleepy, his deep-set eyes a little red, but he was still amused by the whole thing. I wasn't smiling. This was such tiresome business, and talking to her would be the worst part.

"Look," I said. "You're too young to be here, your papers are fake."

"The shit I am!" she said. "I'm twenty-one. I was trained by Ari Hassler and I can . . ."

"Did you talk to Hassler?" I asked Richard.

"He denies everything, says she fooled him completely," Richard said wearily. "She has a phony birth certificate and driver's license . . ."

"It isn't phony, I'm plenty old enough to be here, what are you trying to pull!"

"You're a minor and you don't belong here," I said, "and you're going out tonight."

I looked at Richard.

"I can't get anything else out of her, same routine." He dropped his voice. "I'll wager you she's not the only one."

"Well, then, find the others!" I said crossly. "Submit the entire group to another examination. If there are any minors, I want them out."

"Please . . ." She leaned forward, her hands clutching almost modestly at her robe. "Let me stay, you've got papers saying I'm twenty-one, what are you scared of? You can't tell me you don't want me. Look at me. I saw the others. I'm as good as any . . ."

"Pick a town," I said coldly. "A nice private flight to Miami and first class from there to wherever you want to go. You're leaving now."

"I wanna stay here! You don't understand what this means to me, talk to my handler, he'll tell you I was perfect. Look, I'm ready, I'm telling you, I've been trained by the best."

"Okay, dump her in Los Angeles."

"No!" she screamed. She bit her lip, eyes becoming a bit vague and probably a bit practical. She said in a mumbling voice, "New York."

"Okay, New York. Give her the usual two nights at the Plaza, and a thousand dollars." I looked at her. "Use it wisely, as the old saying goes."

"Bitch!"

"Oh, I'd love to teach you some manners before you go," I said under my breath.

She studied me, calculating desperately.

"Get her out of here," I said.

"Just give me one good reason why you're doing this to me," she pleaded. The tears were very pretty sliding down her rounded cheeks, but her eyes were like two stones. "You know good and well the members would love me, admit it. What the hell's the matter with you that you want somebody six years older than me, for Chrissakes?"

"Honey, it's a cruel world. But have you ever heard the words 'consenting adults'? We don't deal in crazies, we don't deal in minors, we don't deal in unwilling slaves. Come back in five years, and maybe, just maybe we'll talk to you. But don't try to fool us under another name. Now, get her out of here. Fly her to Miami as soon as you can."

"I hate you, you bitch!" she screamed. The trainer tried to lift her and she sank her elbow into his belly. "You can't do this to me, my papers are in order. Call Ari!" The other trainer had slipped her arm around her waist. "I'll tell the goddamn fucking *New York Times!*"

"Don't bother," I said.

She was trying to unbuckle the trainer's arm.

"But if you're really serious, we have two *New York Times* reporters in Bungalow H. And there's a guy from NBC in the main building on the fifth floor."

"You think you're so smart. I'll blow the lid off this place!"

"Everybody's done stories on us, darling. Go to the library and look it up. And when a slave 'tells all,' I'm afraid it's the back page of the tabloids, right along with the tearjerkers by the ex– call girls and porno stars that have found Christ. As for the *Times,* you really can forget it. Ever hear the phrase, 'all the news that's fit to print'?"

The handlers lifted her off the floor. She kicked furiously as they carried her out the open door.

When it closed softly behind her, Richard and I glanced at each other.

"Ari's on line one."

I picked up the phone.

"Honest to God, Lisa, I don't understand this. That girl can't be sixteen. If she is, I'm losing my mind."

"Ari, I just saw her. Miss Teenage America. Cut the crap."

"I'm telling you the truth, Lisa, this is over my head. She had papers all over the place. Did you test her, Lisa? She's been working as a cocktail waitress for two years in the Village. Lisa, she's a stick of dynamite, I'm telling you, she can't be sixteen, she taught me tricks."

"We don't buy from you again, ever, Ari," I said.

"Lisa, you can't do this to me. You don't understand . . ."

"Not if it's Racquel Welch's body and Greta Garbo's head."

"Lisa, she could have fooled God. I've sold you the best merchandise this side of the Rockies, you can't get slaves out of the eastern states from anyone . . ."

"Ever hear of Gregory Sanchez in New Orleans, or Peter Slesinger in Dallas? You sold us a minor, Ari, a sixteen-year-old girl. We can't trust you, Ari. Good-bye."

I put down the phone.

I leaned against the high back of the chair and looked at the ceiling.

"I've pulled the files on the other two he sold us," Richard said, sauntering towards the desk with his hands in his pockets. "No other questions, really. The male slave is at least twenty-three, probably a little bit older, and the woman is twenty-nine." He was watching me. "It's top merchandise," he said with a little tilt of his head.

I nodded.

"What about the money?"

"Let it go," I said. "She won't ever see a nickel of it if I know Ari, and I don't want any more conversations with Ari. I don't like playing policeman for children and liars."

"But that's just it," Richard said coolly, "she was no child." He squinted the way he always did when he was serious, making his eyes smaller, more bright. "She probably menstruated when she was eleven, lost her virginity, if they still use that barbaric expression, when she was thirteen. She was everything she said she was. Probably worked Ari's private rooms for six months. She had an orgasm when I touched her. You smack her with the paddle and the skin comes alive right before your eyes."

I nodded.

"I know all these old arguments. From Kathmandu to Kansas, our name means no minors, no crazies, no captives, no drugs. Consenting adults!"

He looked away a little wistfully, eyes narrow again and distant, all the deep lines in his face emphasizing his expression as they always did. He raked his fingers back through his hair.

"Don't be so abrasive," he said under his breath. "She was my pick. I turned her in."

"I don't like to praise people for doing the least that's expected of them. Shall I make an exception now and praise you?"

"But is it fair, the rule? I mean after what she's been doing and what she's learned?"

"You're going to make me into a schoolmarm or a sociologist," I said. I felt angry. "Let me remind you, in case you've forgotten, what this place is. It isn't a chain of dimly lit rooms to which you retire on Saturday night to act out the rituals of which you've dreamed all week. It's total. It's an environment that engulfs you and obliterates the reality of any other environment you've ever known. It's your fantasies made real!"

I stopped. I was really steaming. I tried to keep my voice down.

"You have to remember what those years are," I said. "I mean the years between sixteen and twenty-one—what they mean."

"They don't mean chastity and obedience anymore," he said.

"They aren't just ordinary years in a person's life! It's her youth she'd be spending on us, and we don't need anything that valuable from her or from anyone else. We can fuel our fires with much cheaper and more negotiable energy. I don't care how pliant she is, how beautiful, how ready! What do you think she'd be like . . . after two years?"

"I understand," he said.

I wasn't sure I did. There had been a touch of hysteria in my voice. I kept seeing the estate in Hillsborough again, my first master, that highway down which we'd come in the limousine. The arguments with Jean Paul. Oh, if only there had been a Martin Halifax then.

The sheer size and weight of The Club oppressed me suddenly. How many more things would happen before the new season settled in?

"I don't know what's the matter with me," I said under my breath. "Maybe once in a while this place gets on my nerves."

"Well, adolescence was pretty complicated for all of us, I suspect. Maybe we all have our regrets about those teenage years . . ."

"I don't have any regrets," I said. "But I wasn't in The Club when I was sixteen or eighteen or twenty, that's the whole point. I could come and go, in and out. No high wires for me without a net."

He nodded.

"But it's not just a matter of the minors themselves," I said. "There's more written about us every day. We're almost common knowledge now in certain circles. I'd be willing to bet anyone—and I mean anyone—who sets out to get in touch with us could do it. And nobody must ever be able to cook up a story about minors, or crazies, or captives in this place."

It was surprising actually that no one had fabricated such things before now. Because every story about us had been written "around us," that is without our acknowledgment or consent. There had never been a scrap of proof behind anything that was written except blurry aerial photos that revealed nothing at all. No reporter had ever gotten inside.

But there were a lot of reasons for this. Members were blackballed without refund of fees if they were connected to the slightest public mention, and the enormous fees they paid, as well as our investigative process, thoroughly eliminated reporter spies.

Cameras weren't allowed on the island. Our own monitoring equipment did not record, so there was nothing to steal. And the electronic devices at virtually all exit points thoroughly ruined any smuggled film or magnetic tape.

As for the slaves, the handlers, and the drivers, and all the other employees, it was simple economics. They made fabulous salaries, and the fringe benefits were intoxicating, to say the least. Booze, food, slaves when they wanted them, the employees' pool, the beach. Nobody could pay them enough for an exposé, because the exposé itself wasn't worth that much, and they were washed up at any club in the world if they "talked." Only a disgruntled few, ones who'd been fired, had ever broken the silence, and the unsubstantiated accounts were badly written, sordid, poor-grade stuff even for the tabloids that ran them, as I had indicated to the girl.

But when people write "around" you, they can say anything, and there had been amazingly few distortions in the big *Esquire* and *Playboy* stories, and even in the tabloids there were no out-and-out lies.

"It's not a matter of whether the girl is ready," I said. "It's a matter of being careful, of being completely clean."

"I agree," he said. "But there is too much money now in this place to get so worked up about it. And all I'm saying is that some of these minors are no more minors than I am."

"Don't kid yourself. Not everyone in this world is afraid of money." It had a sneer to it. This was all getting too rough. "Look, Richard, I'm sorry," I said. "I'm not myself tonight. My vacation was too damned long. I hate going home. The outside world got on my nerves."

"Of course . . ." he said softly.

An odd feeling was creeping over me again. I saw Elliott Slater's face, felt his mouth. I had an unexpected memory of that guy in the bar in San Francisco, Mr. Straight. Three days down there. God, I was tired. Now maybe I could sleep. Maybe all the memories would just pack up and go home.

"Well, for tonight, you've done your duty to your slaves and their masters," Richard said. "Why don't you get out of here and have some fun."

Subtle change in Richard's face.

And I realized that it was purely a reaction to the change in my face. I was aware that I had shifted my gaze to him and I did not feel at all like myself.

"Have some fun?" I asked.

He was studying me. He nodded. Worry in his face.

"Is that what you said. Have some fun?" I asked.

He waited.

"I want an exception made, Richard," I said. "Elliott Slater. I want him reprieved and brought to my quarters tomorrow afternoon."

"Hmmmmm, you are not yourself, as you said. You'll have the young man in three days."

"No," I said. "You made your little stand for the rules in front of everyone. Now make the private exception. I want Slater tomorrow afternoon. They aren't to touch him in the morning; bath and rest by ten. My room at one P.M. Put the order through now. No one is going to know the difference. The other postulants are too damn busy, and the trainers are overworked as we well know, and I don't give a damn."

He didn't say anything for a moment. Then he said: "You're the boss."

"Yes, the boss and the mastermind . . ." I said.

"But of course," he said quietly. "If you feel that strongly about it. Tomorrow, after lunch."

I rose and started towards the door.

"Something's really wrong, isn't it?" he asked.

"What?"

"And it didn't start on your vacation," he said softly. "It's been brewing for a while."

"No," I said. I shook my head. "Just tired. Make sure they send Slater to me at one o'clock. Will you do that?"

"Very well, my dear. Hope it does the trick."

Welcome to
the The House

SOMETHING WRONG, SOMETHING brewing for a long time? Regrets about those teenage years? There had to be some reason for this ambush of memories, didn't there?

Hope it does the trick.

I stood in the garden outside the administration building, and I looked up at the stars, always so brilliantly clear when there were no clouds, as if the sky were sliding down to the sea. Japanese lanterns gave off their low flicker in the flower beds. Lilies under the dark lace of the crepe myrtle were as white as the moon.

My mouth started tingling as if I were kissing him again. And he was only steps away, wasn't he?

Do you know there are three thousand members here tonight, Elliott Slater? Oh, we are such a success.

Distant sound of the plane from the far side of the island. Miss Teenage America already taking off, back to the hypocrisy and the absurdities of adolescence. Sorry and good luck.

But I hadn't any regrets, it wasn't that. Richard was wrong, at least on that score. It would be a terrible lie to say I hadn't done what I wanted from the beginning with those early lovers, and in fighting Jean Paul finally, refusing to go on.

Something was brewing maybe, something I didn't understand, but I had made my own choices always.

And certainly I made my own choice on the night when Martin Halifax had first called.

Of course I'd heard of him, the mysterious owner of the place they called The House. In a moment of exquisite ambivalence I'd almost put down the phone.

"No, I have a different sort of opportunity for you, Lisa," he had said. "Something you might find easier just now. You might try it from the other side, you see."

American voice. Like the older priests in childhood, the ones who didn't sound like Protestant ministers, the ones who were real old-guard Irish-Catholic priests.

"Other side?"

"The finest slaves make the finest mistresses and masters," he said. "I would so love to talk to you, Lisa. About your becoming, shall we say, a part of The House? If you're afraid for any reason to come here, I'll meet you wherever you like."

The basement den of the Victorian that they call The House. Strangely, amusingly, like my father's library except it was filled with more expensive things, more cut off from the noise of the world outside. None of the Catholic books on the walls. No dust.

Martin himself. That wonderful voice connected at last with the friendliest face I'd ever seen. Simple, unaffected, amazingly straightforward.

"It was strictly a belief, a suspicion the way that it began," he said, with his fingertips touching for an instant before he folded his arms on the desk. "That out there, caught in the web of modern life there were hundreds of other men like me, maybe thousands really, roaming the bars, the streets, looking—in spite of danger and disease and ridicule and God knows what—for the place to enact those little dramas, those rich and frightening little dramas we have known over and over in our souls."

"Yes." I think I smiled.

"I don't believe it is wrong, you see. I never believed it was wrong. No. Each of us has within him a dark chamber where the real desires flower; and the horror of it is that they never see the light of another's understanding, those strange blooms. It is as lonely as it is dark, that chamber of the heart."

"Yes." I sat forward a little, unexpectedly disarmed, interested.

"I wanted to create a very special house," he said, "as special as is the chamber inside us. The house where the desires could come to the light. A house that would be clean and warm and safe."

Are we all poets, we masochists? Are we all dreamers, dramatists at heart? There was something so innocent about his expression, so matter-of-fact. There was not the faintest hint of coarseness to him, or subterfuge, or the dark humor that shame can produce.

". . . and over the years I've discovered that there are more of us than I can ever admit or satisfy here, that the range of desires is far more intricate than I ever supposed . . ."

He had paused, smiled at me.

"I need a woman, Lisa, a young woman, but she can't be just a hireling. There are no pure hirelings in The House. She has to know what we feel to work with us. You understand this is no ordinary brothel, Lisa. This is a place of elegance and sometimes beauty. And you might think me mad for saying so, but this is a place of love."

"Oh, yes."

"In love there is understanding, there is respect for the innermost secrets. There is compassion for the very root of desire itself."

"I understand. I know."

"Come upstairs with me. Let me show you the rooms. We are not therapists here. We are not doctors here. We ask no questions as to why or wherefore. We are only believers in this refuge, this little citadel for those who all their sexual lives have been in exile. We exist for those who want what we give."

Old-fashioned rooms, high ceilings, dim lamplight on the papered walls. The solarium, the schoolroom, the master's bedroom, and now the boudoir, waiting for me, satin slippers, the whip, the paddle, the strap, the harnesses, and the illusion perfect to the daguerreotypes in their little golden ovals on the dresser, the silver-backed hairbrush, the bottles of perfume catching the light in their crystal facets, the roses fresh and moist and nodding amid the wreath of fern in the silver vase.

"Now for the right person the pay is excellent, if I do say so myself, but you see it's rather like joining a club . . ."

"Or a religious order."

Soft respectful laughter. "Yes."

Weekend after weekend, I made the drive across the bridge to those mysterious rooms, the doomed and fragile strangers, the ambience of loveliness and sensuality, the place they call The House. My House.

Oh, I know exactly what they feel, know what to say and the words sometimes are everything, know when to exert the pressure, know when to give the tender kiss.

Maybe things were under control, the way I had always wanted them, at last.

And then the mysterious night flight to Rome two years later, Martin and I getting pleasantly drunk in first class, and the long limousine ride to Siena through the rolling, green Italian countryside.

A weekend conference with other talents in the secret world of exotic sex: Alex from the The House in Paris, one of Martin's old protégées, Christine from Berlin. I don't even recall some of the others, except they were all so refined, so clever, the wine flowing in the villa above the city, with all the good veal suppers, and those young dark-eyed Italian boys slipping like shadows through the hall.

Mr. Cross had come in his own plane with five bodyguards. Three Mercedes-Benz limos winding up the hill, towards the villa. "When is somebody going to tell me what this is all about?"

"But you've heard of him, surely," Martin said. The hotel chain and the sex magazine empire—*Dreambaby, Xanadu*—and the wife from Mississippi who didn't understand anything that was happening and wanted pizza to eat.

"Unreal money," Martin sighed with a slight lift of the eyebrows. "The best kind."

Was it possible? We were all gathered around the sixteenth-century table to discuss it.

A posh club, set somewhere in the world where the laws would in no way intrude, and all the pleasures that Martin Halifax and others like him had so cleverly invented. Think of it . . .

"Well, you know, a real getaway," Alex was saying. "Deluxe accommodations, food, swimming pools, tennis, the works. And then the sex. Any kind of sex. Something absolutely therapeutic if you think about it. Doctors will send their patients to us."

I winced at the word therapeutic. Martin hated it.

And the quiet voice of Mr. Cross, the man at the end of the table, our financier.

"You see, there is this possibility, a Caribbean island. Well, it would be almost as if we were an autonomous country, with our own laws. But we would still have the protection of the government that I've been talking about. I mean like there is no way that we would have to worry about any sort of intervention or any, you know, underworld muscle coming in. I mean where we would be, we would be strictly legit. We would have our own clinic, a decent police force if we ever needed it . . ."

Stunning sum of money. Everyone silent.

"You see," Mr. Cross again, "our research indicates that there are thousands of people, potentially millions, who will pay a great deal to have the sexual vacation of their dreams. Sado-masochism, kink, discipline, and bondage—whatever you call it, they want it, especially when it's well done and perfectly safe."

"And we offer them a clean, well-run place that is absolutely luxurious," Alex said. "An experience they can't get anywhere else at any price."

"It's an atmosphere of sexuality we're talking about," Mr. Cross continued. "An atmosphere where it is fashionable for you to act out anything you please."

Martin was uneasy.

"But there is something here you don't seem to understand. The majority of those who want this kind of thing are masochists. They're passive. And that is something they can't even admit to their husbands and wives."

"They can admit it to us," Mr. Cross said.

"No," Martin answered. "You are talking about people with money, position, the kind who can afford this sort of holiday. What makes you think they will come to an enormous resort like this where they may see others whom they know? In The House our biggest problem is secrecy, keeping one guest from seeing another. People are too ashamed of masochistic desire."

"But there are ways to make the thing fashionable," I said. Little silence. The idea was tantalizing me. It was marvelous.

"Yes, but how? How do we make it fashionable?" Alex looked

at me. "How do we staff it, arrange it, offer it to the public so to speak?"

"Okay," I said. "We want famous people, rich people, people who don't want to be the butt of jokes about their masochistic habits, the fact that they like to be whipped, tied up. Okay. You make a situation in which they don't have to admit it, in which being a member of The Club doesn't mean that that is happening at all. The members who come to the island are all 'masters' and 'mistresses' to be waited on hand and foot in public and in private by a staff of well-trained male and female slaves. They're guests of Kubla Khan in Xanadu, there to enjoy the dancing boys and girls, and the harem, unless of course they want to retire to the privacy of the soundproof bedroom, and ring the bell for a slave who can serve as 'master or mistress' with all the appropriate flair."

Mr. Cross smiled.

"In other words, all the members are dominant."

"Macho," Alex said with a raise of the eyebrows, a dry derisive laugh.

"Exactly," I answered. "That's how we sell it worldwide. Come to The Club and live like a sultan, lord of all you survey. Being seen at The Club doesn't necessarily mean anything except that you're there to enjoy the little spectacles, swim, get a tan, be waited on hand and foot."

"That could work," Martin said. "That could work beautifully, I think."

"But the slaves themselves," Mr. Cross asked. "This staff you're talking about."

"That's no problem at all," Alex said. "You're talking now about a different class. Young people from all walks of life, the 'singles' that live in every big city, the young women who sportfuck and the young men just out of the closet."

"Yes," Martin said. "The good-looking kids who would have been the starlets, the high-class hookers, the dancers in a Las Vegas or Broadway show. Offer them room and board in paradise, and a hefty salary to live out their wildest fantasies, and believe me they will be beating down the door."

"I think we have to start small to do it right," I said. "It has to be carefully structured, really clean. Nothing shabby. This sort of sex has its rituals, its limits, and its rules."

"Of course, that's why we sent for you," Mr. Cross answered. "Let's think about a little beachfront club . . ."

And five years later look what you have around you. Three thousand guests on the island this very night.

And the imitators, the "resort" in Mexico and the one in Italy, and the posh big city clubs in Amsterdam and Copenhagen, the one in Berlin where all the members were slaves and the staff were the masters, and the vast spa in southern California giving us the most competition. The inevitable auction houses, and the private trainers. And that mysterious legion that had always existed, the private owners.

Was it inevitable? Was it the right moment? Would someone else have organized it, discreetly advertised it, made it big business? If we hadn't been the first?

Who cares? Were codpieces inevitable in their time, or castrati singers, or the sky-high white wigs of the Ancien Regime, the bound feet of Imperial China, or the witch trials, the Crusades, the Inquisition? You set something into motion. It gains momentum. *It is.*

Momentum. For me, year after year, it was mania.

Meetings and draftings and drawings and discussion, inspecting the buildings, picking out fabrics, paint colors, shapes for the swimming pools. Hiring the physicians, the nurses, training the best slaves to be dominant, to "handle" the masochistic members who didn't even know their own desires. Executing, correcting, expanding. First two buildings, then three, then the compound. Motifs, ideas, fees, contracts, agreements.

And the same old heady gratification of seeing one's fantasies, one's secret dreams, made into a dizzying reality. Only it was now on an almost incalculable scale.

I could always think of better things than what my masters did to me. More elaborate things. The source is virtually endless. All life is variation upon certain themes. Now I saw others swept up in it, dazzled, amazed, adding to it, varying it. The flame burns ever brighter and brighter.

But passion for me?

Passion? What does that mean?

Certainly there were never again masters. Sometime or other

that kind of intimacy had been utterly forfeited and there are times when I do not know why. Was it because I really liked it better when I was the mistress, because it was not merely the old excitement, it was that divine sense of knowing what my slaves, my lovers, really felt? I mean I really had them. My knowledge and my understanding penetrated them. They belonged to me inside and out.

As for love, well, now, that had *never* happened, had it? Not in the conventional way. But what is love, if it's not the love I feel for every one of them in those moments?

And in the shadowy alcove of my veiled bed, I had had the best of the male slaves, bodies you wouldn't believe.

There are exactly thirty seconds between wanting and having at The Club.

Lashing them into submission, ordering them to fuck, astonished at their heat, their power, that strength under my command, that extraordinary masculine body belonging to me.

Noting their responses later in the computer files. Learning how better each time to manipulate them.

And then the women slaves with their silken fingertips and lapping tongues. Leslie, Cocoa, the lovely and presently neglected Diana, my darling, who nestles with me in the dark, which is possibly the same dark from one end of the world to the other, soft on soft.

Midnight in Eden. *But is it Eden?* Somewhere an old-fashioned clock chimes.

Twelve hours until Elliott Slater. And what is so special about that blond-haired, blue-eyed man? Won't he be like all the rest?

Elliott

12

White Cotton

THE CORRIDORS WERE a labyrinth. Bits and pieces of The Club passed me without making any real impression. I knew only that she was at the end of the string that was pulling me through this. She had gotten me out of the lower depths, and they were taking me to her.

I'd awakened in a half dream of desire for her. There was no use pretending it was anything other than that. All morning, I'd seen her face in flashes, fragments of the dream letting go, feeling the lace of her blouse against my chest, feeling the almost electric touch of her mouth.

Who the hell was she, really? What was she all about?

Then something unusual had happened. We had started cleaning on our hands and knees at daybreak, but the attendants had gone easy on me. No clever insults, no straps.

Must have been her doing, but what did it mean? Too easy to think about it in spite of the scrubbing. Too easy to think about her.

It had occurred to me when we were being given our noon meal in the barren little refectory—on hands and knees, of course

—that nothing here was turning out the way I'd thought it would.

No matter what Martin had told me, I'd expected protracted periods of boredom, an inevitable inefficiency that would dilute the whole thing.

Well, there was no boredom. And I hadn't been on top of what was happening since the start. And now this rather calamitous desire for her, this unpredictable reaction to the scent or the sight of her, her touch.

I had to get this part, at least, under control. I mean, she must have trained a thousand slaves like me, and she probably didn't give a damn about any of them, really, any more than I give a damn about the "masters and mistresses" who had worked me over under Martin's watchful eye at The House.

I didn't even give a damn about Martin when it came right down to it. I liked him, of course, maybe even loved him; and true, I got turned on thinking about him. But when it came to the sex part, the lovely nit-grit of sado-masochistic ritual, I didn't give a damn who did it, except in the most decorative way.

And now my mind was attaching itself to *her*. She was taking over. It was like she was materializing where there had been only a dark figure. I didn't like this at all.

Yet the low, pumping excitement had gotten worse, the sense of being a real slave, of being in real danger from her, as my hands and knees got more and more sore.

Then when I'd been taken to the bath I knew I was going to her. Delicious hot shower, expert massage—this was how the good guys lived.

And there had been the added tease of seeing so many other polished bodies on the massage tables, and the bath slaves a flock of little nymphs and fauns among the potted fuchsias and ferns, all reassuring patter ("You can talk now, Elliott, if you want to.") and toothpaste-commercial smiles.

Why had I been scared to ask what was happening? Why had I waited for the handsome little Ganymede who was working on me with his steel fingers to say: "You're going to the boss lady, Elliott, better get some sleep."

If I had been dozing before, that brought me up wide awake.

"The boss lady?" I asked.

"That's what she is," he had answered. "She runs The Club. She practically created it. And she's your trainer. Good luck."

"The top lady," I murmured. A whole string of firecrackers had gone off in my head.

"Close your eyes," he had said. "Believe me, you're going to need your rest."

I had slept. I must have. The sheer exhaustion must have done it, because all of a sudden I was staring up into the great pattern of leaded glass that made up the ceiling, and the handler was standing there and he said, "Come on, Elliott, we don't keep the Perfectionist waiting."

No, of course not.

And so the labyrinth with my last moments of Life Before Lisa slowly ticking away.

We stopped. White hallway, a pair of heavily carved double doors. Silence. Okay. You're much too stable for a total psychotic break.

The handler snapped his fingers:

"Go inside, Elliott, and wait there silently on your knees."

The doors closed behind me. He was gone, and I felt the panic rising as keenly as ever before.

I was looking at a large room done entirely in blue tints with violent splashes of bolder color that caught the light. There was no electric illumination here. Only the sun filtered through the blue-and-violet flowered curtains over the french doors.

Yards of deep vermillion carpet, and on the walls giant Renoirs and Seurats intermingled with Haitian paintings—brilliant works full of Haitian sky and green hills and dark stick-figure Haitians at work, at play, in the dance.

There were long-faced African masks as well as Indian masks in bright enameled green and red. Graceful, serpentine African sculptures of wood and stone rose here and there out of banks of potted palms and ferns. And to my left, its head against the wall, loomed a large four-poster brass bed.

The thing reminded me of a giant gold cage. It had drapery rods and scrollwork, and it was hung all in white cotton lace even to the sheer curtains that enveloped it in a diaphanous cloud. Heaps of lace-trimmed pillows lay piled on the ruffled cotton spread. A bower is what it was, the kind of fanciful thing men often love but can't arrange for themselves, leaving it to the women in their lives to create.

I saw myself walking towards it. I was dressed in a black tuxedo and I had a bouquet of flowers in my hand, ordinary daisies, and I bent down and kissed a girl who was sleeping in the bed.

That kind of bed. But there wasn't any "girl" in it. She wasn't anywhere in sight.

Time just to enjoy the intensity of the room, the way it so marvelously suggested the forbidden, even in this forbidden place. The slight movement of the green tree branches beyond the flowered gauze of the window curtains was something like a dance.

I felt a rush of blood to my head, a sudden disorientation. A trap door had opened and I had stumbled into some secret chamber. And the whole room distressed me suddenly for no apparent reason: the mess of silver articles before the circular mirror on the dresser, boxes, perfume bottles, brushes. A black satin high-heeled shoe lying on its side by a chair. All that snow-white lace.

I sat back on my heels looking around, wishing my face wasn't so hot, and the rest of me wasn't so hot. I had been in stuffy feminine Victorian bedrooms at Martin's house, but this was different, uncontrived, even a little insane. Not a stage set for all the craziness here, but a real place.

There were lots of books. Shelves of them on a far wall, and they were all chewed up like somebody really had read them all to death. Paperbacks stuffed in with hardcovers, some of them patched up with tape.

I stared forward, at nothing and everything; at a white leather chain dangling from the ceiling with a pair of leather handcuffs attached to it, at that black satin shoe lying on its side.

And when a door opened somewhere with a soft, almost inaudible click I felt the hairs rise on the back of my neck.

She had come out of the bath; I could smell the perfumed steam of the bath, one of those piercingly sweet floral scents, very nice, and some other aroma, something clean and smoky and mingled with the perfume: her smell.

She moved across the room into my field of vision without making a sound. She was wearing spike-heel slippers of white satin, like the black one discarded by the chair. And above that she wore nothing but a little lace-trimmed slip that came halfway down her thighs. The slip was cotton, bad luck.

I don't really care one way or the other about the feel of a body through nylon. But a body under sheer cotton drives me out of my head.

Her breasts were naked under the slip, and her hair hung down in a dark shadow about her shoulders, something like a Virgin Mary veil, and through the slip I could see the dark triangle between her legs.

Again I had that sense of a force emanating from her. Beauty alone couldn't account for the effect of her presence, even in this insane room, though beauty she certainly had.

I never should have sat back without her permission. And to look at her directly, that was a violation of the rules of the game, yet I did.

I looked up at her, though my head was slightly bowed, and when I saw her small, sharply angled face, her large brown eyes almost brooding as we stared at each other, the sense of her force intensified.

Her mouth was indescribably luscious. It was rouged without gloss so that the deep red appeared natural and the bones of her delicately sloping shoulders were for some mysterious reason as enticing to me as the full slope of her breasts.

But the current coming from her was not the sum of all the splendid physical details. No. It was as if she gave off invisible heat. She was smoldering in the skimpy little slip and the fragile satin slippers. And you couldn't see the smoke but you knew it was there. There was something almost inhuman about her. She made me think of an old-fashioned word. The word lust.

I looked down deliberately. And going on my hands and knees towards her, I stopped when I had reached her feet. I could feel the force coming from her, the heat. I pressed my lips to her naked toes, to her instep above the band of satin, and I felt that strange, baffling shock again that left a tingling in my lips.

"Stand up," she said softly. "And keep your hands clasped behind your back."

I rose as slowly as I could without breaking the movement, and when I obeyed, I was certain my face was really red. But it wasn't the old ritualized emotion. I stood over her, and though I didn't look at her again, I could see her perfectly, see the well between her breasts, and the dark rose-colored circles of the nipples under the white slip.

She reached up, and I almost backed away from her, feeling her fingers move into my hair. She clasped my head tightly, massaged it with her fingers, sending the chills down my back, and then brought her fingers slowly over my face the way a blind woman might, to see it, feeling of my lips and my teeth.

It was the touch of someone burning with fever, the hot dancing tips of her fingers, and it was further heated by some low sound she made, like a cat's purr without opening her lips.

"You belong to me," she said in something lower than a whisper.

"Yes, Madam," I answered. I watched helplessly as her fingers dropped to my nipples, and pinched them, pumping them as my body tensed. The sensation shot down through my cock.

"Mine," she said.

I felt this compulsion to answer her, but I didn't say anything, my mouth opening and then closing as I stared at her breasts. That sweet, clean smoky scent came to me again, flooded me. I thought, I can't bear this. I have to have her. She is using some altogether new weapon on me. I can't be tormented like this, in this silent bedroom, this is too much.

"Back up, there to the center of the room," she said in a low monotone, advancing as she spoke, her fingers still pressing and pulling at my nipples, pinching them hard suddenly so that I gritted my teeth.

"Oh, we are sensitive, aren't we?" she said. And our eyes met again, the heat blazing in hers, her red lips just parted to show the barest flash of white teeth.

I almost begged her, said "please." My heart was skipping as if I'd been running. I was on the very edge of bolting, just backing off from her—I didn't know what exactly—trying to shatter her power. Yet there wasn't the remotest possibility that I would or could.

She rose on tiptoe in front of me. I could see she had hold of something above me, and I glanced up to see the pair of white leather handcuffs with buckles dangling at the end of the white leather chain.

That I had forgotten about that stuff seemed a fatal error. But what did it matter, after all?

"Lift your hands," she said. "No, not too high, my tall beauty. Just over your head a little where I can still reach them. Fine."

I heard myself shudder. Little symphony of stressful admissions. I think I was shaking my head.

The leather went round my left wrist first, buckled very tight, and then around the right. My wrists were crossed, bound together. And as I stood as helplessly as if six men were holding me there, she went to the far wall, and pressed a button that silently made the leather chain above me retract into the ceiling, causing the cuffs to pull my wrists up well above my head before it stopped.

"It's very strong," she said, coming towards me again, her grace perfect in the spike heels. "Would you like to try to break loose?" The little petticoat slid up on her thighs, the little nest of hair prickling under the white cloth.

I shook my head. I knew she was going to touch me again. I couldn't stand the tension.

"You're impertinent, Elliott," she said, her breasts almost grazing me. Her fingers were spread out flat on my chest. "It is 'No, Madam' and 'Yes, Madam,' when you speak to me."

"Yes, Madam," I said. The sweat had broken out all over me. Her fingers moved down over my belly, her right forefinger pressing into my navel. I couldn't keep quiet. Quickly, she dropped her hand to touch my cock.

I moved my hips back away from her. And her left hand went up behind my neck. She moved to my side, her right hand pinching the loose skin of my scrotum very hard, the fingernails biting into it. I tried not to grimace. "Kiss me, Elliott," she said.

I turned my head towards her, and her lips nudged at my mouth, opening it, and that electric shock came again. My mouth locked tight on her. I kissed her like I wanted to swallow her. I kissed her like I had her on a hook. I could hold her that way, no matter how helpless she had me, that's how strong the current was. I could lift her by the sheer power of it, draw her out of herself, and when through this delirium I felt her breasts against my side, I knew I'd done it, that I had her. And the kissing was wet and luscious and sweet. Her nails pinched the flesh around my scrotum harder, but the pain mingled with the force passing out of me into her. She was up on tiptoe with her whole weight against my side, her left fingers clasping my neck, and I was feasting on her, my tongue inside of her, and my wrists ground into the leather cuffs trying to break loose beyond my control.

She pulled away, and I closed my eyes. "God," I whispered.

And I felt her wet sucking mouth on my underarm, pulling at the hair so hard that I winced. I was moaning out loud. She'd gathered my balls up in her right hand, was massaging them, gently, ever so gently, her lips sucking on the skin of the underarm and I thought I'd go mad. My skin, all over, had come alive. She bit into the flesh, licked at it.

My body went rigid, my teeth gritted. I could feel her fingers letting go of my balls, and closing around the shaft of my penis, and stroking it upwards. "I can't . . . I can't . . ." I said between my gritted teeth. I danced backwards, straining not to come, and she let go, tugging my face around and kissing me again, her tongue going into my mouth.

"It's worse than being whipped, isn't it," she purred under the kisses, "being tortured with pleasure?"

I broke away this time, pulling free of her, and then I kissed her all over her face, sucking at her cheeks and her eyelids. I turned and thrust my cock at her, against the thin cotton of her slip. The feel of her through the cotton was too exquisite.

"No, you don't!" she drew back with a low, sinister laugh, and smacked my cock with the flat of her right hand. "And you never do that, until I tell you that you can do it." She slapped my cock again, and again.

"God, stop it," I whispered. My cock was pumping, hardening with each slap.

"You want me to gag you?"

"Yes, gag me. Do it with your tits or your tongue!" I said. I was shaking all over, and without meaning to, I yanked on the leather handcuffs as if I meant to try to break loose.

She laughed a low, vibrant laugh.

"You bad boy," she said. And there came those taunting, punishing slaps again. She brought her nail across the glans, and then pinched it shut. Yeah, just a rotten kid, I wanted to say but I swallowed it. I ground my forehead into my forearm, deliberately turning away from her. But she took my face in her hand and pulled it around.

"You want me, don't you?"

"Like to fuck the shit out of you," I whispered. In a quick darting motion, I caught her mouth again and drew on it before she could get away. I pumped at her again. Backing away, she walloped my cock again with a broad sweep of her hand.

She drew back, silently, across the carpet.

About six feet away she stood just looking at me, one hand out on the dresser, her hair fallen down around her face, partially covering her breasts. She looked moist and fragile, her cheeks beating with a deep flush, and the same flush on her breasts and her throat. I couldn't catch my breath. If I'd ever been this hard before I couldn't remember it. If I had ever been teased to this point before, I'd blotted it out.

I think I hated her. And yet out of the corner of my eye I was eating her up, her pink thighs, the arches of her feet in the white satin, spike-heeled slippers, the way her breasts swelled under the cotton lace, even the way she wiped at her mouth with the back of her hand.

She'd picked up something from the dresser. It looked at first glance like a pair of flesh-colored, leather-clad horns. I opened my eyes to see it clearly. It was a dildo in the form of two penises joined at the base with a single scrotum, so damned lifelike the cocks seemed to be moving of their own volition as she squeezed the soft massive scrotum the way a child would squeeze a rubber toy.

She brought it closer, holding it up in both hands like it was a sort of offering. It was marvelously well defined, both cocks oiled and gleaming, each with carefully delineated tips. For all I knew there was some fluid in the big scrotal sac that would come through the tiny openings in both of the cocks when she gave them the right twist.

"Ever been fucked by a woman, Elliott?" she whispered, tossing her hair back over her shoulder. Her face was moist, eyes large and glazed.

I made some faint protesting sound, unable to control it. "Don't do that to me . . ." I said.

She gave another one of those low, smoldering laughs. She went back for a small padded stool that stood beside the dresser and she brought it with her and set it down behind my back.

I pivoted to face her, staring at that thing like it was a knife.

"Don't push me," she said cruelly, her eyes narrowing. And her hand flew up and smacked my face.

I turned a little, weathering the stinging shock of the slap.

"Yes, you'd better cower," she whispered.

"I'm not cowering, cutie," I answered. There came the slap again, amazingly hard, my face throbbing.

"Shall I whip you first, *really* whip you?"

I didn't answer her but I couldn't make my breathing quiet, couldn't stop my body from shuddering.

Then I felt her lips on my cheek, right where she had slapped it, her fingers stroking my neck, and a low, thumping feeling rolled through me, intensifying the sensation in my cock. Soft, silky kiss, and the knot in my penis doubled, and in my head something snapped.

"You love me, Elliott?"

Some protective membrane had been ruptured. My mind couldn't catch up with it. My eyes were wet.

"Open your eyes, and look at me," she said.

She had stepped up on the little stool, and she was only inches from me, and she held the double phallus in her left hand, while with her right she lifted the lace hem of her slip.

I saw her dark curly hair there, tiny curling wisps against the pink skin, and shy, delicate pubic lips, the kind that are almost demurely hidden by the hair. She lowered the phallus and pushed one end of it up and into herself, her whole body moving in a graceful undulation to receive it, the other end curving outwards, and toward me just exactly as if she were a woman with an erect cock.

The image was stunning: her delicate form and the gleaming cock rising so perfectly from the tangled curly hair, her face so seemingly fragile, her mouth so deeply rose red. I hardly saw her hands move, or reach up, until I felt her thumbs pressed into my underarms, her face very close to mine as she said, "Turn around."

I was making some soft angry and helpless noise. I couldn't move. Yet I was doing exactly what she said.

I felt the cock push against me, and I stiffened, pulling away.

"Stand still, Elliott," she whispered. "Don't make it a rape."

Then came that exquisite feeling of penetration, of being opened, that gorgeous violation as the oiled cock went in.

Too gentle, too delicious, up to the hilt, and then rocking back and forth, and a low buzzing pleasure coursing through all my limbs from that one heated little mouth. God, if she had only rammed it, made it a damned rape. No, she was fucking me. Which was even worse. She worked it like it was part of her, the soft rubber scrotum warm against me, just like her hot naked belly and her hot little thighs.

My legs had spread out. There was that overpowering sensation of being filled, being skewered, and yet that rich, exquisite friction. I hated her. And I was loving it. I couldn't stop it.

Her arms went round me, her breasts against my back, her fingers finding my nipples again and pressing them hard.

"I loathe you," I whispered, "you little bitch."

"Sure you do, Elliott," she whispered back.

She knew where she was driving it, rocking it. I was going to come, jerk right into the air. I was saying all kinds of little curses under my breath. Harder, she pushed, moving me forward, slapping me a little with her hips, then faster, ramming me, her fingers stretching my nipples, her lips open and sucking on the back of my neck.

It was building, and building, and I was making low, stuttering sounds, thinking she can't come like this, against me, with me not coming, and the thrusts started slamming me, almost knocking me off balance. And then she went rigid with a pure woman-in-ecstasy cry. The heat of her breasts beat like a heart against me, her hair falling over my shoulder, her hands holding tight to me as if she'd fall if she let go.

I stood paralyzed with desire and rage. I was locked out of her, and she was inside me. But abruptly, I felt the phallus slip out with a kind of searing sensation, and the soft, hot weight of her body move away.

But she was still very close to me. And unexpectedly, I felt her hands on the leather cuffs above. She unbuckled the cuffs, and released my wrists and laid my hands down at my sides.

I glanced over my shoulder. She had backed away from me. And when I turned I saw her standing at the foot of the bed. She didn't have the phallus in her anymore. Just that little slip barely covering her sex. Her face was rosy and her eyes glittering against all the whiteness. And her hair was a beautiful mess.

I could feel myself ripping off the little slip, pulling the hair of her head back with my left hand . . .

She turned her back to me, one strap of the little slip falling down over her shoulder, and parting the light cotton bed curtains, she climbed on the bed so that I saw her naked bottom and her tiny pink vaginal lips. Then she turned towards me, drawing her knees to one side almost demurely, her hair hanging down over her face, and she said, "Come here."

I was on her before I knew what I was doing.

I scooped her up in my right arm and lifted her up on the nest of pillows, and I drove into her instantly, impaling her, and slamming her as she had me.

The blood flush came over her face and neck instantly, the deceptive look on her face of tragedy, pain. Her arms flung out and she bounced against the mess of lace ruffles like a rag doll.

She was so tight, so wet and hot it astonished me, the sheath of convulsing flesh feeling almost virginal, driving me right up to the edge. I ripped at the slip, tore it over her head and threw it off the bed. And in some mad moment it seemed she had me again, this time with her glove-tight little vagina, and her naked belly and breasts sealed against me, and I was her prisoner, her slave. But I wasn't going to come until she came. I wasn't going to spend until I saw her shuddering and helpless, and I drew up, lifting her bottom with my left arm, lifting her and forcing her down on me, then slamming her under the full weight of my body, grabbing at her mouth with my mouth, kissing her, and making her face be still under mine. When I caught her like that, slamming her and kissing her, she exploded inside, the blood flush going dark, her heart stopping, full throttle into "the little death," her moans animalian, raw. And holding back nothing, I went on fucking her, spending into her, fucking her harder than I ever fucked anything or anyone—male or female, whore or hustler, or powerless phantom of the imagination—in my life.

Elliott
13

Leather and Perfume

I TRIED NOT to sleep, but it was useless. I drifted in and out for a while, feeling this odd anxiety, looking right at her soft profile against the billow of the curtains as she slept. Lovely woman, flawless up close, and menacing in sleep as she'd been awake.

How could she sleep after that? How could she be so sure I wouldn't jump up and drag her all over the room by her hair? I had a near irresistible desire to start kissing her again and fucking her again, and yet I wanted to get the hell out of the room. I folded her against me, giving it all up in an inevitable drowsiness, caressing her breasts and her wet sex very gently, and then dreaming, really slipping away, as if I were knocked out.

When I woke up, it was dark in the room, and she was saying my name. The little danger alarm went off in my head. If she sent me off now, goddamn it, I'd go mad.

There was one distant lamp on the dresser, throwing a yellow light on the hard, angular features of the sculptures and the masks, and gleaming on the brass of the bed. And I was lying flat on the smooth cotton sheets, the spreads and pillows gone, and the curtains had been tied back. It was the familiar feel of leather closing around my left wrist that brought me fully around. She had already tightened the buckle and now, bending over me, her knees against me, she buckled the cuff at the right.

She's going to whip me, I thought. She's not through with me. Quick simmer of excitement. And I really asked for it, didn't I, saying those things, so it's going to be hard. And she'd do it if I didn't ask for it. Did I think that fucking her would stop her? Scared. Slow boil.

I gave a tug to the straps just to test the strength, and realized I couldn't possibly pull loose. My left foot was quickly manacled to the bedpost. And then the right. All this had happened before, it wasn't the worst. In fact, it was the most comfortable kind of whipping. So why the panic inside? Because it was she? Because never before had I ever *had* one of them who tormented me, not the way I'd had her. Beautiful! And all I could think about, in spite of this, was a line out of a bad Romans and Christians movie, where some slave says to the decadent patrician master, "Whip me but don't send me away."

I twisted, pulled at the straps, my cock rubbing the sheets, but I didn't even strain the heavy brass frame.

And she was watching me, standing on my right.

Her back was to the lamp. Her skin looked almost incandescent in the shadows, as if the heat in her had alchemized into light.

I thought of her under me again, her toughness and her softness, and that she was going to whip me, and the boil was rolling. I wanted to say something to her suddenly, pierce the tension. But I didn't dare. And I didn't know exactly what it was I wanted to say. She had a black leather strap in her hand and this was going to be bad. And why the hell would she care if I did say something to her? What did I want to say?

She was dressed all in black now the way all the trainers dress, except for the lace blouse. Piquant, she looked, chic, a tight little leather vest and skirt snug around her body, her high-heeled boots laced to her knees. If I'd seen her sitting in a sidewalk café looking like that I would have come in my pants.

As it was, I was almost coming against the cotton sheet.

She moved towards me, holding the strap at her right side.

Now I pay for it, not just the smart cracks, but having her. That's it, isn't it? I almost cringed. After all, the whipping never feels good. No matter how much you want it or love it, it hurts. And she'd know how to do it; she was the boss.

She came closer. She bent over, the frills of her blouse brushing against my shoulder, and she kissed my cheek. Perfume and silken hair. I shifted against the sheet, thinking I can't come like a school kid from her kissing me, that's nuts.

"You're a smart aleck, aren't you?" she said in a low, almost loving voice. "You've got a real smart mouth. And you're not under my command or under your own."

I almost said, Yes, I am, really, I am. I'll kiss your feet if you let me go, but I didn't say anything at all.

She kissed me again, bringing the tiny hairs up all over my body because it was so maddeningly light. Just a taste of her mouth. Whiff of her perfume again. "We're going to learn a few lessons," she said, "in how a slave talks and answers at The Club."

"I'm a real fast learner," I said. I turned my head away from her. What the hell was I trying to do? It was bad enough. But I couldn't stand it, the sight of her, the tight vest and the plunging neck of the blouse.

"I hope so." She laughed softly. "I'm going to whip the hell out of you if you're not." And her lips touched me again, feeding on my neck. "What is this? All flustered already? You come against the bed while I'm whipping you and what do you think I'll do to you? Take a guess."

I didn't dare say anything.

"Now, while I'm punishing you," she said just as gently, smoothing the hair back from my forehead, "you're going to answer me properly and deferentially every time I address you, and you will control your powerful proud impulses, no matter what the provocation, you understand?"

"Yes, Madam," I said. I turned over and strained forward and kissed her before she could get away. She pulled in again, softening all over, and dropping down on her knees, kissed me, that same scorching current running through it, and the kiss almost touched off the bomb.

"Lisa," I whispered, I didn't even know why.

And she stayed still, very close, looking at me. And there was some instantaneous sense of why this was so horrific, that always before they'd been wearing masks in my imagination, the women and the men who whipped me, or subjugated me. It didn't matter who the hell they were, really, as long as they said the right things, were good. But she wasn't wearing a mask. The fantasy wasn't cloaking her. "I'm scared to death of you," I whispered. I could hear the amazement in my own voice. I was speaking so low I wondered if she could hear me. "I mean I . . . this is difficult, it's . . ."

There was some little change in her face. Some slight snap in her expression. God, she was beautiful. It was like in this moment her face opened up, like it became the inside of her instead of what she wanted it to be to the outside world.

"Good," she said, making her mouth into a kiss that didn't touch me. She drew back slowly. "Are you ready to be whipped?"

I made a little sigh and nodded.

"You have to do better than that."

"Yes, Madam."

She shook her head. She was studying me. I licked my lips a little, looking at her mouth. She was frowning slightly, her eyelashes a dark fringe as she looked down and then back at me. "I like the way you say Lisa," she said, thoughtfully, as if she was considering. "Let's change it to 'Yes, Lisa.'"

"Yes, Lisa." I was trembling. It has always been that way with Martin. Yes, Martin. No, Martin.

"Good boy," she said.

She disappeared to the foot of the bed. And when she started, she swung the strap as hard as one of the male handlers. And there was an efficiency to the way she whipped, making every lash count.

She went to work. It was like an examination, the way that she spread the blows, and the pain built slowly, luxuriously, just the way the pleasure had when she had screwed me with the dildo, and I could feel myself breaking down, a slow exhilaration building under the pain, all the defenses weakening that would have been solid against her, had she gone at it more brutally, swiftly, with more noise.

Then the thrashing started in earnest. I tensed my muscles, rising off the sheet. I couldn't keep quiet. I tried holding out as I always do, unwilling to let go, but it was no good. My body was cooking all over and I couldn't stand it any longer, the dazzling sting of the strap seeking out all the little places it had neglected, the excitement surging even as I tried to hold it back, the strap teasing the big welts again. There came that priceless moment—a moment that doesn't always come—when I knew I had no control anymore, and I felt everything, everything, at the same time.

"You know you belong to me," she said.

"Yes, Lisa," I answered naturally, spontaneously.

"And you are here to please me."

"Yes, Lisa."

"And there will be no more impertinence."

"No, Lisa."

"And there will be no repeat of the impertinence I heard from you this afternoon."

"No, Lisa."

Finally I was moaning outright, and couldn't pretend I wasn't. I kept my teeth shut even when I answered her. I thought of her sex again, her legs spread and that hot little sheath clamped to me. I wanted to see her. I had things to say to her that they hadn't made words for. But I didn't dare say anything except the proper answers, listening through the rain of blows to each question. I was ready for anything she would demand.

Finally she stopped.

My skin was sizzling, every welt and mark steaming as she undid the cuffs with her maddening, delicate, and quick little fingers and told me to get up.

I climbed off the bed drunkenly and I fell down on my knees in front of her, exhausted as if I'd been running for miles. My muscles hurt from the clenching and unclenching all through the whipping, and I wanted to take her in my arms so badly that I pressed my head to the floor. I was weakened with this feeling for her, drugged.

I bent and kissed the smooth leather of her little boots. I curled my hand around her left ankle, and rubbed my face against her. I didn't care anymore about anything in the world, really, except her. There were all these gradations of her. Having her, fearing her, being whipped by her, just holding on to her.

"No," she said, and I drew my hand back, kissing her feet some more. The soreness and the desire came in flashes.

"It was a good whipping, wasn't it?" she asked.

"Yes, Lisa," I nodded, letting out a little laugh in spite of myself. If you only knew—"Very good"—that I want to devour you. That I . . . what?

"Have you had better?" she asked. She nudged my cheek with the belt so that I looked up.

For a moment I couldn't see her clearly. She was all soft at the edges. Then her face burned through. She was a little damp from the exertion, her rouged lips shimmering ever so slightly, her eyes innocent and full of a vague curiosity. It was like Martin's expression, actually, that constant marveling, probing, discovering.

"I asked you a question. Have you had better?" she said politely, but a little impatiently. "I would like to know."

"Longer and louder," I murmured. I knew I was smiling at her, almost ironically. "And harder, but not better, Lisa," I said.

She bent down and kissed me and I thought I would finally spend, couldn't control it, the wet feeding of her mouth, that way of kissing that was unlike any kissing I'd ever had.

I started to get up. I would have picked her up, crushed her to me. But she drew away quickly, and left me sort of shivering on my knees, feeling the warm prickling sensation in my limbs again and that strange numbness in my mouth.

"I could have skinned you alive," she said. "But I only wanted you a little heated. You're going to do things for me tonight."

I looked up at her again, afraid she would tell me to look down. "Would you . . . ?" I whispered. "Might your . . . might your slave make one little request?"

She regarded me almost coldly for a moment. "All right."

"Let me kiss you again, Lisa, just once."

She stared at me. But then she bent to grant it and I reached up and took hold of her and it was like her heat roaring into me, that brutal and that lyric at the same time. I was just this animal that wanted her, nothing else.

"Let go, Elliott," she said, and she sounded strict and disapproving, but her fingers were clinging to me, and she released me as if she was the one who'd been told to do it, not me.

I bowed my head.

"It's time for some real lessons in obedience and manners," she said, but her voice was a little frayed, disconcerted. Nice sound! "Stand up."

"Yes, Lisa."

"Put your hands behind your back, clasped at the waist."

I obeyed, and old rhythms started—*something bad going to happen, well, maybe I should really be going now*—the low, shuddering alarm. But you belong to her, I thought. Don't think of anything else. Oh, yes, you really belong to her. Some fragment of a thought was running through my mind, something about us looking for our ultimate agony, and mine was desiring her, dying for her while she punished me, not just the punishing, but the focus, the desire. Yet that was not quite it.

She moved around me in a little circle that made every nerve in my body come alert. She looked splendid walking in the high-heeled boots, her calves so tense under the smooth kid, the little suede skirt riding beautifully over her little bottom and hips.

She pinched my face lightly. "You blush beautifully," she said very sincerely. "And the marks look good on you. They don't disfigure you. You look now like you should look."

I felt that vague ripple of feeling that the French call a frisson. I looked her in the eye. But I didn't dare ask to kiss her again. She'd say no.

"Look down, blue eyes," she said but she wasn't disapproving. "Now, I won't gag you, your mouth's too pretty. But one lapse, I mean one little flare of the old Elliott I met this afternoon and I'll bit you and harness you, you understand? And I'll be angry with you. Does that mean anything?"

"Yes, Madam!" I threw her another glance, bittersweet.

She laughed the same way she had the other times, in a low riff, and she kissed me on the cheek again, and I looked at her again, with a flicker of something more subtle than a smile. It was like flirting with her in the sliest fashion. *Kiss me again, please*. She didn't.

"Now, you will walk ahead of me," she said, "and slightly to the right. And again, you smart off once and you'll be gagged and on your hands and knees. You understand?"

"Yes, Madam."

Elliott

14

The Sports Arcade

IT WAS DAMNED unnerving to be out of the cocoon of her bedroom and borne again into The Club. And the flickering hurricane lamps and the din of the evening crowd in the garden struck a deep, primal chord of fear.

The number of guests suddenly scattered around us seemed even greater than what I'd seen the first day, and I kept my eyes down, feeling a low-grade buzz all through me at being walked this way, slowly and deliberately, past so many inevitable glances.

I followed the path, Lisa's arm prodding me at the turn, her hand out to point if there was a fork.

We passed the buffet tables and the swimming pools, and made our way along a little path out of the main garden and towards a low, glass-domed building. The lower walls were covered with vines, and the lighted dome glowed like a great bubble. I could hear the muted sounds of shouting and laughter.

"This is the arcade, Elliott," she said. "Do you know what that means?"

"No, Lisa," I said in an amazingly calm voice. *But it sounds awful.* I was sweating already. The welts and stripes from the strap were itching.

"You're a sportsman, aren't you?" she asked. She pushed me a little faster along the path, and a young handler with longish red hair and a pleasant enough smile reached out to open the doors of the strange building, letting out the noise in a deafening blast.

"Good evening, Lisa," he said loudly. "Packed in there to-night, and they'll be glad to see this one."

The light seemed dimmer once we stepped in, but it might have been only the denseness of the crowd, and the smoke. The smell of tobacco mingled strongly with the malty smell of beer.

Only a sprinkling of women as far as I could tell, though the place was immense, a giant covered garden of sorts, with a long bar running along the curved walls. Trainers pushed past us with naked male slaves, some bound, others walking as I was, some obviously worn out and covered with sweat and dust.

A dozen different languages easily were being spoken around us. I could feel the eyes passing over me, lingeringly, and I heard French and German distinctly, snatches of Arabic, and Greek. Well-heeled men all, naturally, expensive sportswear, all the little accoutrements of money and power.

But the appalling part were the shouts coming from up ahead, the familiar deep-throated noises of men cheering on some competition, then guffawing and cursing when it went wrong. I wanted to leave now.

Lisa pushed through the wall of men and I saw a tree-lined avenue of clean, soft white sand before me that led some hundred yards or more ahead before the crowd swallowed it up. There were large airy fountains to the far left and the right, scattered park benches, nude female slaves, all of them extremely pretty, quietly and busily raking the sand, emptying the standing ash-trays and gathering up discarded glasses and beer cans.

The avenue itself was a mall, it seemed, lined on both sides with scattered, neatly whitewashed buildings, each strung with ropes of tiny lights. There were fenced areas in between the build-ings and groups of men leaned on the wooden railings, blocking the view of whatever went on inside. Guests moved in and out of the buildings. And hundreds strolled on the white sand, shirts open to the waist, drinks in hand, only glancing now and then in the open doorways.

I took a step backwards without realizing it, half pretending I had to get out of the way of two men in swim trunks filing past me, and felt Lisa's fingers biting into my arm. My mouth opened with some half thought out plea, like, "I'm not ready for this," but nothing came out.

The crowd thickened around us. I felt claustrophobic as pant legs and boots and coats brushed me. But Lisa had her hand on my·arm, and was pushing me towards the first of the long white booths.

It was shadowy inside, and for a moment I couldn't make out what was there. Mirrored walls and ceiling, glossy hardwood floor, and thin white lines of decorative neon etching the ceiling, the stage. Then I saw it was a typical amusement park game. You paid for several black rubber rings and you tossed them up, trying to hang all of them on one projectile to make a perfect score. Only the projectiles here were the bowed heads of the male slaves kneeling on a conveyor belt that moved them very rapidly across the stage.

To the guests it was a coarse, hilarious pastime, getting a number of rings around the neck of the victim before he vanished into the wings. And for all the simplicity of it, it had a real scariness to it: the submission of the kneeling victims, the way their well-oiled bodies had become mere objects as they passed before the crowd.

I stared at the little stage, the bowed heads, the rings hanging from bent necks. I didn't want to be left here. I couldn't. There had to be some way of making it clear. And without considering it really, I backed up until I was suddenly behind Lisa and I kissed her on the top of the head.

"Outside," she said. "And don't waste your pleas. If I wanted you up there I'd put you up there. I don't."

She pushed me toward the door.

The lights of the avenue flickered against my closed eyelids for a second, then I was moving again, being pushed steadily towards another booth on the right.

This was a much larger booth, with the same glossy high-tech decor, with a bar and brass rail along the wall, about thirty feet deep. It wasn't rings this time, it was brightly colored plastic balls, about the size of tennis balls, pitched towards the moving bull's-eye targets that were painted in thick gleaming colors on the backsides of the male victims, who, with their hands tied over their heads, tried desperately to dodge by constant movement what they couldn't see. The balls stuck to the target when they hit. And the slaves shimmied to shake them loose. So deliciously humiliating and not the slightest real pain involved. I didn't have to see the faces of the slaves to realize they were preening as they twisted and turned. Every lovely muscle was fully alive.

I felt the sweat streaming down my face. I gave a little negative shake of my head. Impossible, simply impossible. Checking out. Out of the corner of my eye I saw Lisa watching, and I made my face blank.

The next two booths were similar games, the slaves being made to run on oval tracks above to escape the balls and the rings, and in the fifth booth, the slaves were hung upside down from carousels and did not have to twist or turn themselves.

I wondered if that was what they did with them when they were tired from the other games, put them on that carousel where they hung helpless? Scrumptious sufferers. And this was regular service in The Club, wasn't it, this place, not punishment like being sent below stairs.

Any memory of a sane world in which these things didn't happen seemed untrustworthy at best. We'd stepped into a Hieronymus Bosch painting, full of lurid silver and red, and my only chance of getting out again was the lady who'd brought me in.

But did I want to get out? Of course not. Or let's just say, not this very minute. I'd never thought of stuff like this in all my sexual fantasizing. I was scared to death and secretly entranced. But it was like the old "Purple Cow" poem by Gellett Burgess: "I'd rather see than be involved."

I moved numbly, through the glare of the lights. My senses were flooded. Even the noise seemed to penetrate me, the sweetish smell of the smoke to drug me slightly, the hands that now and then touched or examined me stoking the mixture of dread and desire that I couldn't hide.

Naked women slaves appeared and disappeared like flickering pink flames in the shifting male crowd, as they offered cocktails, champagne, white wine.

"Aren't we geniuses of exotic sex?" Lisa whispered suddenly. It was startling to hear her speak. But the expression on her face was even more surprising. She was taking in the crowd in the same dazed way that I was taking it in, as if we'd been drifting for hours together at a county fair.

"Yeah, I think so," I said. My voice sounded as strange as hers. I was steaming.

"You like it?" she said. No irony. It was like she'd forgotten who we both were.

"Yeah, I like it," I said. I got a powerful, secret satisfaction from the innocence of her face and voice. And when she looked up at me I winked at her. I could almost swear she blushed as she looked off.

It occurred to me, why not grab her and bend her over my arm, kissing her madly, like Rudy Valentino in *The Sheik?* I mean in the middle of all this exotic sex it would be a scream, at least to me. I didn't have the nerve.

I was going to die if she got pushed out of shape with me. Which meant playing one of these alluring little games if she said to do it, right?

As we started to walk again, I watched her out of the corner of my eye, her jutting breasts under that elegant layer of lace, the vest that made her into a little hourglass. This was heaven and hell.

And as she directed me towards one of the small clearings, I realized she might show me all of the diversions before choosing the one that had affected me the most.

But when I saw the game in the clearing, I couldn't too well cover up what I felt.

There was a race in progress here, men all around the four-sided fenced enclosure with feet on the rail as they might be at a rodeo, cheering on the naked slaves who ran in neat tracks on their hands and knees.

But the slaves weren't simply racing each other for the distance. They were retrieving in their teeth black rubber balls thrown down the tracks by the guests at the railing who would not release a second ball until the first one had been retrieved. And the spectators were whipping them on with leather straps.

It seemed some five balls made up the race, because a winner was pulled up by both arms right after he laid a fifth ball at his master's feet. His face was red, dripping wet, as he was applauded, patted, caressed. He was at once taken out of the clearing, a white towel wrapped around him, but the others, panting and shuddering, were whipped into place for the next race.

I saw the punishment. You raced until you won.

And just as I figured, the slaves were glorying in it, really competing with one another. They knelt poised and desperately ready to begin again, eyeing each other, jaws set.

Again, I backed away, trying to appear casual about it. Weren't we going on to the next clearing, the next booth? I mean, come on, there's lots of stuff to see, right? I think I'll go home and read the *New York Times* now. The noise was like a buzzing in my head.

"It's really tough for you, isn't it?" she said, big brown eyes looking up again. Everything melted in me except what never melts, of course. I thought of a lot of little nasty things to say, but I didn't say them. I felt lusciously subject to her. And defiantly I kissed her cheek.

She backed up and snapped her fingers and made a little gesture for me to get moving. "Don't do *that* again," she said. She was really flustered. Her face was pink.

She led the way down the crowded avenue without glancing back. I told myself I didn't want to look at the clearings on either side, but I couldn't resist. More races. Different lengths of races, variations. But it was more fun watching her beautiful little bottom moving under her skirt, the sweep of her hair that came down almost that far, the little seams of flesh behind her naked knees.

The avenue branched to left and right as we neared a thick crowd before a low, lighted stage. Some eight or ten slaves were on the stage, each naked except for a white towel draped over one shoulder.

Lots of tousled hair and polished muscles and smiles, amazingly provocative smiles, as the slaves apparently taunted the crowd with little gestures and "come on" motions of the head.

I soon saw what was happening. The handlers were selling the slaves for the races or games, and the slaves were lapping it up, vying for the high spenders. Two were sold off while I watched, the result of a little informal auctioning among three bidders, and immediately another pair were led up the steps out of a pen, and started the same preening and good-humored taunting. Hoots, shouts from the guests, and occasional threats like, "I'll work that smile off your face," and "You think you want to run for me?" strengthened the convivial tension.

Lisa put her arm around me and pulled me close to her, the feel of her fingers against me pretty maddening. I stole a couple of glances at her breasts beneath the low-collared blouse. I could almost see her nipples.

"Which one is the most attractive, the most sensuous?" she asked, inclining her head as if we were just a couple at a pedigreed dog show. The feeling of being utterly subjugated by her was getting worse. "Think about your answer, and answer me truthfully," she said. "It will teach me things about you."

"I don't know," I said kind of testily under my breath. The thought that she'd buy one of these brutes and start paying attention to him infuriated me.

"Get your mind on exactly what I'm telling you to do," she said coldly. She reached up and brushed the hair back from my forehead, but her expression was flinty, threatening. "Pick the one you really think is the most handsome, the one you'd like to fuck if I let you do it. And don't lie to me. Don't even consider it."

I was pretty miserable. All I felt was jealousy. But I looked at the men, and things inside me were scrambled. My senses took over and shifting gears this fast felt entirely new. They were all very young, obviously athletic, and they were as proud of their stripes, their welts, the pink blush on their butts as they were of their genitals, the muscles in their legs and arms.

"I think the one on this end, the blond, is terrific," she said.

"No," I shook my head as if this wasn't even discussable. "There's no one on the stage who can equal that guy in the back of the pen, the dark one." He was something special even in a place full of people who were special, a young, black-haired, smooth-chested faun, right out of the forest primeval. He should have had pointed ears. His curly hair was short though full on the sides, and only a little long in back; and his neck and shoulders were particularly well shaped, powerful. His partially erect cock was on the way to being as big around as a beer bottle. He looked part demon, especially when he stared directly at me, his lip curling a little, his sleek dark eyebrows coming together for an instant in a playful frown.

"That would be your choice, you'd like to have him?" she asked, appraising him. He was being moved to the front of the pen, his hands behind his neck, his eyes fixed on us as his cock hardened.

I imagined it, screwing him while she watched, and my mind split in half. That had been hard for me at Martin's, very hard, screwing in front of others. Easier to be whipped, humiliated in a dozen ways than to let them see that. There was a sense in me of something being released. He was making my temperature rise.

Lisa made some little gesture to the handler, like the subtle hand bids made at art auctions. Immediately, he motioned for the slave to come up on the little stage, and then down the steps through the crowd towards us.

On close inspection, he was damn near overwhelming. His olive skin had been darkened by a tan, and every inch of him was hard. He dropped his eyes with perfect courtesy as he approached, his hands still behind his neck as he went down on one knee to kiss Lisa's boot with a grace that was slightly surprising. Even the back of his neck was enticing. He threw me a quick up-and-down look. I looked at her, half wanting him, half hating him, unable to detect what she really thought of him.

She took the towel off his shoulder as he rose, and threw it to the handler. Then she motioned for us to follow her.

We came right away to a very noisy clearing, a large open ring where the loose crowd was roughly three deep right up to a half circle of jammed-packed bleachers.

Lisa pushed her way forward, motioning for us to follow until we were at the railing, the crowd closing around us instantly.

Two obviously fresh and sexually primed slaves on hands and knees were just entering the ring, and the spectators began counting in a low chant, one, two, three, four, five . . . as the pair squared off from one another like fighters. Warily, the slaves peered at each other through tousled hair, their bodies glistening under a thick coating of oil, one a dark-skinned, brown-haired slave, the other a silver blond, with a long mop veiling his face.

But what exactly was the game? Just pin the other guy down for the count or rape?

The brown-haired slave sprang with a hiss at the blond one, trying to mount him. Yeah, it was rape. The thick oil allowed the blond to slide free easily, and as he did so he turned and sprang at the darker one, failing to catch hold in the same way. A real scuffle followed, with oily hands slipping desperately off oily limbs. The chanting count continued now past one hundred, and the struggle intensified, the brown-haired slave getting on top of the other, his arm locked around his throat. But he was shorter than the blond slave and no matter how he jabbed, he couldn't pull it off. The blond rolled over on him trying to force him off, and finally got free just as the count ended with 120.

No winners. Both were booed by the crowd.

Lisa turned to me. "Need I tell you what to do?" she asked. She gestured for the handler. The olive-skinned faun gave me another curling smile as I glared at her.

"Pretty damned old-fashioned stuff, if you ask me," I said. The top of my head was coming off.

"Nobody did ask you," she said. "And you picked a champ, by the way. You better be good."

There was a lot of racket from the crowd as the handler pulled us aside for the oiling. The evil little faun was studying me, sizing me up, his lips curling in that same maddening fashion. He was ready to go. I could hear bets being placed, see men arguing and talking in the crowded bleachers.

And my anger gave way to another more savage emotion. Get him. Fuck him, the bastard. I was ready, too.

Champion, she called him. Probably done it hundreds of times. A goddamned gladiator, that's what he was, and I was right off the bus. Okay. I was getting more and more exhilarated, crazy. It was sublimely brutal and it was galvanizing me, yet another doorway opening on something that had always been locked up.

"Remember," the handler said pushing me towards the ring. "On your hands and knees always, and no hitting. And don't waste any time defending yourself. Get him. Now go to it." And he shoved me down and under the rail.

With a loud clack, the count began.

I saw him moving in front of me, glowering at me from under his dark brows, the oil beaded on his hands and his cheeks. Stockier than I am, just a little muscle-bound, not good for him. The count was up to thirty, thirty-one . . .

Suddenly, he lunged at me as if he'd go over my head, and I spun around sharply to the right just in time to see him land in the dust clumsily. But the secret was to mount him now, without a second's hesitation, and I sprang at him before he could recover, making in effect a complete circle from the time he had rushed for me. I got on top of him, and locked my left arm around his throat, reinforcing it with my right. But it was madness trying to hang on, his body slipping and sliding under me as he bucked in fury, his greased fingers scratching uselessly at my hands. I could hear him snarling.

But he wasn't getting away, not from me. It was the gutter fights I'd never had, the alley rapes I'd never committed, nor ever even truly imagined. And he had it coming, the son of a bitch, he would have done it to me. It was divine. I humped him as if I were already in, clamping down on him like a vise. It was working. He couldn't throw me off and he was weakening. His fingers slipped as they grasped at my arms, and my hands. The crowd was roaring. I rammed him hard. He shook his head savagely and tried to roll over, but I was too heavy for him, too mad and determined for him, and I was in. I had him, and I had both arms around his neck again, and he didn't have a chance now.

The crowd broke its counting—110, 111—to scream and applaud. And his frantic bucking only made it better, the friction gorgeous as he tried to get free. I came, spewing into the heat inside him, shoving his head down in the dirt.

They let me rest for a little while after the shower and scrubbing. I sat on a little patch of soft grass with my arms folded on my knees and my head on my arms. I wasn't really tired or worn out.

I was thinking. Why had she chosen that particular game for me? It had been the very opposite of a humiliation, yet the exposure had been dazzling. And the lessons unique. Rape without guilt. Should every man experience that once in his lifetime, his capacity to use another like that, but in a situation where no real moral or physical damage is done?

I could have gotten addicted to that little game. Except that I was already getting addicted to her. It nagged at me, why had she chosen it? It was too tricky, giving me a chance to master the other one. Was she building me up for a real fall?

When I finally looked up, I saw her leaning against one of the fig trees watching me with her head to one side and her thumbs hooked in the side pockets of her suede skirt. She had the strangest expression on her face, her eyes large, her lower lip very kissable, her face girlish and soft.

I had that odd desire to speak to her, explain something to her, the same urge that had come over me in the bedroom, and again the anguish: what the hell would she care? She didn't want to know me, this woman. She wanted only to use me and that was why I was here.

Yet we were looking at each other over the distance of the little bathing place, oblivious to the racket from the ring where the same drama was being reenacted, and I was scared of her again, just as I'd been scared for hours, scared of what was going to happen next.

When she beckoned to me, there was a stirring in my loins that I could almost hear. I had a real premonition, that it wouldn't be any more macho antics right now.

I rose and walked over to her, the anxiety getting worse.

"You're very good at wrestling," she said calmly. "You can do things that a lot of new slaves can't. But it's just about time to whip you again, don't you think?"

I stared at her boots, the tight fit around her ankles. Back to her room, please, I thought. I could take anything if we were alone there again. Just thinking about it . . . I knew I was supposed to answer her, but I could not make the proper words come out.

"Blond slaves give everything away with their faces," she said, her curled finger stroking my cheek. "Ever been whipped at a real whipping post?" she asked. "For a nice large and appreciative crowd to watch?"

So here it comes.

"Well?"

"No, Madam," I said dryly with a little cold smile. Not ever for any crowd. And God, not for this crowd, not in this place! I had to think of something, something that wasn't an out and out entreaty. But again, nothing came out.

A handler appeared behind her, flash of hairy wrist, the *de rigueur* strap.

She said: "Take him to the whipping post. Let him walk with his hands at his sides. I like the way he looks that way, better than the other ways. And fully shackle him for the whipping. The works."

Total absence of discernible pulse. And the cold realization that if I said no and refused to move, the son of a bitch would whistle up his assistants and probably drag me to it all the same.

Well, that wouldn't happen.

"Lisa . . ." I whispered, shaking my head just a little.

Her hand came towards me again with a distinct whiff of perfume—flashes of the bedroom, the sheets, her naked under me—and closed warmly on the back of my neck.

"Shhhh. Come on, Elliott," she said, her fingers massaging my neck muscles. "You can take it, and you will, for me."

"Merciless," I whispered, clenching my teeth and looking away from her.

"Yes, exactly," she said.

Lisa

15

The Whipping Post

HE WAS GETTING a little scared for the first time now. All the good humor had drained out of his face. And the anger wasn't there either, the way it had been right before the wrestling match. No, something was really working finally. He didn't like the idea of being shackled, whipped in front of spectators. The nerve had at last been touched.

And what a laugh it would be if he knew how scared I was of disappointing him, how damned panicky I was that I just wasn't giving him his money's worth.

I mean all this bull about the slaves existing purely to please the masters and mistresses was just that: bull. We had to give everybody in this place what he or she bargained for, and we knew it. The system absolutely depended on satisfaction all around. What the hell was wrong with me that I couldn't really grind him under, give him what he came here to get?

But now with the whipping we had something. Okay.

I told the handler to lead him in front of me because I didn't want, for just a minute or two, to see his face. I had to break away from him. I had to get myself under command again.

When you train slaves you learn to watch everything, the slightest change in expression or respiration, all the little signals of distress that vary enormously from punishment to punishment, motif to motif. Ideally, you are also involved. Impassioned. But you learn to do it so well that you don't need to be burning anymore. And sometimes the burn is so steady and so continuous that you're not aware how powerful it is until you start to bring it to a close.

But something else was going on here. I wasn't just watching him; I was magnetized by him. It was an agony for me not to look at him every second, not to touch his skin, his hair. I wanted to provoke his rebelliousness again, his absolutely surprising insolence, his sense of his being *right there*.

What I couldn't stand was the idea of conquering him and that was what he had every right to expect me to do.

I let them get several yards ahead of me, just a little amazed by the way that he was looking around. The handler jerked his arm once or twice but it didn't have much of an effect. I could tell just watching his posture, the stiffness of his shoulders, that he was tense as a wire.

And that rational part of me, that part of me that was pure professional, kept trying to figure out what was really going on with the two of us, why I was out of hand.

Okay. He's a thousand times as handsome as the file pictures. Forget early calculations on that score. His hair is thicker, almost bushy, and that softens the shape of the head. And he does have a slightly cruel expression when he isn't smiling, a toughness that he hasn't invented, but on the contrary, tries to conceal. He doesn't like his own toughness all that much. He takes it for granted. Okay. That's nice.

And blue eyes, yes, unbelievable, and infinitely beautiful by sunlight, torchlight, incandescent light, whether or not he is smiling, staring, merely thoughtful, grave. The body is *the* body for a man to have. Say no more.

Now, add in the long fingers, the narrow hands, the manicured nails (almost unheard of among the slaves), the bearing, and the deep inflection of the voice and the way he does almost everything I tell him to do and you have Mr. Macho with inveterate elegance, the square-jawed guy by the fire in the ski lodge in the cigarette commercial, drawing on a Marlboro as if he's lazily recharging his batteries with it, the guy you know will like Mozart as well as Billie Holliday, be a tolerable judge of French wines.

All right, I have that part. And I admit I have never seen a slave quite like that before. That's dream stuff, only I never dreamed it. *Reads Russian novels word for word.*

But what about the rest of it, the look in his eye, the odd and intimate way in which he smiles, the way he *told* me he was scared of me, the damned smart cracks—nobody ever does that with me—and the particular energy that starts burning out the circuits when we touch?

I never fell in love in high school, never believed all that stuff about guys "kissing" better than others. But damned if he doesn't know how to kiss. He kisses the way I imagine men kiss each other, rough and really luscious, and affectionate in a way it can only be between equals, real equals, when there is equal potential for the acceleration and the fulfillment of desire. I could crawl into the back of a Chevrolet with him to kiss like that for an hour. Only guys don't kiss each other in the backs of cars, do they?

What in the hell is going on?

We'd come to the triple whipping post. Okay. He was really uptight.

Flood of white light on the three round cement stages, each slave tethered by the neck to the high post that came almost to the chin. And the line of shackled slaves waiting their turn, only two of them blindfolded, one gagged.

The crowd was the usual nine o'clock five-or-six-drinks-and-nobody-has-to-drive-home-because-we-are-home crowd, the guests at the tables on the raised terraces the ones who make no bones about the fact that whipping, pure and simple, turns them on. They don't need the games and the races. They think they're silly. And never mind that the whipping is 50 percent show and noise.

And the usual drifters, a good hundred or so milling in front of the stage with drinks in hand.

The handler, a very abrupt and rough young man I didn't know, led Elliott to the side, but Elliott was turning his head to look at the slaves who were "getting it," and the handler gave him a corrective crack of the strap.

I drew in a little closer. I half wanted to put the shackles on myself, but the handlers do it better, faster. They have more practice. I came up just close enough so that I didn't interfere.

Elliott looked at me for a second. There was a little muscle dancing in his cheek, and the dark red flush.

The handler put the thick white leather strap around his chest and then laced his wrists to the strap in back. It was driving him crazy. He looked off at the crowd and I could see the glaze over his eyes.

I kept reaching to touch him and tightening my fingers, moving so the gesture wasn't noticed. But now I put my fingers in his hair. He looked at the whipping post steadily, not acknowledging me, and his mouth twisted a little, looked a little mean.

When the handler put the white leather collar around his neck, I thought he was going to struggle. And he almost did.

"Take it easy," I said.

It's a lovely collar, lined in soft fur, and it pushes the chin up gracefully, but it makes you feel fifty times more helpless than you already are, and I could see he was clenching his teeth hard.

"You've been through this before . . ." I said, stroking his back. I was really not liking this so much. And I could see it was killing him that he couldn't lower his head to look at me, couldn't even turn it anymore.

"Blindfold him," I said.

Definitely not expecting it, silently terrified of it. And the handler pulled his head roughly as he slapped the blindfold around his eyes. He went rigid. I could see the thick pads under the white leather, thought how they felt when they were pressed to the eyelids. The handler buckled it tight. And as always happens, the lower part of his face looked irresistible, the lips working nervously, stretching, pressing together, going slack.

He shuddered all over, swallowed, shifted his weight.

I rose on tiptoe and kissed him on the cheek. He moved aside. It was getting worse for him by the second. His body seemed to swell under the shackles, his wrists twisting in the lacings, his lips drawn back in what looked like a bitter smile. But it was really sending him. He was hard and there was no way to hide that, no matter how angrily he turned away from me.

I kissed him again, and felt that shock. I went up on tiptoe and kissed his mouth. He started to pull back, all rage and frustration, but he didn't, obviously couldn't make up his mind to it fast enough, and it started again, that energy, that vibration with the pull of his open mouth.

He stopped it and turned away again. But he was losing control completely. He shook his head as if the blindfold were driving him wild. It looked like a white bandage around his eyes, and with his blond hair over it, he looked boyish and vulnerable, like he'd been wounded and patched up.

"Lisa!" he whispered, barely opening his lips. "Take off the blindfold. Take off the collar. The rest of it I can take." He started struggling against the shackles, his face beet red. The handler gave him a mean tug, kicking his legs apart.

"Shhhh." I kissed him again, pressing against him. "You've had the blindfold on before. You can stand it."

"Not this time. Not here," he said in the same whisper. "Lisa, remove it. It's too much."

Then he went still like a person counting to ten to keep his temper, the sweat draining down the sides of his face.

"I'm taking you up to the head of the line," I said. "They'll whip you next. It's not going to be too much harder than what I gave you in the bedroom."

"Only there's a little matter of two hundred people seeing it," he whispered between his teeth, "and I can't see them."

"I'll gag you if you don't shut up."

That was it for him. He wasn't going to let that happen. Silently, he was really coming apart. When I put my arm around him, he didn't pull away this time. He broke down. He turned towards me, and I rose on tiptoe again, and he kissed my hair.

I felt such a wave of desire for him I could hardly stand it. I motioned for the handler to go up and arrange for the whipping, trying to hide my face from anyone who might look. I didn't want to do all this, but it was what he came here for, goddamn it, what he really wanted, and I didn't dare not give it to him. I didn't know what the hell was really going on.

I loathed all of it suddenly, the artifice of it, and yet the excitement, the sense of the forbidden, the sheer lust at having him helpless . . . well, that was still there. And he was feeling it; he wasn't flagging for a second. But he was really out on the edge.

All right, first-class Club experience, Elliott. This is what it's about.

"You want to please me," I said, close to his ear. That's what the mistress is supposed to say. Go for the Academy Award with it. "Tell me you do. I want to hear it."

But the handler had come back for him, and it was time. Two other fresh slaves were being tethered to the posts. He was to be on the right.

I gave him over to the handler and went up into the highest part of the bleachers to watch.

From there I could see a lot of the arcade, the avenues, the fountains, the booths, and the crowds streaming through the walkways, and radiating out from the raised concrete stage on which the pillories stood.

He was pulled forward by the metal ring on the front of the white collar. Then that was tethered tight to the high post. Quickly, they had the straps around his ankles. Now he couldn't do anything but stand straight, arms tight to his back, and take the blows. He looked noble, actually. Like Errol Flynn in *Captain Blood* when the enemy got hold of him: straight Saturday matinee hero in chains. Grind of desire with a root like a time probe.

Immediately the whipping masters started swinging the straps.

The others took it predictably, with a nice dramatic flair, but he was tensing, shivering, working against it all the way.

A dozen or so guests gravitated to him with an infallible eye for something special. They started taunting him. But I wondered how many of them realized he was really breaking down.

The noise and the rhythm of the straps was hypnotizing. And the longer it went on, the worse it was for him. Obviously, no matter how it excited him, it was devastating him. He couldn't give in.

As soon as it was finished, I gestured for him to be brought to the foot of the bleachers with the shackles and blindfold still on.

He was so hot he was like a man just out of a steambath, his hair soaking, his chest heaving, his breath coming in little pants. I turned him around and there wasn't a particle of resistance in him as I looked at his skin.

He looked just about as enticing as he'd ever looked, and he was silent, licking his lips, only his color and the dancing muscles in his face revealing how miserable he was.

I propelled him carefully down the walkway through the crowd. He was obviously still frantic at not being able to see. He jumped when he was touched. But he wasn't going to beg me again to take off the blindfold. He didn't make a sound. I moved him steadily towards the front floors of the arcade and out into the garden and the quiet.

Lisa

16

Locked Out

HE WASN'T ANY calmer when we reached my room, but he hadn't said a word. The lowest lamps were lighted, the bed changed, the covers neatly turned down for the night.

I led him to the center of the room, where I told him to stand still. I stood back looking at him, just quietly watching him. He was crying under the blindfold. And he tried to swallow it in that classic masculine fashion so that the little soft sounds he made actually gave an impression of strength. His cock was still beautifully hard.

I moved through the double doors, wondering how keen his hearing was, and glancing back at his profile, at the really luxurious sight of him shackled that way against the civilized furniture of the room. The white blindfold made him look all the more ruddy, and his hair more full.

I sat down silently at my desk. I had a pain in my head that wasn't really a pain. It was a great, awful noise. My body was hurting for him, and yet I felt paralyzed, numbed. I reached over and picked up his file and I looked at the big glossy black-and-white photo of him in the turtleneck and the tinted aviator glasses, smiling at the camera. And I shut it and put it back.

I rested my elbow on the end of the desk and pressed my teeth to my knuckles and actually cut them with my teeth before I realized what I was doing, and stopped. Then I stood up and stripped off my clothes, getting impatient with them and almost tearing them, and just letting them fall on the floor.

Naked, I went back into the bedroom. I stood in front of him and looked at his face again, sliding my fingers around it and tilting it up from the rim of the white collar so that I could see it better in the light. I ran my thumbs over his lower lip, stroked his cheeks.

He had silky skin, the kind of skin only men have, not soft like a woman's skin, but silky. The heady sense that I possessed him, could do anything to him, was overpowering, yet the feeling was not what it should have been! It was not, was not . . . I felt locked out of him and he was not the one locking me out. All of this was locking me out! I could have whipped him more, made him crawl. He would have done it. And I would have been locked out!

He was still agitated, almost frantic. And my touching him made it worse. I reached back and undid the strap that was holding his arms and his hands. And before he could work himself free of it, I unsnapped the collar and threw it aside.

His body seemed to sigh all over as the straps fell to the floor, the tension knotting in his cock.

Then his hands came to life. He went as if to rub his wrists, then he reached for the blindfold, his fingers dancing right in front of it without touching it, and then he reached out for me.

I jumped. He caught me by the arms, wrapping his fingers all the way around them and bringing me forward. And then he realized I was naked, and he felt my sides and my breasts, giving a little startled noise. And before I could stop him, he had pulled me to him, forcing me against his chest. His cock was thumping against my sex, and he kissed me in that shocking way and I realized he had lifted me off my feet.

I reached up and shoved the blindfold up and off his eyes and his eyes were like some sort of unearthly part of him, a spectacle of light and blue color unlike anything else on his body, these two living reflecting orbs. I am going crazy, I thought. I am truly out of my head.

But I couldn't see anymore. He was kissing me again and we were going down on our knees, him pulling me, and it was so hot it was like losing consciousness, the lights going out around me, the walls dissolving. He stretched me out on the carpet and then he went in with a fast, thick scraping motion so that I couldn't find myself in it, hold it back. It blazed at once.

I moaned into his mouth, then my breath stopped. I was rigid, the pleasure erupting in waves, one after another, until I almost screamed, certain that it couldn't go on or I really would die. He was driving against me, right against the core of me—I could see the shaft of his cock against the blackness in my head—and I felt that sudden little spurt of my fluids against him, that impossible opening up, the sensation positively raging, as he came, roaring right over it, stoking it and stoking it and driving it further, until I shattered, screaming No, No, No, and God and Shit and Damn and No, Stop and finally giving up, like something broken, smashed to pieces, unable to make a sound or move.

After a long moment, I pushed at him a little, at his shoulder, his chest. I loved the crush of him against me, his head on my shoulder, the sun-cooked smell of his hair. I pushed him a little, loving the fact that I couldn't possibly move him. And then I lay perfectly still.

When I opened my eyes it was to see an almost formless shimmer of light. And gradually the bed, the lamps, my masks floating against the walls, the real faces of myself.

And him sitting up, beside me, his bent knee against my thigh.

He was just sitting there, his hair messed up, his face still moist and florid, and his mouth a little hard. His eyes were large and dreamy, full of whatever he saw. And he was looking at me. And it was like waking on the bank of a stream in a place where you think you are completely alone, and seeing this extraordinary male creature sitting right beside you, this beauty looking at you, like he never saw a female creature before in his life.

He didn't look crazy, or dangerous, or unmanageable. But he looked extremely unpredictable, as he had all along.

I sat up, drawing back very slowly, then rose to my feet. He watched me, but he didn't move.

I went to the dresser and took my negligée off the chair. I put it on, thinking how odd it was, this envelope of cotton and lace, that it was supposed to protect me from him. I pressed the button for the handler, and his face changed.

There was a raw glimmer of fear, and then a look of desperation. And his eyes watered slightly as we regarded each other. I felt this catch in my throat. Everything is coming to an end, I thought. But what did that mean? Why do I say things to myself when I don't even know what they mean? He looked forward, to the left of me, as if considering something, unable to make up his mind.

Daniel came in almost immediately; Daniel always takes care of my room.

And I saw the immediate shock on his face to see a slave sitting there without any manacles, in that outrageously relaxed position, taking not the slightest notice of either of us.

Elliott slowly climbed to his feet. He continued to stare, clearly thinking, still only vaguely respecting the fact that we were there.

Daniel looked relieved, but still unsure.

"Okay," I said. "Take him in for the night. Bath, full massage, healing lamp." I paused, rubbing the back of my head. Schedule for him. Routine. Got to get him away from me or go crazy. And got to give him what he's signed in for. "All right. In the morning, classes with the other postulants. Dana for exercise at eight, food and drink serving with Emmett at nine. I'll call Scott to see if he can take him for a demonstration in his class at ten."

No, no, not Scott. He'll fall in love with Scott. But got to do something, got to . . . Okay. Stick with Scott. Let Scott use him in the class for a demonstration, double whammy, that's something. Scott won't let him down.

"Rest in the afternoon, then he's to serve at the tables or in the bar all afternoon. Everybody can look, but don't touch."

What else? Can't think. He's going to fall in love with Scott.

"Any misbehavior, whip the hell out of him. But no one, I mean no one, not even Scott is to really touch him, I mean . . ."

I was drowning.

"And I want him rested between four and six and then back here at six sharp."

"Yes, Ma'am," Daniel said. Uneasy. Worried expression.

"What the hell's the matter with you!" I said. "Has everybody in this place lost his mind!"

"Excuse me!" He snapped to. Took Elliott's arm.

"Get him out of here!" I said.

Elliott was looking at me. Stop it. The awful, appalling feeling came to me that I'd failed him utterly, that for the first time in my entire "secret life" I hadn't delivered right on the line. It was a pain flashing like electricity through my temples. I turned my back.

Lisa
17

Obsession:
Twenty-four Hours

I WAS SITTING there, just staring at them as though they were living things instead of two large, dirty canvas suitcases with the keys in the locks, and the forbidding little documents case on top. I had the impulse to hide them in the closet, or under the lace skirts of the bed.

It was twelve o'clock. The breakfast tray was cold, untouched. And I was still sitting against the pillows, in my nightgown, drinking a second pot of coffee. I hadn't slept four hours all night. I'd tried to sleep between 10 and 11 A.M. when I knew he was in the classroom with tall, dark, handsome Scott because I couldn't stand the thought of it. But jealousy doesn't make you sleep. It makes you lie awake and stare.

Yet I didn't feel bad now. That was something I was just beginning to realize.

The fact was, I felt better than I had in years and years. I could not remember ever feeling precisely the way I did now. Or could I? It struck me that we didn't have enough words in the English language to describe *excitement*. We needed at least twenty to get the nuances of sexual feeling, and then this sort of excitement, this being swept up and out of yourself and into an obsession, this combustible mixture of ecstasy and guilt. Yes, obsession, that's the word for it.

And now there were the suitcases here, which hadn't been easy to get.

Not enough just to say, "This is Lisa and I want the personal possessions of Elliott Slater. Bring them to my room." You don't bring slaves' clothing and personal possessions into the compound. You don't just send for the documents case. This stuff is strictly confidential, the private belongings of the person whom the slave becomes when he finally leaves here.

And who set up all these rules? You guessed it.

But I'd managed it, by a little mixture of lies and logic. After all, I have my reasons and I shouldn't have to explain things. And the bags had been unpacked, hadn't they, inventoried and the clothes hung up in plastic bags with mothballs, right? So what's the big secret? I have very personal and urgent reasons for requesting all the personal possessions of Mr. Elliott Slater. I will sign for everything in full, including his cash and documents. Pack it up and bring it here.

One of those waves of desire was coming again, something like a scorching wind. I wanted him so badly. I wrapped my arms around my waist and bent over, tensing, waiting for it to pass. And I found myself remembering, quite abruptly, the early high school years when I had known these same agonizing waves of sexual hunger, and they had seemed purely physical and there was no promise of consummation, no promise of love. Ugly memories of feeling freakish, like I carried a secret within me that made me an outcast.

And yet it was exhilarating to feel that young again, that crazy. And frightening at the same time. This time it was hooked to another being, to Elliott Slater, this blast of heat, this physical take-over of body and mind. If I stopped to think about it, really think about it, I could fall into something just as bad as despair.

I slid off the bed and padded silently across the floor to the suitcases. They were filthy, the leather corners scratched and bruised. Extremely heavy. I turned the key in the lock of the one on the left, and undid the straps.

Everything very different inside. A faint masculine perfume rose from the neatly folded clothes. Nice brown velvet coat, leather patches on the elbows. Tweed Norfolk jacket. Two exquisite Brooks Brothers three-piece suits. Blue work shirts starched and ironed under their plastic wrapping. Army surplus turtlenecks, two really beat-up khaki bush jackets with crunched airline tickets and parking lot stubs in the pockets. Church's oxfords, Bally loafers, expensive jeans. Mr. Slater flies first class.

I sat cross-legged on the carpet. I felt the velvet coat with my fingers, smelled the perfume in the tweed. Cologne in the fibers of the turtlenecks. Lots of gray, brown, silver. No real colors except the blue work shirts. And everything immaculate, except the grungy safari jackets. Little plastic case with a fancy Rolex in it. Should be in the documents case. Address book in one of the pockets, and a plain blue business ledger thrown in with the underwear that was a . . . yes, a diary. No, close that, this is going far enough. But don't fail to note that the handwriting is legible. And he writes in black ink. Not ball point. Black ink.

I drew back my hand as if I'd touched something hot. Queasy feeling in the stomach at the sight of his writing. I reached for the documents case. I turned the key.

One-year-old passport, good photo, the smiling Mr. Slater. And why not? He'd been to Iran, Lebanon, Morocco, and half of Europe, as well as Egypt and South Africa, El Salvador, Nicaragua, and Brazil, all within twelve months.

Ten credit cards which would expire before he left here, except for the American Express Gold. And five grand—five grand, I counted it twice—in cash.

California driver's license, handsome face again with the irrepressible smile. Damn near best driver's license picture I've ever seen. A leather checkbook. A Berkeley hills (north campus) address. About five blocks from the house in which I grew up and where my father still lived. I knew those blocks up there.

No student apartments that high up, just those modern weather-stained redwood houses, old stone cottages with peaked roofs and diamond pane windows, here and there a mansion like a giant rock clinging to the cliff, all half hidden by the dense forest that swallowed up the winding sidewalks and crooked streets. So he lived up there.

I drew up my knees and ran my fingers back through my hair. I felt guilty. Like he would suddenly appear behind me in the doorway and say: "Get out of those things. My body is yours. But not those things." But there wasn't anything personal here except the diary. After all, why would he carry copies of his own books? Maybe to remind him who he had been when his two years had passed? Maybe because he always did.

I tipped over the other suitcase and unlocked it and unbuckled it.

More fashionable male finery. A handsome black tuxedo under plastic, five dress shirts. Primo cowboy boots, probably snake-skin, probably custom made. Burberry Raincoat, cashmere sweaters, plaid scarves, all very British, fur-lined driving gloves. And a real camel's hair sports coat, really nice.

And now pay dirt, sort of. Two torn and wrinkled receipts for auto service in a thumbed-up guide to world ski resorts. Mr. Slater drives, or did drive, a fifteen-year-old Porsche. That meant the old-fashioned, upside-down, bathtub-style Porsche, the one nobody ever took for anything else. And two dog-eared Dover paperback copies of Sir Richard Burton's travels in Arabia with lots of private scribbling on the inside cover, and yes, finally, a brand new copy of *Beirut: Twenty-four Hours* still sealed in the plastic wrapping put on by the publisher with a sticker on the front announcing it as the winner of some kind of award. God, if there wasn't plastic all over it.

I flipped it over. The inimitable Elliott, windblown in turtle-neck and bush jacket, looking appropriately forlorn—Ladies and gentlemen, this man has seen disaster, risked his life to take these pictures—the inevitable smile melancholy, wise. I felt the queasy feeling again, like my high school love had just walked past the homeroom door.

Well, I'd gone this far, so what was a little plastic? I mean I'm not going to hurt the book. Feeling like a thief I tore it open, and standing up, I walked back to the coffee and the bed.

Beirut, a city being smashed to fragments by years and years of tribal war. This was strong stuff. The most wrenching kind of photojournalism in which you are spared nothing, and yet the framing of each shot—the juxtaposition of ancient and modern, death and technology, chaos and deliberation—is so fine that it gives you the chilling pleasure that only art can give.

Unerring eye, it seemed to me, for the eloquence of faces, fig-ures in motion. Light and shadow used like paint. The darkroom technique was perfect and he probably did it himself on the black and white. And the color photos made the dirt and the blood embraceable, like the texture on a modern sculpture, the subject of which was war.

I started to read the commentary—he wrote that, too—and it was a hell of a lot more than captions for pictures. Understated, clean, it was almost a parallel story, in which the personal was subordinated to the power of what had been witnessed and recorded.

I put down the book. More coffee. So Elliott's a good photographer and Elliott can write.

But what does he think of himself? Why did he come here? And for two full years of incarceration? What made him do a thing like that?

And why am I rifling his stuff like this, and doing this to myself?

I drank another mouthful of coffee and got off the bed and walked around the room.

This wasn't a good excitement now, it was an uncomfortable restlessness. I reminded myself twice I could send for him anytime I wanted, but that wasn't right, not right for him, not right for me. And I could hardly stand it.

I went to the bedside table and picked up the phone. "Would you get me Scott if he's gettable? I'll wait," I said.

Twelve forty-five. Scott would be drinking his only after-lunch Scotch right now.

"Lisa, I was going to call you."

"What for?"

"To thank you for that little present this morning. I loved every minute of it. But I never expected to get my hands on him so soon. What got into you, giving him away like that? Tell me he disappointed you and I won't believe it. Are you okay?"

"One question at a time, Scott. And let me ask the first one. How did it go?"

"Well, I exhibited him in the trainers' class, you know, lessons in how to read a slave's responses, find his weak points. It drove him nuts. I thought he'd go out of his head when the class started examining him, but he was totally controllable. On a scale of one to ten, I'd say he's a solid fifteen. Why did you let me get my hands on him so soon?"

"Did you teach him anything new?"

"Hmmmm . . . That he could stand more than he thought he could. You know, being examined by the trainers, hearing himself discussed as if he were a specimen. He was delightfully unprepared for all that."

"Did you learn anything about him, anything special?"

"Yes. He's not *in* the fantasy, he's wide awake."

I didn't say anything for a moment.

"You know what I'm talking about," he said. "He's too sophisticated to be imagining he 'deserves' all this, or that he was 'born to be a slave,' or that he's lost in a world 'more noble and moral' than the real world, all the lovely romance slaves like to invent for themselves. He knows where he is and what's he doing to himself. He's about as open as any slave I've ever handled, the kind you think will crack but never cracks. Why did you let me have him? How come you're not really talking to me?"

"Okay. All right," I said. "All right, fine."

I hung up.

I stared at the messed-up suitcases. And the copy of *Beirut: Twenty-four Hours* that lay on the bed. *He's not in the fantasy. He's wide awake.* You said it.

I went back to the suitcases and picked up the worn, dirty paperbacks of the two-volume Burton book, *Personal Narrative of a Pilgrimage to Al-Madinah and Meccah.* I'd read it years ago in college at Berkeley. Burton the wanderer, disguising himself as an Arab to get into the forbidden city of Mecca. Burton, the sexual pioneer. Obsessed with the sexual practices of peoples who differed so dramatically from the proper English class he came from. What did that mean to Elliott? I didn't want to read Elliott's notes. It would be like reading the diary.

But I could see that he had been over these books thoroughly. Passages were underlined, circled, double marked in red and black, the flyleaves were covered with markings. I put the books back carefully and I put back *Beirut: Twenty-four Hours.*

I had to send for him. Yet I couldn't. Had to keep the desire in check.

I took another walk around the room, trying to feel something other than desire, and little spasms of jealousy over the details that had come tripping off Scott's tongue, trying to feel something a little easier than this obsession.

Once again: why would a man who could produce something like *Beirut: Twenty-four Hours* come as slave to The Club? Did he have to escape the ugliness of something like Beirut?

There are of course thousands of reasons why slaves come here. In the early days of The Club, they were mostly marginal beings, the half-educated, quasi-artistic, highly imaginative creatures whose careers in no way absorbed their exotic energies. Sado-masochism was a cultural world to them, utterly divorced from their dreary jobs, or repeated failures to get into music, theater, some artistic profession.

Now they were generally better educated, and usually enjoying the freedom of a protracted adolescence in their late twenties, ready and willing to exploit and explore their desires at The Club, just as they might study at the Sorbonne for a couple of years, undertake Freudian analysis, go to California and live in a Buddhist monastery.

But they were people by and large who lost themselves in what they did because they had not become themselves yet. Elliott Slater's life was going full tilt.

What was his reasoning? Had he been lured into our fun and games, and slowly addicted to it so that he was losing touch with everything out there that was waiting for him, the books he could write, pictures he could take, the assignments that would take him around the world?

The clash between our little universe and the raw reality of Beirut unnerved me. It gave me the shivers.

Yet the book was not raw. The book was art. And this place was art. And it struck me that Elliott's reasons for coming here had nothing to do with escape or renunciation of who he was. His reasons maybe had more to do with the pilgrimage by Burton, and Burton's obsessions and quests.

If you have landed in Beirut in the very middle of a war, where you might be killed by a bullet or a terrorist bomb, what is it like to come here where you know you won't ever be injured—on the contrary, you will be nurtured, watched over, babied—yet all these things will happen to you, these raw humiliations and exposures that most human beings could not possibly bear?

What had Martin written in the file? "Slave says he wants to explore what he fears most."

Yes. This had to be a sexual odyssey for Elliott, a deliberate violence to himself, a plunge into the things he feared in a place where he couldn't be hurt.

And the eerie thought came to me that he was really *disguised* as a slave the way that Burton had been disguised as an Arab when he penetrated the forbidden city. The disguise was nakedness. And I had found his identity in the things he owned, in his clothes.

Eerie thought, because as far as I knew he was being the perfect slave. He was in tune with us all the way. And I was the one with the jammed gears and the screaming engine. I was dreaming up all this shit about him. I ought to leave him alone!

I poured a fresh cup of coffee and made a slow promenade of the room.

Why weren't we obscene to him compared to the suffering of Beirut? Why wasn't our sexual paradise the worst sort of decadent contrivance? How could he take it seriously on any level when he took pictures so skillfully of all that?

I put down the cup of coffee and put my hands to my temples. It was as if the thoughts were hurting my head.

It came to me again, as it had on the vacation in California and on the plane coming home, that something was very wrong, that something was happening in me, a momentum building that I didn't understand, to which I didn't want to lose control.

The Club: Twenty-four Hours. Was it all equal in his mind? But the pictures would never tell the tale.

I think for the first time in all the years since it had begun, I hated The Club, at least for a moment. I hated it. I had this irrational desire to push out the walls that surrounded me, push up the ceiling, get out. *Something brewing, and for a long time.*

The phone was ringing. For a long moment I just stared across the room at it, thinking somebody should answer it before I realized the somebody was me.

I had a sudden fear that it would be about Elliott, Elliott had "cracked."

Very reluctantly, I picked up the phone.

Richard's voice: "Lisa, have you forgotten our appointment?"

"Our what?"

"With the pony trainer from Switzerland, Lisa. You know our friend with the elegant human stable . . ."

"Oh, shit."

"Lisa, the man really has something here, something rather marvelous if you could . . ."

"You handle it, Richard," I said. I started to put down the phone.

"Lisa, I spoke to Mr. Cross. I told him you weren't feeling too well. Needed some rest. Mr. Cross says it's up to you to approve all this. You should see the slave ponies, review the whole . . ."

"Richard, tell Mr. Cross I've got a hundred-and-three temperature. You play the ponies. Sounds just great to me."

I hung up the phone, shut off the bell, pulled the plug, and knelt down and hid the disconnected phone under the bed.

I went back to the suitcases. I picked up the silver turtleneck that I had unfolded before, and I pressed it to my face, smelling the rich cologne. I slipped off my negligée and my nightgown. And I pulled the turtleneck over my head. It was like having his skin on, to feel it on my arms, over my breasts, and smell that perfume.

Elliott
18

Lisa on My Mind

AFTER SEVERAL VISITS to Bath Heaven and its choir of little Bathangels I knew nobody was going to tell me much about her, who she really was.

I did worm it out of Mr. Iron Fingers Masseur that there was a gorgeous female slave named Diana mixed up in it who was in tears someplace because the Boss Lady–Perfectionist hadn't sent for her in two whole days.

"But where does she come from, what kind of jokes does she laugh at, you have to know something about her that's not classified, come on."

I kept doing inventories of her possessions, those sculptures, that shelf of books.

"Those paintings, the masks, how did she get those?"

"Elliott, this is like a stuck record," he said, working my skin like it was clay. "Get your mind off her. Male slaves don't get close to her. Think about all the beautiful ladies and gentlemen she's training you for."

"What do you mean, she doesn't like men, is that what you're saying, that she and this Diana slave . . . ?"

"You're getting yourself wound up over nothing. She doesn't like anybody. She just knows how to handle everybody better than anybody else could handle them, get the point?"

But the one thing they didn't mind confirming, over and over again, was that she was the real creator of The Club.

Almost every little game she had invented; the sports arcade was entirely her idea, and she had some other elaborate trips on the drawing board right now.

And I kept thinking about the way she looked last night when she stood in the middle of the arcade and said in that strange ironic voice, "Aren't we geniuses of exotic sex?" She was some kind of genius all right. But I was building up a suspicion about her. How did she feel about what she had accomplished? Was she one-tenth as impressed with it as I was? I didn't think so. I wish I had grabbed her and kissed her like Rudy Valentino in *The Sheik*.

But it was too crazy. I mean I was fantasizing about her, imagining she could love, she could feel, that I could affect something in her. I mean it was . . . like the goddamned song . . . almost like falling in love.

What the hell had Martin said, about sado-masochism maybe being a search for something. *You might be searching for a person, Elliott, rather than a system and at The Club the system is what you get.*

I didn't need Martin to tell me not to fall any deeper into this trap.

Listen to what Mr. Iron Fingers is saying to you. You're supposed to want the system. You're supposed to prove Martin was wrong.

But all day long I was playing this maddening little game of watching for her. Watching for her in Scott's class, half relieved she wasn't there to compound that little torture-chamber nightmare. And half disappointed she wasn't. And seeing her in the crowds all around while I mixed drinks and carried drinks and set down drinks, trying to properly wallow in the pinches and the compliments and the smiles.

But then there were those final confusing moments last night, when she was standing there naked in that open negligée, all moist and sweet and pink, with that handler gaping at her, stammering all those directions like the building was on fire. Damn her. I wanted to grab her, just hold her. I wanted to say just let me stay here and let us talk together for a little while, let us . . .

I wished I could talk to Martin. Ask him what to do about this. Emergency. Help. Something dangerous was happening in my head, the thought that I could make her love me, make her really love me. Ah, pride before the fall as all know.

And now and then, I thought of screwing up to disgust her and get away from her, to be sent back below stairs.

But it was really too late for that.

During the trainers' class, when I had almost bolted away from the hands examining me, I had been terrified of being sent back down again, separated from her. And there had been the electrical fire in my brain when Scott, that dark, feline trainer had whispered in my ear: "Thinking about her, Elliott? Dreaming about her? What would she do if I gave a bad report on you, Elliott?"

Martin, I am in trouble. And the trouble is, it's too late.

Elliott
19

Dress Up

SIX O'CLOCK AND no chimes anywhere on the island. Just the thumping in my chest. The handler glanced at his watch, and then told me to go in and wait right beside the door.

More than anything, I wanted to savor the first glimpse of her, wanted to slow things down so at that moment I could truly see her and hear what was in my head.

I have this theory actually, that after an absence you discover in that first glimpse what you really think and feel about another person. You know things you couldn't know before.

Maybe I wouldn't be so stark raving mad about her; she would be a little less dangerous, less pretty. I would start to think more about the others; like, who knows, maybe I'd start thinking about Scott.

The door closed behind me. The handler was gone. And the room looked warm in the soft electric light, the sky beyond the lace curtains a leaden gleam. Dreamy place. Like a chamber of the heart.

I heard some sound so unobtrusive that I wasn't even sure of it, and I turned my head towards the open parlor doors.

She was standing there all right. And I was in love with her. So much for the first glimpse. And the really wonderful thought came to me that she was quite deliberately trying to drive me out of my mind.

She was in a man's suit, a tight-fitted little three-piece number, except it was made of dark, dusty lilac velvet, so deep that in the creases it was an ashen gray. And knotted very loosely under the white collar of her shirt was a pale pink silk foulard. Her hair was swept up and back in a twist, and she was wearing a fedora of the same dusky mauve with a dark charcoal silk band. It was right out of the forties gangster movies, the shape of the hat, the way it dipped over one eye, and she was all cheekbones under the shadow of the brim, the mouth a kind of pouting glimmer of red.

The lust I felt for her was so total I could hardly keep still. I wanted to bury my face in her crotch, pull her down on top of me. In love with her, love her, the words were caught up in the lust.

I could see her eyes now, clearly, and feel that force emanating from her, see the hair swept up from her naked neck, her naked ear. She looked delicate in the suit, downright breakable.

"Come closer," she said. "And slowly turn around. I want to look at you. Take your time."

The pants were so snug on her they must have been made for her, and her breasts were pushing at the covered buttons on the vest.

I did as she said. I wondered if they'd given her the details, about the trainers' class, what that little adventure had been like.

And I could feel her coming closer, as if she affected the air around her, feel her perfume before I smelled it, feel that force again when I saw her angular shadow in the corner of my eye.

I inclined my head to the side rather deliberately and glanced down at her, sucking up her appearance before I looked straight ahead. Shiny little pointed toes peeking out of the pant legs, high heels, pants tight enough in her crotch to make her feel the seam between her legs.

I saw her hand move and I thought I can't stand it. She has to touch me. I have to touch her. Rudy Valentino, the sheik, is going to kidnap her and take her off to his tent in the desert. But neither of us moved.

"Follow me," she said, snapping her fingers lazily, the light glinting on her fingernails for a second, and she turned and went through the pair of double doors.

It was the parlor I'd glimpsed last night. I watched the easy shift of her little hips, wanted to touch the back of her naked neck. She looked like a little manikin in the suit. I mean a baby man, a supernatural creature, something not a woman yet just as little and lovable and soft.

Large desk, massive African sculpture in one corner, and a really terrific Haitian painting in six panels of scenes from the French colonial days, something to look at later when she wasn't blinding me, in all the thousands and thousands of times I'd be in these rooms kissing her naked insteps and her naked calves and her naked crotch that ought to be freed from those tight little pants and let to breathe in my face. Nothing really feminine in this room, except her steaming in the mauve velvet, turning back to me and then staring quite deliberately to her left.

I looked in the same direction, and for one moment it didn't register. "Those are my suitcases," I said.

Martin had said that your clothes are locked up. It's the strictest security because if you can't get your clothes and your papers then you can't possibly escape from The Club. He said they weren't even on the island, the clothes, they were stored in a special place. And I remember I had pictured bank vaults.

Yet there were my suitcases unlocked and open and I could see my passport and my wallet on top of the clothes. It was almost embarrassing looking at those personal, otherworldly things.

"I want to see what you look like," she said, "in clothes."

I looked at her, trying to figure what this meant. And the surprising thought came to me that that would be too humiliating to be dressed in front of her. But it was kinky, divinely kinky. And I could feel her trembling though she didn't appear to be trembling at all.

"I want to see you in this," she said. She bent over the suitcase and pulled out a gray turtleneck shirt. "You like gray, don't you? And you don't like colors. If you belonged to me in the outside world, were my slave utterly and completely, I'd dress you in colors. But put this on for me now."

I felt absolutely strange taking the shirt from her. I jerked it down over my head as if I'd never done anything like that before. It was incredible, the liveliness of the sensation as the cloth touched my skin all over. And my lower half felt ludicrously naked. My cock looked illegal. I felt like a centaur in a porno-graphic sketch.

But she handed me a pair of brown pants before I had even pushed the sleeves up a little, and I put them on, feeling the rougher cloth scratch at my backside, come up uncomfortably tight around my cock and balls. I didn't think I could close the zipper. I put my hand in trying to shift the painful erection, flashing a little smile at her, feeling her eyes on me.

"Zip it," she said. "And don't come."

"Yes, Madam," I said. "Just wondering if Adam and Eve felt this way in Eden the first time they got dressed."

I took the belt from her and that was a trip, holding the leather myself for once, sliding it through the loops. I shouldn't have spoken to her like that. It was the clothing doing it already. But this was all madder even than the sports arcade and the damned whipping post and everything else that had gone down.

"You're blushing again," she said. "It always makes your hair look terrific, really blond, when you blush."

I made a little gesture of mock modesty, like golly gee, I just couldn't help it.

She handed me a pair of socks and the brown Bally loafers I didn't like very much. I had to make myself stop staring at her and put them on.

Really weird, even the fraction of a difference in height, the leather against the sole, the smooth feeling of it all, like it was a casing, like it wasn't natural—all this clothing, like it was a form of being shackled and harnessed, just being dressed.

She held out the brown wool jacket.

"No, not that . . ." I said.

Hesitation. She looked suddenly blank, lost.

"I mean it's too precious, the jacket matching the pants and the shoes. I'd never wear that."

"What then?"

"Give me the Norfolk jacket, the tweed. I mean if you don't mind, if I have something to say about it."

"Of course," she said. Apologetic! She put the brown back on the hanger and took out the Norfolk jacket. I love belted jackets. I really wanted one of my filthy old safari jackets, but I didn't think she'd go for that.

"You happy now?" she asked. Tough again, slightly sarcastic.

"Not till I comb my hair. It's kind of a compulsive thing, you know, after I put on my jacket, I comb my hair." My butt was burning under the cloth of the pants. I thought my cock would go off. I was literally tied in knots. When she reached into her back pants pocket just like a man would do it and drew out a black plastic comb, all her gorgeous little curves jiggling like crazy, I couldn't help shifting my weight, trying to get more straight with not coming. "Thanks."

"There's the mirror," she said, pointing to a rather small narrow one between the two doors that led to the hall.

And there was Elliott Slater in it, combing his hair, looking like he had two million years ago in San Francisco when he headed out to catch a movie on his second to last night as a free man.

I looked down when I was finished, and then up again slowly as I handed the comb back to her, letting my fingers linger on hers for a second, and then staring at her. And she backed away. She almost jumped. But she realized what she'd done, and she stiffened as if she had to take command again, deny that she'd showed this little glimmer of fear.

"What's the matter?" I asked.

"Shhh. Walk up and down so that I can look at you," she said.

I walked very slowly away from her with my back to her, feeling everything pulling and rubbing and burning and cramping me, and then I came around again towards her, getting closer and closer, until she put her hand up and said sharply, "Stop!"

"I want to kiss you," I whispered as if the room were full of people.

"Shut up," she said, but she had backed away again with two little anxious steps.

"Are you afraid of me, just because I'm dressed?" I asked.

"Your voice is changed, and you're talking a lot and acting different!" she said.

"What did you expect?"

"You have to be able to play it both ways for me," she said raising her finger and pointing at me threateningly. "And you behave yourself, dressed or undressed. You make one impertinent little move, and I'll press one of some ten different buttons in this room, and you'll be running races in the sports arcade all night."

"Yes, Madam!" I said again unable to stop a little smile. I shrugged. But then I looked down again, trying to show that I wanted to please her. If she pressed one of those buttons, well . . .

She turned her back on me, and I had a feeling it was kind of like a young, inexperienced matador turning his back for the first time on the bull.

She walked around in a little circle, and when she glanced at me again I lifted my right hand very stiffly to my lips and I blew her a little kiss. She stood there staring at me.

"I did something," she said suddenly. She put her left hand on her hip and she looked uncomfortable, very uncomfortable. "I found this book in your luggage and I unwrapped it so that I could look at it."

"Fine," I said. Don't try to figure this out, I was thinking. She can't really be interested. "I'd like you to have it, if you want."

She didn't answer. She just studied me for a moment. There was all sorts of light and heat playing in her face. She went over to the table and she picked up the book.

It gave me a mild shock to see it—Elliott the photographer, Elliott the correspondent—but not as bad as I would have thought. She had a fountain pen in her hand and she said, "Sign it?"

I took it from her, trying very discreetly just to touch her hands when I did it and not managing it, and I went over to the couch and sat down. I can't sign books standing up.

I went suddenly and totally on automatic pilot, like I didn't know what was going to come out as I moved the pen. I wrote:

> To Lisa,
> I think I am in love with you,
> Elliott

And I stared at it. I gave the book back to her. I felt like I had just done something really stupid that I'd regret till I was ninety years old.

She opened it and when she read the words, she was beautifully stunned. Beautifully!

I was still sitting on the couch, and I put my left arm up along the back of it and tried to look very casual, but my cock was pumping like something with a mind of its own that wanted to get out.

Everything was rolling together, this insane lust for her, this love, this love for her, and this absolute exhilaration that she'd read this and she was blushing and she was afraid.

I think if there had been a brass band in the room at that moment, I wouldn't have heard it. I would have heard only this pumping of my own pulse in my head.

She had closed the book and she was looking glaze-eyed almost like someone in a trance. For a second, she was unrecognizable to me. I mean it was one of those moments of "the absurd" when people look not only like strangers but strange beasts. I saw all the details of her as if she'd just been invented, and I didn't know what she was, whether she was a man or a woman, or what.

I wanted to shake myself out of it, but what shook me out of it was the sudden scary feeling she was going to cry. I almost got up and grabbed hold of her, or said something or did something, but I couldn't move. The spell went as fast as it had come. She was all woman again, looking unaccountably soft in the masculine pants and jacket and she knew things about me nobody knew, no other woman knew, and there was this sense of dissolving into her. Maybe I was the one, sitting there on the couch looking casual, who was about to cry.

I could understand this, really understand it, if I pressed just a little further with it, I felt. But then maybe I would cry.

She licked her lips slowly, and again, she didn't seem to see anything. Then hugging the book to herself she asked: "Why did you get so scared? I mean last night in the arcade when I made you wear the blindfold?"

Shocking, real shocking. Like somebody throwing a bucket of cold water over me, but then that would make me go limp. This didn't make me go limp. Just feel naked as hell in these damn clothes. And like a dangerous rapist.

"I didn't like it," I said. Funny monotone voice. I mean this isn't exactly the conversation you have at a restaurant table, for God's sakes. And we're dressed like we were having lunch at Ma Maison. What was it going to be like, taking *off* these damned clothes? "I wanted to see what was going on," I said. Shrug. "Isn't that typical?" When in the hell had I ever wanted to be typical, I thought.

"It's usually a turn on," she said. But her voice was distant, not listless, exactly like somebody talking in her sleep.

Her eyes were really round. Most beautiful women have almond-shaped eyes, but hers were round, and that and the pouting lip gave her some kind of almost uncivilized look, even though she was so slender, angular, high toned.

"Wearing a blindfold . . . it can make it easier. You can surrender," she said.

"I'm all yours," I said, "as it is." And you did that to me and I let you do it, and I think I love you, I thought.

She took a step backwards, stopped. She held the book to her even tighter, like it was a baby. Then she went to the desk and picked up the phone.

I started to get up. It was pure craziness. She wasn't going to send me away like this, I'd rip the fucking phone out. But before I was on my feet even, she'd said something into the phone that didn't add up.

"Get ready for takeoff in five minutes. Tell them the rest of the luggage is ready to go." She put down the phone and she looked at me and her mouth moved, but she was silent for a second. Then she said, "Put your wallet and your passport in your pockets and take out whatever you want to carry with you from the bags."

"You're kidding," I said. But it was too gorgeous, like somebody saying, We're now taking off for the moon.

The doors opened and two young flunkies—white clothes but no leather—came in and started packing up the bags.

I put my watch on, slipped the wallet in my pants pocket and the passport in my coat pocket. I saw my diary in the bottom of the suitcase, and glancing at her, I took that out. It meant I needed my shoulder bag, a kind of crushed canvas bag I carried with me all over, and I got that out from underneath everything, put the diary in it, and slung it over my shoulder.

"But what the hell's going on?" I asked her.

"Hurry up," she said.

The two flunkies were taking out the suitcases.

She started walking after them. She still had the book in her left hand.

She was positively marching down the corridor when I caught up with her.

"Where are we going?" I asked. "I don't understand."

"Be quiet," she whispered, "until we get outside."

She cut right across the grass, and through the flower beds, her shoulders very square, her walk jaunty, almost swaggering. The flunkies were loading the bags into a little electric cart on the path up ahead. They both took the front seat as she gestured for me to get into the back.

"Will you tell me what it is we're doing?" I said squeezing in beside her.

My leg was crushed up against her and I had a sense of how small she was as the cart took off a little too fast and she fell against me, her hand on my thigh. She was like a bird next to me, and I couldn't see her face under the brim of the hat. "Lisa, answer me! What's going on?"

"Okay, listen to me," she said. But she stopped. She was flashing as if she was angry, hugging the book to her chest. And the cart was tearing along now at a good twenty miles an hour right around the edge of the crowded pleasure gardens and past the pool.

"You don't have to go if you don't want to," she said finally. Her voice was unsteady. "It's heavy duty, going in and out, stripped down one minute, dressed the next. I can understand if you're not ready for it. So if you want, you can go straight back to my room. Strip down again. Hit the button on my desk for the handler, and they'll take you right off to Scott or Deena or one of the others. I'll call from the gate. You want Scott, you can have him. Scott's the best. He's impressed with you, he wants you. He would have chosen you when you first got here, but I got you first. But if you want to come with me, then come with me. We'll be in New Orleans in an hour and a half. There's no big mystery. We're just doing what I want to do. And we come back when I say we come back."

"Hmmmm, shrimp creole and coffee with chicory," I said under my breath. Going to the moon all right and on to Venus and Mars.

"Smart ass," she muttered. "What about crawfish etouffée and Dixie beer?"

I started laughing. I couldn't help it. And the more solemn she got the more I laughed.

"Well, make up your goddamn mind," she said.

The cart came to a halt at a pair of gates beside a lighted glass booth. We were between two banks of electronic scanners. And I saw another higher fence beyond.

"There's nothing like time to ponder big decisions," I said, still laughing.

"You can walk back," she said. She was really shaky. Her eyes were glittering under the shadow of the hat brim. "Nobody will think you tried to run away or stole the clothes. I'll call from the booth right there."

"Are you crazy? I'm going with you," I said. I went to kiss her.

"Go on," she said to the driver, giving me a hard shove in the chest.

The plane was a turbo jet monster, engines roaring as we drove up. She jumped out before we stopped and started up the metal steps. I had to run to catch up with her again—I think she moved faster than any woman I'd ever seen—the goons coming behind us with the bags.

The interior was all brown and gold plush, luxurious, some eight or so club chairs arranged in a half circle in the salon. There was a bedroom opening off to the back, and a full-scale billiard room with a big TV monitor to the front.

Two older men, both very properly dressed in ugly dark suits, were talking in Spanish to each other in hushed voices over their drinks. They both started to rise but Lisa gestured for them to sit down.

Before I could say or do anything she slipped into the single seat between the pair and the windows, leaving me no choice but to sit opposite her a miserable four feet away.

A voice crackled over the speaker system: "Ready for takeoff. Call for Lisa on line one."

I could see the phone light blinking silently beside her. And the little intercom she opened with a touch of her hand.

"Take off, we're ready," she said. "Buckle up, Mr. Slater." She turned to the pane of thick, murky glass.

The voice came again over the whine of the engines. "They say it's urgent, Lisa, would you pick up line one?"

"Can I get you a drink, sir?" The flight attendant bent down close to my ear.

The two Latin Americans—I was sure that is what they were —had turned a little more sharply to face each other, the conversation rising to shut everything out.

"Yeah," I said disgustedly, glaring at the two lumpy men and

Lisa sitting next to them. "Scotch, if you've got a single mash, two fingers with a little ice."

"I'll call them later," Lisa said into the intercom. "Go." She turned her head to the window and pulled her hat down over her eyes.

Elliott
20

On the Loose

BY THE TIME we landed, I was ready to murder somebody. I was also a little drunk. She wouldn't move out of that window seat next to the two creeps from Argentina, and I nearly tore the felt on the pool table playing eight ball with myself while the flight attendant, who looked good enough to rape, kept filling my glass.

La Poupée, a terrific surreal French movie that I used to love, starring a dead Czech actor whom I also used to love, kept blazing silently away, ignored by everybody, on the giant picture screen.

But as soon as we set foot outside the New Orleans airport (naturally it was raining, it is *always* raining in New Orleans), the two Argentinians vanished, and we were sliding *alone* into the back of a ludicrously enormous silver stretch limousine.

She sat smack in the middle of the gray velvet seat staring at the blank little television set in front of her, with her knees very close together, hugging my book like it was a teddy bear, and I put my arms around her and knocked off her hat.

"We're going to be at the hotel in twenty minutes, stop it," she said. She looked terrible and beautiful, I mean like somebody at a funeral looks terrible and beautiful.

"I don't want to stop it," I said, and I started kissing her, opening her mouth, my hands all over, feeling her through the velvet, through the thick seams of the pants and the heavy sleeves of the jacket, and then reaching inside and pulling open her vest.

She turned towards me, pressed her breasts against me and there came that fatal voltage, that annihilating heat. I was rising up, pulling her up and against me and then we went down together full length on the seat. I was tearing at her clothes, or just sort of pushing them and shoving them, trying not to really hurt them but to get them open and I got a real taste of how hard it is to get a man's shirt off a woman or to really feel a woman through a man's shirt.

"Stop," she said. She had pulled her mouth away and she turned to the side, her eyes shut, panting as if she had fallen down from running. I tried to lift up a little so as not to hurt her with my weight, and I kissed her cheekbone and her hair and her eyes.

"Kiss me, turn around, kiss me," I said, and then I forced her head towards me, and that current started again. I was going to come in my pants.

I sat up and kind of turned her around and she scrambled into the corner, her hair spilling out of the twist.

"Look what you did," she said under her breath, but it didn't mean anything.

"This is like fucking high school, goddamn it," I said.

I looked out at the sagging, delapidated Louisiana landscape, the vines covering the telephone wires, the broken-down motels melting into the grass, the rusted fast food stands. Every emblem of modern America looked like a missionary outpost here, a piece of junk left over from a colonization attempt that had failed over and over again.

But we were almost into the city proper, and I love the city proper. She had her brush out of the overnight bag. And she whipped at her hair, her face flushed, the pins flying out as she brushed her hair free. I loved seeing it come down like a shadow enfolding her.

I grabbed her and started kissing her again, and this time she backed up, pulling me with her, and it seemed we were circumnavigating the whole car for a few minutes, me kissing her and kissing her, and just eating the inside of her mouth.

She kissed like no woman I'd ever kissed. I couldn't figure out exactly what it was. She kissed like she'd just discovered it or something, like she'd fallen from another planet where they never did it, and when she shut her eyes and let me kiss her neck, I had to stop again.

"I feel like I want to tear you to pieces," I said clenching my teeth, "I want to just break you into pieces, I want to just get inside."

"Yes," she said. But she was trying to button her shirt and her vest.

We were lumbering along Tulane Avenue in that silent unreal way limousines travel, like they are tunneling unseen through the outside world. And at Jeff Davis, we turned left, heading for the Quarter more than likely, and I grabbed her again, gauging, well, at least another delicious dozen kisses, and when she pulled away this time, we were in those narrow claustrophobic little streets of row houses, heading towards the heart of the old town.

Elliott
21

Over the Threshold

WHEN WE WENT into the office of the hotel, she was all lovely with her hair pushed back over her shoulder and the hat askew and her shirt collar undone, but she was trembling so badly she could hardly hold the pen.

She wrote Lisa Kelly in a scrawl like an old lady would write it and when I fought with her about who was going to use whose American Express card, she got all flustered and shut up, like she wasn't sure what she wanted to happen. I won and they took my American Express card.

The place she'd chosen was perfect, a renovated Spanish townhouse about two blocks from Jackson Square, and we had the servants' quarters cottage in back. The purple flagstones were uneven the way they always are in these old New Orleans court-yards and the garden was a thicket of enormous, wet, gleaming, green banana trees and pink oleander and jasmine crawling over the brick walls with a few electric lights here and there like lan-terns.

The fountain nymph was covered with green moss and the water choked with irises, but I loved it. The thump of a jukebox came from somewhere on the block: "Beat It" by Michael Jackson, which brought back the real life I'd left in California a little more vividly than anything else around here. And there was a nearby racket of restaurant pots and pans and the smell of coffee.

She was shaking even worse when we got to the door, and I just held onto her for a moment, the light rain pelting us, the little yard a kind of symphony of water sounds with the rain on the banana leaves and the roof and the plants, as two of the most beautiful mulatto children I'd ever seen in the whole world put the bags inside.

I didn't know whether these kids were girls or boys, and I still don't know. They were wearing khaki shorts and white T-shirts and they had waxy oily skin and dark liquid eyes like the Hindu princesses in Indian paintings, and they glided almost sleepily into the big whitewashed room with one load of bags after another until they had it in a heap.

Her luggage was the kind you have when you travel private planes, all matched caramel leather with gold initials on it, and she had about as much as people used to take with them on the grand tour of the Continent in 1888.

I gave the kids five bucks and they said something in voices you only hear in New Orleans, real soft and French and lyrical and almost drugged out, and they went off looking like old men for one second when they smiled back at me.

She was staring into the room as though it were a cave full of bats.

"You want me to carry you over the threshold?" I asked.

She looked at me as if I'd startled her. And something surfaced in her for a moment, a wild look I couldn't interpret. I felt the heat again. I didn't wait for her to answer. I scooped her up and carried her inside.

She positively blushed. She started laughing and trying to conceal it, like she wasn't supposed to, or something.

"So laugh," I said as I set her down. I smiled at her and I winked at her, like I had at all those women in the garden pavilion back on the island. Only this was from the heart.

Then I made myself stop looking at her long enough to look around.

Even in these old servants' quarters the ceilings soared to fourteen feet. The mahogany four-poster was immense and there was an old silk wedding tester over it complete with cherubs and cabbage roses and old stains, as if the rain had seeped into it somewhere along the line. You couldn't have gotten a bed like that into most of the houses I'd lived in.

And there was a mirror that rose all the way from the marble mantel to the ceiling, and a couple of high-backed walnut rocking chairs on the edges of a worn Persian rug. Big, wide, uneven cypress boards, floor flush with the flags outside and french doors all the way down the length of the room just the way they had been in her room at The Club.

The bath and the kitchen broke the spell a little, same white tile and chrome fixtures, microwave oven, electric coffeepot you find in any luxury motel. I shut the doors.

It wasn't hot enough for the air conditioning and the smell of the rain was exquisite, so I turned off the machine and I went outside and closed up all the big green shutters over the french doors so that nobody could see us if they wanted to. And then I went inside and opened all the glass doors that nobody opens with the air conditioning anymore, and latched the shutters and opened the slats and at once the room was warmer, steamier, sweeter. The noise of the rain was really loud. I locked the main door.

She was standing with her back to the lamp, just staring at me.

She was damp and mussed. Her lipstick was a little smeared and her shirt was open all the way into the vest and she had taken off her shoes so that she looked sort of fragile.

I came towards her and put my arm around one of the pillars of the bed and just studied her, letting the lust come up, double, triple, until it was molten lava again.

So here we were and there weren't any trainers or any handlers and no buttons to summon help and just the two of us in this room. And I knew she was thinking about it just like I was thinking about it.

But what did she want? And what did I want? That I tear her clothes off? That I rape her? That I act out some little tableau of revenge for all the things she'd done to me? They say when a man is really sexually aroused he doesn't "think." Well, I was thinking of every moment with her, of the sports arcade and the harness and the way the blindfold felt when she put it over my eyes, and the belts, and her naked breasts, how hot they were, and what I'd said to her in the limousine, that I wanted to break her open, get inside of her. Only I hadn't meant rape when I'd said that. Was I going to let her down?

I wanted to say something, but there weren't any words. It was that baffling desire I'd had before in her rooms at The Club to confide something to her. I think I wanted to invade her, but not with meanness, not with cruelty, not with violence, not with strength, but with something else, more vital and more important and private than that.

She made some little uncertain movement towards the bed. And I could feel her heat again, see it dancing under her skin, and her pupils were kind of dancing in the same way as she looked at me.

I went towards her and I took her head in both my hands, and I just kissed her, the same open-mouth, wet kind of slow kiss we'd been doing over and over, and she went limp against me, moaning out loud and I knew everything was going to be perfect.

I pulled off her jacket, broke open the vest, starting pulling the shirt off her. When she bent to unbuckle her belt, her hair fell down over her naked breasts, and something about the movement, the bent head, her hands loosening the tightness around her waist, breaking open the pants, went right to my brain. I pulled the pants down and lifted her out of them, crushing her naked bottom in my fingers.

I went down on my knees in front of her, burrowing my head into her sex, and then my face and licking her and kissing her.

"I can't, I can't stand it," she whispered. She was clawing at my head, pressing me against her and then pushing me back. "It's too intense, stop it. Come into me," she said, "It's too, it's too . . ."

I had my own clothes off in a second. And I pushed her up on the bed, so that she was sitting at the very foot of it, and I pushed her legs apart and looked at her naked sex and the way that it was breathing, moving, the hair glistening, the lips pink and secret and quivering.

"I want you inside of me," she said, and I looked up at her face and it seemed for a second too exquisite to be human, just as the sex seemed too savage, too animalian, too secretly different from all the rest of her to be human. We moved back on the bed together, kind of rolling over, kissing and just rubbing against each other naked.

I went down on her again, spreading her wide apart and this time she didn't resist.

But she couldn't keep still. She started thrashing under me. I was licking her and kissing her, and diving my tongue into her, drenched in her clean, salty, charcoal smell, and licking at the silky hair, and she was going absolutely crazy. She clawed at me again, and told me to get on top of her. But I couldn't stand not doing it, I had to do it just a little bit more, taste her, have her like that, get into her.

I turned around and I got into the 69 position and I felt her mouth take hold of my cock, and then she was all right with me suckling her and licking her. She was locked on, sucking strong and passionately as a man, as if she liked to do it. She sucked stronger and stronger, her hand around the base of my cock, her mouth really wet and steady and I was plunged into her sex, stroking the depth of it with my tongue, really wet with her, saturated with her, while her fingers were pinching the welts on my backside, stroking them and scratching at them. I moved back to let her know I was going to come, but she locked her arms even tighter around me and when I came in her, I felt her delicious little cunt contracting, her hips thrust against me, this little mouth of her shuddering under my mouth, her whole body burning up. It went on and on, and I could hear her moaning, giving the same cries again against my cock. She came like a chain reaction of explosions. I came until I couldn't stand it any longer.

I lay back thinking I had never done that with a woman. With at least 568 men, probably, but never in that position with a woman. And I had always wanted to do that. But I was mainly thinking I loved her, that I really loved her.

The second time it was a lot slower. We didn't start right away.

I think I slept maybe a half hour, I don't know how long it was, under the covers, with the dim lamp on still and the rain falling a little slower, the sounds that same symphony of the rain on a hundred surfaces and the water flowing in the rain pipes and the gutters.

Then I got up and turned off the lamp. And we snuggled together again, only now I was fully awake. I could see the raindrops like tiny silver lights clinging to the slats of the green wooden shutters and hear all the other rough, mingled sounds that make up the French Quarter, the dim blast of the Bourbon

Street clubs only a block away, the loud roar of cars in the narrow streets, that jukebox pumping out some older, more deep-throated rhythm and blues song that almost brought back with it a memory. Smell of New Orleans. Smell of the earth and flowers.

When we finally started again it was tender. And we were kissing each other all over. We kissed each other under the arms and on the nipples, and on the belly. On the inside of the thighs and in back of the knees.

I went into her and she broke loose, her head all the way back, her cries like they'd been before, Oh God, Oh God, Oh God, as I came in her.

When it was finished, I knew I was going to sleep for a million years and I got up on my elbow and looked down at her, cradling her in my arms, and I said, "I love you."

Her eyes were closed. She squeezed her eyebrows together for one instant, and she reached up to pull me down against her. She said "Elliott" like she was scared, really scared, and she just lay there under me, holding onto me.

A little while after, dreamily, it occurred to me to tell her that I'd never said this to anyone before, but that seemed arrogant. I mean why was that special? All it meant was that I was a jerk of sorts. And I was too sleepy with her next to me, curled up against me, to say anything. She hadn't answered me, really, but then why should she? Or maybe she had. Think of it that way.

And she was petal soft now and sweet and her perfume and her juices mingled in this overpowering aroma that kept bringing the pleasure back in waves over me.

I woke up very abruptly two hours later. I didn't want to be asleep anymore no matter how tired I was.

I got up and opened my suitcases and started to put some of the clothes away, my eyes used to the dark, and the light through the slats of the blinds enough to see everything. But I realized I didn't know how long we were going to stay here. I couldn't think about going back to The Club right now. What had she said, it was "heavy duty" switching back and forth.

She sat up and sat still with her arms around her knees watching me.

I put on a white turtleneck shirt, khaki pants, and the only clean safari jacket that was in the suitcase. It was the best of the bunch actually, the military khaki jacket from the army surplus store, and it wasn't badly wrinkled. And I loved it. I never put it on that I didn't think of some of the places around the world I'd been in it, El Salvador, for instance. Not too good to think of that one. But Cairo, okay, and Haiti, sure, and Beirut of course, and Teheran and Istanbul and dozens of other strange memories.

She got out of bed and I think a tight wire in me snapped rather comfortably when I saw she was unpacking just about everything. No leather skirts or boots. She hung up gorgeous little velvet suits and skimpy gowns and threw dozens of high-heel shoes on the floor of the closet.

Then she put on a little dark blue polka-dotted silk dress that went down over her angles and curves softly and beautifully, with long cuffs at the wrists that made her hands look longer and full sleeves and a little smocking at the shoulders. She tied the cloth belt around her waist, which brought the hem up nicely over her knees and made her breasts into two dark points under the silk, and she didn't bother with pantyhose, thank God, and she put on a pair of navy blue leather shoes with heels like ice picks.

"No, don't do that," I said. "The thing about this city is it's great to walk in. We can take a walk after we eat. It's utterly flat. We can walk anyplace. Put on some low shoes so we can walk."

She said all right. She put on a pair of natural brown leather sandals with lower stacked heels. She brushed her hair loose, and put her sunglasses up on the top of her head to hold her hair back some out of her face and changed all her personal things from a black leather bag to a brown leather bag and we were ready.

"Where are we going?" she asked.

The question surprised me. Wasn't she going to tell me?

"Well, Manale's on Napoleon," I said. "It's nine o'clock, we might have to wait for a table, but we can have some oysters in the bar."

She gave a little nod of approval and smiled uncertainly, very pretty smile while it lasted.

"You didn't keep the limo, did you?" I asked, moving towards the phone. "I'll call a cab."

Elliott

22

The First Layer

IN THE CAB we didn't say anything to each other. I didn't know what to say to her. There was just the pounding excitement of being with her and the fun of being back in New Orleans, riding up Saint Charles Avenue under the oak trees towards Napoleon and thinking of all the things we could do if she let us stay here. Let us, let us, let us. I almost asked her if this was done often, but I didn't want to just yet. Or maybe not ever.

Years ago when I discovered Manale's you never had to wait, but now the whole world knows about it. The oyster bar was so crowded we could hardly hear each other, but we started right into two dozen raw oysters on the half shell and two beers.

"How did you first come to New Orleans?" she asked, drinking the beer fast the way I did, and devouring the oysters. She sounded natural, like we were just a couple on a date. "I found it on my first vacations from The Club," she said. "Fell in love with it. And after that every time I had to get away from The Club for a few days I came here."

"Vacations with my mom and dad," I said. "For Mardi Gras mainly." The beer and the oysters were too good to be food for humans. "They'd take me out of school to come down for that week every year."

I told her about the little mansion hotel on Saint Charles Avenue where we stayed—she knew it, great place, she said—and then making the oyster festivals and the gumbo festivals in Cajun country.

"Yes, I want to do that too," she said. "Go into the Cajun country. I almost did it several times. But I'm so in love with the town . . ."

"Yeah, I know what you mean," I said. And I kissed her on the cheek.

"I do photo stories all the time on New Orleans just to get down here," I said. The kiss had caught her off guard. Every time I kissed her it caught her off guard. "The pay's lousy," I said. "I usually lose more than I make. But I can't resist it. I've done ten articles in the last five years."

"So you're glad . . . that we're . . . that we came here?"

"Are you kidding?" I tried to kiss her again, but she turned away like she hadn't seen me, but she had. She took a deep drink of her beer.

She said she spent six weeks down here once all alone in a Garden District apartment right off Washington Avenue doing nothing but reading and taking walks in the afternoon. Yes, it was great for walking, this city. I was right about that.

She was softening all over, her manner changing. She was smiling. Her cheeks were just a little flushed.

I think at The Club she was always aware of people watching her, probably more so than a slave would be. Now she just got lost in what she was saying and she ate the oysters and drank the beer just like I thought she would, sensuously and enjoying every morsel, every drop.

By ten o'clock I was deliriously high, that kind of high you only get from beer, and when you haven't had anything to drink for a while.

We were in the crowded dining room under the glaring lights and everybody was talking loudly and she was buttering the bread and going on rapidly and easily all about her one big side trip, this plantation house out in the country that she went in by herself when she rented a car and drove to Saint Jacques Parish alone not knowing how she had managed to do it.

She just wanted to see the old ruined house and there was

nobody to go with so she went by herself. She talked about this powerless feeling she'd always had, even in California where she grew up, that she couldn't do anything unless there was somebody with her, and how this was one city where for some reason she didn't have it. She did things by herself. I wondered if the noisiness of the dining room wasn't helping both of us. She was beautifully animated and her neck and her hands were extraordinarily graceful and the dress made all these shadows in the right places in the glare of the lights.

And then came the barbecue shrimp, which was nothing short of fantastic, and she started in at once.

I don't think I could love a woman that couldn't eat this barbecue shrimp. First of all the dish isn't barbecued at all. It's a mess of giant whole shrimp, with their heads on, baked in the oven in a deep dish of peppery marinade. They bring it to the table just like that and you tear off the heads of the shrimp and peel them and eat them with your fingers. It turns you into a gourmet, then a gourmand, and then a barbarian. You can enjoy it with white wine or red, it's so peppery, but the best way is with beer, she agreed with me, and we had three more Heinekens each and dipped the french bread in the marinade and cleaned up both the dishes when we were finished. I wanted some more.

"I'm really starving," I said. "I haven't had anything but slop since I went to prison. I saw what the members were eating. Why do you have to feed the slaves such slop?"

She laughed out loud.

"To keep your mind focused on sex," she said. "Sex has got to be the only pleasure you have. We can't have you looking forward to dinner, you know, when you're supposed to be making love to a new member in Bungalow One. And don't call it prison. It's supposed to be heaven."

"Or hell anyway," I said laughing. "I've always wondered how we masochists that managed to get saved would ever explain to the angels that we would rather be tormented by a couple of devils, you know, I mean, if it's supposed to be heaven and there are no devils, then it's really going to be hell."

That really broke her up. Next best thing to making a woman come is making her laugh.

I ordered another dish of shrimp and we both dug into it. And by this time the dining room was thinning out. In fact, we were closing down Manale's and I was doing all the talking about

photographing New Orleans and the way it should and shouldn't
be done, and then she started asking me how I got into photography, when I had the Ph.D. in English and what they had to do
with each other, the Ph.D. and photography.

Nothing, I said. I just stayed in school as long as I could, really
got a gentleman's education, read all the great books three times.
It was photography that I worked at, that I did well, that I liked.

We had two cups of coffee before we left and then we went
outside and started walking down Napoleon Avenue towards
Saint Charles. It was just about a perfect New Orleans night, not
hot at all, and no wind, just the air almost inviting you to breathe
it.

I said again there was no city in the world like this for walking.
When you try to walk in Port au Prince you get stuck in the mud,
and the sidewalks are no good and the kids won't leave you alone,
you have to pay one of them to keep the others off; and in Cairo
you get sand in your hair and in your eyes. And in New York it's
usually too hot or too cold or you get mugged. And in Rome you
get almost run over at every intersection. San Francisco's too
hilly to walk anyplace except Market Street; the flat part of
Berkeley is too ugly. London is too cold, and despite what anybody says I have always found Paris an inhospitable place to
walk, all concrete and too crowded. But New Orleans.
The pavements are warm and the air is silk and there are big,
drowsy, drooping trees everywhere that have thrown out their
branches at precisely the right height for you to walk under them,
as if they knew you were coming.

And all the way down Saint Charles Avenue we would see
beautiful houses.

"But what about Venice?" she asked. "How can you beat walking in Venice?" She slid her arm around me and pushed her body
against mine. I turned and kissed her and she said underneath
her breath that maybe in a few days we'd go to Venice, but why
think of that now when we're in New Orleans.

"Do you mean this?" I asked. "We can stay gone that long?" I
kissed her again, and put my arm around her.

"We go back when I say we do, unless you want to."

I took her face in my hands and kissed her. I figured that was
my answer, and just thinking of who we were and where we'd
come from got me excited again. I didn't want to be anyplace on

earth where she wasn't. But the place on earth I wanted to be with her most was here.

She kept us moving, tugging on me, her right hand on my chest, her weight against me slightly. We were on Saint Charles now and the streetcar went rocking past, a lighted string of empty windows. The domed roof was wet and that reminded me that it had been raining. It was probably still raining downtown. So what? The rain was like everything else here in that it didn't stop you from walking.

"Okay, so you started photographing people, faces in San Francisco," she said, "but how did you start working for Time-Life?"

I told her it wasn't as hard as she might think, that if you had a good eye you could learn very fast, and I had the added luxury of not needing the money. I covered local stories for two years, rock shows and even some movie stars and writers for *People,* really dull stuff while I was learning my craft and getting familiar with every kind of camera and doing a lot of my own work in the darkroom. But you don't do your own darkroom work for the big magazines. You just send back the film. They pick what they want and then you can sell the rest someplace else if you want. It's not so interesting.

By the time we got to Louisiana Avenue, I had made her start talking again, and she was telling me rather disturbing and upsetting things like that she never had any life outside The Club actually, that she had done the four years at Berkeley kind of in a dream, mainly carrying on S&M work at Martin's in San Francisco on the sly.

What the university meant to her was sort of what it had meant to me, finding secluded places in which to read.

A funny embarrassment came over me that she knew The House in San Francisco where I'd been first turned on to S&M, that she knew Martin. But she not only knew Martin, she was friends with him, had worked with him. She knew the rooms in the house and we talked about that for a while, but I kept asking her personal things, like where did she live in Berkeley, and how did her family get there. When she spoke of Martin there was a reverence in her voice.

"I was no good at normal life at all," she said. "And I was really lousy at being a child."

"I never heard anyone say that before," I laughed, hugging her and kissing her.

"I couldn't figure out what childhood was supposed to be. I had dark, strange sexual feelings when I was very little. I wanted to be touched and I made up fantasies. I thought childhood was a perfect crock, if you want to know the truth."

"Even in Berkeley with all the liberalism and free expression and intellectualization of every step you take?"

"It wasn't like that for me," she said. "Martin's was the place that was intellectually free." She walked with nice easy strides beside me. We were making good, exhilarating time down the avenue, under the lacy shadows of the leaves beneath the street lamps, past the big white front porches, the little iron fences, the garden gates.

Her dad was an old-guard Irish Catholic who worked his way through college in St. Louis, and taught at the Jesuit college in San Francisco, her mother one of those old-fashioned women who just stayed home until her four children were grown up and then went to work in the public library downtown. They moved to the Berkeley hills when Lisa was a little girl because they liked the heat in the east bay and they thought the hills were beautiful. But they hated the rest of Berkeley.

I knew her street, her house even, a big ramshackle brown-shingle place on Mariposa, and I had even seen the lights on lots of times in the big garage library when I drove by.

That is where her dad was always reading Teilhard de Chardin and Maritain and G. K. Chesterton and all the Catholic philosophers. He would rather read than talk to people, and his rudeness and coldness were legends in the family. On sex he was Augustinian and Pauline as she described it. He thought chastity was ideal. But he could not practice it. Otherwise he might have been a priest. When you stripped all the language away, sex was filthy. Homosexuals should abstain. Even kissing was a mortal sin.

Her mother never voiced a contrary opinion; she belonged to all the church organizations, worked on fund-raisers, cooked a big dinner every Sunday whether the kids were there or not. Lisa's younger sister got perilously close to being a Playmate of the Month for *Playboy* and it was a family tragedy. If any of his girls had an abortion or posed nude for a magazine her father said he would never speak to that girl again.

He didn't know anything about The Club. He thought Lisa

worked for a private membership resort somewhere in the Caribbean, and that the people who went there were being treated for various illnesses. We both laughed at that. He wanted Lisa to quit and come home. Her older sister had married a sort of dull real estate millionaire. They all went to Catholic schools all their lives except Lisa, who laid down the law that she go to the University of California or she would not go to college at all. Her father sneered at the books she read, the papers she wrote. Lisa did S&M when she was sixteen with a student at Berkeley. She had had her first orgasm when she was eight years old and she had thought she was as a freak.

"We were what they used to call Catholics in nineteenth-century France," she said, " 'immigrants of the interior.' If you think of devout Catholics as simple, stupid people, you know, peasants in the back of big city cathedrals saying their rosaries before statues, then you don't know my dad. There is this awesome intellectual weight to everything he says, this constitutional puritanism, this languishing for death."

But he was a brilliant man, loved art and saw that his daughters learned a great deal about painting and music. They had a grand piano in the living room, they had real paintings on the walls, Picasso etchings and Chagall etchings. Her father had bought Mirandi and Miro years and years ago. They went to Europe every summer after Lisa's younger sister was six years old. They lived in Rome for a year. Her father knew Latin so well he kept his diary in it. If her father ever found out about The Club or her secret life it would kill him. It was damn near unthinkable, his finding out.

"There is one thing I can say for him, however, and you might understand it, if anybody would understand it, that he is a spiritual man, truly a spiritual man. I have not met too many people who really live by what they believe as he does. And the funny thing is I live by what I believe, absolutely what I believe. The Club is the pure expression of what I believe. I have a philosophy of sex. Sometimes I wish I could tell him about that. He has these aunts and sisters who are nuns. One is a Trappistine nun and another is a Carmelite. These are cloistered nuns. I would like to tell him that I too am a sort of nun, because I am saturated in what I believe. You must know what I am talking about. It's kind of a joke in a way, if you think about it, because when Hamlet said to Ophelia, as I am sure you know, when he said, 'Get thee to a nunnery,' he really meant a whorehouse, not a nunnery at all."

I nodded. I was dazzled a little.

But her story frightened me, and made me hug her tightly as she talked. It was exquisite, her animation and intensity, and the simplicity and the honesty of her face. I loved the details she described, her first communion, and listening to opera in the library with her father, and sneaking away to Martin's in San Francisco and feeling then and only then that she was truly alive.

We could have talked like this forever. She had said in a rush at least sixteen things that I wanted her to explain. We would need a year or so to know each other. This was just peeling back the first layer.

She wasn't really finished before we were trading facts and I was telling her all about my father, who was an atheist and believed totally in sexual freedom, how he'd taken me to Las Vegas to get laid when I was still a teenager, and how he drove my mother crazy demanding she go with him to nude beaches, and how she finally got a divorce, a little disaster from which none of us had recovered. She taught piano in L.A., and worked as an accompanist for a voice teacher and fought constantly with my father over a measly five hundred bucks a month spousal support because she could barely support herself. My father was rich. So were his children because his father had left us money. But my mother didn't have anything.

I was getting mad talking about this, so I got off it. I had given my mother a check for a hundred grand before I left for The Club. I had bought her a house down there. She had a whole bunch of gay men friends I couldn't stand, hair dresser types, and she was still pretty in a pale sort of way. She didn't believe in herself.

My father would keep the community property that belonged to my mother tied up in court forever. He was a big conservationist in northern California, chained himself to redwoods when they were about to be cut down, owned a big Sausalito restaurant, a couple of bed and breakfast hotels in Mendocino and Elk, and acres and acres of Marin County land that was almost beyond realistic appraisal. He worked all the time for nuclear disarmament. He had the largest collection of pornography outside of the Vatican. But he thought S&M was sick.

Again we started laughing.

He thought it was disgusting, perverted, childish, destructive, made speeches about Eros and Thanatos, and the death wish, and when I told him about The Club—I had told him it was in the Middle East (this *really* cracked Lisa up)—he threatened to have me committed to the state mental hospital in Napa. But there wasn't time.

My dad had married a twenty-one-year-old girl just before I left; she was an idiot.

"But why did you tell him about The Club!" She couldn't stop laughing. "You told him the details, about the things you'd done!"

"Why not? He's the one that stood outside the hotel room door in Las Vegas when I slept with the hooker. I tell him everything, if you want to know."

She was still laughing. "I wonder what you and I would be like," she said finally, "if our fathers had abandoned us when we were kids."

We had come to Washington Avenue and we cut over across Pyrthania Street to see if the bar at Commander's Palace was open. It was and we had two more beers, talking steadily all the time about our parents and the things they'd said to us about sex and about scores of other things that had nothing to do with it. We'd had the same teachers at Berkeley, we'd read the same books, we'd seen the same movies.

If it hadn't been for The Club, she hadn't the faintest idea what she would have been—the question made her anxious—maybe a writer, but that was just a dream. She'd never created anything but an S&M scenario.

Her favorite books kind of amused me, but they made me love her, absolutely love her. They were pretty muscular things like Hemingway's *The Sun Also Rises* and Hubert Selby's *Last Exit to Brooklyn* and Rechy's *City of Night*. But then she also loved Carson McCullers's *The Heart Is a Lonely Hunter* and Tennessee Williams's *A Streetcar Named Desire*.

"In other words," I said, "books about sexual outlaws, people who are lost."

She nodded, but there was more to it than that. It was a question of energy and style. When she felt bad, she would pick up *Last Exit to Brooklyn* and she would read in a whisper the "TraLaLa" story or "The Queen Is Dead." She knew the rhythms so well she could practically recite them from memory. It was the poetry of darkness and she loved it.

"I will tell you," she said, "what it is that has made me feel like a freak most of my life, and it wasn't having the orgasm at eight years old or listening furtively and shamefully to other little kids describing spankings or slipping off to San Francisco to be whipped in a candlelighted room. It's that nobody has ever been able to convince me that anything sexual between consenting individuals is wrong. I mean it's like part of my brain is missing. Nothing disgusts me. It all seems innocent, to do with profound sensations, and when people tell me they are offended by things, I just don't know what they mean."

I was engrossed. In the light of the bar she looked exotic, her face all angles, her voice low and natural, and it was like drinking water to listen to her.

Before we left New Orleans, she said, we had to make the transsexual shows on Bourbon, the really raunchy ones with the female impersonators who are actually taking hormone shots and getting operations to turn them into women. She loved these shows.

"You must be kidding," I said. "I wouldn't get caught in those joints."

"What are you talking about?" she said. She got furious. "These people are putting their sexual principles on the line, they're acting out their fantasies. They are willing to be freaks."

"Yes, but those are dives, tourist joints. How far from the elegance of The Club can you get?"

"Doesn't make any difference," she said. "Elegance is just a form of control. I like those joints. I feel like a goddamned female impersonator and I like to watch them." Her whole manner changed when she said this, and she started trembling a little and so I said, well, of course, if she wanted to see them.

"I'm confused," I said. My tongue was getting thick. I had drunk two Heinekens since we came into the bar. "You're writing the ticket. Why don't you just say where we're going?"

"Because I just did. And you said, 'You gotta be kidding,' and besides I do not just want to tell you what to do, and I am not writing a scenario!"

"Let's get out of here," I said.

We cut out again, and hung around the gate to the Lafayette Cemetery across the street for about twenty minutes, talking about whether or not we should climb over the wall and walk through the graves. I love these above-ground graves with their Grecian pediments and columns, and broken-down doors and rusted coffins. I had half a mind to climb the fence. But then we might get arrested.

We decided it was a good time to go all through the Garden District instead of doing that.

And so we wove back and forth from Saint Charles to Magazine on the various streets, here and there to look at a particular antebellum house, white columns in the moonlight, wrought iron railings, old oaks so big around I couldn't span them with my arms.

There is maybe no neighborhood on earth quite like this, these giant sleepy houses, these relics of a former time, all spruce and serene behind their immaculate gardens, here and there the hum of an automatic sprinkler, the faint shimmer of the spray, in the dense and leafy dark. The sidewalks alone are beautiful, made up as they are of long stretches of herringbone brick, and purple flagstone, patches of cement broken into little hills over the roots of the giant trees.

She had favorite houses, houses she used to come to look at when she lived here in the apartment and did nothing but read and walk; and we went visiting them now. We found two houses with For Sale signs on the fences, and one house in particular entranced us, a tall narrow Greek Revival house with the door on the left side and two french windows on the front porch. It had been painted a deep rose color with white trim, and now the paint was peeling softly all over it except where it was covered in vines. It had Corinthian columns and long front steps, and a string of old magnolia trees inside the fence. There was a side garden behind a brick wall that we couldn't see.

We stayed a long time, leaning on the gate and kissing each other, and not saying anything until I said we should buy the house. We would live there happily ever after and we would travel all over the world together and we would come home to our house. It was big enough to have wild parties and houseguests and a darkroom and sit-down dinners for both our families from California.

"And when we get bored with New Orleans," I said, "we'll fly to New York for a couple of weeks or down to The Club."

She looked irresistible, smiling up at me in the half dark, her arm wound around my neck.

"Remember, this is our house," I said. "Of course we can't live in it for two years, until my contract's up at The Club. But I don't see why we don't make the down payment now."

"You're not like anybody else I ever knew," she said.

We started walking again, kissing in a soft, dreamy, drunken way without urgency; we would walk a few steps, kiss, lean against one of the trees. I messed up her hair hopelessly. She didn't have any more lipstick on, and I could reach under her dress very quickly before she had a chance to stop me and feel the smooth cotton of her panties between her legs, wet and hot and I wanted to fuck her right where we were.

Finally we managed to pull ourselves across Jackson Avenue and we wandered into the Pontchartrain Hotel, where the bar was still open too, and we had some more drinks, and when we came out we figured everything from then on was rather ugly and seedy so we took a cab back downtown. I was feeling manic, like this night was momentous, and every time I felt it I would grab her and kiss her again.

Those horrible joints on Bourbon were closed already, thank God.

It was three o'clock and we went into some comfortable enough place with a couple of gas lamps and several square wooden tables and we got into our first argument. I knew I was drunk. I should have shut up, but it was over a movie called *Pretty Baby,* all about the old Storyville red light district in New Orleans, directed by Louis Malle. I hated it and she said it was a great film. It had Brooke Shields as the little-girl whore in it and Keith Carradine as the photographer Belloc and Susan Sarandon as Brooke's mother and I thought it was worse than a flop.

"Don't call me an idiot just because I like a movie you don't understand," she was saying, and I was stammering, trying to explain that I didn't mean she was an idiot. She said that I said that anybody who liked a piece of garbage like that was an idiot. Did I say that?

I had another Scotch and water, and I knew what I was saying was brilliant, about how that whole movie was a lie, and nothing in it had any substance, but when she started to talk it was sexual outlaws again, that the movie had been about these women prostitutes and the way that they went on living and loving and experiencing day-to-day life though they were outcasts.

It was all about flowers blooming in cracks; it was about life being unable to crush out life. And I started to understand everything she was saying. She knew how Belloc the photographer felt, he was in love with the little-girl prostitute (this is the Keith Carradine character in love with the Brooke Shields character) and how he got left by everybody in the end, but the best scene was when the whore played by Susan Sarandon was nursing the baby in the whorehouse kitchen.

She was saying how you cannot just make people shut up and die because they are sexual outlaws, that you wouldn't know now that that was what The Club was all about because all you saw was rich people sitting around the pools and you had to have money to go there and be young and be beautiful, but there was an idea and the idea was that anybody could come here and act out his or her sexual fantasy, and you still could, you still could, you still could.

The slaves didn't have to be rich, and if you weren't beautiful enough to be a slave you could be a handler or a trainer, all you had to do was really believe in the idea of The Club, and you had to be in the fantasy. And a lot more happened at The Club than people realized. Because a lot of the members admitted in private that they wanted to be dominated and punished by the slaves. So a good many of the slaves knew how to take the dominant role on demand. It was a hell of a lot freer than it looked. Her eyes were really dark now, and her face was drawn and she was talking rapidly in silvery riffs, but she started to cry when I said: "Well, goddamn yes, that's just what I'm doing at The Club, acting out my fantasies, but what's that got to do with the whores in *Pretty Baby*? It wasn't their fantasy they were acting out, it was somebody else's."

"No, but it was their life and it was life, and they went on hoping and dreaming and the movie caught the day-to-day life. The photographer in the movie saw in them images of freedom and that is why he wanted to be with them."

"But that's stupid. All the Susan Sarandon character wanted to do was get married and get out of the whorehouse and Pretty Baby was just a kid and . . ."

"Don't tell me I'm stupid. Why the hell can't a man argue with a woman without telling her she's stupid?"

"I didn't say you were stupid, I said that was stupid."

The bartender was suddenly leaning in my face saying, sure this was an all-night bar, and he hated to ask us to leave, but this was the hour between four and five when they did the cleaning. Would we maybe go around the corner to Michael's?

Michael's was a real dump. No sawdust, no pictures, no gas lamps. Just a rectangular room full of wooden tables. They didn't have any Johnny Walker Black Label. Lisa was not really crying. "You are mistaken!" And something kind of interesting was happening in Michael's.

The people who were coming in had just woken up or something. They hadn't been carousing all night as we had. But what kind of people get up at five o'clock in the morning when it is still dark and start immediately drinking in Michael's? There were two incredibly tall drag queens in wigs with pancake makeup on their faces talking to one of those thin young men who has drunk and smoked so much that he looks one hundred years old. His face was shrinking over his skull and his eyes were totally bloodshot. I wished I had a camera. If we were going to go to Venice I was going to get a camera.

Everybody coming in knew everybody else. But they didn't mind us being there.

"What do you mean you're not writing a scenario?" I asked. "When are you going to tell me what you are doing? You mean people just take off from The Club like this and go back? If you have a slave, you can just take the slave out like this, and then bring him back? But what are the rules? Suppose I just split out of here right now, you know, left? I've got all my personal belongings . . ."

"You want to do that?" She was rubbing the backs of her arms, and she looked gorgeous to me in an Italian way, her dark hair really a mess now, her eyes getting bigger and bigger as she got drunker, her speech just a little slurred.

"No, I don't."

"Then why did you say it?"

We were outside again. The rain had stopped. I couldn't remember the rain starting. We were in the Café Du Monde next to the river, across the street from Jackson Square, and we were in a wash of white light, and there were already big noisy delivery trucks roaring through the Rue Decateur.

The café au lait was wonderful, hot and sweet and perfect, and I was eating dozens of hot little sugar-covered beignets, and telling Lisa all about cameras, and things about shooting faces and getting people to cooperate.

"You know I could stay here forever," I said. "This is a seedy place, but it's a real place. California isn't real. Did you ever think it was real?"

"No," she said.

I wanted more Scotch, or several cans of beer. I got up and went over to her side of the table and pulled a chair up right beside hers and wrapped my arms around her and kissed her and hugged her and lifted her out of the chair, and we stopped on the street corner realizing neither of us knew where the hotel was.

When we got there, the phone was ringing and ringing. She got furious.

"Did you call every goddamned hotel in New Orleans to find me?" she said into the phone. "And you call me at six o'clock in the goddamned morning!" She was walking up and down in her bare feet with the phone in her hand. "What are you going to do, have me arrested!" She hung up. She tore up the phone messages that had been tacked to the outside door.

"It was them, wasn't it?" I think I asked her.

She had her hands up, rubbing her temples, and she sounded like she might cry.

"What are they so uptight about?" I asked her.

She leaned against my shoulder and I hummed something under my breath, very low, "I Can't Give You Anything but Love Baby," and we sort of danced for a long time without moving our feet.

It was daylight and I was making a speech.

The garden was wet and more lush and fragrant even than it had been in the dark and all the windows of the little servants' quarters house were open and she was sitting on the high four-poster bed in her white cotton slip. I could smell flowers everywhere. Flowers in California never smell the way they do in Louisiana. This was intoxication, the pink oleander and jasmine and the falling-apart wild roses. I called her "pretty baby" and I was explaining to her that I loved her, and I was making long intricate points about what the love was and why it was different from anything that had ever happened to me before, that we had peeled back this skin at The Club, and that she knew things about me and my secret desires that no woman had ever really known, no woman who knew me, and that I loved her. I loved her.

I loved who she was, that she was this small, dark-haired, dark-eyed, intense person who believed so passionately in what she was doing and that she wasn't just a mystery to me like other women, that I knew what she was, I knew all about her, things she hadn't even told me, that inside her was this locked-up place into which nobody could get, but I was going to get there. And it was even all right her thinking *Pretty Baby* was a good movie because she was projecting on it all her purity and defiance.

She was terribly upset. But she might as well have been behind glass. I was too drunk to stop.

She was taking off my clothes, and we were lying on the bed together and the phone was ringing, and I reached over, almost falling off the bed, and pulled the phone jack out of the wall. We were necking again, and I told her it was all right if she hurt me, really hurt me, that I was figuring on it, expecting it. It was worth it to love somebody like this. I said, "I am really drunk. I will not remember this."

Elliott

23

Spies and Revelations

I DID REMEMBER. Every single word.

I went out to breakfast at ten o'clock because I still couldn't get her up, and there was no food in the hotel and I was starving.

She kissed me. I told her the coffee was perking right by the bed and that I was going to the Court of Two Sisters and she should come down there when she woke up or I'd be back when I was finished.

I went immediately to a newsstand for magazines and papers, and then to a camera shop to buy a Canon AE1—simple, reliable, and not so expensive that I wouldn't mind giving it away to some kid before we went back to the island. You couldn't bring a camera into The Club even in your luggage, otherwise my luggage would have been full of them.

By the time I reached the Court of Two Sisters on Royal, I'd shot a full roll and I knew that I had a blissful, psychedelic hangover. No headache at all, just this light-headedness, this happiness, and everything looked marvelous.

And I wanted to get drunk again, but I didn't. These moments with her were too extraordinary. Today was going to be everything it could be with her, that is, if she wasn't packing when I got back to her.

I told the waiter she might join me, to show her to the table if she came in. Then I devoured a couple of Eggs Benedict, two extra orders of sugared ham, had three bottles of Miller's beer which the hangover absolutely, unequivocally required and deeply appreciated, and settled back with a pot of coffee to tear through the latest *Esquire, Playboy, Vanity Fair, Time,* and *Newsweek* magazines.

The world was in the same mess it had been when I left, naturally, since a full week hadn't passed, and look how long it took the world to get that way.

There were at least two new movies I really regretted not being able to see. *Time* had used three pictures of mine in an article on San Francisco gay writers. Okay. Death squads still operating in El Salvador, but of course, war in Nicaragua, marines still in Beirut, etc., etc.

I shoved all this aside and just drank the coffee. The open garden of the Court of Two Sisters was fairly quiet and I tried to think rationally about last night and what had happened. I couldn't. I could only feel a purely irrational love, and a happiness and an extraordinary sense of well-being. It occurred to me that I ought to pick up the phone and dial my father in Sonoma and say, "Guess what, Dad, I found the girl of my dreams." *And you'll never guess where.* He'd never know how funny it was, or that the joke might be on me.

The realities started coming back.

Like, what does all this mean to her? And what if when we get back to The Club, she presses that button on her dresser and she says to Daniel when he comes in: "Take him. I'm finished with him. Give him to one of the other trainers." Or, "I'll send for him in a couple of weeks." She could certainly do that if she wanted to, and maybe that was just what she did every time she took a slave out.

Maybe it was like checking out a book from the library and when you'd read it you were through.

No, this was not something to think about, that she could do that. And why think about it when we were here and I had her? As she put it, why think of Venice when you are in New Orleans? But I had to think about it, and when I did I remembered those last lucid moments, saying to her that she was going to hurt me, and there was this exhilaration, this sense of well-being still, of walking into it.

I wanted to get back to her.

But something else was bothering me too. It was the phone call and the way she'd said, "What are you going to do about it, arrest me!" I was sure that's what she'd said. And what did it mean? I kept telling myself she was just drunk, angry. But what did the words mean?

There was the other possibility, the grand possibility, that what she'd done, taking me out of The Club, was strictly against the rules, and they'd been looking for us.

But that was too farfetched, too purely, wonderfully romantic. Because if she'd done that, well . . . no. That was absurd. She was the boss lady. *It's heavy duty, going in and out . . . I can understand if you're not ready for it.* And why would she blow her cool like this when she was a scientist of sex, and had been all her life?

No, there was a good streak of the poet in her as there is in any good scientist, but a scientist is what she was, and she knew all about what she was doing. She'd just forgotten to check in, administrative responsibilities. *So they call her at six o'clock in the morning?*

This line of thinking was depressing me enormously. I poured another cup of coffee, gave the waiter a five dollar bill and asked him for a pack of Parliament 100s. I thought about her last night when we had been walking together through the Garden District, and my arms were around her, and there had been no Club, just us.

The waiter was coming back with the Parliament 100s when something startled me. On the very edge of the courtyard, near the Bourbon Street gate, was somebody I knew from somewhere and he was watching me. He had his eyes right on me and he didn't look away for a second when I looked at him. And very quickly, I realized he was wearing white leather pants, and white leather boots. He was all done out exactly like one of The Club handlers. In fact he couldn't be anything else. And I knew this guy. I remembered him. He was the good-looking blond young man with the sea tan who had greeted me in San Francisco, and said "Goodbye, Elliott" on the deck on the yacht the first day.

But he wasn't smiling now the way he'd been on those occasions. He was just looking at me, and leaning against the wall, and there was something almost sinister about his stillness and his steadiness and his presence in this particular place.

I felt a chill pass over me looking at him, and then a slow boiling rage. Hold it. There are two possibilities, right? This was usual, the surveillance when you took a slave out. Or, she'd bolted against the rules. *And they had come looking for* us????

I could feel my eyes narrowing, my defenses rising. *What the hell are you going to do, have me arrested?* I crushed the cigarette out and I rose slowly, and I started towards him. And I could see his face changing. He drew back a little against the wall, and then his face went blank. And he turned and went out.

When I got to the street, naturally I couldn't find him. I stood there for a couple of minutes. Then I went back into the men's room which was just inside the entrance. He wasn't in there. He was just gone.

I looked across the courtyard.

Lisa had come in. The waiter was taking her to my table. She stood there, a little anxiously, obviously waiting for me.

She looked lovely enough to make me forget everything. She had on a white cotton A-shaped dress, with a high frilly neck and leg of mutton sleeves, and she was wearing white sandals. She even had a white straw hat, which she was holding at her side by the long ribbons attached to it. And when she saw me, her face brightened exquisitely and she was like a young girl.

She came to meet me halfway, and put her arms around me just as if there were no one around to see us, or to care, and she kissed me.

Her hair was still just a little damp from the shower and full of perfume. And she looked fresh and curiously innocent in the white dress, and for a moment I just held her, aware that I wasn't hiding too well all the things that were on my mind.

She kept her arm around me as we went back to the table.

"So what's new in the world?" she said, shoving the magazines aside and for a second she stared at the camera.

"I know, I can't take it back," I said. "So I'll give it to somebody on the street, or some interesting looking student in the airport on the way."

She smiled at that. She told the waiter she wanted some grapefruit and some coffee.

"What's the matter?" she said suddenly. "You look really upset."

"Nothing, just that guy you sent to watch me. The handler. He startled me. I guess I thought they'd be invisible or a little more cool than that." I studied her as I said this.

"What guy?" she asked, her head a little to the side. Her eyes narrowed just the way mine had about five minutes ago. "If this is a joke, I don't get it. What are you talking about?"

"One of the handlers from The Club. He was right over there. He left when I got up to ask him what he was doing. Then you came in."

"How do you know he was a handler?" she asked. Her voice had dropped to a whisper, and her face was reddening slightly. I could see her temper rising.

"White leather drag, the works. Besides I recognized him."

"You're sure."

"Lisa, he had on the full drag," I said. "What kind of guy goes around in white leather boots and pants, unless he's got a sequined cowboy shirt to go with it? And I remembered him from the boat coming in. No question, it was the same guy."

The waiter set down the two halves of the grapefruit in their silver dishes of ice. She just stared at them. Then she looked at me again.

"He was over there, watching me. He wanted me to know he was watching. But obviously . . ."

"Damn bastards," she said under her breath. She stood up and called out for the waiter. "Where's the telephone?"

I followed her into the alcove. She put a couple of quarters down the slot.

"Go back to the table," she said, glancing up at me.

I didn't move.

"Please," she said. "I'll be there in just one minute."

I backed out into the sunlight again, still watching her. She was talking to somebody now with her hand cupped around the receiver. I could hear her voice peak, shrilly, and then die off. Finally she put down the phone and came racing towards me, her bag nearly falling off her shoulder.

"Pay the check, would you?" she said. "We're going to change hotels." And she started across the court, not waiting for me.

I caught her wrist and very gently I drew her back towards me.

"Why change hotels?" I asked. I had an odd, light-headed feeling, and it wasn't the hangover any more. I kissed her cheek and her forehead, and I could feel her very slowly and reluctantly relax, sort of give in to me.

"Because I don't want their goddamned surveillance!" she said, and she gave a little tug to free herself. She was more upset than she looked. I could feel it.

"What's the difference?" I suggested softly. I had my arm around her and I squeezed her shoulder, urging her towards the table. "Come on, have some breakfast with me. I don't like to run away from people. I mean what are they going to do? What are they supposed to do?" I was studying her. "Think about it. I don't want to leave that little place. It's our place."

She looked up at me and I felt for a moment that everything was just the way I dreamed it was. But it was a dream so complex that I didn't begin to understand it. I kissed her again, vaguely aware that more and more people were filling the court now and that some of them were watching us. I wondered if it made them happy, to see a young woman like this, so fresh and lovely and a man kissing her as if he didn't give a damn about anything in the whole world but her.

She sat down and she bent her head forward leaning on her elbows. I lit a cigarette and watched her for a minute, my eyes slowly scanning the court to see if the handler had come back or if anyone else had taken his place. I didn't see anyone.

"Is it the usual thing, on trips like this?" I asked. "That they follow and watch so that I don't bolt?" Almost fatalistically, I felt I knew the answer. This in and out thing wasn't done with new slaves. It was done with those who had been there for months and months and knew the rules and could be counted on to behave. She'd done it a bit early with me, that's all.

But there was something deliberately ironic in her expression as she looked up, her lowered lids rising languidly, her eyes almost black.

"It isn't usual," she said in a voice so low I could hardly hear her.

"Then why are they doing it?"

"Because what I've done isn't usual either. In fact, nobody's ever done it before."

I sat silently, weighing that for a moment. My heart was speeding up. I took a slow but nervous draw on the cigarette.

"Hmmmm."

"Nobody's ever taken a slave out of The Club," she said.

I didn't say anything.

She sat still, her hands slipping over the backs of her arms, as if the place was cold. She didn't look directly at me. She wasn't looking at anything.

"I don't think anybody else could even pull it off," she said, "if you want to know." Her voice was raw, and her lips gave a little bitter twist of a smile. "I suppose I'm the only one who could get everything going like that." She looked at me slowly, with the same languid rise of the eyelashes. "Send for the plane, get them to load your stuff; get you onto the plane."

I tapped the ash from the cigarette.

"They didn't know you were gone till three o'clock this morning. You were checked out to me. I was gone. Nobody could find you. I left with a man on the plane. Who was the man? I had sent for your luggage. It took them a few hours to figure it all out. Then they started calling hotels all over New Orleans. And they found us a little before six. You may or may not remember the call."

"I remember," I said. And that said that I remembered everything else, including telling her again that I loved her.

I looked at her. She was really on thin ice. She wasn't trembling so it could be seen. But I could see it. She stared at the food like it was something slightly horrifying to her. But she was staring at the table in the same way, and the vines twining around the wrought iron posts holding the ceiling of the porch above us.

"Why did you do it?" I asked.

She didn't answer. She went very rigid, staring off to the right, past me. And then without the slightest movement or sound from her, her eyes moistened and glazed over.

"I wanted to," she said.

Her lower lip started quivering. She took the napkin from the table and folded it and touched it to her nose. She was crying.

"I just wanted to," she said again.

I felt like somebody had hit me in the stomach. I mean watching her break up and start to cry was awful. And it was so damned sudden. One moment her rigid face and the next moment the tears just spilling down her cheeks and her lips quivering, and her expression completely crumpled.

"Come on," I said. "Let's go back to the hotel where we can be alone." I signaled the waiter for the bill.

"No, no. Wait a minute," she said. She blew her nose hard and buried the napkin in her lap.

I waited. I felt like I should touch her, reach over and hug her, or something, and yet I didn't because we were in this damned public place. I felt really stupid.

"I want you to understand a few things," she said.

"I don't want to," I said. "I don't care."

But that was not true at all. I just didn't want her to cry like this. She was all broken up now, though she wasn't making a sound. She looked hurt, positively hurt.

All I wanted to do was hold her right now. Probably everybody who'd been looking at us before was thinking what's that bastard done to make her cry?

She blew her nose again and wiped it and sat quiet for a moment. She was having a terrible time of it. Then she said: "Everything's okay as far as you're concerned. They know I tricked you. I led you to believe it was something we did. I told them that. And I'll make double sure they know when I talk to them again. They're pretty damned persistent. I expect they're calling the hotel now. But the main point is, they know I took you, that you were the victim of the whole thing, it was my idea. I kidnapped you."

I couldn't help but smile at that.

"And what do they want you to do?" I asked. "What are the consequences?"

"Well, they want me to bring you back, naturally. I broke the rules. I violated your contract." The tears welled up again, but she swallowed and made her face very calm deliberately as she looked away from me. "I mean this is a pretty terrible thing to do, you know."

She looked at me for a second and then away as if I was going to say something terrible and accusatory to her. I had no such intentions. In fact, the idea was perfectly ludicrous.

"They want me back at work," she said. "There're all kinds of problems cropping up. We bounced a teeny bopper night before last and it seems it wasn't the fault of the trainer who sent her. She'd switched with her older sister, and it turns out the older sister is married to some guy at CBS. The whole thing looks prearranged. And CBS is really pressuring us for an interview. We've never given anybody a real official interview. And everyone is really pissed about what I've done . . ." She stopped as if she had suddenly realized what she was doing now, telling me all this, and she glanced at me directly again, and then away. "I don't know what is the matter with me!" she whispered. "Taking you out of there like this."

I leaned across the table, and I took both her hands, and though she resisted just a little, I brought them together and pressed them together, and kissed her fingers.

"Why did you do it?" I asked again. "Why did you want to, as you said?"

"I don't know!" she said, shaking her head. She was starting to cry again.

"Lisa, you do know," I said. "Tell me. Why did you do it? What does it mean?"

"I don't know," she said. She was crying so that she couldn't really pronounce the words. "I don't know!" she insisted. She was breaking down completely.

I put a couple of twenties on the table, and I took her out of there.

Elliott

24

Literal versus Symbolic

THERE WERE MORE phone messages tacked to the door when we got back.

She was fairly calm now and she didn't tell me to go out of the room while she called.

But she looked defeated and miserable and very pretty, and I felt miserable seeing her with that expression on her face.

In fact, I was completely and quietly unglued.

It was clear within a few minutes that she was talking to Richard, the Master of Postulants, and she was refusing to give him the exact time that we would come back.

"No, don't send the plane yet!" she said at least twice.

I could tell by her answers she was insisting nothing bad was happening, that I was with her, that I was okay. She said she'd call tonight again, and tell them how much longer it would be.

"I will," she said. "I will. I'll stay right here. You know what I'm doing. Now what I'm asking you for is a little time."

She was crying again. But they could not possibly have known it. She kept swallowing it, and her voice was very steady and cold. Then they were talking about this teeny bopper exchange and the CBS interview thing and I knew she wanted me to go out so I did. I heard her say: "I cannot give those kinds of answers now. You're asking me to virtually create a public philosophy, a public statement! That takes time and it takes thought."

I took some pictures of the yard, the little house in which we were living.

As soon as she came out into the yard, I stopped snapping, and I said immediately, "Let's take a good walking tour of the Quarter, I mean really check out all the museums and the old houses, spend a little mad money in the shops."

She was startled. She had a lost and chilled look, but her face became a little animated, and she hugged the backs of her arms nervously and studied me as if she didn't quite understand what I said.

"And then after that," I said, "let's make the two-thirty steamboat cruise. It's dull, but hell, it's the Mississippi. And we can get something to drink on the boat. And I have an idea for tonight."

"What?"

"Dancing, straight conventional old-fashioned dancing. You've got some gorgeous dresses in there. I have never gone out dancing with a woman in my life. We'll go up to the River Queen Lounge at the top of the Marriott and we'll dance till the band stops playing. We'll just dance and dance."

She stared at me as if I were crazy. We just looked at each other for a moment.

"You mean it?" she said.

"Of course I mean it. Kiss me."

"It sounds great," she said.

"Then smile," I said. "And let me take your picture."

To my absolute amazement, she let me do it. She stopped in the door with her hand on the frame and she smiled, and she looked wonderful in her white dress, with the hat hanging by the ribbons from her arm.

We made the museum in the Cabildo first and then all the restored old houses that are open to the public, the Gallier House and the Herman Grima House and Madame John's Legacy and the Casa Hove, and stopped in just about every antique shop and gallery we saw.

I had my arm around her again, and she was getting lighter and happier, and her face was smooth again, like a young girl's face. With the white dress, she should have had a ribbon in her hair.

I thought if I do not love her forever, if this ends in some shabby and stupid disaster, one thing is certain: I will never be able to look at a woman in a white dress again.

By one o'clock, when we had lunch at the Desire Oyster Bar, we were talking again just as we had been last night. It was as if the handler and the phone calls had never intervened.

She was telling me as much as she could tell me about how The Club was organized and built. There were originally two financial backers and they had been in the black by the end of the first year. It was now impossible for them to satisfy the demand for memberships and they could pick and choose. She told me about the other clubs that were imitating them, the big one in Holland that was all indoors, and the one in California and the one in Copenhagen.

She was always getting offers to leave for higher pay, but with profit sharing she was now making half a million a year, and she never spent a penny of it except when she was on vacation. It just piled up.

I told her about the sports obsessions I had, how I'd almost cracked up an Ultralite plane in Texas, and the two winters I spent skiing the most dangerous mountains in the world.

I hated this part of myself, always had, and loathed the people that I had met through these activities because I felt like I was playing a part. It was a hell of a lot better photographing people diving off cliffs in Mexico than diving off yourself. I thought I'd gotten interested in photography because it was a way out.

But it had backfired.

I took every war assignment Time-Life would give me. I freelanced for two newspapers in California. The Beirut book took nine months of work night and day after the original shooting, and nothing dangerous happened to me in Beirut, but I came close to dying both in Nicaragua and in El Salvador. I had come really close in El Salvador. It was the incident in El Salvador that slowed me down and made me start to think.

I was kind of amazed as we talked about all this that she knew what was happening in these places. She didn't just know the outlines; she knew about the religious factions in Beirut, the history of the government. I mean, Club or no Club, she read more than most people would have in the daily papers.

It was two o'clock and we had to hurry to catch the steamboat for the river cruise. The day couldn't have been better, blue sky, the lovely fast-moving clouds that I never really see anyplace but in Louisiana, only little fits now and then of light sunshine rain, and not too many people on the boat because it was a weekday.

Together we leaned against the rail of the top deck just watching the city until we were well downriver and the view became industrial and pretty repetitive and the thing to do was to sit back in a couple of deck chairs, have a few drinks, and feel the movement of the steamboat and the river breeze.

I hated to admit it, I told her, but I love these steamer trips, commercial and dull as they seemed. I loved just being on the Mississippi, and there was no other river that engendered that kind of reverence in me except the Nile River.

She'd been in Egypt two years ago at Christmas time. It was one of those periods where she just couldn't stand to be near her family, and she'd stayed at the Winter Palace at Luxor for two weeks by herself. She knew what I meant about the two rivers, because every time she crossed the river, she would think, "I am on the Nile."

But every time she crossed a river she had a particular excited feeling, whether it was the Arno or the Thames or the Tiber, like she was touching the passage of history itself.

"I want you to tell me," she said, rather abruptly, "how you nearly got killed in El Salvador. And what you meant when you said it made you think."

She had that same intense and almost innocent expression on her face that she had had last night when we talked. And both of us were going really slowly with our drinks. She was not really like my conception of a woman when she talked. But I knew this meant I had a pretty lousy conception of women. I mean she was sexless or something, interesting, without conscious seduction. She could have been anybody. And I found that extremely seductive.

"It wasn't anything you couldn't read in the papers," I said. "It was nothing. Just nothing." The truth was I did not want to describe it blow by blow, build to the moment of climax, reliving every second. "I was with another reporter and we were in San Salvador and we stayed out after the curfew. We got stopped, and we nearly got shot. And we knew it."

I could feel myself getting that ugly, absolutely abysmal feeling again that had been with me for six weeks after I'd gotten out of El Salvador, that sense of the futility of just about everything, that transitory despair that can come on you any time in life, actually, that you just don't let in most of the time.

"I don't know where the hell we thought we were, in some café on Telegraph Avenue in Berkeley, couple of upper middle class white liberals, talking Marxism and government and all that rot to other upper middle class Berkeley liberals. I mean I guess we felt that safe, nobody was going to hurt us in some foreign country, it wasn't our war. Well, we were coming back to the hotel and we got stopped in the dark by two guys, I don't even know what they were, national guard, death squad goons, whatever, and the guy we were with, the Salvadoran we'd been talking to all night, got fucking terrified. And after we had showed our identification and everything, it got pretty clear that we weren't going to be let go. I mean this kid with this M-16 rifle just backed up and looked at the three of us. And it was pretty damn clear that he was just standing there thinking about shooting us."

No desire to recapture the pure white tension of that moment, the stink of real danger, the absolute helplessness of not knowing what to do, to move, to talk, to remain still, when the slightest change of facial expression might have been fatal. And then the rage, pure rage, that follows that helplessness.

"Well, anyway," I said. I took out a cigarette and packed it lightly on my knee. "He and the other guy he was with got into an argument, all the time the kid was aiming this gun straight at us, and something happened at that moment, like a truck appeared, and they were supposed to go, and they both looked at us, and we didn't move or say anything. I mean frozen, man."

I lit the cigarette.

"It was about two seconds there, and we knew what they were thinking about, at least it seemed again that they were going to shoot us. And to this moment I can't tell if it was true, not true, and if it was true, why they didn't. But they took the Salvadoran with them. They took him right in the truck while we stood there and did nothing. And we'd been in his mother's house all night talking politics, mind you. And we did nothing."

She sucked in her breath with a scorched sound.

"Christ," she whispered. "Did they kill him?"

"Yeah, they did. But we didn't find that out until we were back in California."

She murmured something under her breath, prayer, curse, something like that.

"Exactly," I said. "And you understand, I mean we did not even argue with them," I said. This was why I did not want to talk about this, did not, absolutely did not want to talk about it.

"But you don't think you should have argued . . ." she said.

I shook my head. "I have no idea whether I should have or not. I mean if I had had an M-16, you know, it would have been different." I took a draw on the cigarette. The smoke vanished in the river breeze and the cigarette, for that reason, seemed tasteless. "I got the fucking hell out of El Salvador immediately."

She gave a little nod.

"And that's when you started thinking."

"Well, I think for the first week or so, I just kept telling people the story. I kept going over it in my mind, what happened, and thinking what if, what if, what if, you know this guy had just let go with the M-16 and we were another couple of dead American newsmen. I mean one half-inch column in the *New York Times* or something, and then it was over. It was like the damn thing kept happening. It was a fucking tape loop in my mind. I couldn't get rid of it."

"Naturally," she said.

"And what became clear to me, really clear, was that I had been doing all kinds of dangerous things. That I'd been walking through these countries like they were Disneyland rides, like I was, you know, asking for assignments to get in where the action was, and I didn't have the faintest notion what I was doing. I was using these people. I was using their wars. I was using everything that was happening."

"How do you mean using them?"

"Honey, I didn't give a damn about any of them. It was talk. Berkeley liberal talk. Inside here, it was all a three ring circus for me."

"You didn't care about them . . . the people in *Beirut: Twenty-four Hours?*"

"Oh, yeah, I *cared* about them," I said. "They ripped me apart. I mean I wasn't some stupid shutterbug just photographing these things as if they didn't mean anything. In fact the agony was the way the photographs cooled everything down, abstracted everything. You just cannot get it on camera. You can't get it on video. But in a very real way, I didn't give a damn about it all. I had no intention of ever doing anything about it, what was going on! I was riding these experiences, like they were the roller coaster. I was skiing downhill. I was, in my heart of hearts, glad the war and the violence and the suffering were there so that I could experience them. That's the truth!"

She stared at me for a second. Then slowly, she nodded.

"Yes, you understand," I said. "Like when you're standing by the track at Laguna Seca and you think, well, if there's going to be a car crash, well I hope it's right here so I can see it."

"Yes," she said. "I know."

"But even that was not enough," I said. "I was one step from getting involved in the action itself. And not because I gave a damn or thought I could change anything in this world, but because it would have been a perfectly legal license to . . . do things I couldn't do otherwise."

"Kill people."

"Yeah. Maybe," I said. "In fact, that was exactly what was coming and going through my head. War as sport. Didn't matter what cause, really, except, you know, they should be the good guys, what we liberals call the good guys, but it really didn't matter finally. Fighting for the Israelis, fighting in El Salvador, what the hell." I shrugged. "Pick a cause, any cause."

She nodded again in that same slow way, like she was thinking it through.

"Now if you get to be my age, and somebody has to stick an M-16 rifle right in your face for you to know what death really is, for all this to come home, well, I think you're a pretty hard-headed individual, frankly, the kind of literalist who just might be dangerous."

She was puzzling this.

"Well, I had to think about it. Why was I seeking it out, literal death, literal warfare, literal suffering and starvation, and grooving on the pure reality of it, as if it were merely symbolic, the way people groove on a film."

"But the act of reporting, getting the story . . . ."

"Ah," I waved that away, "I was a beginner. There are too many others."

"And what did you conclude about it all?"

"That I was a pretty destructive guy. That I was a kind of a doomed person."

I took a swallow of my drink.

"That I was a damned fool," I said. "That's what I concluded."

"What about the people who *were* fighting in these places? I don't mean the soldiers of fortune or the mercenaries. I mean the people who believe in the wars? Are they damned fools?" She asked this very politely, truly inquisitively.

"I don't know. In a way, it doesn't really matter in my story whether or not they're fools. The fact was my death wasn't going to change anything for them. It would have been gratuitous, utterly personal, the price of the sport."

She nodded, slowly, her gaze moving past me over the deck and the distant banks of the river, the low, olive drab swampland falling right into the brown water, the swift panorama of the gliding clouds.

"This was after you did *Beirut: Twenty-four Hours?*" she asked.

"Yes. And I didn't do any *Twenty-four Hours in El Salvador.*"

When she turned to me again she was as serious as I'd ever seen her, unselfconscious, completely absorbed.

"But after what you'd seen," she said, "of real suffering, real violence—if it did mean something to you for whatever reason—how could you stand the scenarios at Martin's?" She hesitated. "How could you stand the rituals of The Club? I mean how did you make this transition?"

"Are you kidding me?" I asked. I took another swallow of Scotch. *"You're* asking me that?"

She looked genuinely confused by the question.

"You saw people who were really being tormented," she said. She was picking her words slowly. "People who were, as you said, immersed in literal violence. How could you justify what we do after that? Why weren't we obscene to you, decadent, an insult to what you'd witnessed? The guy getting put into the truck . . ."

"I thought I understood what you were asking," I said. "Nevertheless I'm amazed." I took another little drink, thinking about how to approach the answer. Whether to take it slowly or to come right out.

"Do you think that the people on this planet who are fighting literal war are superior to us?" I asked.

"I don't know what you mean."

"Do you think that people who do literal violence, either defensively or aggressively, are better than those of us who work out the same drives symbolically?"

"No, but God, I mean there are those who are swept up in it for whom the suffering is inescapable . . ."

"Yes, I know. They're swept up in something that is as ghastly and destructive as it was two thousand years ago when it was fought with swords and spears. It is not too different from what was happening five thousand years before that with rocks and clubs. Now why does something that primitive, that ugly, that horrible, make what we do at The Club obscene?"

She understood me, I knew she did, but she didn't commit herself.

"Seems to me it's the other away around," I said. "I have been there and I assure you it is the other way around. There is nothing obscene about two people in a bedroom trying to find in sadomasochistic sex the symbolic solution to their sexual aggressions. The obscenity is those who literally rape, literally kill, literally strafe whole villages, blow up busloads of innocent people, literally and relentlessly destroy."

I could almost feel her thinking as I watched her face. Her hair had fallen down over her shoulders, and against the whiteness of her dress, it made me think of her little joke last night about the nunnery, it made me think of a nun's veil.

"You know the difference between the symbolic and the literal," I said. "You know what we do at The Club is play. And you know the origins of that play are deep, deep inside us in a tangle of chemical and cerebral components that defy competent analysis."

She nodded.

"Well, so are the origins of the human impulse to make war as far as I'm concerned. When you strip away the current politics, the 'who did what to whom first' of every small and great crisis, what you have is the same mystery, the same urgency, the same complexity that underlies sexual aggression. And it has as much to do with the sexual desire to dominate and/or submit as the rituals we play at The Club. For all I know, it is *all* sexual aggression."

Again, she didn't answer. But it was like she was listening out loud.

"No, The Club is no obscenity compared to what I've seen," I said. "And I thought you more than anyone else would know that."

She was looking out at the river.

"That is what I believe," she said finally. "But I wasn't sure that someone who had been in Beirut and El Salvador would believe it."

"Maybe somebody that has had that kind of war done to them, somebody who has been ground under by it for years and years, maybe they would have no use for our rituals. Theirs is a different life than anything you or I have ever known. But that does not mean that what has happened to them is superior, either in origin or effect finally. If it makes saints out of them, that's wonderful. But how often can the horror of war be counted upon to do that? I don't think anybody on the planet anymore really believes war is ennobling, or that it has any value."

"Is The Club ennobling?"

"I don't know. But for my money, it certainly has value."

Her eyes seemed to brighten a little at that, but whatever she was really feeling was deep inside her.

"You came there to work it out symbolically," she said.

"Of course. To explore it, to work it out, without getting my head blown off or blowing off somebody else's. You know this. You must know it. How could you create this intricate island paradise if you didn't?"

"I told you. I believe it, but I've never lived in any other way," she said. "My life's been too much of a self-created vocation. And there are times when I think I have done everything in the name of defiance."

"That's not what you said last night. Do you remember what you said? About feeling no disgust for anything that two consenting individuals could do together, that it had always been innocent to you? You know as well as I do that if we can work out our violent feelings within bedroom walls where no one is hurt—no one really frightened, no one unwilling—then we just might be able after all to save the world."

"Save the world! That's a tall order," she said.

"Well, save our own souls anyway. But there isn't any other way to save the world now, except to create arenas to work out symbolically the urges that we've taken literally in the past. Sex isn't going to go away, and neither are the destructive urges wound up in it. So if there was a Club on every street corner, if there were a million safe places in which people could act out their fantasies, no matter how primitive or repulsive, then who knows what the world would be? Real violence might become for everybody a vulgarity, an obscenity."

"Yes, that was the idea of it all, the idea." Her brows came together, and she seemed lost for a moment, and strangely agitated. I wanted to kiss her.

"And it still is the idea," I said. "People say S&M is all about childhood experiences, the battles with dominance and submission we fought when we were little that we are doomed to reenact. I don't think it's that simple. I never have. One of the things that has always fascinated me about sado-masochistic fantasies, long before I ever dreamed of acting them out, was that they are full of paraphernalia that none of us ever saw in childhood."

I took another drink, finishing the glass.

"You know," I went on, "racks and whips, and harnesses and chains. Gloves, corsets. Were you ever threatened with a rack when you were a kid? Did anybody ever make you wear a pair of handcuffs? I was never even slapped. These things don't come from childhood; they come from our historic past. They come from our racial past. The whole bloody lineage that embraces violence since time immemorial. They are the seductive and terrifying symbols of cruelties that were routine right up through the eighteenth century."

She nodded. She seemed to be remembering something, and her hand touched her waist lightly, her fingers stroking the fabric of her dress. "The first time," she said, "I ever put on one of those black leather corsets, you know . . ."

"Yes . . ."

"I had this feeling about the time when all women wore things like that, you know, every day . . ."

"Of course. When it was routine. All the paraphernalia is the flotsam of the past. And where is it routine today? In our dreams. In our erotic novels. In our brothels. No, in S&M we're always working with something a hell of a lot more volatile than childhood struggles; we're working with our most primitive desires to achieve intimacy through violation, our deepest attractions to suffering and inflicting pain, to *possessing* others."

"Yes, possessing . . ."

"And if we can keep the racks and the whips and the harnesses forever relegated to the S&M scenario—if we could relegate rape in all its forms to the S&M scenario—then maybe we could save the world."

She looked at me for a long time without saying anything. And she nodded just a little again, finally, as if nothing I said shocked her or surprised her.

"Maybe it's different for a man," I said. "Call the San Francisco police any night of the week and ask who's committing the robberies and assaults. It's the people with testosterone in their blood."

She gave a little polite smile to that, but lapsed back immediately into seriousness.

"The Club is the wave of the future, babe," I said. "You ought to be more proud of it. They can't sanitize or legislate our sexuality out of us. It's got to be understood and contained."

She made some little accepting sound, her lips pressed together, her eyes narrowing slightly, then brightening again.

I finished the drink, and was quiet, watching the movement of the clouds across the sky.

I could feel the vibration of the steamboat all through my body, feel the dull surge of the engine and even the great silent pull of the river, or so it seemed. The wind had picked up but only a little.

"You aren't really proud of what you've done, are you?" I asked. "I mean, in spite of what you said last night."

She looked darkly troubled and indescribably lovely sitting next to me, the hem of her dress fallen back from her bare knees, her long, lean calves so beautifully shaped, her face so still. I could feel her brooding, her agitation, and I wished she would talk to me, say what she really thought about this.

"Well, I think you're terrific," I said. "I love you. Just like I told you last night."

She didn't answer. She was staring at the blue sky over the shore, as if her thoughts had snared her.

Well . . . so what?

After a while, she turned to me again.

"And you were always fully aware of what you wanted from The Club," she said. "It always had this therapeutic quality for you."

"Therapeutic, hell," I said. "I'm only flesh and blood, and I listen a lot to the flesh, maybe more than most people do." I touched her cheek very lightly with my fingers. "I've had the feeling most of my life that I was a little more physically there than most people."

"So have I," she said.

"Uh huh, very hot," I said, meaning it straight, not playfully.

"Yes," she said, "like I could explode if it didn't get out. Like my body had made me a criminal even when I was a little kid."

"Exactly. And why do we have to be criminals?"

I sat up and lifted her hair back from her face, and let my lips just lightly brush her cheek.

"Let's just say after that experience in El Salvador," I said, "I got hooked on symbolic violence. Therapeutic? Who knows. I got obsessed with violent films and TV shows that I wouldn't have even glanced at before. I got hooked on my own violent fantasies and when I heard somebody talking about Martin's place again for about the thirtieth time, I did what I never thought I'd ever do. I said: 'Tell me about that place. Where is it? How do you get the number to call?' "

"You can't believe it's real when you first hear about it," she said, "that others are doing it."

"Right. And it wasn't therapy, really. That was the best part. Martin said in one of our first little conversations that he never tries to analyze anyone's sado-masochistic desires. He doesn't give a damn why one person has fantasies that are full of whips and chains and another person has never thought of such a thing in his entire life. 'We'll work with what you are now.' I guess I just started working with it, peeling back the layers. Going deep into it, through one scary moment after another. I found it was as scary as anything I'd done. It was fucking awful and fucking delicious. It was the grandest and most interesting experience I'd had so far."

"An odyssey of sorts," she said. She had slipped her hand up around the back of my neck, and her fingers felt warm in the cool river breeze.

"Yeah, like that," I said. "And when I heard of The Club, well, I couldn't quite believe that somebody had had the guts to create it on that scale. I was dazzled. I was crazy. I knew I would get into The Club no matter what I had to do."

I closed my eyes for just a second as I kissed her. I slipped my arm around her, lifting her towards me, kissing her again.

"Be proud of it," I whispered.

"Of what?"

"Of The Club, baby doll. Be brave enough to be proud of it," I said.

She looked vague and a little bruised, and softened all over from the kissing.

"I can't think about it all right now," she said. "I can't figure it out." I could feel her heating up, lips taut, luscious.

"Okay. But be proud of it," I said, kissing her just a little harder, opening her mouth.

"Don't talk anymore about it," she said, drawing up closer, her arm around my waist.

We were our own little heat wave on the deck. Anybody coming around might get burnt.

"How much longer do we have to stay on this tub?" I asked, whispering in her ear.

"I don't know," she said. Her eyes were closed. She was kissing my cheek.

"I want to be alone with you," I said. "I want to be alone with you back at the hotel."

"Kiss me again," she said.

"Yes, Madam."

Elliott
25

"The Lady in My Life"

WE STOPPED ON the way back for some wine and a load of delicacies—caviar and crackers, apples, sour cream, smoked oysters. I bought some cinnamon and butter and bread, lots of French yogurt, a cold bottle of Dom Perignon (the best they had, $50) and a package of liquor store wine glasses.

When we got to the room, I ordered an ice bucket, turned off the air conditioner again, and latched the shutters the way I had the first time.

It was just getting dusk, vivid, sweet New Orleans dusk with the sky blood red and the pink oleander glowing in the tangle of the garden. The heat lingered in the air the way it never does on the coast. There was a velvety feel to the warmth and the room was full of dusty shadows.

Lisa had crumpled up all the telephone messages and thrown them away. She was sitting on the bed, the white dress up on her thighs, her shoes tossed in the corner. She had a large crystal bottle of perfume in her hand and she was smoothing the perfume into her skin all over. She massaged it into her neck, and into calves. She rubbed it into the spaces between her toes.

When the exquisite little mulatto child brought the ice he brought more messages.

"Will you throw those away?" Lisa asked. She didn't look at them.

I opened the champagne and got it to bubble just about perfectly into the two glasses.

I sat down beside her and reached lightly, slowly, for the buttons down the back of her dress. The perfume wasn't Chanel this time. It was Chalandre. Blissfully overpowering. I took the bottle from her and put it on the table, gave her the champagne.

The perfume mingled with the sunny smell of her hair and her skin. Her lips were wet from the champagne. She said, "Do you miss The Club?"

"No," I said.

"You know, the paddles and the straps and all that, do you miss it?"

"No," I said again kissing her. "Unless of course you have the overwhelming desire to beat the hell out of me. In which case, I'll throw myself on your mercy as a gentleman should. But I have something else in mind, something I've always wanted to do."

"Do it," she said.

She slipped off the dress. Her tanned skin was very dark against the white spread, and the light was good enough still to see the strawberry pink of her nipples. I ran my hand down between her legs, cradling her, touching her soft, secret hair, and then I slipped away from her, and went quietly out of the room into the dark little kitchen.

When I came back I had the butter with me and the little box of ground cinnamon.

I stripped off my clothes. She was leaning back on her arms, and the thrust of her breasts, and the long delicate curve of her flat belly to that secret mound of dark hair, was gorgeous.

There was a bashful flush to her cheeks.

"What are you going to do?" she asked, looking at the things I'd brought in, almost timidly.

"Just this little thing I've always wanted to do," I said, lying beside her, stretching her out, cradling her head, kissing . . . ight arm I reached over her, and gathered up some . . . fingertips. It was already nice and soft from . . . oothed it over the pink nipples of her breasts, . . . les and stretching them a little as I did it. She was breathing deeply, the heat rising from her invisibly like the perfume. I put the little box of cinnamon to my lips. I smelled it, that delicious Eastern smell, that forbidden smell, about the wildest aphrodisiac fragrance I've ever smelled except for the smell of pure male or female body. I rubbed the cinnamon onto her nipples.

And rolling on top of her, crushing her a little, my cock hard against her thigh, I started to suckle her breasts, lick them.

I could feel her tense under me, the heat from her sex incredible, and she moaned, struggling it seemed not to lift her arms, and then she clamped her hands around my head. She was wildly excited yet somehow resisting, frightened.

"It's too much," she said, "too much." I drew up and smoothed the hair back from her face. I was pure animal now, and all I wanted to do was have her. I thought of what she'd said about the blindfold before, how it should have made things easier. And I reached down and picked up the little sheer cotton slip she'd worn under the dress, and I stretched it out until it was a gathered band of white cloth and then I tied it around her head, blindfolding her. I crushed the knot in back until it was flat. I placed her head on the pillow.

She took a long, languorous deep breath. Her mouth lost its tenseness. It was pouting and soft and luscious and I felt her whole body relax under me. I felt it grow warm and open to me. She wound her arms around my neck, and her hips moved against me.

She said something soft under her breath, a murmur. And this time when I licked her breast, when I closed my mouth on it and sucked on it, and let my teeth close on the nipple, stroking it, she moaned and pressed herself against me. I was going crazy doing this to her, just this, and had to rise up a little to keep my cock off her thighs, away from her wet heat, or I'd come and it would be too quickly over. She was giving hoarse cries, cries that would have made a child or a nun think she was in pain. There was something being cut loose in her.

I took the soft butter on my fingers again, and I went into her with it, rubbing it into her pubic hair, and into the lips of her vagina. I rubbed the cinnamon on her, onto her clitoris as she spread her legs, all the resistance utterly gone out of her.

"Do it, do it . . ." she whispered, or at least the words sounded like that.

I was so hot now I didn't think I could stretch it out much longer. I pushed my face into her, covering myself with her scent, her clean scent and the scent of the butter and the cinnamon.

I started licking up under the clitoris, opening her with my tongue, scraping upwards, and then closing my mouth on her completely, closing it over her lips, and then sucking on her.

She was flung out as if she were bound that way and couldn't lift her arms or her hands, or struggle to close her legs. She was mine completely. She writhed under it, lifted her hips, but she didn't resist. She belonged to me. I ate out the butter, ate the cinnamon, tasted that crazy aphrodisiac taste, the spice and her charcoal fluids and the heat of her. It sounded like she was crying. She struggled; she said she was going to come.

I climbed up on top of her and when my cock went in she was so tight, so hot I exploded in her. She was coming and coming, as I came, her face scarlet, the blindfold of white cotton glowing in the dark, her lips shuddering, some little curse or prayer coming out of her with the word God.

I said, "Say my name, Lisa."

"Elliott," she said. She said it again. Her sex was locked to me, shuddering like her mouth as I lay still inside of her.

After a little while, I got up and turned on the shower. Nice, good blast of warm water, the little white tile bathroom full of steam immediately. I was soaping all over and thinking about everything, trying to shake off my postfuck, drug-sleep feeling.

She startled me when she appeared outside the glass door, and then I opened it for her.

She came in, sleepy-looking too, her hair all tangled, and I put her right under the torrent of water. I rubbed the soap well into the washcloth and I started to bathe her. I rubbed it over her shoulders and her breasts, gently washing off all the butter, and I could see her awakening, losing all control.

She kissed my nipples, then stroked them with her hands. Then she wrapped herself around me. I kissed her neck as the water flowed over both of us. I caressed her sex with the soapy cloth, washing her sex in slow, rough strokes with it.

"Come," I whispered, "come in my arms. I want to see you come." I didn't think I wanted to make it so soon again. I figured you had to be in prime shape for that, coming three and four times a day, the way I did at The Club. I felt happy. I loved the feel of her against me, naked and slippery and shivering, the water flooding over her hair. I felt her sex open as she went up on tiptoe. I felt her arm go down my back, her fingers moving into my backside, massaging, then opening me and slipping very gently inside.

That raw, inexpressible feeling of being opened up, being fucked there. She had two fingers inside me. She went deep, deep, easy as she had with the phallus before in that first scene at The Club, touching just the right place, finding the gland, pressing it.

I dropped the washcloth and went into her. She came in violent red shivers. Her mouth was open against my cheek. The sobs were caught in her throat. I fucked her against the white tile, her fingers still inside me. She came again, if she'd ever stopped coming, her breasts as red as her face, her face speckled with water droplets, her hair flowing down her shoulders and her back as if it was water.

"I meant it when I said I love you," I said.

No answer. Just the heat of the shower flooding us and our own heat and then her upturned face and her lips kissing me, and her head on my shoulder. Good enough for now, beautiful. I can wait.

The River Queen Lounge was pleasantly crowded when we got there, but she was easily the most ravishing woman in the room.

She had on a little black Saint Laurent dress, and spaghetti strap heels, and her hair was all tousled and witchy. The diamonds around her throat made it look long and exotic and positively biteable. I guess I was no slouch myself in a black tuxedo either. But that wasn't what made everybody look at us.

We were like a honeymoon couple, necking almost as soon as we had our drinks, and pushing onto the dance floor glued to each other, in a swoon among the polyester husbands and wives.

The place was softly dim, full of pastel light, the city of New Orleans an ocean of glitter outside the plate glass windows, the band Latin American, steady and sensuous, real dance music with all those extra rhythmic sounds.

The champagne went to our heads. I kept them playing through the break with a couple of hundred dollar bills, and we did rhumbas and cha-cha-chas and all kinds of stuff I'd never have been caught dead doing before. Her hips swung gorgeously under the black dress, breasts shivering in the silk, feet pivoting on the stiletto heels.

We had fits and fits of laughter.

We went back to the table bent double laughing after we did the cha-cha-cha.

And we drank all the gooey, disgusting, ridiculous tourist cocktails. Anything with pineapple or little paper hats or colored straws or salt or sugar or cherries or Sunrise or Voodoo or Sazarac in the name of it, we wanted it. Bring it right here to this table now. But we had the best time at the break when the band went into Bossa Nova. The singer was not a half bad imitation of Gilberto, with the lulling Portuguese words and the druggy rhythms, and we were really wailing, drifting in it, and barely stopping to sip our drinks standing up.

By eleven o'clock we wanted something a hell of a lot noisier. Yeah, come on, let's blow this place.

I carried her into the elevator. She was giggling against my chest.

We went down into Rue Decateur and found one of the new discos, the kind of place I never connect with New Orleans, like a thousand discos the world over with the stifling crowds and the flashing colored lights. The dance floor was packed, the crowd was young, the music deafening, the giant video screen flickering with Michael Jackson screaming out "Wanna Be Startin' Something" and we went into it immediately, pumping and twisting, and flung into the sea of bodies, grabbing hold of each other, and necking again with a new heat. Nobody, but absolutely nobody in this place was dressed as we were. And they were staring at us. And we were having fun, pure fun.

No sooner did we have our drinks than the slower sound of Eddie Grant's "Electric Avenue" was dragging us back out again. We were making it up, what we were doing, didn't matter what anybody else was doing. Right into the Police: "Every Breath You Take" and the "King of Pain." And then the screen went black for the Doors' "L.A. Woman." This wasn't dancing, it was total madness, convulsions, whipping and gyrating, holding up Lisa when she was off her feet, her hair clinging in wet strands to the side of her face.

I hadn't done anything like this in years since the big rock concerts in San Francisco when I was a student. We belted down the drinks, the colored lights making the place flash on and off the way a place can do when you're so drunk you're about to slide off the barstool. The mandate was to keep dancing. Gliding through David Bowie and Joan Jett and Stevie Smith and the Manhattan Transfer, and back to Jackson again with one of those soft melodic cheek-to-cheek numbers, and we were in a sweet, slow embrace on the dance floor, as they sang "The Lady in My Life."

I was singing it to her in her ear. I wasn't with the rest of the human race anymore. I had everything from the earth I had wanted. We had our arms around each other, and we were just one body, one warm body, a satellite, broken free forever from its orbit, unwinding forever into its own celestial path.

"Pity the rest of the human race," I said, "that they don't know this is heaven; that they don't know how to get in."

At one o'clock we glided out, our arms around each other, and just drifted through the narrow streets, the passing headlights cutting a path over cobblestones and gas lamps and the old Spanish galleries and green shutters.

We were wilted and exhausted, and when we came to one of those phony lampposts made to look like an old gas lamp (I actually love these lampposts), I put my arms around her and kissed her like I was a sailor with a girl he'd picked up. Real messy, wet kisses, gnawing at the sweet inside of her mouth, feeling her nipples through the black silk.

"I don't want to go back to the hotel," she said. She was all disheveled and lovely. "Let's go someplace different. I can't walk. I'm too drunk. Let's go into the Monteleone."

"Why don't you want to go back?" I asked. She was supposed to call The Club. I knew she hadn't. She'd never been out of my sight except for the brief moments when she went to the ladies' room.

She said: "I just don't want to hear that phone ringing. Just anyplace, let's go into the Monteleone, just a hotel room, you know, like we just met." She was too anxious. "Please," she said, "please, Elliott."

"Okay, sweetheart," I said.

We turned around and went to the Monteleone.

They gave us a room on the fifteenth floor, the pearl gray velvet, wall to wall carpet type with a little double bed, like a million old-fashioned, faded at the seams hotel rooms in America. I shut off the lights and opened the drapes and looked out on the low roofs of the French Quarter. We drank Scotch out of the bottle we'd bought on the way, and then we lay down, dressed, on top of the covers.

"One thing I want to know," I said in her ear. I was running my finger around the rim of her ear. She was a little limp sack of sweetness and heat tumbled next to me.

"What?" she said. She was almost gone.

"If you were in love with me, if you brought me here like this because you were, if you were just busted up in love with me the way I am with you, instead of this just being a fling, a bizarre little fling, or nervous breakdown or something for you, a crack-up or something, would you tell me?"

She didn't answer me. She lay still like she was already asleep, the shadow of her lashes dark against her cheeks, the little black Saint Laurent dress soft as a nightgown. She was breathing deeply. Her right arm was over me, and her fingers tightened on my shirt, but the way a hand can do in sleep, trying to pull me closer.

"Damn you, Lisa," I said.

The headlights of a car below slid over the papered ceiling, down the wall.

"Yesss," she said. But it was a sleep voice. She was out of it.

Elliott

26

Desire Under the Oaks

WE WERE THE only people touring plantations the next day in evening clothes. But what the hell, we'd been the only people at the drugstore soda fountain eating breakfast in evening clothes, too.

The private limo took us north to Destrahan Manor and then to San Francisco Plantation, and on to Oak Alley in Saint Jacques.

We snuggled together in the big gray velvet seat and we traded stories again, of childhood and disappointment and dreams. It was supernatural, flying at sixty miles an hour through the low Louisiana landscape, the levee always concealing the Mississippi, the sky frequently completely overlaced with green.

The air conditioning was silent, deliciously icy, and we tunneled through time itself as surely as we tunneled through the verdant and lush subtropical land.

We had plenty of liquor in the little icebox. We had cold beer and some caviar and crackers. And we turned on the little color TV set and watched the game shows, soaps.

And then we made love, really wonderful hangover love, with

no blindfold and no nothing, stretched out all the way on the big wide soft seat.

But a mood came over me at Oak Alley, maybe because it is one of the most glorious Louisiana plantations I've ever seen. Or maybe because I finally had some time to think.

Oak Alley does truly have an avenue of oaks going to the front door, and inside it is one of those perfectly balanced houses, with a central hallway and stairs that makes you feel every other kind of house is a mess. But there is more than grandeur to Oak Alley. There is the color of the light coming through the oaks, the tall grass in which you seem to sink as you walk around the house; there are black angus cows silently fixed in the distance, staring at you like ghosts from an exotic past; and there is the scale of things, the round columns, the high porches, and the silence of it all, that makes you feel as if you have gone one more step through the otherworldly quality of New Orleans to yet another enchanted place.

I got stubborn and silent as we roamed around it because I had to make up my mind about what I thought.

I was in love with her. I'd said that to her and to me at least three times. She was everything I had ever wanted in a woman, mainly because she was sensuous and she was serious, and she was smart and she was straight and painfully honest in her own way, which must have been why she was so silent now. On top of all that she was beautiful, unrelentingly beautiful. And whether she talked about her father or the movies she loved, or she said nothing, whether she danced or laughed or looked out the window, she was the first woman I had ever found as *interesting* as a man.

Perhaps if Martin had been here he would have said: "I told you so, Elliott. You were looking for her all the way along."

Maybe, Martin. Maybe. But how could you or anyone else have predicted this!

Okay. All that was marvelous. And she had busted us out of The Club in a violent, spontaneous, and romantic fashion just as I had hoped the first night. But it was clear there could have been three reasons, just as I suggested when I tried to talk to her on the bed in the Monteleone when she fell asleep. Either she loved me. Or she was having a nervous breakdown. Or she was just really having a fling. I mean if The Club is where you lived for six years, you are really into acting out your fantasies, right? Or are you?

But whatever the case, she was not going to tell me.

When I had told her I loved her, her face was as vulnerable and responding as I could want it to be. But she hadn't answered. She didn't commit. She didn't explain. She either wouldn't or couldn't cop to what was going on inside.

Okay. So what was I going to do? The funny part is that even stubborn and silent and thinking, I was just as charged with love for her and with the madness of the whole thing as I had been when I was talking and kissing. Nothing went sour or dim. But what was I going to do?

It seemed to me, by the time we left Oak Alley and the limo rocked its way out of the drive onto the river road, that the situation was pretty much what men say they want: sex and fun without a commitment, an affair with no strings attached. And here she was the one acting like the man. And I was the one acting like the goddamned woman, wanting her to tell me where we stood.

And I was pretty sure that if I pressed her, if I took her by the arms and said, "Look, you have to tell me. We can't go one more step without your telling me where we stand," I had a fifty-fifty chance of destroying the whole thing. A fifty-fifty chance. Because she just might tell me something so disappointing and simple that I would come totally apart.

Okay. It wasn't worth it, not as long as she was with me. Not as long as she was snuggled up against me, and I could kiss her and fuck her and love her and talk to her like this. And think silently that she just might be altering the course of my entire life.

So I made up my mind to go on loving her and not say anything more. It was sort of the way I'd felt the first drunken morning when I'd said that she was going to hurt me, and that it was okay. Sort of. Except I was too excited now and too many things were occurring to me, for me to think of it in that sentimental way.

My mind was getting busy. I should call the real estate agents about that house for sale in the Garden District. I had to give my dad a call and see if he was alive, or if he'd killed my mother. I had to get another camera.

What was all this?

I wouldn't even ask her why we were not going back to the

hotel, what we were really avoiding, what The Club was likely to do.

But when we left Oak Alley and she told the driver to go into the bayou country to St. Martinsville, I knew we were definitely "running away from home."

We stopped in one of those big, purely American roadside discount stores and we bought cosmetics and toothbrushes and the cheapest clothes you can probably find anywhere in the States.

At the motel in Saint Martinsville we put on khaki shorts and white T-shirts and then we went walking together, arm in arm like lovers, into damp, green depths of the quiet and endless Evangeline State Park.

This was another haunted place, because there are three- and four-hundred-year-old oak trees here, leaning their great, enormous and beautiful elbows on the ground, which are true wonders of the world. The grass is velvet, and the sky comes right down through the trees like bits and pieces of polished porcelain glimmering through the clumps of leaves, and the moss drifts like the hair of ancient women all the way to the ground. The whole world seems, as it did at Oak Alley, to be a dark and silent and verdant place.

There wasn't any cinnamon or butter when we made love, just the two of us in the tiny little wallpapered motel cabin like it had been in the limo, and this time with the beer in the ice in the bathroom basin, and the little ruffled curtains moving in the moist current of the rattling air conditioner, we went right to the moon and the stars.

Slower, sweeter, wilder, it went on all the late afternoon, the kisses and the sighs and the soft words spoken amid the battered doll-house like furniture and the light through the dirty, brittle old yellow window shades under the ruffled curtains getting more and more golden until it was dark.

Conversation about the kind of woman I always thought I'd marry: some primitive woman, deeply foreign, like the woman I'd lived with briefly in Saigon, waiting on me hand and foot, and never asking any questions, Goethe's flower girl, Gauguin's Tahitians, ah, the sadness, the hostility of it, the lockout and the despair of such ideas. I had never been stupid enough to call that a dream.

She did not say anything about that. She looked adorable to me in the khaki shorts and the T-shirt and the thong sandals we'd bought in the discount mart. She wore Chantilly perfume, real cheap and sweet, that she'd bought there also, and I wanted to photograph her face, the way her face looked in the shadows, the cheekbones, the shadows in the hollows of her cheeks, the lovely pout of her red mouth.

Finally she said: "I never thought I'd get married at all. I never thought I would really love someone. I never thought . . ." She sat still looking horror-struck and I felt stubborn looking at her, thinking, "The hell, I am not going to say it again."

I was hungry. I wanted some Cajun food, real Cajun jambalaya, and shrimp and red beans. And to hear some goofy, shrill, nasal, high-pitched Cajun music and singing, maybe even find a little bar somewhere where we could dance.

"I'm going to buy that house in the Garden District," I said.

She woke up like somebody had pulled a string attached to her, as she sat there, staring off.

"It will cost a million dollars," she said. Her eyes were glassy and strange.

"So what?" I said.

We showered together and we put on more of the discount store shorts and shirts and sandals. And we were pretty much ready to go out.

Then something stupid happened, well, more or less.

One of those big brown horrible Louisiana roaches got into the room, and Lisa jumped up off the bed screaming, absolutely screaming, when the roach came waddling over the bumpy polyester carpet across the room.

Now these are actually waterbugs or so I am told. But no one that I have ever known from Louisiana ever called them anything but roaches and just about everybody I know who was born there, with these roaches, goes screaming mad like this when they come into a room.

I myself have no fear at all of roaches. So as Lisa was screaming her head off, I mean going to absolute hysteria, screaming, "Elliott, kill it! Kill it! Kill it!" it was a great pleasure for me to go and get the thing, pick it up off the carpet in my hand, and get ready to throw it out the door. It was a damn sight better idea than smashing it, because they give off an appalling popping noise if you smash them directly, and a squashed one is worse to look at than a moving one as far as I am concerned. I don't like these things, but I don't mind picking them up.

But this act of picking up the roach, catching it like a moth in my right hand, brought Lisa into a catatonic state of silence with her hands clamped over her mouth. She stared at me as if she could not believe what I was doing, and I stood still staring at her. Then she put her hands down, and white faced and sweating and shaking she said, "Well, if it isn't the goddamned samurai himself, Mr. Macho Man, picking up the goddamn roach in his bare hand!"

I don't know what exactly she was feeling. Maybe she was just so shaken up and so scared and so upset, and here I was holding the roach in my hand. I don't know.

But whatever it was she sounded furious and contemptuous and ironic, and I said, without thinking about it, possibly unconsciously irritated by her incredible screaming: "You know what, Lisa? I'm going to put this roach down your shirt."

She went totally and completely nuts.

Screaming the same way she had before, really screaming, she rushed into the little ratty closet of a bathroom and slammed the door and pushed the latch. And there came through the door the most hysterical condemnations and pleading and miserable choking-and-sobbing crying I'd ever heard.

Well, very plainly this was not funny to her, not funny at all. She was just too scared. And I was a rat.

But for one solid hour I could not persuade her to come out. I had thrown the roach outside, and then killed the sucker. He was dead, dead, dead. No more would he scare gorgeous little girls from roachless Berkeley, California. Not enough of him remained for a roach funeral. He was dead. I was sorry, I told her, I wouldn't do such a thing, really, it was bullying and mean.

But just when I would get her calmed down and believing in me, that I knew I had behaved terribly, I couldn't, just couldn't resist throwing in some little teasing remark, like, "Of course I would never put a big, sticky, ugly, multilegged, squirming brown cockroach down your shirt!"

I knew I shouldn't do this, it was *so* sadistic, but it was also so damned funny and I just couldn't stop myself, and of course *I* knew I wasn't going to really do it, and the next time I said, "Of course I wouldn't, Lisa, do you think I would expect you to work out your fear of roaches in an S&M scenario with me putting a roach down your shirt, the way you made me wear that blindfold at the whipping post in the sports arcade, no Madam!"

But finally I was begging her to come out.

"Lisa, come out of the bathroom. I swear I would never do something like that to someone. I have never and I would not. It's mean. I wouldn't do it." I had come completely straight. She still wouldn't open the door.

"All right, Lisa. This is Louisiana. Now what are you going to do the next time one of those critters gets in?" (Crying.) "What did you do when you were here before and I wasn't here?" (More crying.) "But I am here and I am going to get rid of them when they come in, right? Now you better make up with me immediately or maybe I just might not." (Terrible crying.) "Like what if there is one in that bathroom right now, coming right out from under the linoleum or something right against the wall?" (Awful, sad, terrible crying.)

"I hate you, Elliott," she said in the most deep and resonant and feelingful voice. "You don't understand this. You don't know what it's like. You can't imagine how I feel. I swear to God I hate you right now. I really do hate you. I do."

"Lisa, I'm sorry! It's seven o'clock. It's dark. We're in this shit-kicking bayou town. I'm hungry. Come out! Okay. If you don't come, Lisa, Mr. Macho Man is going to break down the fucking door right now."

She didn't come out.

I broke down the door like I said I would.

Actually, this was very easy. The hinges were rusted and corroded, and when I slammed the door with the one wooden chair in the room, the hinges broke right out of the jam. And there was Lisa standing on the toilet top, with her arms folded, and the door lying in front of her with the paint scraped off it, and she was just staring at me. And the door jamb was a splintered mess.

"Look, Ma," I said and I opened both my hands. "No roaches. I swear." I stood still and I smiled at her and silently pleaded with her. I made motions to her to please get down and come to me, and then she broke and jumped off the toilet top and ran down the sloping ramp of the door into my arms.

"I wanna get out this ratty motel," she said, and I held her and kissed her and smoothed her hair back from her face, while I apologized again. And softly, hotly, helplessly, she burst into new fits of tears.

This was an extraordinary, luscious moment, and I felt like a rat.

The manager was banging on the front door. His wife was shouting.

We got everything together. The driver was already outside. I gave the manager a hundred-dollar bill to cover everything and said in a sneering, imperious voice, "That will teach you to rent to rock stars again."

We were doubled over laughing as we got in the car.

"Goddamn hippies!" the manager said.

That sent us into hysteria.

Twenty miles out of town, we found a great roadside restaurant with freezing air conditioning and we had everything I wanted to eat, crawfish done six different ways on a platter, and jambalaya and cold beer, with the jukebox playing the most cacophonous Cajun music I could have asked for. I ate like a pig.

Hour by hour we rode north.

Necking, talking now and then, as the night fell down around us and it didn't really matter where we were or where we were going, and the movement of the car was like the movement of a ship.

When we got faintly hungry again (It was I, not she. She was astonished that I could be hungry.) we pulled in at a drive-in movie, let the driver get in the back to go to sleep, and loaded up on hot dogs and popcorn to watch *The Road Warrior* with Mel Gibson, an Australian film directed by George Miller that despite the ironic, sarcastic, anti-macho wisecracking coming from the female occupant of the car, I found terrific.

I must have drunk a six-pack of beer. I was drifting off when the second feature ended and she started the car.

"Where are we headed?" I said sleepily. I could hardly see.

"Go on to sleep," she said. "We're bound for parts unknown."

"Parts unknown." I loved it. The cool air from the vent was rushing over me. I was snuggled up against her with my legs stretched out to the side. The night was a mirage.

Elliott
27

To Keep Warm

WHEN I WOKE up, the sun was cutting through the windshield and we were going at least one hundred miles an hour. The chauffeur was still asleep in the back.

I took one look at the land and knew we weren't in Louisiana anymore. And one look at the road ahead again, and knew that the skyline could only belong to one city on earth. We were driving into Dallas, Texas, and you could almost see the heat rising off the road.

Without looking at me or letting up on the accelerator, her naked legs long and brown and soft coming out of the khaki shorts, she picked up a silver canister off the seat and thrust at me. "Coffee, blue eyes," she said.

I took a big hot swallow of the coffee, and stared forward, positively humbled by the Texas sky in front of us, the unbelievable height of the voluminous clouds. Somebody had opened up the whole world. Stacked to the stratosphere the clouds were, with the morning sun driving shafts right through them, turning the rolling white terrain to pink and yellow and gold.

"And what exactly are we doing here, beautiful?" I bent over to kiss her smooth soft little cheek.

We were already mounting the tangle of immaculate Dallas freeways, sliding through the wilderness of towering glass and steel monoliths. Everywhere I saw futuristic buildings with an almost Egyptian purity and massiveness, flawless reflections of the cloudscape gliding across a hundred polished walls.

She was weaving in and out of the traffic like a race car driver.

"Ever hear of Billy Bob's Texas?" she asked. "In Fort Worth? Wanna go dancing there tonight?"

"Hot damn, you're my kind of girl," I said. I took another swallow of the coffee. "But I left my snakeskin boots back in New Orleans."

"I'll buy you some new snakeskin boots," she said.

"What about some breakfast?" I kissed her again. "This boy needs some grits and eggs and ham and flapjacks, the works."

"All you really think about is food, Slater."

"Don't be jealous, Kelly," I said. "Right now, you're the only thing in this world I love more."

We stayed in the big gaudy silver Hyatt Regency long enough to make love in the shower, stash the driver in his own room in front of a color TV, and then we took off for Neiman's, Sakowitz, and the swanky sci fi shopping malls with their glass ceilings, fountains, and fig trees, and silver escalators, and everything for sale from diamonds to junk food.

I loaded up on good books at the B. Dalton, mainly some old favorite stuff I thought I might read to her, if she'd let me. And she kept picking out blue and lavender and purple clothes for me —turtlenecks and velvet jackets, dress shirts and even suits. I made her buy kinky high-heel sandals, strapping them on for her myself in the store, and she had to at least try on for me every pretty white dress we saw.

Then late afternoon we hit Cutter Bill's for what we really wanted—pearl button cowboy shirts, fancy belts, skin-tight Wrangler jeans, and Mercedes Rio boots.

It was dark when we got to Billy Bob's Texas and the place was jammed. We had on matching everything, including hats, and we sauntered in like a couple of natives, or so we figured it. Who knows what we really looked like? Two people crazy mad in love?

It took me a moment to realize we'd entered a city-block-sized compound, with souvenir shops, billiard tables, restaurants, and bars—even an indoor rodeo arena—and thousands eating and drinking and crowding onto the dance floor while the seamless sound of the live country-western band rolled over everything, going at once to my head.

We danced every number the first hour, fast, slow, in between, drinking beer right out of the bottle, and just copying the dancers around us until we had it down. We slunk around the floor with our arms around each other's necks, waltzed, swung, danced cheek to cheek, smooched. It seemed insane that women had ever worn dresses, that lovers had not always worn exactly the same clothes. I could hardly keep my hands off her gorgeous little bottom in the tight jeans, her breasts bulging under the tight shirt. And her hair was still that feminine mane, that silky dark veil over her shoulders, that was the final touch. When she pulled her hat down over her eyes, leaned against the wooden railing with her ankles crossed and her thumbs hooked in her pockets, she was too damned pulchritudinously fuckable for me to stand it. Nothing to do but dance.

The rodeo in the little indoor arena was the real thing and not half bad. I loved the smell of it, the sound of those stomping animals. She covered her face a couple of times when the guys were almost trampled, and then we wandered into the restaurant part for some big juicy hamburgers and french fries, and around eleven, I discovered she knew how to play pool.

"Why the hell didn't you tell me?" I said. Time for some serious gambling. And by midnight she'd won three billion dollars from me. I wrote her a check.

My feet were killing me. But I was still grooving on the dim yellow lights, the endless thumping music, the deep, sweet, sentimental voice of the baritone singing Linda Ronstadt's old "Faithless Love." One last dance.

"S&M boots," I said finally. "Why don't you lasso me and drag me to the car so I don't have to walk?"

"You're not kidding," she said. "Guess who's walking out of here in her sock feet? Come on, cowboy. Time for the proverbial roll in the hay."

A little after eight when I was doing laps across the pool, singing "Faithless Love" with a lot of bubbles in it, she came out, dressed up in jeans and boots again, and said we should take off for

Canton right now. Only it wasn't Canton like in China, but Cant'n.

"Post haste, wherever the hell it is," I said, climbing out of the water. "But an emergency ration of eggs Benedict and Miller's beer first, okay?"

I also wanted to cut off her Wranglers with a scissors and make love to her before we left. We compromised on that.

(We didn't have a scissors.)

Canton was a town an hour south of Dallas where every first Monday of the month for one hundred years they have held a gigantic flea market which attracts people from all over the States. And by ten we were rocking south in the limo again, the driver in the back, Lisa at the wheel as before.

"Quilts," she said, "that's what I'm looking for, the last genuine batch from the thirties and forties, made in Kansas and Texas and Oklahoma, where the women still knew how."

It was ninety-eight degrees when we got out of the car.

But from eleven until one we shuffled through the dusty dirt paths of an endless sprawling marketplace past thousands of tables and booths full of beat-up furniture, prairie antiques, dolls, paintings, carpets, trash. Quilts we found by the pound. I know because I was carrying them over my shoulder in a green plastic sack.

"What would you do without me?" I asked.

"Gee, Elliott, I don't know," she said. "Hold still and let me wipe the sweat from that brow."

But I'd also kind of fallen in love with the quilts by that time, learned about the old patterns—Dresden plate, and wedding ring, and flower basket, and lone star, and postage stamp. I was loving the colors, the stitching, the feel of these old things, their clean cotton smell, and the gentle way that the vendors bargained with Lisa and she got them for the price she wanted every time.

We ate hot dogs from one of the stands, and dozed for a while under a tree in the shade. We were all dusty and sticky and just watching the families pass—the barrel-shaped guys in short-sleeve shirts, the women in shorts and sleeveless tops, the little kids.

"You like it out here?" she asked.

"I love it," I said. "It's like another country. Nobody could ever find us here."

"Yeah. Bonnie and Clyde," she said. "If they knew who we really were, they'd kill us."

"I don't know about that," I said. "I could handle them if they got rough." I got up and bought two more cans of beer and sat down again beside her. "What are you going to do with all these quilts?" I asked.

She looked weird for a moment as though she'd seen a ghost or something. Then she said, "Try to keep warm."

"That's not a very nice thing to say, Bonnie. What about old Clyde here, he can't keep you warm?"

She turned one of her rare smiles on me that was pure loveliness.

"You stick with me, Bonnie," I said. "And I swear, you'll never be cold again."

On the back to Dallas, we made love on all the quilts in the back of the car.

We put them on the bed when we got to the Hyatt and they really classed up the place. Then we swam, had dinner in the room, and then I read aloud to her as she lay beside me on the bed.

I read a couple of short stories I loved, and a funny part of a James Bond thriller, and my favorite paragraph from a French classic, things like that. She was a terrific listener. I'd always wanted a girl I could read to, and I told her that.

It was midnight. We got all dressed up again, and went up in the elevator to the Top of the Dome and we danced till the band quit.

"Let's go for a drive," she said. "See the mansions of Turtle Creek and Highland Park by moonlight, you know . . ."

"Sure, as long as we wake up Rip Van Winkle and make him do the driving so I can snuggle with you in the back."

I felt like we had been together for years and years. It couldn't have been any better for me, the way it was moment to moment.

We stayed in Dallas for four more nights like that.

We ate take-out chicken and watched the basketball games on TV, and we took turns reading aloud the short stories in the *New Yorker,* and chapters from the books. We swam in the pool.

At night we went out to the big glossy Dallas restaurants and the discos and the nightclubs, and sometimes we went for long rides in the clean countryside looking to spot old white farm-houses or old overgrown cemeteries with Confederate dead.

We walked through old-fashioned streets of little towns at sun-set, when the katydids were going at it in the trees and we sat on benches by the town square and we watched slowly, thoughtfully, as the sky lost its color and its light.

We watched old movies on cable at two in the morning as we snuggled together under the quilts, and we made love all the time.

Love in the American Hyatt Regency spaceship where every-thing is brand new and nothing is permanent and the windows are imitations of windows and the walls are imitations of walls, and the lovemaking is so real it is like a thunderstorm, whether or not it is in the spotless bed or in the spotless shower or on the deep, spotless, carpeted floor.

Off and on we talked. We talked about just the worst things that had ever happened to us, school things, and parent things, and the things we thought were beautiful: paintings, sculptures, music.

But gradually our conversation started to wind away from our-selves. To cling to other subjects. Maybe she was afraid. Maybe I didn't want to say any more until she said something very partic-ular that I wanted to hear, and I was being stubborn. I don't know. We still talked plenty, but it was about everything else.

We argued Mozart versus Bach, and Tolstoy versus Dostoev-sky, whether or not photography was an art—she said yes, I said no—Hemingway versus Faulkner. We talked like we knew each other very well. We had a horrible fight over Diane Arbus and over Wagner. We agreed on the genius of Carson McCullers and Fellini and Antonioni and Tennessee Williams and Jean Renoir.

There was a splendid tension, a magical tension. Like any mo-ment something could happen. Very important something either good or bad. And who was going to tip the scales? Like if we started to talk about ourselves again it would have to go a step further and we could not go that step. But hour by hour, it was remarkably wonderful, remarkably good, remarkably just plain all right.

Except when the Warriors lost to the Celtics in a really crucial play-off game, and we were out of beer and room service was taking forever and I was really, really pissed off. She looked up from her copy of the newspaper and said she had never heard a man shout like that over a ball game, and I told her that this was symbolic violence in all its glory and please shut up.

"A little too symbolic, don't you think?" She locked me out of the bathroom and took the longest shower in history. Just to have the final say, I passed out.

In the middle of the third night I woke up and I realized I was alone in the bed.

She had pulled the drapes and she was standing at the window looking out at the great steel wilderness of Dallas in which the lights never go out.

The sky was enormous above her, a deep midnight blue with a panorama of tiny stars. And she looked tiny against the window with her head bowed, and it seemed she was singing something to herself under her breath. Too faint to be sure of. Like the scent of her Chanel.

When I got up, she turned silently and came to meet me in the middle of the room. We put our arms around each other and just held each other.

"Elliott," she said like she was working up to tell me some dreadful secret but she just laid her head on my shoulder, and I held on to her stroking her hair.

Under the covers again, she was shuddering and yielding like a half-frightened young girl.

When I woke up later, she was sitting in the far corner away from the bed, with the silent TV turned towards her, so the light wouldn't bother me, I guess, just watching it, the blue light flickering on her face, and she was drinking Bombay gin straight with the bottle next to her and smoking my Parliament cigarettes.

The driver said next afternoon that he had to get home. He liked the money and all and the traveling and the food was terrific, but his brother was getting married at Redemptorist Church in New Orleans and he had to get back.

But we knew we could have let him take the limo back and just rented a car.

That wasn't why we were going back.

She fell utterly silent at dinner and she looked tragic, which is to say that she looked beautifully, exquisitely, heartrendingly, frighteningly, and wrenchingly sad. And I said, "We're going back, aren't we?"

And she nodded her head. Her hand was shaking. We found a little bar on Cedar Springs where there was a jukebox and we could dance all by ourselves. But she was too tense, too unhappy. We went back before ten o'clock.

We were both wide awake at four in the morning when the sunlight came down on the glass city. We got dressed up again in our evening clothes and checked out of the hotel. She told the driver to get in the back again, that she wanted to drive.

"That way you can read to me if you want," she said.

I thought that was a great idea, and we hadn't even tapped Kerouac's *On the Road,* my favorite of all the books, which to my amazement she'd never read.

She looked wonderful as she drove. Her black dress slipped down back from her knees into her lap and her legs were lovely, and she stabbed at the pedals with her stiletto heels, and she drove the big limousine like a suburban girl who'd learned to drive when she was teenager, that is, with more gusto and ease than most men could have driven it, parallel parking it in three seconds when we had to, without a whimper, using only one arm, and never hesitating to pass, and running yellow lights every time there was a chance, and never unnecessarily letting somebody go first or get ahead, and rolling through stop signs.

In fact, she maneuvered the car so easy and so fast, she made me a little bit nervous, telling me to shut up more than once. What she really wanted to do was go faster than the driver would have gone, and pretty soon we were roaring towards New Orleans at ninety miles an hour when there wasn't any traffic and a good seventy when there was. Once she pushed to one hundred ten and I told her to slow down or I would jump immediately.

I told her this was a damn good time to read *On the Road.* She couldn't even smile anymore, but she tried. She was trembling. When I said it was a marvelous and poetic book, she only nodded.

I read her all my favorite passages, the truly dazzling and original parts, though all of it is really dazzling and original, and pretty soon she was really enjoying it, nodding and smiling and laughing and asking me little questions about Neal Cassady and Allen Ginsberg and Gregory Corso and the others who had inspired the book. These were the beat poets and writers of the fifties in San Francisco who were for all practical purposes swept off the popular scene by the flower children of the sixties before we had gotten old enough to know what was going on. They were the most fragile of subjects, recent literary history, when we were in school. And I wasn't really surprised at how little she knew of them, and how thrilled she was by Kerouac's prose.

Finally I read her a hilarious part of the book where Sal and Dean are in Denver and Dean gets all excited and steals one car after another so fast that the cops cannot even figure what is happening, and after that I got to the passage where they were actually driving a limousine to New York, and Dean tells Sal to imagine what it would be like if they owned the car they were driving, that there's a road they could take through Mexico and Panama and maybe even to the bottom of South America.

I stopped.

We had just roared past Shreveport, Louisiana, and we were headed straight south.

She was staring straight forward, her eyes wide, blinking suddenly as if she was trying to see through a fog.

She glanced at me for a split second, and then back at the road.

"That road's still there, gotta be," I said. "Through Mexico, Central America, down to Rio . . . And we could rent a better car than this. Hell, we could take a plane, we could do anything . . ."

Silence.

This was what I'd told myself I wouldn't do. I sounded too angry. It would never work.

The speedometer was climbing to a hundred again. She took a swipe at her eyes. Tears all right. But she had seen the speedometer and slowed down.

And then she clamped shut again, white faced, lip quivering. She looked like she might start screaming or something. Then she was gone again, stony eyed, into the miles.

After a while, I put the book away, opened the flask of Johnnie Walker I'd bought back somewhere in Texas, and took a little taste. I couldn't read anymore.

Just after Baton Rouge, she said: "Where's your passport? Have you got it with you?"

"No, it's in the room in New Orleans," I said.

"Damn," she said.

"And yours?"

"I have mine."

"Well, hell, we can get mine," I said. "We could check out and go to the airport and take the first plane to anyplace."

She flashed her big round brown eyes on me for so long I reached out to steady the wheel.

It was just before dark when we were barreling through the narrow streets of the French Quarter, and she was telling the driver over the phone in the car to wake up.

We got out of the car, mussed-up, tired, hungry, with a bunch of tacky paper bags full of junk, and started into the flagstone carriageway of the little hotel.

She turned around before we got to the desk.

"You wanna do it?" she said.

"You bet I want to do it," I said.

I looked at her for a second, her white face, the pure fear in her eyes. I wanted to say what are we running from? Why does it have to be like this? Tell me you love me, goddamn it, Lisa. Let's get it all out!

"Lots of phone messages for you all," said the lady at the desk.

I wanted to say all that and more to her, but I didn't. I knew I'd settle for it on any terms she laid down.

"Go in there, get your passport," she whispered. Her fingers were actually biting in my flesh of my arm. "I'll wait for you in the car. Come right back out."

"And company too for you all," said the woman. She craned her neck to look through the glass doors into the yard. "Two gentlemen still waiting for you all. Been waiting all day."

Lisa spun around and glared through the doors.

Richard, that tall Master of Postulants, was standing there in the little garden watching us with his back to the doors of the cottage. And Scott, the unforgettable Trainer of Trainers, was just getting up and crushing out his cigarette.

Elliott
28

The Walls of Jericho

THEY WERE BOTH dressed in dark suits, rather somber and immaculate, and they greeted us very courteously, if not downright cheerfully, as we crossed the yard and went into the cottage and turned on the lights.

Everything was orderly and cool and normal-seeming except that they had been in the cottage, obviously, and the rooms were still full of cigarette smell. There was something perfectly sinister about it, about them being here at all.

Richard, bushy browed and smiling, looked enormous, which to be more specific means he was still a couple of inches taller than me. Scott, a shorter and much more graceful man, looked equally as physically powerful under the Madison Avenue drag.

I realized I was sizing them up.

Lisa was really shaking now. And she did this very peculiar thing of walking all the way across the bedroom and standing against the wall. This was something like a hysterical action. And I realized I was really rattled myself as I nodded to them both and took the sack of junk we had with us into the other room.

Actually I wanted to see if there was anyone in the bath or th
kitchen. There was not.

Scott, who was rather fantastic looking in the slim-fitting blac
suit, came slowly into the kitchen—all of their movements an
gestures were calculated to put somebody at ease, it seemed—an
told me they would like to speak to Lisa alone. There was a
obvious anguish in his face. He looked at me and I wondered if h
was thinking what I was thinking, that the last time he'd seen m
we'd been playing master and slave for an audience of twent
novice trainers in his class.

I did not really want to think of that at this moment. But
could feel it, like somebody had just opened the oven door an
the oven was on full blast. He was one of those men who looks al
the more like an animal when he gets dressed up.

"We just have to talk to her for a little while alone," he said i
a low, almost purring chest voice.

"Well, sure, of course," I said.

He put his left hand on my neck and gave it a soft pressure
and he smiled, a flash of agreeable dark eyes and white teeth, an
went back into the other room.

I went out of the kitchen into the courtyard and I sat down o
the wrought iron bench that was farthest from the rooms.

But I knew that Lisa could see me where I was sitting. Ther
were lights scattered around this little garden, which had jus
come on with the slow deepening of the evening, and I was sittin
in the light. I put my foot up on the bench, and I lit a cigarette.
wished I had brought out the bottle of Scotch.

But really it was better not to drink. I could see them throug
the lighted french windows, against the backdrop of the rose
colored walls and the immense four-poster bed and the antiqu
mahogany chairs, and the two men in their black suits were talking to Lisa, walking back and forth and gesturing and she wa
sitting in the rocking chair holding the backs of her arms. All o
them in black, curious, the way that they stood out, and the ligh
of the lamp skittering on her blackish-brown hair.

I couldn't hear anything because of the goddamned air conditioner, but I could see that Lisa was getting more and more upset
Finally she was on her feet and she was pointing her finger at
Richard, and Richard had his hands up as if her finger was a
loaded gun. That perpetual smile had left his mouth, but his eyes

were still crinkled as if he was smiling. But deep-set eyes like his with bushy eyebrows often look like that.

Then she was screaming and the tears were sliding down her face. I could see the veins standing out in her neck, and her face was twisted, and even her legs stretched by the high stiletto heels were taut and shaking. She looked like she was all wires.

I couldn't stand this much longer.

I crushed out the cigarette and stood up, facing the doors. Lisa was pacing the floor and tossing her long hair back and really shouting. Still I couldn't hear the words that were exchanged. It looked to me like Scott had told Richard to back off and Scott was taking over. Lisa was calming down. Scott was moving about with that feline fluidity, palm up as he gestured. She was listening and she was nodding, and then it seemed she saw me through the glass door. We were just staring at each other through the glass.

Scott turned and he looked at me. And I just stood there, waiting, not willing to turn around or walk off.

He came over to the window and, gesturing for my patience, he started to pull the drapes.

I went to the door and opened it.

"No, man, I'm sorry," I said, shaking my head. "Can't do that."

"We're just talking, Elliott," Scott said. "You're kind of a distraction out there. And it's very important that we have this talk."

Lisa, who had sat down in the rocker with her knees drawn up, wiping her nose with a linen handkerchief, looked up and said softly. "It's okay, Elliott. Believe me. It's okay. Go into the bar and have a drink. It's okay."

"Well, let's get some things straight before I do," I said. "I don't know what's happening, but nobody is going to force anybody . . ."

"Elliott, we don't do that kind of thing," Scott said. "We don't force people to do anything at all. Now, you know who we are." He looked just a little injured and painfully sincere. His black eyes were easily expressive, and his mouth moved into a similar easy and somewhat sad smile. "But there is something here at stake that is very important to us. We have to talk to Lisa about this."

"It's okay, Elliott," she said, "really it is. I'll call you in the bar. I want you to go. Would you do that because I ask?"

It was the longest forty-five minutes I ever spent. I really had to remind myself every thirty seconds that I didn't want to get drunk. Otherwise I would have been gulping the damn Scotch. Everything that had happened was going off like firecrackers in my brain. Through the open door I could see a slice of French Quarter street, a long rose-wreath wrought iron railing on a gallery over the narrow sidewalk, couples walking arm in arm past the gaslights of a restaurant door. I kept looking at this as though it meant something, the dark green of the shuttered doors, the flickering light.

Finally Scott came gliding in. The human panther, with a sleek head of curly black hair, eyes quickly scanning the place.

"Let's have *our* talk now, Elliott," he said. Hand on the back of the neck again, hot silky fingers. Everybody at The Club has hot silky fingers, I thought.

Richard was waiting in the room, and he explained that Lisa was in the kitchen and it was our turn to talk now. Those stiletto heels of hers, the rhinestone straps glittering, were lying on the rug. Like the slipper on the floor of her bedroom that first time. Icepick right through the head.

I sat down in the armchair. Scott was in a little straight-back chair by the secretaire. Richard, with his hands in his pockets, leaned against the post of the bed.

"Elliott, I want to ask you a few questions," Richard said. Face pleasant, manner a lot like Martin's, deep-set eyes cheerful, smile a little tight.

Scott seemed lost in his own thoughts.

"Were you happy at The Club before you left? I mean were things popping, were they working out?"

"I don't really want to talk like this without Lisa," I said.

He shook his head, just a touch of impatience.

"We can't solve this, Elliott, unless you come straight with us. We have to know what's going on. Now, from all our reports, and we're awfully good judges in these situations, you were doing beautifully at The Club. We were both getting our money's worth." Narrow eyes. Pause that said Let's hear you contradict that.

"Now when a slave gets to The Club, Elliott, I mean before anything happens, if a slave gets as far as The Club grounds, Elliott, that slave is pretty deep into S&M. I mean he knows a lot about his sexuality and what he wants. I mean you don't wind up

ull time at The Club because you had a weird weekend in the
Castro District of San Francisco with a kinky friend."

I nodded.

"I mean you have an individual that is not only interested in
acting out his fantasies, but one who is committed to living them
in a very intense way for a long period of time."

Again I nodded. Where was Lisa? Was she in the other room? I
did not hear a sound. I shifted uneasily in the chair. I asked very
politely, "Would you get the point?"

"I am getting to it," he said. "What I am trying to say is the
experience of The Club usually means a great deal to the slave or
he or she would not be there. I mean we are not some run-of-the-
mill whorehouse in . . ."

"Believe me," I said, "we are in total concurrence on this.
There is no need to go on."

"All right. Now what I am going to tell you is going to sound
harsh, but you have to understand why I'm saying it and I want
you to keep quiet until I speak my peace. If you do not leave and
come back with us now on the plane of your free will—and I
assure you no one is going to lay a hand on you to try to force
you to do that—you will be blackballed utterly and entirely and
forever from The Club. You will never see The Club again, as a
slave there, or a member, or an employee on any level, at all."

Pause. Slow breath. Voice a shade calmer, slower as he went
on.

"You will be blackballed from every place like The Club with
whom we have connections around the world. You will be blackballed from the houses of the trainers who sell to us as well. That
includes Martin Halifax. He will never let you in the front door
because if he does, we won't deal with him ever again, and Martin will not risk that.

"Now, what that means, Elliott, is that for the rest of your life
you will remember this remarkably intense experience that you
had. But you will never be allowed to have it again. As The Club
gets bigger, as it branches out, as more clubs open, you will read
about them but you will never be allowed in. I ask you to think
about that."

I didn't nod or say anything.

Again he said: "I ask you to think about that. I ask you to
think about your sexual history, your background, how you came
to us. I ask you to think about all the preparation you went

through for the moment that you docked at our gates. I want you to think about what you were expecting, what you had a right to expect before Lisa took you out. You don't have to answer me at this moment. But just think about what I have said."

"I think there is something here that you don't understand," I said. "And if you'd let me talk to Lisa—"

"You're going to have to forget about Lisa for a moment, Elliott," Richard said. "This is between us. We are giving you a choice . . ."

"But that's what I don't understand." I stood up. "Are you trying to tell me that Lisa is out of The Club, that Lisa's been fired from The Club!" I knew I sounded angry, belligerent. I tried not to. I tried to calm down.

"No, Lisa has *not* been fired," he said. "Lisa is in a category unto herself. And if there are any allowances to be made, they will be made for Lisa."

"Well, then, what's this about?" I was getting even more angry and quite suddenly I was getting angry with her. What had she told them? I was trying to protect her and I didn't even know what she had told them.

"It was my understanding," I said, "that she explained to you the circumstances under which I left. You're talking to me like I broke out or something. And you won't let me talk to her to find out what she'd told you. I don't understand what's going down . . ."

"She can't help you now, Elliott," Scott spoke up.

"What do you mean, help me?"

"Elliott," Scott said in a matter of fact way, rising and taking a couple of steps in front of me, "Lisa has cracked."

The word set up an immediate jarring vibration in my head.

"At The Club," Scott said, "we have our own meaning for the word cracked."

He glanced at Richard. Richard was watching him.

"It doesn't mean that somebody has gone crazy," Scott continued, "lost their marbles, anything like that. It means that somebody cannot function in our environment anymore. And to be absolutely candid, it rarely happens to staff members. When it happens, it happens to slaves. I'm not talking about ordinary resistance, anxiousness, cold feet. We know those symptoms when we see them in all their variety, but now and then a slave really cracks. He just stands up and says in his own way, 'Guess

what, fellas, I can't do this anymore,' and we know how to recognize it when it happens for just what it is. And it is useless to
. . ."

Richard suddenly put up his hand. He made a little gesture at Scott that was perfectly eloquent of "There is no point to telling him all this."

"I understand," I said. "This was bound to be part of it and you just don't tell all the slaves this or as soon as the going gets rough . . ."

"Exactly," Scott answered. "And this is very definitely related to what concerns us here. When you come to The Club you are told there is no escape, no release, no chickening out. That is part of the contract you sign to give us your services in a very special arena of human behavior. But it is also part of our guarantee to you: that you will not be allowed to have second thoughts, that you will not be allowed to get out. Now the reasons for this are obvious, Elliott. If you do not know that your incarceration is absolute, *then you cannot relax and enjoy what is going on.* You are going to start thinking: 'What I'm doing really feels great, but I feel stupid doing this! What if my Aunt Margaret saw me in these harnesses and chains? Golly, this is great but I better get out of here. I haven't got the nerve for this.' Guilt would do that to you, Elliott, self-consciousness, the natural ambivalences to which we're all prone. But when you're incarcerated and there is no alternative, then you can really experience the interplay of dominance and subservience that is The Club. And it is absolutely imperative that no escape be possible, or contemplated or dreamed of. Which is why you must come back to The Club."

He paused, glancing at Richard.

"Elliott, every trainer and handler on the island knows about you and Lisa," Richard said. His voice was a little tireder than Scott's. "They knew Lisa had busted you out before we knew it. And I have little doubt that a good many of the slaves know it too. Now, we cannot allow this to happen, Elliott, and I think we have explained enough. We cannot have people bolting, breaking contracts, blowing to smithereens the most fundamental and important agreements of The Club. The Club works like a Swiss watch, Elliott, it is that regular, that complicated, that precise."

I looked at both of them. I understood what they were saying about all of this. There wasn't any argument, no need for questions. I had understood before I ever got on the yacht.

"But you're saying," I asked, glancing slowly from one face to the other, "that Lisa is *not* going back to The Club."

"She refuses to go back," Scott said.

I stared at him for a long moment.

"I have to talk to her," I said. I started for the kitchen door.

Scott approached very cautiously, and put his hand out for me to wait.

"I want you to think about all this. I want you to take your time," he said.

"Gotcha," I said and I tried to guide him to the side.

"Wait."

We looked at each other for a couple of seconds.

"It's no fun being excluded by any group of people, Elliott," he said. "But think about who we are, and who you are. I am not lying when I tell you you will never know anywhere else what you knew with us. And don't think that we can't make the exclusion stick."

"Some things might be worth that," I said.

Richard moved between me and the kitchen door.

"Elliott, this had to be arbitrary. The fabric has been ripped, dangerously ripped, and it's got to be restored."

"Would you get out of the way?"

"There's one thing more," Scott said, motioning for Richard to back off. "And this is pretty important. We should get it straight now."

He slipped his left arm behind my back, and he was exerting that same gentle pressure as before. His black eyes were fairly calm, and when he continued, his voice was low again, caressing, very much the way it had been in the trainers' class.

"Nobody's going to get rough with you, Elliott," he said. There was nothing mocking or ironic in his tone. "Nobody's going to force you into anything really heavy when we get back. We're going to reindoctrinate and we'll do it as slowly as the situation requires. You can rest for a week, live like one of the guests on the island, full privileges, as long as it's on the q.t. After that we proceed at your pace."

He was very close to me and he moved just a little closer until our bodies were touching, that hand steady still against my back.

"If you want my opinion, when you finally see the landing strip on the island, you'll feel considerable relief. And then something else, something really nice, is going to happen in your head. But if you don't feel that, we'll go very slow. We're experts at this, Elliott. It's going to be good, I promise you. I'm going to see to that."

I could feel the electricity coming from him, the energy that underlay his manner, the sharp sincerity of the look on his face. I think some acknowledgment passed between us then, something much darker and simpler than a smile, a slow silent concurrence, without irony or humor, that the statement had its charms. I felt power coming from him, and confidence in that power, and there was a powerful, seductive intimacy to the manner in which he spoke again.

"You're worth it to us, Elliott, whatever time and effort it takes. This isn't bullshit. I am talking business now, plain and simple, and you know what our business is."

"The important thing," Richard said, "is that you come back on the plane with us now."

"Got you loud and clear," I said. "Now, please, get out of the way.

But the kitchen door opened before either of them could move, and Lisa was standing there, in the light from the bedroom against a darkened room, with her hand on the knob. One strap of her dress had fallen down over her shoulder. Her hair was tangled and lifeless as though the whole shape of it depended somehow on the condition of her soul. She was barefoot and she looked broken and ragged in the beautiful little black dress. Her face was red and streaked from crying and her mascara was smudged, but she wasn't crying now.

"I want you to go back with them, Elliott," she said. "They are right in everything they're saying and the important thing is for you to back now."

I looked at her for a long moment and then I turned and glanced at the two men. I felt like I was swallowing a rock.

"Go outside," I said.

There was a moment of hesitation, then Scott gestured for Richard to follow him and they went outside into the yard.

Angrily, quickly, I pulled the drapes over the windows, and when I turned around, she was still standing in the door.

I stood staring at her across the room, my back to the door as though as long as I stood there, they couldn't get back in.

For a moment I was too upset—call it anger, call it hurt, call it confusion—to speak. Then I said, "You are telling me you want me to go back?"

She looked amazingly calm now, as though my anger was calming her. But her teeth bit into her lower lip a little just for an instant as if she was going to cry.

"Talk to me, Lisa!" I said. "Are you telling me you want me to go back!" My voice was incredibly loud.

She didn't move, but she seemed somehow to get smaller, to be clinging, without even moving as she stood at the door. She started forward, blinking a little, as if the volume of my voice had hurt her.

I tried to get calmer. "Is that what you are saying?" I couldn't help shouting. "That you want me to go back?"

"Yes," she said, her mouth twisting. "I think it is absolutely mandatory that you go back." She looked up and her eyes got steady now. "I broke a contract with you, Elliott," she said, her voice getting lower as if she was swallowing. "I fucked up something very important to you. Now I want you to go back to The Club and let Scott and Richard have a chance to mend the damage that I have done."

"I don't believe you!" I whispered. "Important hell!" I moved towards her, but I didn't trust myself to touch her. "Now, that is not everything that you want, not everything that you feel! Don't do this to me, Lisa! Don't do this!" I was really shouting again.

"It is exactly what I want and what I feel," she said. Her lips were trembling. She was about to break.

"Don't cry again," I said. "Don't dare! Don't cry, Lisa," I said. These weren't words, they were sputtering noises. I was moving back and forth and I knew I was going right over the top. I was going to hit something. I stopped in front of her, just about as close to her as I trusted myself to be. I dropped my voice, and I bent close to her until I was staring right into her eyes. What I had to say wasn't for anybody listening at the door, if it mattered now.

"Lisa, how many times have I told you how I feel about you? I've copped to everything inside me from the start. I love you, Lisa, are you listening to me! I have never said that to any woman or man in my life before. Now, you look at me and you talk to me! And don't tell me that you want me to go back to the goddamned Club! Fuck the goddamned Club!"

It was like looking at someone who was frozen, somebody

playing that kid's game of statues where you have to stand absolutely still. A waifish, black-eyed, barefoot woman just staring at me, her wet eyes smeared with black mascara, mouth frozen with lips apart.

"What did this mean to you, Lisa?" I was clenching my teeth so hard I was hurting myself. And I could hear my voice breaking up. I could hear myself imploring. "Lisa, come straight with me. *Come straight!* If you can tell me that you just cracked, that you just fucking cracked and I was just part of it, if you can say that, that I was just an escape route, then say it out loud to me now!"

I couldn't go on. I couldn't speak anymore, and that awful feeling came back to me right out of the long night of drunkenness of telling her that she was going to hurt me, that she was going to do it, and the awful realization that it was happening now.

"Oh, Jesus Christ, oh, God," I was cursing, muttering. I was walking in a circle, and then I went for her, catching her as she backed into the dark kitchen, and holding her by the arms. "Tell me you don't love me, Lisa!" I was roaring at her. "If you can't say you do, then say you don't. Say you don't. Say you don't. Say you don't. Tell me that!"

I pulled her towards me, and with all her strength, it seemed, she tried to pull back. She had her eyes shut, and her hair was in her eyes and she was gasping, choking, as if I had my fingers around her throat. I didn't. I was just holding her arms.

"Scott!" she shouted suddenly. "Scotty!" And she jerked away as I let her go. "Scotty!" she screamed.

She caved in onto one of the kitchen chairs, heaving, dry sobs coming out of her, her hair hanging down in front of her face.

Scott and Richard were in the room, and Richard went around me, with a darting motion and came up behind her shoulder and asked her very softly if she was all right.

The very sight of him bending over her, the solicitous sound of his voice, made me go right out of my head.

I didn't do anything. I just turned and I went out of the room. I was in a blind rage. I wasn't walking on the same earth with anybody else. I could have knocked a brick wall down with one blow. That she could call out for that guy, that she could call out like I was hurting her!

The next thing I knew I was sitting in the courtyard on the

little wrought iron bench and I had somehow managed to light a cigarette and I was staring at the dark glossy tangle of the little overgrown yard. My face was pumping with heat. I couldn't hear anything. I was deliberately memorizing the fountain, the broken-down little cherub in it, the conch and the slimy water, and the choke of spiderwebs in the cherub's eye. I don't know whether they were talking to me or not.

But a long time passed, maybe twenty minutes or so. My heartbeat was pretty regular again. And I was so miserable and getting so much more miserable by the moment that I thought I was going to break. I was going to go to pieces or something.

I mean like I might really, really hurt somebody. These geniuses of pain, for instance, these clever, sophisticated masters of The Club. These guys! These fucking bastards! I swallowed it over and over. And then I heard someone coming out of the room, and I looked up and saw it was Scott, the guardian angel.

"Come inside," he said. You would have thought somebody had just died and I was the chief mourner, and he was the undertaker. And here I was ready to commit murder. "She wants to talk to you. She has something to say."

She was sitting in the rocker again with the linen handkerchief in her hand. She had for reasons utterly unbeknownst to me put on her shoes. And Richard was standing behind her like another guardian angel, and Scott hovered around me like I might all of a sudden take a poke at somebody. I might.

"I don't blame you for being mad, Elliott," she said.

"Save it, lady," I said. "Don't say anything else like that."

She winced like I'd hit her right between the eyes. I couldn't stand looking at the way she bowed her head. But she looked at me again, very straight, right through a fresh film of tears.

"Elliott, I'm begging you to go back," she said. "I'm begging you for my sake to go back to The Club and wait there for me."

Tears sliding down her face, quavering voice.

"I'm begging you to go back," she said again, "and wait for me just a couple of days till I . . . till I come."

I hadn't expected this. I looked at Richard. A model of candor and compassion. And Scott, who had slipped in along the wall behind me, just watching her with his head lowered and to the side, rather sad.

"They won't make you do anything, Elliott. They won't, you know . . . nothing."

"Absolutely correct," Scott said under his breath.

"Just let everyone see you get off the plane," Richard said. "And it's your choice what you want to do after that."

"Elliott," she said, "I promise you I will be back." Her mouth was working again, twisting the lower lip pressed between her teeth. "I just need those days. I need them alone to understand why I cracked, why I did this. But I promise you that I will come back. Whatever you think about this, I will be back and you can tell me. You can tell me just what you think I deserve to be told. And if you want to leave The Club then, it can be arranged properly and officially for you to leave."

I glanced at Richard, and he nodded.

"Just cooperate a little with us," Scott said.

"I'm begging you," she said. "Will you do it for me?"

I didn't answer for a minute. It seemed like it was crucial to wait that one moment, just looking at her, the little wet-faced, straggle-haired waif, shoes or no shoes, with the rhinestone straps fallen down off her ankles, as she huddled, knees bare, dress all messed up, on the edge of the chair.

"Are you absolutely sure," I asked as quietly as I could, "that you want me to leave you here?"

"Believe me, Elliott," she said in the same tremulous voice, her eyes black and glistening. "It is the *only* thing I want."

For a second I couldn't breathe.

I was so hurt and the pain was so pure that I guess my face was blank. The pain felt like a mask that was spreading and tightening over my face. I didn't look at the other men, but I knew that Richard was looking at me, and that Scott had respectfully bowed his head and moved closer to the door.

There was an astonishing innocence to her expression, her large eyes so beautiful even with the smudges of mascara and so tired.

The mask of pain was getting tighter and tighter. I could feel it pull at every tissue, feel it close over my throat. But gradually it broke and it melted, and I felt like something was being comfortably, miraculously drained away.

"It's just like everything else you've said and done," I said to her. "It could mean at least two different things!"

We looked at each other, and I could have sworn something happened, some little private thing. Maybe that her eyes softened, that it was just the two of us for one split second, or maybe it was only that I had caught her off guard with some little idea she didn't expect.

When she spoke again now, she had to take her time and the tears rose up in her eyes.

"My life's falling to pieces, Elliott," she said in a near whisper. "It's just coming down around me like the walls of Jericho. I need you to go back and wait for me to come."

Richard and Scott both took that as a cue. Richard bent down and kissed her on the cheek, and Scott was gently pushing me towards the door.

I stepped out into the garden, a little baffled that I was doing it, and I stood there looking at nothing, thinking nothing, hearing Richard talking to her behind me, something cold and reserved in the tone:

"Now are you certain that you . . ."

"I will be all right," she said, wearily, in an almost sing-song voice. "If you will just go. I promise you. I won't leave this hotel. I'll plug in the phone. I'll be here. Station one of the goons out there, but tell him to stay out of sight. Just let me have what I need right now."

"Very well, my dear. You call us day or night."

I was staring at the distant glass doors to the front hall of the hotel. The soft heat of the night was pulsing with the sounds of the katydids. The sky had a violet light to it still in a sharp rectangle formed by the high brick walls.

"Look, this is going to work out," Scott said. He looked perfectly miserable for what it was worth.

"Leaving her here like this?" I demanded.

"We have a man watching her. He's in the bar. She's going to be okay."

"Are you sure about that?" I asked.

"Listen, man, this is what she wants," Scott said. "She's okay, I know her."

You know her.

I took a few steps away from him across the flags. I lit another cigarette. Private gesture that, lowering your head, cupping your hands around the flame. Just for a second blow them all way.

Richard had come out and he appeared beside me, glancing back at her furtively as he spoke under his breath.

"You're doing exactly the right thing," he said.

"Back off, asshole," I said.

"You love this woman?" he asked, deep-set eyes narrowing, voice like ice. "You want to ruin everything for her? She won't come back to The Club unless you're waiting for her there."

"Play this one out with us, Elliott," Scott said, "for her sake."

"You guys have got everything figured, haven't you?"

I turned around and looked back at her. She had risen and come towards the french door, her ankles unsteady in the perilous shoes. She had her arms folded, and she looked shattered, absolutely broken to bits.

I stamped out the cigarette on the stones, and pointed my finger at her.

"In a couple of days," I said.

She nodded.

"I won't break my word," she said.

I wanted to tell her coldly and calmly that I didn't care whether or not she ever came back. I wanted to call her every bad name for a woman I knew, every snarling bad name in every language that I had ever heard. But she wasn't all those names to me. She was Lisa. And the one lie she had told, she had admitted to that first morning at the Court of Two Sisters. And there had never been any lies from her after that, or any promises, or any commitments of any kind.

Yet I had the feeling of something so vital and so precious being destroyed, something so extraordinary and so crucial, that I couldn't even look into her face anymore. It was like some door had opened, and the horror that had always been behind the door, the awful thing I'd feared all my life was finally standing there.

Lisa

29

Visit to Church

All we are asking is that you explain it to us, that you let us try to understand. How could you do it?

It was a dump, a hole, joint, any name you can think of for a seedy tourist trap built like an alleyway with a bench down one wall for the customers, and the stage a garishly lighted strip behind the bar opposite.

And a man who looked exactly like a giant of a woman was dancing, if you could call it that, or more truly shuffling back and forth in satin mules, the light flickering on her white satin gown, her heavily made-up cheeks, the spun glass of her white wig, her vapid unfocused eyes. She/he was watching herself in the mirror, dancing with herself, mouthing the words to herself of the recorded song as it crackled through the speakers, a dreary leakage of rhythmic sound, the silver boa shivering over her smooth and powerful arms, her whole appearance strangely, undeniably sensuous as it was manufactured, beautiful as it was ghastly.

To me anyway. You are all angels. You have transcended everything into the pure theater of yourselves. I am worshipping.

I mean, you are the mentor, the guardian angel of this whole system, and you tell me not to ask you any questions!

I sat motionless against the wall, watching her, the heavy, almost lumbering steps of her big feet, dime-store pink of her waxed mouth, dull, straight-ahead stare beneath fringe of false lashes. Reek of urine from the little bathroom just beyond the filthy red velvet curtain. Stench of dirty carpet, damp, mildewed on the narrow floor. Faint sweet stink of pancake makeup, dirty costume. Like the giant marble angels in church who hold out the shells full of holy water for us to dip our fingers. Larger and smoother than life, undeniably perfect creatures.

It had been hours that I'd been sitting here.

How could you do it to him, to him, I mean whatever the reason? Play games with him like this? What do you think this guy is that you can manipulate him, use him like this? You are the one who taught us to never, never underestimate the psychological dynamite we are dealing with.

Two hundred-dollar bills to keep the place open. Ten, eleven, twelve rip-off seven-ounce nightclub bottles of beer, Bourbon Street almost empty outside, and only one other person in The Club, I mean this dump, not the club, this hole, this dive, this alleyway, this chapel of the perverse, this catacomb, an emaciated man hunched over his drink at the end of the bar, checkered jacket. *How could you do it?*

Now and then the barker came in. Nobody bothered me.

One female/male after another gliding back and forth on the tinseled strip over the rows and rows of dimly lighted bottles, bare shoulders, sleek pink arms, hint of cleavage under the dirty strip of sequined satin, shoes down at the heel, high sheen of artificial estrogen all over.

Like what is this guy supposed to do now? Like he gets ready for the sensuous experience of a lifetime and you up and yank him out of it? You unilaterally decide that you will bring down the curtain? I want to be understanding, but how much understanding would I have gotten from you if I had done it, if I had up and taken Diana or Kitty Kantwell or any one of them out like this? Do you think you would have flown a thousand miles to talk it over with me, Miss Perfectionist?

I was no longer at all certain that I could walk back. I had to stop and think to remember where it was, a map I drew in my mind. Like two blocks that way and then this way. And what about the goon they have hiding out there somewhere, would he appear if I fell on my face in the street? *It's not a matter of the expense, or the talk on the island. Think of this man and what you have done to him. What the hell are we going to say to Martin? Martin sent him to us.*

I got up to see whether or not I could walk, and then I was standing on the sidewalk and asking the barker where I could find a phone. I looked down and I saw the most peculiar thing, that I was wearing those ugly, tacky thong sandals we'd bought in the discount store. Elliott looked terrific in the safari shorts and the white shirt and the white tennis shoes.

What we are asking is why? Why did you do it? What we are asking is that you just come back, now, that you get on the plane, help us to get him back, sit down and talk this thing over . . .

I was out in the street in these awful sandals, and I had some sort of raincoat on, some burgundy-colored poncho raincoat that I vaguely remembered getting in San Francisco at a store on Castro Street called the All American Boy with my sister saying, "I don't care, being right in the middle of them makes me nervous." She meant the homosexuals. She should see these angels, my angels. It was too heavy for New Orleans, this raincoat, even on this spring night when it was not hot, it was as Elliott had said, sublime, but I remembered now why I was wearing it. I didn't have anything on under it.

When I had started to throw up, I had torn off that lovely dress, my favorite dress, my very best favorite dress. I had ruined that dress and it was the dress I'd worn when we went dancing, and when we made love in the back of the car, and when we slept on top of the sheets at the Monteleone together, and when we drove back.

That dress was just gone forever, ripped up and ruined forever on the bathroom floor. When I had gotten up off the bed I had thought, I will simply put this on, this poncho. This is fine. I did have the cotton slip on under it.

And no underwear, that secret naked feeling of no underwear. It doesn't matter. All opened up by love, that wonderful naked feeling of no covering there.

You owe him that, you owe us that. Get on the plane with him now. God, that is the least you can do! Come with us.

So I was standing on Bourbon Street and I was drunk, and I was in this burgundy-colored rain poncho with nothing but a slip on under it. I had money in my pockets, too much money. I had hundred-dollar bills and coins and coins. I had given out the bills the way Elliott did it, folding the bill in half and just slipping it to the person, making no big deal of it, smiling, and that was all. And one of those girl/men, the big beautiful brunette with the voice stuck right in the top of her throat like the throb of a kid's toy electric organ, had sat down by me and called me honey and talked to me. Pink and sleek, like an angel or a giant seal, depending . . .

. . . Doesn't anything mean anything to you? Do you know what you are jeopardizing if you do not come back with us?

They were all of them having operations, the girls. The angels. They did it piece by piece. She had her balls still, tucked up someplace into her body, and her penis all bound down so that it wouldn't show when she stripped down to the G-string, and she had breasts and the estrogen injections.

She knew she was beautiful, that she looked like some lovely Mexican woman who knows she's prettier and smarter than all her sisters and brothers, the one who gets the job as the hostess in the roadside restaurant so that she wears the low-cut black dress with the cleavage showing and gives out the menus while all the rest of them are working as cooks and busboys, that kind of beauty, the Miss Universe of the pots and pans. *Look, we're trying to understand, we're trying.* Castration for this?

"You don't really let them, I mean, they won't cut off your balls, will they?"

"Honey, we don't think those things are very ladylike!"

He said, "There's the phone."

"What did you say?"

"The phone, honey. Honey—" (confidential, like we'd just fallen in love, slimeball) "—is there somebody who can come down here and meet you?"

Well, what do you call it then, if not flat-out victimization? You took advantage, you just took total advantage of your position and your power. You want to hear the truth, you acted like a god-damned stereotypical, selfish, and emotional woman.

"What time is it?"

"Two o'clock." He looks at his cheap watch. Two o'clock in the morning. Elliott gone now exactly seven hours. We could have been to Mexico by now. And headed for Panama. Bypassing El Salvador.

What do you think is going on in his head right now? Two years he absents himself from his business, his career, his life, and the boss lady wants a fucking five-day fling in New Orleans?

"Honey, we're closing now."

Go ahead and close up the Dreamgirls Club. See if I care. Crackly music playing to the empty stage behind the bottles. Now they all grow white satin sequined wings and they fly out the back door and up into the dark damp sky over the rooftops of New Orleans and they are gone out of the squalor of the chapel forever. (Though in the distance and under cover of night they do look to mortals remarkably like giant flying roaches.) Mirrors reflecting the empty rows of benches and tables where I had just been sitting at the very end, unbothered, by myself. The street full of garbage, enormous, glistening, green-plastic sacks of garbage. Roaches. Don't think of roaches.

Reek of Chinese food from the booth, a couple walking together, girl in white shorts and halter and man in short-sleeve shirt, drinking beer out of big paper milk-carton-type containers. Lots of beer. Get some beer, enough to really swallow. Beer would taste wonderful. Miller's beer. Elliott says the best American beer is Miller's, best foreign Heineken's, best worldwide Haitian. Wake up Elliott and we'll drive all night and in the morning we will be in Mexico. If only he had had that passport. We could be in New York by now, waiting on a flight to Rome. They could never have caught us.

It's the inconsideration of it I don't understand, it is the betrayal of the trust, the absolute disregard for the delicate mechanism, the degree of vulnerability, the . . . STOP IT!

Then on from Rome to Venice. There is no city on earth for walking like Venice. And relatively small roaches.

"Where is a phone? Can you tell me where I can find a phone?"

Open corner bar. Not the same bar. Yes, the same bar. The same bar where we had the argument about *Pretty Baby*. The same bar where we drank the Scotch and the gin before we went to Michael's and Elliott said . . . everything that Elliott said.

Taste of Elliott, feel of Elliott's turtleneck pulled tight across Elliott's chest. Elliott's mouth, Elliott smiling, blue eyes, hair full of rain, Elliott smiling. Kiss of Elliott.

"Right there, honey."

("She's really drunk." "She's okay. She's okay.") Nooooo, she's not!

I put the quarters in the phone, one after the other, one after the other. I do not believe actually that it's necessary to put this many quarters in at the outset. Very brief lapse of memory. Focus. Probably you put in one quarter and wait for the operator. The truth is I haven't made a call from a pay phone since . . . three days ago? If after seven years it's the same phone number, but why wouldn't it be the same phone number, nothing has changed, nothing has moved. Phone ringing in San Francisco. It is two o'clock here, well it will only be twelve o'clock there. And at twelve o'clock Martin Halifax is never sleeping.

A man in a really appalling polyester suit has come out of the bar. Straw hat, sheer white shirt thinly concealing undershirt, Shriner on convention from Atlanta. Oh, the things we make up about people whose clothes we don't like. But he looks a little too neat, everything being pressed, for a native.

Ah, but there he is by the lamppost, the Club goon, and how do I know? He's the only guy on Bourbon Street at two o'clock in the morning with the million-dollar tan, the straight white teeth and the designer jeans and the pink tennis shoes! We don't hire slobs, do we? (Ringing in San Francisco.) Not people who go around in ponchos and thong sandals with no underwear on.

"Hello."

"Martin!"

"Yes, this is Martin. Who's is this?"

"Can you hear me all right? Martin, you have to help me. Martin, I need you." *(Martin will have to know about this. Martin sent him here. What the hell are we going to say to Martin? She just up and kidnapped Elliott Slater!)* "Martin, I need you like I never needed you before. I have to talk to you."

"Is this Lisa? Lisa, where are you?"

"I'm in New Orleans, Martin. I'm on Bourbon Street, and I'm wearing this rain-poncho and these sandals. And it's two o'clock. Martin, help me please. Please come. I'll cover it, every penny of it, expense is no object, could you just get on the next plane and could you come? Martin, I know what I am asking. I know what I am asking. That I am asking you to drop everything and fly two thousand miles to help me. I'm not going to make it through this one, Martin. Will you come?"

"Have you got a room in New Orleans, Lisa? Can you tell me exactly where you are?"

"The Marie Laveau court, Rue Saint Anne, the cab driver will know it. I'm in the servants' quarters suite in back under the name Mrs. Elliott Slater. Will you come?"

"Mrs. Elliott Slater?"

"I did this terrible thing, Martin, I did it to Elliott Slater. I betrayed everything, Martin. Everything we believe in. I need you so badly. Please help me."

"Lisa, I'll be there as soon as I can possibly get there. I'll call the airport now, and I want you to go directly back to the hotel, Lisa. Do you think that you can manage to get a cab? I can have people come pick you up where you are . . ."

"I can make it that far, Martin. I made it that far a week ago. I can make it again." And there is that goon standing there, that bright shiny muscular goon with the white teeth and the shirt unbuttoned down the front, and the tight jeans over his hips, and his cock shoved up in front under the jeans so that he looks like he's got a hard on when he hasn't. I have just dropped the entire contents of my purse. No I haven't. I don't have a purse. I just dropped several quarters. He is picking up the quarters. Fine strapling of a youth.

"Go back to the hotel and go to sleep. And I'll be there as soon as I can, I promise. I'll be there before you wake up, if I can manage it."

"I did a terrible thing, Martin. I did it to Elliott Slater. I don't know why I did it."

"I'm on my way, Lisa."

The man in the polyester suit was standing right up against the glass of the phone booth. The goon was nearby counting the quarters. He has to be from The Club. What perfect stranger in designer jeans would steal a woman's quarters?

"You sure are a pretty little girl, you know that? You just about the prettiest little girl I've seen in this town all night." Nice man. Like the man who sells your parents a vacuum cleaner or mortgage insurance.

Table in the bar to sit down. No. Don't go to the bar. Go directly home. Turn the corner. Beer in the icebox. Nope, drank the beer. Elliott's clothes. No, they took them.

"How'd you like to come have a drink with me, pretty girl?"

The goon is sidling up. Wink of the eye. "Good evening, Lisa."

Gotcha.

"A pretty girl like you all by yourself. Why don't you come have a drink with me?"

"Thank you. You are very kind."

The goon moves in.

"But I belong to a very strict religious order and we are guarded night and day by young men. You see, here is one of them now. And we are not allowed to talk to strangers."

"Do you want me to walk you back to the hotel, Lisa?"

"If you don't find me a six-pack of Miller's beer somewhere in this town before we get to the hotel, you can just forget it."

"Good night, honey."

"Come on, Lisa."

Good night, angels.

Lisa
30

Love and Ideals

"WHY DON'T YOU start from the beginning?"

We were sitting in the corner of the little Italian restaurant, and he looked so calm, so infinitely reassuring. There was more gray at his temples than there had been, and a touch of gray in his eyebrows that strengthened the inquisitiveness, the openness of his gaze. But otherwise he was simply Martin, unchanged, and he was holding my hand in his very firmly and there was no indication he would let it go until it was okay.

"They called you, didn't they?" I asked. "When they were looking for us."

"No, they didn't," he answered at once.

"Well, that shows you the magnitude of it. They didn't want you to know what I'd done. You trained Elliott and you sent him to us They probably didn't want anybody to know. It was crazy of me to think they'd call you."

I sipped the white wine, trying not to feel sick from last night's drunk and the long ride to the airport—I had made myself go to the airport as soon as I confirmed that he was on the incoming flight—trying to let the food and the wine do what they were supposed to do. Elliott and I had not discovered this place and it was just around the corner, really good veal, Elliott would have loved it.

Martin drank his coffee and tried not to make a face.

"Ah, New Orleans," he shook his head, the smile easy, wonderful. "Coffee and chicory." He made a mock scowl.

"I'll get them to bring you some good coffee," I said.

"No, you won't. We masochists love wretched coffee." His left hand squeezed just a little tighter. "Tell me about Elliott. Tell me the whole thing."

"I don't know what went wrong. I don't know how it ever went so far. It was like something happened to me and I didn't have any control, I just lost all control. I betrayed everything I believed in, everything I taught others to believe."

"Lisa, talk to me. Make sense."

"I busted him out, Martin. I got his clothes out of storage. I told him to get dressed. I got him on the plane with me. I led him to believe this was 'done' at The Club, that you could take a slave out and bring him back. I came here to New Orleans and for five days . . . I don't know . . . maybe longer . . . we just, we just did things. We went dancing and we made out and we even went to Dallas for a while and . . . God, there were so many things we never got to do . . ." I stopped. It was happening again.

I was losing the damned thread of it in a dissolve of emotion.

"I did a terrible thing," I said. "I broke his contract. I betrayed him, Martin, and I betrayed The Club and I betrayed you."

He narrowed his eyes and it seemed the politest of gestures. The way he let the other person know that he was really listening, though his face was as placid and accepting as ever.

"Where is Elliott now?" he asked.

"At The Club. They came and got him and took him back. It was incredible. They were like a pair of cops, Richard and Scott. I mean they looked like they worked for the fucking FBI. The board of directors is up in arms. Of course they are saying I'm not fired. Mr. Cross said if there is one person who is indispensable around here, it is Lisa. They just want me to come back. They took Elliott back and God knows what's going on in his head."

Suddenly I couldn't talk. My voice just gave out, like someone had put a hand on my throat. I didn't look at him. I looked at the silver-edged plate. I wanted to reach for the wine, but I couldn't. It seemed impossible to even do that.

"Why did you stop?" he asked. Warm dry fingers. He lowered his head slightly to look into my eyes.

"Help me, Martin," I whispered.

"I'm no doctor, Lisa. You know that. But I'm a good listener and I want you to take it from the top, and tell me everything, every last detail."

I nodded. But that was almost too painful to contemplate, recapturing those five days, making anybody understand them. Crying again. In this place. Cried in the Court of Two Sisters. Cried in the motel. Crying in this place. That's more crying than I have done in ten years.

"Martin, I want you to tell me something first." I took his hand now in both of mine. "With all my heart I have to know this."

I could see the worry in his face, but he didn't look as scared as Elliott had when I cried in the Court of Two Sisters. Elliott had looked like he was going to pass out.

"Is what we do right, Martin? Or is it evil? Are we the good thing that we tell ourselves we are, are we the healthy thing we say we are to others? Or are we some evil, twisted thing that never should come to be? Are we bad?"

He looked at me for a long moment, obviously suppressing his surprise at the question, and if he was offended he concealed that as well.

"Lisa, you are asking me this?" he answered slowly. "The night you first came to The House in San Francisco, I told you how I felt about all this."

"I have to hear it again, Martin, please, as if I never understood before."

"Lisa, as far as I'm concerned, The House is proof of my refusal to be a bad person—my refusal to be made to look bad, feel bad, or sound bad because of the brand of sex that I want. You know that."

"But is it bad or good, what we do?" I asked again.

"Lisa, we have taken the search for exotic sex out of the bars and off the streets and out of the shabby rip-off hotel rooms; we've taken it away from the hard-bitten prostitutes and the tough little hustlers, and all those who made criminals and beggars out of us in the past. How could that not be a good thing?

But you understood this when you first came to The House, and nothing has changed since then. The Club itself is a masterpiece built upon the same principles with stunning controls, and it's never failed anyone who ever passed through its gates."

"Well, it failed Elliott Slater," I said.

"Hmmm. I wonder. But what's happened to change you so that you don't believe in what we've done?"

"That's just it. I don't know! I don't for the life of me understand. Everything just fell to pieces. One moment I knew where I belonged and who I was, and the next moment I wasn't anybody I knew and I didn't understand anything that was going on."

He watched me. He waited. But I knew if I said anything it would be the same stuttering repetition. He said begin. How to begin?

"Lisa," he said patiently, "it's been years since we really talked, years since that first night when we got together in the basement den and I explained to you about The House. But I remember you as you were then perfectly. You were a lovely young girl, though nothing as pretty as you are now. And there was something so wise and almost seraphic about your face that I wound up talking to you that night the way I've talked to very few people in my life."

"I remember that night," I said.

I wanted him to bring it back, the wonder, the sense of discovery, the great reassuring illusion of The House, of something already realized, established.

"I talked to you about love and about ideals," he said, "and about my belief that some day people everywhere would stop leaving the crucial business of aberrant sex to riffraff and policemen."

I nodded.

"I remember I asked you if you could love the people who came to my house," he said. "Do you remember your reply? You told me that in a very real way you loved all the sexual adventurers who didn't hurt others, that it was impossible for you to feel any other way towards them. You felt love and pity for the old flasher in the park who opens his coat, the guy on the bus who rubs against the pretty girl, never daring to speak to her. You felt love for the drag queens and the transvestites and the transsexuals. You said that you were they and they were you. It had been that way ever since you could remember."

He pushed the coffee cup to the side and leaned a little closer across the table.

"Well, when you told me that," he said, "I thought here is a girl who is as romantic as I am, and fifty times as innocent as I ever was, and possibly a little bit crazy. I could see that a powerful sexuality had shaped you, perhaps even embittered you. But that you'd managed to invest it with an almost unaccountable spirituality. Yet I couldn't quite believe you that night."

Lovely words. But for me it was more the way I'd described it to Elliott, that some vital imprinting had never taken place, some message about sex being bad had failed over and over to reach its destination in my head.

"But two years later," he went on, "when you had been working at The House every weekend, when you knew the 'guests' as well as I did, I knew that you'd meant exactly what you'd said. It wasn't only that you could act out a scenario of dominance and submission with flawless conviction. It was that you loved. You really loved. Nothing sexual disgusted you or confused you or turned you off. Only real violence, real hurt, the real destruction of another's body and will were your enemies, the same as they were mine. You were just what you said you were. But it is entirely conceivable, entirely, that a love like that could not endure forever."

"But no, it's not that," I said. "It wasn't like they changed or I changed in that way. It was like something altogether inexplicable intervened."

He drank a little of the wine that had gone untouched during the meal, and lifted the bottle to fill the glass again.

"All right, then," he said. "Just start talking about the first moment when things went bad. And let me listen as I have to a thousand stories."

I put my hands to my head and I leaned forward on the table and let my eyes close.

"I think in some way it started when I was on vacation," I said. "When I was on the way home, and I holed up in this luxury hotel in Dallas and I was watching this movie on video disc. It was about the gypsies in New York—it was called *Angelo, My Love*—and they were so alive, these gypsies . . . they were so undeniably wholesome no matter what they did. You know, they stole and they bullshitted and they lied, but they lived within this incredibly vital closed society and there was a gorgeous continuity to their lives. You didn't want anything to happen to them to ever make them be part of the herd."

"The way you were at The Club."

"Well, normally, I would have thought so. That's their world and this is mine. But it didn't feel like that anymore. It was like they had something that I never had. It was like when I was a kid and I wanted this, you know, the secret life, our life, and I thought, God, maybe I'll never have it. It will always be fantasies in my head, you know. That desperate feeling."

"Of course."

"Well, anyway. I was in this hotel and I was crazy to get back to The Club. I had to get inside The Club. And then this photograph, this picture in the file of Elliott. I mean this has nothing to do with the movie, you understand, but when I saw it something snapped in my head."

"Keep talking."

"You know, I've always concurred that women aren't visually stimulated the way men are. You know, that old argument, but when I saw this picture. Just this picture . . ."

Lisa
31

"Death of a Traveling Salesman"

IT WAS GETTING dusk. And we were still talking.

We had drifted from one little place to the next, having a drink here, a cup of coffee there. And now we were walking back through the streets to the hotel, and the whole city was glowing in the waning sun, the way only New Orleans can. Maybe in Italy the light is this color, I didn't know at this exact moment. *Why think of Venice when you are in New Orleans?* But it was too beautiful now, the soft variegated walls of the old building, the chalky green paint on the long shutters, the purple flagstones with their tracery of green moss.

And I was still spilling out all the things that had gone on, the things that Elliott had said, every stupid detail. The way we danced, those long, long talks. And the lovemaking. About the house that he had said we would buy, the programs we watched on TV, and the cornball things that happened.

Martin had his arm around me, his raincoat and his jacket and sweater over the other arm, all the dark San Francisco layers having come off one by one in the balmy heat, though he had never complained about it.

He had listened and listened, stopping only now and then to ask the oddest questions.

Like, "At the Marriott, what were the songs they played?" And "Which Warriors game was it?" How the hell would I know which Warriors game it was. And "What part of the book did he read to you by the pool?" And "How did it make you feel when he smiled like that?"

Whenever I got upset he'd wait and then coax gently.

But I was winding down now, and it had been exhausting, frightening, reliving it.

We came to the hotel and went into the long dark ground-floor bar. We ordered our drinks, his usual white wine, my usual Bombay gin with ice and we went out into the little courtyard and sat down at one of the little wrought iron tables. The yard was empty.

"I just don't know how I could have done it," I was saying. "I know the reason for the rules better than anybody else knows it. I made the rules. I invented the whole thing. But that isn't the worst part. The worst part is that if I went back there, if he was all right—reoriented, integrated, whatever the hell terminology we have to adopt for this situation—I think I'd go crazy the minute I saw him. I don't think I could stand any of it again, not a single solitary aspect of it. And that is what I just can't understand. That's why I can't go back, patch it up, go back and talk as Richard and Scott keep telling me to do, work it out. I know I'll go mad if I see Elliott, if I see that place. I'll go stark raving mad. No question about it."

I looked at him, the way that he sat with his right hand curled just under his lip, his eyes narrow and accepting as before, his long, lanky body so relaxed in the wrought iron garden chair as if he was perfectly at home and could go on listening forever.

"You know, it was the damnedest thing about him," I said. "It was as if he could do anything. He was so damned sensual. I mean plain sensual. You wouldn't believe the way he ate, for instance. He didn't just eat. It was like he was inhaling the food, making love to it. It was the same way when we danced. Oh, you wouldn't have believed that. People were stepping back just to watch us. I didn't know what we were doing. I didn't care. I'd never danced like that. And the sex, it was like he could play any way that he wanted. It had been heavy S&M and then it could be on the natch and it was so hot, it was like when you get a shock from static electricity. Yet it was so, so . . ."

"So?" he prodded.

"So damned affectionate! Sometimes we'd be holding each other in the dark, I mean when we were half asleep, and it was like just holding on to . . . I don't know . . . I don't know . . ."

"And how was it for you?" he asked under his breath. "I mean when it was on the natch"—he took the question slowly—"when it was without the rituals and the paraphernalia?"

I was quiet, because maybe all afternoon I'd known I was coming to that. And I felt as shaky suddenly as I had every time during this week when I'd considered that very question.

"You want to hear something crazy?" I said. "Crazy as all the rest? It was the first time I'd ever done it like that." I looked at him, wondering if he could ever guess the extraordinary quality of saying this, confessing it. "I won't say there weren't the fantasies, the bits and pieces of things running through my brain. I think there will always be that, some ironclad connection between pleasure and pain that can't be broken. But there were these moments, these flashes, even these long, slow periods of times when there was just me and him in that bed and I have never known that before. Never."

I looked away from him. It was as if the silence around me was getting louder and louder. I lifted the drink and felt the ice-cold scald of the gin, the heat in my throat, my eyes faintly watering. Shattering to feel as if Elliott were here, as if we were together. And the anguish at the sheer impossibility of all of it.

Martin was quiet, no longer prodding.

We were still alone in the little garden, the noise from the bar very faint, and the night was stealthily coming on as it does in the South, with no chill, the cicadas come alive, the dark red-brick stain of the walls deepening. The small patch of sky overhead was shot through with red and gold, a rippling stream of clouds bleeding away from the riverfront.

Soon would come that moment of real darkness, when the leaves on the trees would sharpen and contract and the light behind would be white and everything would be distinct in silhouette for a few seconds. And then the dark clumps and shapes would grow thicker and merge with one another. I couldn't bear it, bear the beauty of it suddenly. Slow, ugly pain of crying again. It was getting too familiar.

Martin moved to take a drink of his wine, and then settling back with his long legs out, his ankles crossed, he spoke in a low voice as if the silence and the dusk required it.

"Is it really possible you *don't* know what happened?" he asked.

"God, I've told you that over and over again," I said. "I don't understand any of it. It was like I fell apart, like I never really was anybody and I suddenly discovered it. Like the walls were scrims and everything was a fraud from start to finish. I got on that plane with him like somebody jumping off a cliff. And yet I wouldn't be any other human being except the one I am. God! I have won in the course of my life some extraordinary victories."

He studied me for a moment before he nodded.

And he drew back a little, obviously into his thoughts. It seemed he would say something, and then he was quiet for a long moment, drinking the wine, savoring it, and finally setting it down as he turned to me and touched the back of my hand lightly with his fingers.

"All right," he said as if he had made some quiet decision. "Don't be impatient when I say this. But all through the afternoon, as I've listened to this story, I've found myself reminded again and again of another story. A short story I read some time ago. It was beautifully written by a true genius of prose, an author named Eudora Welty. And there is no way that I can do justice to it, really, in the recounting of it now. But I want to tell it to you as best I can."

"Tell me then," I said all too quickly.

"All right," he said again. And there was a momentary pause in which he seemed to gather himself together. "It was called 'The Death of a Traveling Salesman.' And if memory serves me right the salesman was on the road again after a long debilitating illness during which he'd been nursed in a hotel room by strangers. He was out in the heat again, in the country, and lost, and his car got snagged on a cliff so that he had to stop at a lonely house to get assistance. There was a woman in the house and later a man joined her. And though the man managed to free the salesman's car, nevertheless the salesman wanted to stay on in this little country house, and have supper.

"But almost from the moment the man arrived he thought

there was something mysterious happening in the house, something he couldn't quite fathom. Every detail of the place seemed to profoundly affect him, to be almost hallucinatory. The simplest words of the man and the woman seemed somehow to contain an enormous import. There was a moment early on in fact when the salesman even felt the presence of danger.

"But before the night was over, the salesman realized what it was that was going on in this house that struck him as so mysterious. It was very simply that the man and woman were married, and going to have a baby. It was merely ordinary love between two people who were expecting a child that had struck the salesman as so unusual, so almost terrifying and magical. He had traveled so long and so far from that simple intimacy in life that he could scarcely recognize it when he saw it.

"Well, it seems to me, that something of the same thing has happened to you with Elliott Slater. Lisa, you simply fell in love. For all the complicated and personal and irreducible reasons, you fell in love.

"You recognized something in Elliott that meant everything that love can mean. And when you were swept up by that love, you went with it instinctively, exactly where you thought it should go. And to your astonishment that love didn't die; it flowered. It positively expanded, until all its possibilities were beyond escape.

"Now that is bound to be an overwhelming thing. It is the basis upon which lives are subverted and hearts broken. And there are people who live out their whole lives without ever knowing it even once. But I cannot believe that you, who've devoted yourself to exploring love under all its names, can't recognize normal love for what it is. You know. You've known all along."

It seemed I focused purely upon the words he'd said, that just for a split second the meanings were beyond me, and there came a flood of images that had to do only with Elliott. Elliott saying, "I love you" that first drunken night and me sitting silent on the bed as if my lips couldn't move, as if I'd swallowed some drug that left me like a statue.

I thought I was going to burst inside. And now as then, it was as if my lips were sealed shut. I couldn't talk. I wanted to, and yet I couldn't. When I heard my own voice it was like something breaking, ripping.

"Martin," I said, trying to keep calm, trying not to crack. "Martin, I can't love a man like that. I can't. It's like I'm dissolving. I am coming apart, like I am a mechanism dependent upon a thousand little wheels and springs, which is suddenly breaking down, each part beginning to run at its own speed, uncontrollably. I can't love like a normal person at all."

"But you can and you have," he said. "All these hours, it is normal love that you have been describing to me. That is all there is to it. And you know that what I'm saying is true."

I tried to say no. It was important to say it. To get to the elusive and horridly complex reasons why he was making it all too simple.

He drew closer to me, his face shadowy in the half-life from the distant glass doors, and I could feel his fingers closing on my arm, that wonderful reassuring touch.

"You didn't need me to tell you this. You know it yourself. But something else here is wrong."

"Yes . . ."

"Somehow or other you feel this love disenfranchises the secret life, the life of The Club, that the two can't mix. If this *is* love— what you and Elliott have—then all the things you have done are bad. That simply is not so, Lisa. You cannot make that terrible, damning judgment upon yourself."

I put my hand over my eyes and turned my face away from him. I felt we had come immediately to the knife edge of it, and I had not thought really that all the talking in the world was going to bring us there.

"Lisa, don't run away from this," he said. "Don't question it and don't run from it. Go back to The Club, and tell Elliott exactly what you've been telling me, what he wanted to hear when he told you he loved you."

"Martin, it's impossible," I said. It was absolutely essential to stop this disintegration, this horrid sense of breaking down forever.

But I was thinking the strangest thing: what if, what if it really was something that could happen? What if Martin was right and Elliott and I could have each other like that? What if it was half that good for only a year, a fourth that good for a decade? Christ, that was worth the death of everything I'd ever been before, wasn't it? But that was the very problem.

"You know what I am," I said. I pleaded for him to understand. "You know the paths I've traveled."

"But don't you see?" he answered. "So does Elliott. Lisa, this love was born at The Club. It was born in the very fulcrum of your secret life. Do you think it could have happened to you anywhere else? And what about Elliott? Do you think this has happened to him before?"

"I don't know."

"Well, I know. Elliott loves you, knowing exactly what you are, and you love Elliott, knowing full well what he is. It isn't an either/or situation of normal love versus exotic love. You have the thing all men and women strive for: the lover from whom you do not have to hide anything."

I put up my hands in a little gesture for silence. It was moving too fast for me to catch up.

"Then why can't I go back there!" I asked. "Why the hell am I terrified of the very sight of the place?"

"Why did you have to get out when you took him on the plane?"

"Because the person I am there couldn't know him the way I knew him here! I couldn't mix the two. God knows other people can. Scott can. Richard can. You can. You can sleep with your lovers and talk to your lovers and snap right back into it . . ."

"But the rituals were always protecting you from that very thing."

"Yes!"

We stared at each other for a moment. I had lifted my hand to my lips. What I said astonished me. But there was the overwhelming sense of injustice, that it was nothing so simple, and yet I was struck by the violent simplicity of what I'd just said.

"I can't think," I said. My voice was breaking and it infuriated me, the crying, the endless crying. "I can't reason, I can't believe somebody who has done the things I've done can have love!"

I heard his reaction though it wasn't in words, the soft murmur of shock.

I struggled to get a handkerchief out of my purse, and I hid my face behind my hand for a moment. For the first time all day I wanted to be alone.

"You know, it's as if I made this choice early on, it's as if . . ."

"But there was no reason for that choice!" He started to say something more but he stopped. Then he spoke again very softly. "I never knew you felt so guilty about all of it. I never knew you felt so bad."

"I don't," I insisted. "Not when I am doing what I am supposed to do at The Club. I do not feel bad. I believe in what I do. The Club is the veritable externalization of what I believe. It is my vocation, The Club."

Again, I stopped, mildly shocked by what I had heard myself say. And yet these were words I'd used many times over the years, to others, as well as in my own head. The Club was my nunnery. *But the rituals were always protecting you from that very thing.*

I had been staring ahead in the darkness and I turned and looked at him now, a little amazed at the alertness and the calm of the expression on his face. The sheer habitual optimism of his expression.

"That vocation requires an awfully stiff amount of self-sacrifice, doesn't it?" he asked.

"I never thought so," I said. But I felt flattened, absolutely flattened and strangely excited at the same time.

"Maybe it was a moral deal all along," he said.

I nodded.

"And it was never meant to be that, was it? It was done in the name of freedom and as we have said a thousand times, in the name of love."

I shook my head, and again that quick little gesture for silence.

"It's all happening too quickly," I said. "I need time to think." But that was a lie. I couldn't think when I was alone. That's why I sent for him. And to tell him so, I reached out and I took hold of his hand. I held him so tight I was probably hurting his hand a little, but he didn't pull away.

"You know, Lisa, very few of us anymore get through life without a dramatic bid for freedom. That dramatic bid is the hallmark of our times. But most of us never really reach our goal. We get stuck halfway between the morass of myth and morality we left behind and the utopia on which we've set our sights. That's where you are, stuck between that dismal, repressive Catholic morality you came from and the vision of a world in which no form of love is a sin. You've scored your victories and they've been spectacular, but if you think you cannot love Elliott, you've paid an awfully high price at the same time."

I didn't speak. But every syllable had struck home.

For a long time, I sat still, not even trying to think consciously about the words, and feeling only sadness, sadness like grief, and that stealthy surge of exhilaration struggling as if to get free of the grief.

The moments passed in stillness.

The sweet subtropical night had fallen and the few scattered lights of the garden had come on beneath the shivering branches of the ferns, the drowsy fronds of the banana trees. The sky overhead was blackness. There were no stars.

He was still holding my hand and he gave a gentle, kind pressure.

"I want you to do something for me," he said.

"What is it?"

"When you called me I came just as you asked me to. Now you do this for me."

"You're scaring me," I said.

"Go back to The Club. Go in there and call Richard and tell him you're coming back and to send the plane now. And when you get there, do two things. Clear up the outstanding business or what it is so that Mr. Cross is happy, so that The Club and you remain on good terms. Then go to Elliott. Tell him all the things you've told me. Tell him why you held back, why you couldn't commit yourself, why it started to fall apart."

"That would feel awfully good . . . to tell him. To explain." I knew I was crying again, positively gushing. Awful. But I just nodded and covered my eyes with my hand. "I wish he were here now."

"He's not very far away. And my suspicion is he'll understand this situation, maybe even better than you do." His grip tightened. "In the best of all possible worlds there wouldn't have to be this choice. Like you said, he could have it either way. But if you can't for now, tell him that. I think when you tell him that he'll understand what's happened. And he will want you the way you are now."

"That's the crux of it," I said, but I could hardly hear myself. "Only it's got like sixty cruxes, and each time we hit on one I think I'm coming apart. What if he wants The Club again, Martin? The way things were before I messed them up for him?"

"Well, then, he can tell you that. And you can bow out and let them reindoctrinate him. But I don't think that's what he wants.

I never did think so. If The Club was what he'd really wanted, he would have given you a thousand signals from the start. And things would never have happened the way they did. You would never have gotten so far together."

"You believe that?"

"Think on it. Think on the story the way you've told it to me. Every step of the way it was the two of you. I suspect that as far as The Club is concerned, he got his money's worth."

"God . . ." I whispered. "If only that were true." I just held tight to his hand.

"But you see, these are things you have to verify with Elliott."

I didn't answer.

"Lisa, nothing is going to happen until you go back there and talk to Elliott."

He waited silently for a few moments.

"Go on," he said. "Remember he knows more about you than any man has ever known. You've told me that yourself."

"Yes, that I can't deny," I said. My voice sounded tired to me, and very afraid. "But what if . . . What if it's too late?"

Too awful to think of that. All the missed opportunities, those last moments, the things not said.

"I don't think it's too late," he said unobtrusively. "Elliott— and I know he would love to hear me say this—is an awfully tough young man. I think he's waiting for you. Probably hurt. Probably mad as hell. But most definitely waiting for you. After all, you did promise that you'd come back. Go in there and call for the plane."

"Give me a minute."

"You've had your minute."

"It could all be a horrible mistake!"

"Either way it could. So make that mistake in the direction of Elliott. You know all about the rest. There's nothing new there."

"Don't push!" I said.

"I'm not. I'm simply doing what I do best: helping people to realize their fantasies. You've been telling me your fantasy all afternoon long. Now I'm going to help you make it come true."

I smiled in spite of myself.

"That's why you sent for me, wasn't it?" he asked. "Go in there and call. And I'll go with you. I'll help you. I don't really want a little vacation in the Caribbean with two dozen naked young men stumbling all over themselves to please me, but I'll put up with it for you."

He leaned over and kissed me on the cheek.

"Go on."

I snapped on the light and sat down before the bedside telephone. Six o'clock by my watch and the travel clock on the dresser. I picked up the phone and dialed.

Three minutes and forty-six seconds before the inevitable connections were made.

Then Richard's voice.

"This is Lisa," I said. "I'm ready to come home. Do you want to send the plane here, or for me to meet it in Miami?"

"We'll send it immediately."

"I want to meet with the board, and with Mr. Cross. I want to clear up my desk and talk about taking a leave of absence. That is, if you were serious about not firing me."

"Give us a break. We'll do whatever you want us to. I think the leave is a good idea. Mr. Cross will eat out of your hand as long as you come back."

"How's Elliott?"

"You sound better. You sound like yourself."

"How's Elliott?" I asked again.

"That's it, the old impatience, the old air of command."

"Knock it off, Richard, and answer the question. How is Elliott! Give me a full report."

"Such a sweet girl," he sighed. "Elliott is in the best of health, I assure you, though reorientation is at something of a standstill. To be more specific, he's out on one of the yachts at this moment deep sea fishing, and when he's not deep sea fishing, he's playing tennis hard enough to decapitate his opponent, and if he's not playing tennis, he's swimming laps fast enough to clear the pool. And if he's not swimming laps, he's in the lounge dancing with two and three slaves at a time. He won't drink Chivas Regal Scotch. He has to have single mash or Johnny Walker. He's given us a list of some twenty films he wants on video disc, and the steaks aren't good enough for him. He wants us to send to a special cattle ranch in California for the beef. He doesn't like the library. We should redo the library. People don't want to fuck and swim and eat every minute. They ought to have good books to read. And he has dreamt up a dazzling addition to the sports arcade called The Hunt in the Maze, which Scott is developing right now. He and Scott have become 'buddies' it seems."

"Are you telling me that he is balling Scott?"

" 'Buddies' do not ball each other," he said. " 'Buddies' play poker, drink beer, and talk with their mouths full of food. What I am telling you is that Mr. Slater knows he has us by the balls. And Scott, his 'buddy,' is recommending that we change Mr. Slater's status from slave to member with all fees waived."

I covered the mouth of the phone. I didn't know whether I was laughing or crying.

"He's okay, then."

"Okay? I would say that is an understatement. As for the gossip on the island . . ."

"Yes . . ."

"It has been effectively shushed by the rumor Mr. Slater is and has always been on the staff, testing The Club's systems on the sly."

"Brilliant!"

"Yes, he thought so too when he suggested it. And highly probable, I might add! He'd make an excellent staff member. He has an absolutely extraordinary gift for shoving people around. By the way, he has a message for you. In fact, he made me swear I'd give it to you as soon as you called."

"Well, why the fuck didn't you say so? What message!" I demanded.

"He insists that you will understand what it means."

"So tell me."

"He says that he should have put the roach down your shirt." Silence.

"*Do* you understand what it means? He seems to think it is *very* important."

"Yes," I said. It means he still loves me. "I want to come back now."

Lisa

32

Final Report
to the Board

THE PLANE DIDN'T reach New Orleans till three in the morning. It landed at The Club at 8 A.M. And I went directly to work.

Mr. Cross, Richard, and Scott were in my office when I got there, and over a round of Bloody Marys for breakfast we began clearing everything up.

Yes, we would take on trial fifteen of the pony slaves from the stables in Switzerland. And we would use them here exclusively as draught animals, and we would house, feed, and punish them in keeping with this highly specialized sense of themselves. All terms acceptable. Scott and Deena: work up list of possibilities.

Yes, we'd do business with Ari Hassler in New York again, as it had been proven beyond doubt that the teeny-bopper we'd bumped had actually been the younger sister of the slave Ari trained and recommended in good faith to us. Better photo checks on board the cargo yacht recommended. Avoid fingerprinting for the present. Slaves don't want to be fingerprinted and who can blame them?

Yes, on the new saltwater swimming pool, the coast view apartments on the south side of the island.

Polite but absolute No on the requested "official" interview with reporters from CBS. Permission denied to CBS to bring their boat to any point within our waters.

Full concurrence of all board members, however, that official interviews cannot be avoided forever. Going public with a well-prepared statement, very possibly a full brochure, is preferable to continued pressure from outside reporters to breach The Club's security. Begin preparation of such a public statement. Consult or hire outright Martin Halifax to do this. He just happens to be here.

Yes, on the insistence of the female slaves that they be allowed into the sports arcade. But use only those who request it. Watch carefully! All women must work as servers of drinks in the arcade to become familiar with its particular masculine ambience before being used there. Study ambience after inclusion of the women to see if it changes for the men. Advise. Yes, on the new roller rink games, and development and construction of the jungle maze for slave hunt adjacent to the arcade.

Yes, on the indefinite leave of absence for Lisa Kelly with full pay though she is not requesting full pay. And yes, she will be within reach by phone of The Club wherever she is on a twenty-four-hour basis. (Private note to file by Mr. Cross: Try not to disturb Lisa Kelly during her leave unless absolutely necessary.)

Yes, on the plane to take Lisa Kelly alone or accompanied on a direct flight to Venice, as soon as clearance can be arranged for that. Please book the Royal Danieli Excelsior, a suite facing the lagoon.

Yes, I will talk to Diana, the slave I have had for four years, before I leave the island and I will explain everything. My rooms, in one hour.

Yes, on full Club membership for Elliott Slater. Investigative processes already more than adequate. All fees for the first year waived. Retirement of Elliott Slater as slave.

Consider strong possibility of staff position for Elliott Slater, part time, advisory, etc. The idea for the jungle maze, and the crude drawings presented to the board for same, originated in conversation between Elliott Slater and Scott.

Present Location of Slater?

Unknown

"Unknown?"

Lisa

33

In Sickness
and in Health

"HE SPLIT AN hour before you arrived."

"You told him I was on my way in?"

"Yeah, we did." Scott glanced at Richard. I wanted to hit both of them.

"Goddamn you. And you didn't tell me this, you let me believe he was still here!"

"Look, Lisa, what were you going to do, chase him to Port au Prince? You went right into the boardroom. I didn't even have a chance to tell you. He was so damned anxious to get off the island he wouldn't even wait for the Cessna. He had to have the copter take him to Haiti and from there he went to Miami and then on to the West Coast."

"But why did he go? Did he leave any message for me?"

Disgusting exchange of glances between the two of them.

"Lisa, we didn't do anything bad here," Scott said. "I swear to God. I went into his room this morning and told him you'd left New Orleans. He'd been drinking all night. He was in a real mean mood. He was watching that *Road Warrior* movie. He's nuts about that movie. And he just turned off the screen and started pacing the floor. And then he said, 'I have to get out of here. I want to get out of here.' I tried to talk him out of it, to get him to stick around for an hour, for Chrissakes. But it wasn't any good. He called the Time-Life office back there. They gave him some assignment in Hong Kong. He said he'd be there day after tomorrow, had to go home for his equipment. He called some guy to bring his car to the San Francisco Airport and open up his house."

"The Berkeley house."

I hit the intercom. "Send Diana to my room immediately. And change the flight plan to San Francisco. And get me the file on Elliott Slater. I want the address of his Berkeley house."

"It's here," Scott said. "He left it with me. Just in case anyone should want to reach him, he said."

"Well, why the fucking shit didn't you say so?" I grabbed the paper out of his hand.

"Lisa, I'm sorry . . ."

"The hell you are," I said, heading for the door. "And to hell with you, and to hell with The Club."

"Lisa . . ."

"What?"

"Good luck."

The limousine was on the Bayshore Freeway fifteen minutes after we landed, burrowing north through a light evening fog into San Francisco and towards the Bay Bridge.

I don't think the craziness of it hit me, however, until I saw the ugly urban squalor of University Avenue: that I was back in my own hometown. This little chase, that had begun in another galaxy, was leading me right back into the Berkeley hills where I'd grown up.

Nice going, Elliott. Only for you.

The limo swayed awkwardly as we started up the steep, winding streets. It was worse than familiar. The very sight of the overgrown gardens, the houses nestled among the tangled oaks and Monterey cypresses, curdled my soul. No, not just home, this place: rather the landscape of an identity, a period of life that was almost indistinguishable from constant pain.

I had the terror suddenly that someone would see me in spite of the darkened window glass, and know who I really was. I hadn't come this time for a wedding or a funeral, or a week of vacation. I was Sir Richard Burton slipping into the Forbidden City of Mecca. And if I got caught I'd be killed.

I looked at my watch. Elliott was two hours ahead of me. Maybe even not there.

And in an instant of sheer perversity, I told the driver to turn and take me down my own street. I didn't know why I was doing it. But I had to just stop for a moment at my own house. We cruised slowly downhill until I saw the lights on in my dad's library. I told the driver to stop.

Quiet here under the black acacia. No sound but the lawn sprinkler spinning its shower of light across the dark, glossy grass. Blue-white flicker of a television in my little brother's upstairs bedroom. A shadow moved against the library shades.

The panic mellowed out into melancholy, that awful sadness that always came over me when I saw this overgrown corner of the world, the old peeling shingles, dim lamps that meant home.

No one was going to see me. No one would ever know I'd been here. All the things Martin had said were turning round and round inside me. Not a bad person, Lisa, just a different person, and maybe someday that person would have the courage my father had not merely to live by what he believed, but to talk about it, admit it, challenge the world with it. And maybe when that happened, the pain would stop for reasons that would never be clear.

Right now just settle for the fear going away, for the sadness melting, for another private farewell.

Elliott was five minutes up the street.

It was just the kind of house I imagined it would be. One of those little stone cottages with the rounded door and the tower that made it a diminutive castle, hanging on to the edge of a cliff. Garden neglected; chinaberry tree almost blocking the front door; white daisies falling down on the flagstone path.

Beyond I could see the ink-black water of the bay and the distant skyscrapers of San Francisco rising out of a layer of rose-tinted fog. The two bridges arcing over the darkness, and to the far right the vague outline of the hills of Marin.

All the familiar things and yet this was so unfamiliar. The real me in the real place. And the real him in there, because the upside-down, bathtub-style Porsche was rammed into the impossibly narrow driveway, and lights were on all over the little house.

When I touched the knob, the door opened a little.

Stone floors, big hole of a fireplace in the corner with the fire blazing, a few dim lamps scattered about under the low beam ceilings. And the leaded-glass windows showing the spectacular view of city, water, and night sky.

Nice place. Beautiful place. Smell of burning wood. Lots and lots of books on the walls.

And Elliott sitting at the table in the little dining room, with a cigarette on his lip, talking on the phone.

I pushed the door open just a little wider.

He was saying something about Kathmandu. That he would probably leave Hong Kong before the end of the week and he wanted a full three days in Kathmandu.

"Then maybe Tokyo, I don't know."

He had on his bush jacket and a white turtleneck and he was very brown, hair streaked with white, like he'd been swimming and sunning the whole time we were apart. In fact, I could smell the sun on him almost, and he looked slightly out of place in these dark, wintry rooms.

"You come up with the assignment, fine," he was saying. "But if you don't, I'm going just the same. Call me. You know where I'll be." He was loading a camera as best he could, reaching up to steady the phone receiver when it almost slipped. He clicked past the first few frames of exposed film.

Then he saw me. And he didn't have time to hide the surprise.

I tightened my grip on the doorknob as my whole arm started to shake.

"Yeah, get back to me," he said and he hung up the phone. He stood up and he said very softly, "You came."

I was shaking all over now. My knees were knocking. And the air from outside felt suddenly cold.

"Can I come in?" I asked.

"Sure," he said. Still amazed. He wasn't even trying to be tough or mean. But then I'd just chased him over two thousand miles. Why should he be, I thought. He was just standing there looking at me, the camera around his neck, as I closed the door.

"The place is musty," he said. "It's been locked up for a couple of weeks. And the heat's not working. It's kind of . . ."

"Why didn't you wait for me at The Club?" I asked.

"Why didn't you talk to me when you called?" Instant flare of temper. "Why did you talk to Richard instead of me? And then Scott comes in and tells me you called the night before and you were on your way."

Red to the roots of his hair.

"I felt like a goddamn eunuch waiting around there. I didn't know what I was waiting for."

Then the red started to fade a little.

"Besides, I was finished with The Club," he said.

Silence.

"Aren't you going to sit down?" he asked.

"Rather stand," I said.

"Well, come in."

I moved a little ways into the room. Big curving iron stairs to the far right, tower room overhead. Smell of incense mingled with the smell of the fire. Smell of books.

The distant lights of San Francisco seemed to pulse more strongly beyond the leaded glass.

"I have some things to say," I said.

He got a cigarette out of his pocket and had a little trouble closing in with the lighter. Glad to see that. Then he threw me a glance the way people throw a punch. Eyes very blue thanks to the darker tan. Got to be one of the handsomest men I've ever seen. Even when the mouth is mean.

I took a deep breath.

"So go ahead," he said. He looked directly at me this time and held it.

Chills from his voice.

"I ah . . . came here . . ." Stop. Breathe. "I came here to tell you that I . . ."

Silence.

"Well, I'm listening."

". . . that I love you."

No change in his expression. Then the cigarette rising very slowly to the lip.

"I love you," I said again. "And I ah . . . I loved you when you told me you loved me. I just couldn't say it. I was afraid."

Silence.

"I fell in love with you and I lost my head. I ran away with you and I fucked everything up because I didn't know how to handle it, didn't know what to do."

Silence.

Face changing slightly. Softening, or it might have been an illusion. Head cocked to the side just a little. Temper and the coldness melting so slowly that I really couldn't be sure.

The fire hurt my eyes suddenly, like there was smoke in the place or something. But what the hell damn difference did it make, whether he was still mad?

I was going to say it all no matter what he did. No matter what he said. I knew that it was right to say it, it was right to come and tell him everything, and right in the middle of it all, dead center in the pain, I felt this strange elation, this relief.

I stopped looking at him. I just looked past him at the glittering outline of the Golden Gate, at the city lights.

"I love you," I said again. "I love you so much that I am willing to make a fool of myself coming here. I don't want ever to be separated from you. I'd have gone after you to Hong Kong or Kathmandu to tell you these things."

Silence.

The lights seemed alive along the curve of the bridge, alive in the skyscrapers that climbed like ladders to the stars.

"I ah . . . I owe you all kinds of apologies," I said, "for what I did, for spoiling The Club for you."

"To hell with The Club," he said.

I looked at him slowly, cautiously, so that if he looked really mean, I could quickly detach, look away. But I couldn't tell with the flicker of the fire and the shadows. All I could clearly see was that he was Elliott and that he was a little closer to me than he had been a moment ago. But my eyes were watering badly now and I knew I had to take out the goddamned handkerchief for the umpteenth time.

"I mean somebody else would have handled it all better," I said. "Somebody else would have known what to say, what to do. All I knew was I couldn't stay at The Club with you and be in love with you. I couldn't love you and be the person that I was there. I know I should have told you in New Orleans, but I was so afraid that you wanted to go back to The Club. I knew I couldn't do it anymore, the roles and all. I thought I was going to disa . . . I was going to disappoint you. Make things even worse than they were. Really let you down."

Silence.

"Well, the fact is I still can't do it. Even now. Something's snapped in my head that makes all that impossible. I can't do it anymore with you. And I don't know if I can ever do it again with anyone else. It became artificial. It became like a trap."

I shut my eyes for a second. He was just staring at me when I opened them again.

"But you were never an escape route. It was you—you who made it fall apart—you and me."

He was staring, but the face softened, becoming obviously emotional yet in a secretive way.

"And if you don't want me this way," I said, "the way it was those last few days, I understand. I mean it's not what you came for, right? I understand if you don't answer me. I understand if you call me names. But that's what happened. And I love you. I am in love with you and I've never said that to anyone else."

I blew my nose and wiped my eyes.

And I stood looking at the floor, and thinking, well, it's done. Whatever happens, it's done. The worst was over. And I had a splendid sense of that, that it was over. It had its chance now, whatever it was going to be. There was no impediment now.

So let him blow up.

Silence.

"Well, anyway. That's what I had to tell you," I said. "That I love you, that I'm sorry for what I did."

Tears again.

"This is really something," I said, "this crying at regular four-hour intervals. It's getting almost to feel natural, like a new kind of sado-masochism, the heat and the chills."

The room was fading like the light was being closed off. And then coming back gradually and brightly. He had come closer, blotting out the light of the fire a little, and now he was right in front of me, and I could see the light over his shoulder. I could smell his cologne and the sea salt smell of his hair and skin.

I was disintegrating. It was as bad as I told Martin it was. I wanted to reach out for him, to hold on to him. But we were both standing there, not moving. And I couldn't, didn't dare be the first one to touch.

"You know, I ah . . . I booked the plane to Venice," I said. "I had this idea, that maybe somehow we could get it going again. And this time we could really take off. In Venice, we could just walk and we could talk things out. I mean if it could be patched up between us, if you . . . I mean if it isn't totally fucked."

Silence.

"You remember you said there is no city in the world other than New Orleans for walking quite like Venice."

Silence.

"You said that," he said.

"I did? Well, you know the food in Venice, well, I mean the pasta and the wine and all." Shrug from me. "Well, I thought it was worth a try." I looked directly at him. "I thought it was worth anything and everything actually . . . I'd do anything to get you back."

"Anything?" he asked.

"Yeah, anything, except . . ." Be the Perfectionist. You wouldn't ask me to be that . . .

"Like marry me? Be my wife?"

"*Marry* you!"

"That's what I said."

For a second I was too stunned to answer. He looked as if he was perfectly serious, and he was so beautiful that I could hardly stand it.

"Marry you!" I said again.

"Yes, marriage, Lisa," he said with the smallest smile. "You know, like walking down the hill and introducing me to your dad? And later driving up to Sonoma and meeting mine? And maybe having a little wedding in the wine country, with your family and my family and—"

"Hold it!" I said.

"I thought you said you loved me. You wanted to be with me forever . . . You'd do anything to get me back. Well, I love you, you know that, you're probably sick of hearing it by now. And I want to get married to you, Lisa. That's what forever means to me! That's what love means, too." His voice was getting louder, more determined. "No more just screwing around like we did on the road. It's you and me married, with the rings and the vows and all the rest."

"You're shouting at me, Elliott," I said. I backed away from him. It was like somebody had hit me. Go down the hill and meet my father! Get married. For Chrissakes.

"I'm not shouting," he said.

He took a drag off the cigarette and went and smashed it out in the ashtray on the table, all of these gestures like some kind of preparation for a barroom fight.

"I mean I am shouting at you, because you're so stupid," he said. "Because you don't know yourself, who you really are. Because I was stupid not to tell you in New Orleans that I didn't want for either of us to go back to the fun and games at The Club. I let those sexual whiz kids talk me into leaving you there, which was punk as far as I'm concerned. And I don't like to be ashamed of myself. I want to marry you. That's what I want."

"Look, Elliott. I'm so in love with you that I'm going to pieces," I said. "I'm walking away from everything I've done since I was eighteen. My life, the career I built, crazy as it was. All gone because of you! But marriage? Old-fashioned marriage? Ceremonies and rings and vows . . . ?"

"Wrong. All wrong," he said. "Not old-fashioned marriage. Our marriage." He took out another cigarette and struggled with the lighter. "And who asked you to turn your back on your career for me?"

"What are you trying to say?"

"That I want to marry you, the person you are! And that means Lisa, the brains behind The Club as well as the woman standing here, the woman I was with in New Orleans. You're the one who's ashamed of what you do, damn it, and you have been from the start. I never asked you to give it up. I'm not asking you now."

"Be married and work at The Club? You're talking crazy."

"No. I'm talking the way life is. Lisa, neither of us gives a damn about The Club now. We have what we want. We're clear on that. But the time is bound to come when you'll think about going back there."

"No."

"Yes," he said. "You can't create something that complicated, that successful for so many others and not feel some pride, some involvement still in what you've done . . ."

"And what about you?" I countered. "Will the time come when you'll want the fun and games again? Are you missing them now?"

"No," he said calmly. "But to be perfectly frank, I don't know what may happen as time goes on. Right now it doesn't seem possible to go that route again. I want you. But whatever happens, I want us to have a bond between us, a contract, if you will, that makes us our own little club of two. I'm talking about the strength to handle things together. I'm talking about fidelity, but I'm talking about honesty, too."

"Elliott, let's just leave here. Let's just go and . . ."

"No way, Lisa."

I stood glaring at the fire, watching him out of the corner of my eye.

"We've been down too many kinky roads, you and me. An affair with us wouldn't have a chance. You'd wake up one morning, start thinking about The Club, and go catatonic. I'd never know from moment to moment whether I still had you. No way. But marriage, that's different. We will have our rituals and our contract, and we'll give it all we've got. And that's what it's going to need to have a chance."

I turned around and faced him. And I don't think I saw all the marvelous physical details, the blue of the eyes, the soft line of the mouth. I wasn't afraid he'd touch me or kiss me and mix me up. I saw only somebody that I knew really well, that I had been closer to than anyone else I'd ever known. In spite of the tension between us, I felt almost safe.

"And you believe it could work?" I asked.

"Of course, I do," he said. "If you can make a place like The Club, you can do anything you want."

"Oh, you're putting me on."

"No, I'm not. Just giving credit where it's due." He had a defiant look. His eyes were large the way people's eyes get when they are daring somebody. "Let me love you," he said. "After all the risks you've taken, can't you trust me this much?"

He came forward and put his arms out, but again I turned away and stepped back.

"Okay!" he said angrily. He put up his hands and backed off. "You think it over. You stay here and think it over. The freezer's full of steaks. There's wood for the fireplace. The house is yours! I'm going to Hong Kong. You call me if you want to get married. You say I do. We do. I'll come right back."

He marched over to the table, crushed out the second cigarette like he was murdering it, and picked up the phone. He was blazing red again.

"Wait a minute," I said.

"Nope, got to go to Hong Kong," he said. "No more waiting on the boss lady who's always got to run the scenario, have things her own way."

He was punching in the number.

"That's not fair," I said.

"The hell it's not."

"You wanna ride to Hong Kong?" I asked. "In a nice cushy private jet?"

He stopped punching the buttons.

"Nice ride after that to Kathmandu? And maybe Tokyo after that?"

He turned and looked at me.

"We'll steal the plane," I said. "We'll go to Venice and— Hey, I know what we'll do. We'll go to the film festival at Cannes!"

"Can't get into the Carlton now. Everything's booked. Let's go to Hong Kong."

"The hell with the Carlton. The Club has its own houseboat there. We'll go there first, then we'll steal the plane and go to Hong Kong. It's going to make them furious when we steal the plane."

"And we get married in Cannes. Maybe in a little French church."

"Jesus Christ. A church."

"Come on, Lisa!"

He slammed down the phone hard enough to break it.

"Martin was right about you," I said. "You're a romantic. You're mad."

"You're figuring it wrong," he said. "I just like it when things are a little risky. I like it when it's a little dangerous. You know what I mean?"

He looked ominous for a second, his eyebrows knotted, his mouth just a tiny bit hard.

Then the smile came back, sort of irresistible.

"Like skydiving off a cliff . . ." I said.

"Kind of . . ."

"Like pushing an Ultralite plane as high as it will go . . ."

"Sort of . . ."

"Like wandering around El Salvador and Beirut with a war on . . ."

"Maybe, a little . . ."

"Like signing up as a slave for two years at a place like The Club."

"Yeah." He laughed, but very quietly, almost as if it was meant to be secret, as if the joke was something I couldn't really fully appreciate the way he could. He was next to me in a second, his arms right around me, and didn't give me a chance to turn away.

"Don't do that," I said. "I'm trying to think."

Those blot-out kisses, scent, taste of Elliott, Elliott's lips, Elliott's skin.

"Now you know it's going to be worth it," he said.

"Stop," I said softly. I couldn't see anything. Absolutely paralyzing kisses. "I wonder why the hell I'm bothering to fight."

"Hmmmm. I'm wondering the same thing," he said. "God, I missed you. And you wore this damned white dress just to drive me out of my head, didn't you? And this damned white hat."

He wouldn't stop kissing me. He was undoing the buttons at my neck.

"Stop it, wait till we're on the plane."

"What plane?" he said. He was reaching up under my slip, pulling at my panties, ripping the zipper down the back of the dress.

"Will you cut it out, you're tearing the dress, damn it. All right, I'll do it. Now, stop it. Wait till we get on the plane."

"Do what?" he asked. He was pulling my hair down, pulling off my hat.

"Get married, damn it!" I shouted. "That's what!" I went to slug him but he ducked.

"You will. You'll marry me!"

"Well, that's just what I was trying to say while you were tearing my clothes to pieces, for God's sakes."

"Oh, my God, you mean it. You'll do it! Oh, shit, Lisa, I'm scared to death."

"Goddamn you, Elliott." I swung at him with the purse and got him as he put up his arms. He was laughing.

"Well, come on then for Chrissakes," he said ducking the next swing and catching me by the waist. "Let's get out of here. Let's go to Cannes, baby doll. And Hong Kong, and Venice—I don't care where we go!"

He pulled me towards the door.

"You're breaking my ankle!" I said.

I tried to fix my zipper while he and the driver threw his bags in the back of the car. He ran back into the house to lock up.

It was really night now, and the view of San Francisco was burning out there beyond the edge of the garden, and when the house went dark, it was the only light I could see.

My heart was pounding the way it had that very first time years and years ago when I had crossed the bridge into the city with Barry, that faceless kid whom I never knew. It was pounding the way it had the day I went to meet Jean Paul, or drove south with him to the master's estate in Hillsborough, or went to see Martin at The House.

But this time the old raw excitement was mixed with a new emotion, too rich and exquisite to be anything but pure love.

Elliott was two steps away from me and the driver had started the engine. And I was holding on to my hat and looking up at the constellations the way I had a thousand times on this mountain ever since I was a little girl.

"Come on, Mrs. Slater," he said.

He picked me up the same way he had in New Orleans and set me down inside the car.

I clung to him as the limo made its awkward lumbering turn on the narrow hillside, tumbling us even closer together.

"Tell me again that you love me," he said.

"I love you," I said.

DISCOVER THE TRUE
MEANING OF HORROR...